The Game

1885-1906

Thomas W. Campbell

Publishing Information

This work is a fiction based primarily on the characters created by Sir Arthur Conan Doyle. The narrative explores an imagined relationship between Arthur Conan Doyle as the chronicling author, Dr. Watson as the provider of case information, and Sherlock Holmes as the consulting detective. While drawing inspiration from Doyle's original characters and Victorian London setting, all events, dialogue, and character interactions depicted herein are products of the author's imagination and should not be construed as historical fact or canonical representations of Doyle's original works. The author utilized spell check, grammar check, sentence composition tools, and artificial intelligence during the writing of this book.

The Game 1885-1903
First Edition: September 30, 2025
ISBN: 979-8-218-73771-9

Published by:

Sherlock Holmes Society USA
P. O. Box 347
Carolina Beach, NC   28428

Contact:
SHolmesSociety@gmail.com
Printed in the United States of America

2 21B

Sherlock Holmes Society USA

Playing the Game

For generations, readers worldwide have enjoyed what they correctly understand to be the fictional adventures of Sherlock Holmes and Dr. John Watson, as created by Arthur Conan Doyle. Historical examination confirms beyond doubt that Holmes and Watson were indeed literary characters, products of Doyle's imagination rather than flesh-and-blood individuals who walked the streets of Victorian London.

Yet there exists a venerable tradition among devoted enthusiasts—known to Sherlockians as playing "The Game" - that deliberately embraces a far more intriguing premise: what if Holmes and Watson had been real people whose remarkable exploits genuinely occurred in the gaslit streets of Victorian and Edwardian England?

THE GAME 1885-1906 is a work of historical fiction, based on the life of Arthur Conan Doyle. It features Doyle's marriages, his children, and his medical practice. It also includes the first 39 Sherlock Holmes stories published before 1906.

To many serious Sherlockians, this imaginative exercise represents more than mere entertainment. These dedicated scholars have constructed elaborate theories supporting the delightful fiction that the greatest detective stories ever written were never fiction at all, but rather the product of an extraordinary collaboration between three remarkable men who actually lived and worked together in late Victorian England.

According to this carefully crafted premise, Dr. Watson would have provided the meticulous documentation, his medical training lending precision to his observations of each case. Sherlock Holmes himself would have contributed his analytical insights and methodological expertise, ensuring the accuracy of every deductive process recorded. And Arthur Conan Doyle, rather than being their creator, would have served as their trusted literary partner, applying his narrative skills to transform their factual accounts into stories that would captivate the reading public while preserving the essential truth of each investigation.

This would have been no mere ghostwriting arrangement, but a true meeting of minds: Watson's detailed chronicling, Holmes's intellectual rigor, and Doyle's storytelling artistry combining to create something unprecedented in the annals of criminal literature. Each man would have brought his unique strengths to their shared endeavor—Watson's humanity and perspective, Holmes's brilliant deductions and scientific approach, and Doyle's ability to craft their experiences into compelling narratives.

The present volume fully embraces this imaginative premise. Here, we encounter what would have been the fruits of their collaboration: accounts that bear the authenticity of Watson's firsthand observations, the precision of Holmes's methodology, and the accessibility of Doyle's prose. These are presented not as stories, but as chronicles—not as entertainment, but as history rendered in vivid detail by three men committed to preserving the truth of their extraordinary partnership.

In these pages, we witness their alliance as it might have unfolded: Holmes with his unparalleled analytical genius, Watson with his courage and unwavering loyalty, and Doyle with his commitment to ensuring their achievements would be remembered accurately by posterity. Together, they would have revolutionized not only the science of detection but the very way such groundbreaking work could be shared with the world.

This is their story as it might have been—the imagined account of how three exceptional individuals could have joined forces to bring justice to countless victims and illuminate the darkest corners of human criminality. Within these pages, the collaboration is real, the friendship authentic, the methods revolutionary.

Table of Contents

The Marriage of Arthur and Louisa

August 6, 1885

The morning mist clung to the Yorkshire dales like a gentle blessing as St. Oswald's Church in Thornton-in-Lonsdale prepared to witness a union that would bind two hearts together for life. August 6th, 1885, dawned crisp and clear, the kind of day that seemed to promise new beginnings and bright futures.

Arthur Conan Doyle stood at the altar, his tall frame slightly rigid with nervous anticipation. At twenty-six, he had established himself as a dedicated physician in Southsea, Portsmouth, but today he found himself far from his practice, in the Yorkshire countryside where his beloved mother had made her home. It was Mary Doyle's presence in Thornton-in-Lonsdale that had drawn them to this charming village church for their wedding, rather than celebrating in the familiar surroundings of Portsmouth. Arthur's thoughts were entirely consumed by the woman who would soon become his wife, his dark eyes—usually so keen and observant in his medical practice—now searching the church entrance with barely contained emotion.

The small congregation that had gathered in the ancient stone church represented the most important people in both their lives. Mary Doyle, Arthur's devoted mother, sat in the front pew, her face radiant with joy for her son. How fitting it seemed that they should celebrate this momentous occasion in the place she now called home, surrounded by the Yorkshire dales that had embraced the Doyle family. Beside her, young Innes Doyle shifted restlessly, proud to serve as witness to his older brother's happiness. Constance Doyle, another of Arthur's siblings, dabbed at her eyes with a delicate handkerchief, already emotional before the ceremony had properly begun.

Bryan Waller, Arthur's dear friend and mentor, stood nearby as a witness, his presence a testament to the deep friendship that had shaped Arthur's early years. Julia Waller, accompanying her husband, smiled warmly at the proceedings, remembering the young man Arthur had been when he first came into their lives.

But it was Emily Hawkins who perhaps felt the deepest mixture of joy and melancholy. As Louisa's mother, she had watched her daughter blossom into a woman of remarkable intelligence and grace. Louisa had captured Arthur's heart not merely with her beauty, but with her sharp wit and gentle understanding of his ambitions as a physician. Emily knew that in Arthur, her daughter had found not just a husband, but a true partner in life's grand adventure.

The Reverend S. R. Stable, resplendent in his ceremonial robes, had known this small community for many years. He had baptized children, married couples, and laid the elderly to rest within these hallowed walls. The choice of St. Oswald's Church for this union spoke to the importance of family ties and the special place Yorkshire held in the Doyle family's heart. There was something particularly moving about this wedding. Perhaps it was the way Arthur's eyes lit up when Louisa appeared at the church door, or the quiet confidence with which she walked down the aisle, but he sensed he was witnessing the beginning of something truly special.

Louisa moved gracefully down the aisle, her wedding dress rustling softly against the stone floor. Though Arthur's medical practice awaited him back in Portsmouth, she understood the significance of celebrating their union here in Yorkshire, where his mother had found peace and happiness. She was ready to embark on a new chapter alongside the man whose dreams seemed as vast as the dales themselves. Her mother's eyes followed every step, remembering the little girl who had grown into this radiant woman.

As the ceremony commenced, Reverend Stable's voice rang out clear and strong, the familiar words of the Anglican service echoing through the ancient stones. "Dearly beloved, we are gathered together here in the sight of God, and in the face of this congregation, to join together this man and this woman in holy matrimony..."

Arthur's hand found Louisa's, and in that moment, the nervous tension that had gripped him all morning melted away. Here was his anchor, his inspiration, his beloved Louisa. The woman who understood his dedication to healing others, who encouraged his medical practice, and who saw in him not just the man he was, but the man he could become.

When the time came for vows, Arthur's voice was steady and sure. Louisa's response was equally clear, her words carrying across the small church with quiet conviction. Bryan Waller and Julia stood as witnesses to Arthur's promises, while Emily Hawkins and the Doyle family members bore witness to Louisa's, creating a circle of love and support around the couple.

The exchange of rings was simple but profound. Arthur slipped the gold band onto Louisa's finger with reverent care, and she accepted it as the symbol of their shared future. In that moment, surrounded by family and friends in the Yorkshire church that had welcomed the Doyle family, they became husband and wife.

After the ceremony, the small wedding party gathered outside St. Oswald's Church for congratulations and farewells. The Yorkshire air was sweet with the scent of heather and the promise of a beautiful day ahead. Arthur and Louisa accepted the well-wishes of their loved ones, their faces glowing with happiness.

Mary Doyle embraced her new daughter-in-law warmly, welcoming Louisa into the family with genuine affection. How wonderful it was to have her son's wedding celebrated here in her Yorkshire home, surrounded by the landscape she had grown to love. Emily Hawkins kissed her son-in-law's cheek, trusting him with her daughter's happiness. The Waller family offered their congratulations and support, knowing that their friendship with Arthur would continue to flourish.

As the day drew toward its close, Arthur and Louisa prepared to depart for their honeymoon journey to Dublin. Ireland beckoned with its rolling green hills and vibrant culture, a perfect destination for a couple beginning their married life together. The crossing would give them time to adjust to their new status as husband and wife, away from the familiar surroundings of both Yorkshire and Portsmouth.

Standing before the church where they had pledged their love, Arthur took Louisa's hand one more time. The witnesses who had signed their marriage certificate—Bryan and Julia Waller, Emily Hawkins, Innes and Mary and Constance Doyle—had given them the greatest gift of all: their presence and blessing on this most important day.

As their carriage rolled away from St. Oswald's Church, carrying them toward their new life together, Arthur and Louisa Conan Doyle looked back only once at the small Yorkshire church where their love had been blessed. They would return to Arthur's medical practice in Portsmouth after their honeymoon, but this day in Yorkshire, in the place his mother called home, would forever hold a special place in their hearts. Ahead lay Dublin, and beyond that, a future filled with adventures neither could yet imagine. But whatever challenges or joys awaited them, they would face them together, bound by the vows they had made in the sight of God and in the presence of those who loved them most.

The mist had lifted from the Yorkshire dales, and the sun shone brightly on Mr. and Mrs. Arthur Conan Doyle as they began their journey into married life, carrying with them the love and blessings of that perfect August day at St. Oswald's Church.

Watson meets Doyle

January 25, 1886

Dr. James H. Watson adjusted his collar against the January chill as he walked down the quiet residential street in Southsea, his leather satchel heavy with notebooks and loose papers. The modest Victorian terrace houses stood in neat rows, their windows glowing warmly against the winter afternoon, and Watson found himself hoping that this meeting would prove more fruitful than his previous attempts to find literary assistance.

At the address that his long time friend Dr. Stamford had provided, Watson paused before the front door to gather his courage. Inside lay either the solution to his problem or another disappointment to add to his growing collection. He knocked firmly.

"Come in," called a rich Scottish voice from within.

Watson entered to find a young man with a thick dark mustache hunched over a writing desk in a cozy study lined with bookshelves. Arthur Conan Doyle looked up from his papers, his keen hazel eyes immediately assessing his visitor with the practiced observation of a medical man.

"Dr. Watson, I presume?" Doyle rose from his chair with an easy smile. "Our mutual friend Dr. Stamford spoke very highly of you. Please, take a seat." He gestured to a comfortable leather chair positioned across from his desk. "My wife has just put the kettle on—would you care for some tea?"

"Thank you, yes, Dr. Doyle." Watson settled into the offered chair, noting the medical diploma on the wall alongside what appeared to be certificates from literary publications. "Dr. Stamford mentioned you've managed quite successfully to combine medicine with writing."

"Indeed, though I confess the doctoring pays more reliably than the letters—so far." Doyle's eyes crinkled with humor as he moved to prepare tea from a service set on a side table. "Please, call me Arthur. If we're to discuss potential collaboration, formality seems rather unnecessary."

Arthur poured tea from a well-used pot into two cups, his movements efficient and practiced. "But Stamford was intriguingly vague about your literary aspirations. He mentioned something about detective stories?"

Watson accepted his cup gratefully, using the moment to organize his thoughts. "Not exactly detective stories in the conventional sense, Arthur. More... chronicles of actual criminal investigations." He leaned forward slightly, his weathered hands steady despite his inner nervousness. "You see, I've been sharing lodgings with a most extraordinary fellow—a consulting detective named Sherlock Holmes."

"Consulting detective?" Arthur's eyebrow arched with interest. "I must confess, I'm not familiar with the profession."

"That's because Holmes essentially invented it," Watson replied, warming to his subject. "When the official police are baffled, private individuals bring their problems to him. He possesses the most remarkable powers of observation and deduction I've ever witnessed." Watson's voice grew more animated as he continued. "I've been present for dozens of his cases over the past year, and I've kept detailed notes of his methods and solutions."

Arthur set down his cup, his interest clearly piqued. "What sort of cases?"

"Everything from missing persons to murder most foul. Just last month, we assisted in the matter of a stolen racehorse that Scotland Yard had given up as hopeless. Holmes solved it in an afternoon by examining a single hoofprint and some tobacco ash." Watson opened his satchel and withdrew a thick, leather-bound notebook. "I have the complete account here—how Holmes determined not only which horse had been stolen, but where it was hidden and who took it, all from clues the police had trampled over for days without seeing their significance."

"Fascinating." Arthur reached toward the notebook, then hesitated. "May I?"

"Of course." Watson handed over the notebook with obvious pride. "Holmes is quite methodical in his approach—every detail matters, every observation contributes to the solution."

Arthur chuckled as he opened the notebook, his eyes scanning Watson's neat, precise handwriting. "Your documentation is remarkably detailed. You've captured not just the facts of the case, but the atmosphere, the characters involved..." He paused to read aloud: "'Holmes stood perfectly still for nearly ten minutes, his sharp profile etched against the lamplight as he examined the fragments of cigar ash, his keen mind clearly processing every detail with systematic precision.'"

Arthur looked up with genuine admiration. "You write with the eye of both a medical man and a natural storyteller, James. These aren't just case reports—they're glimpses into the mind of a genius at work."

Watson colored slightly at the praise. "Holmes insists that I focus on his logical processes rather than what he sometimes calls unnecessary embellishment. He believes the methods themselves are sufficiently compelling without dramatic flourishes."

"But that's precisely what would make these stories compelling to readers!" Arthur's enthusiasm was becoming evident. "The logical deduction provides the intellectual foundation, but the atmosphere, the character development, the human drama—that's what transforms a mere puzzle into literature."

He turned several pages, reading silently for a moment before continuing. "This case of the Boscombe Valley Mystery—you've structured it almost like a novel. The tragic family history, the apparent impossibility of the crime, Holmes's systematic demolition of the obvious solution..." Arthur closed the notebook carefully and fixed Watson with an intent stare. "How many such cases do you have documented?"

"Nearly three dozen complete investigations, with notes on perhaps twenty more." Watson gestured toward his bulging satchel. "Some are brief affairs—matters resolved in a single afternoon. Others are quite complex, involving international conspiracies or family secrets stretching back generations. There was the matter of the Red-Headed League, the Five Orange Pips, the Adventure of the Speckled Band..." He paused, suddenly self-conscious. "I realize it must sound rather fantastic."

"On the contrary, it sounds like exactly the sort of thing readers are hungry for." Arthur stood and began pacing behind his desk, his mind clearly racing. "Crime fascinates the public, but most detective fiction is pure sensation with no logical foundation. Your Holmes provides both rigorous reasoning and genuine mystery." He stopped pacing and leaned forward intently. "Tell me, James, what does Mr. Holmes think of your literary ambitions?"

Watson's expression grew more cautious. "I confess that was a delicate conversation. When I approached Holmes about the possibility of transforming our cases into publishable stories, his initial reaction was... less than enthusiastic." Watson shifted slightly in his chair. "Holmes is quite ambivalent about public attention. He values his privacy and has little interest in fame or recognition."

"But he didn't forbid it entirely?"

"No, though it took considerable persuasion." Watson's tone carried a note of diplomatic careful. "Eventually, Holmes reluctantly agreed to allow me to proceed, provided certain conditions were met. He insists that any published accounts must maintain complete accuracy regarding his deductive processes, and he's quite adamant that his actual identity and location remain protected through appropriate changes to names and peripheral details."

"And his reasoning for allowing it at all?"

Watson considered his words carefully. "Holmes acknowledges, somewhat grudgingly, that properly presented accounts might serve to educate the public about scientific investigative methods. He's quite critical of the detective stories that appear in the penny press—calls them 'sensational rubbish' that misleads people about actual investigative work. I believe he sees some merit in correcting those misconceptions, though he remains skeptical about the entire venture."

Arthur resumed his pacing, his expression growing more thoughtful. "So he's given his permission, albeit reluctantly?"

"Yes, though I suspect his tolerance for the project may depend entirely on how respectfully his methods are presented." Watson's voice carried a note of warning. "Holmes is not a man who suffers fools gladly, and any sensationalization or inaccuracy would likely end his cooperation immediately."

Arthur stopped pacing and turned to face Watson directly, his expression growing more serious. "James, before we proceed further, I need to understand exactly what you're looking for from this meeting. Are you seeking someone to edit your existing notes to make them more acceptable to the reading public? Or is it something else entirely?"

Watson leaned forward, grateful for the direct question. "Not editing, Arthur. I'm looking for a collaborator who can write the stories using the elements from the notes I provide." He paused, choosing his words carefully. "You see, I don't want to be the author of these stories—only the source of the material that makes them possible."

Arthur's eyebrows rose with interest. "You want someone to take your detailed case documentation and craft it into publishable fiction?"

"Precisely." Watson's voice grew more confident as he explained his vision. "I can provide extraordinarily detailed accounts of Holmes's investigations—every conversation, every deduction, every piece of evidence and how it fits into the solution. But transforming that raw material into stories that will captivate readers? That requires literary skills I simply don't possess."

Arthur returned to his chair, his expression showing growing understanding. "So you'd provide the factual foundation, the investigative content, the character insights..."

"Everything that makes the stories authentic," Watson confirmed. "What I need is a writer who can take that material and craft it into compelling narratives that will both entertain readers and educate them about proper detective methods."

"And you have no desire to be recognized as a co-author?"

Watson shook his head firmly. "None whatsoever. My role would be entirely behind the scenes—providing source material, ensuring accuracy, perhaps reviewing drafts to confirm that Holmes's methods are presented correctly. But the actual writing, the literary craftsmanship, the public recognition—all of that would belong entirely to my collaborator."

Arthur leaned back in his chair, his mind clearly working through the implications. "That's a remarkable offer, James. Most men would want credit for such contributions."

"Most men don't have my particular constraints," Watson replied with a slight smile. "I need the income that successful stories might provide, and I want to see Holmes's methods properly presented to the public. But I also need to protect my medical career and respect Holmes's privacy. Anonymous collaboration serves all those purposes."

Arthur stood and moved to the window, gazing out at the winter afternoon as he considered Watson's proposal. "So you're essentially offering to provide a professional writer with an almost unlimited supply of authentic detective stories, fully researched and documented, in exchange for complete anonymity and a share of the profits?"

"That's exactly what I'm offering," Watson confirmed. "The question is whether you're interested in such an arrangement."

Arthur turned back to face him, a slow smile spreading across his features. "James, I believe you may have just presented me with the opportunity of a lifetime."

"Then you're willing to consider it?"

"More than consider it." Arthur returned to his chair with obvious enthusiasm. "But I'd need to see more examples of your work, and we'd have to discuss the practical matters—how to present these cases, whether to use real names, the question of legal liability..."

"I've given considerable thought to those concerns," Watson interjected. "Holmes and I agree that some creative license with names and locations would be essential, both for privacy and to avoid potential legal complications. The methods and solutions would remain exactly as they occurred, but the details that might identify actual persons would need modification."

"Precisely what I was thinking." Arthur dipped his pen in ink and positioned it over the paper. "And the structure of the stories... would you be amenable to my making editorial decisions about how to present the material for maximum literary effect?"

Watson nodded eagerly. "That's exactly what I'm hoping for, Arthur. You would have complete creative control over the presentation, provided the essential investigative elements remain accurate."

Arthur went on to ask, "And that editorial freedom you are offering me includes the dates surrounding each case?"

"Yes! Most definitely. In order to maintain anonymity, I hope that you will change the dates when the cases took place."

"Excellent." Arthur positioned his pen over the paper. "Then I propose we begin with a trial arrangement. You'll select your strongest case—something with compelling mystery, clear deductive reasoning, and interesting characters. I'll craft it into a proper story, then we'll attempt to place it with one of the better magazines."

Watson leaned forward, his expression growing more serious. "Arthur, before we proceed further, I must mention certain conditions that any collaboration would require."

Arthur's pen paused above the paper. "What sort of conditions?"

"Two essential requirements, actually." Watson took a careful breath. "First, any stories that are eventually published must list you as the sole author. My name must not appear anywhere as co-author or collaborator."

"But surely you deserve recognition for—"

"No," Watson interrupted firmly. "I'm a physician with a professional reputation to maintain. Being publicly known as a writer of sensational fiction, however well-crafted, could seriously damage my medical career.

More importantly, my association with Holmes must remain completely discreet for his protection as well."

Arthur nodded slowly, understanding the professional concerns. "I can appreciate the need for discretion. And the second requirement?"

"You must agree never to disclose publicly that I am providing you with case material or assisting in any way with the writing process. To the reading public, these must appear to be entirely your own creations—works of imagination that happen to demonstrate realistic investigative methods."

Arthur set down his pen, studying Watson's face intently. "You're asking me to take complete public credit for what is essentially a collaboration."

"I'm asking you to protect both my professional standing and Holmes's privacy," Watson clarified. "The stories themselves will provide adequate compensation for me. Seeing Holmes's methods properly presented to the public, perhaps inspiring more scientific approaches to criminal investigation—that's reward enough."

"And when people ask where you acquired such detailed knowledge of investigative procedures?"

Watson managed a slight smile. "You're a medical man yourself, Arthur. You can speak knowledgeably about scientific observation and logical deduction. Most readers will assume you've simply conducted thorough research into police methods."

Arthur was quiet for a long moment, clearly weighing the implications of such an arrangement. Finally, he extended his hand across the desk. "James, I accept your conditions completely. Your discretion and Holmes's privacy will be absolutely protected."

He paused, then continued with obvious sincerity. "However, I have one essential condition of my own."

Watson raised an eyebrow. "What sort of condition?"

"While I understand and respect your need for anonymity, I absolutely insist that any income we receive from these stories be divided equally among the three parties involved." Arthur's voice carried firm conviction. "You're providing the source material, Holmes is providing the cases and methods, and I'm contributing the literary craftsmanship. Without all three elements, there would be no stories to sell."

Watson looked genuinely surprised. "Arthur, that's extraordinarily generous, but I hadn't expected—"

"It's not generosity, it's simple fairness," Arthur interrupted. "You may need to remain a silent partner for professional reasons, but you deserve equal compensation for equal contribution. I won't accept any other arrangement."

Watson was quiet for a moment, clearly moved by the offer. "That's... that's very fair of you, Arthur. I agree with the principle completely." He paused, his expression growing more thoughtful. "However, I should discuss this arrangement with Holmes before committing him to any financial agreements. While he's given permission for the literary venture, he hasn't specifically agreed to profit from it."

Arthur nodded approvingly. "Of course, that's quite proper. You shouldn't commit him to arrangements he hasn't approved."

"I believe Holmes will find your proposal reasonable," Watson continued, "especially since you're insisting on fairness rather than taking advantage of our situation. But I want to ensure he's comfortable with receiving payment for his contribution."

"Then shall we say that the three-way division is contingent upon Holmes's agreement?" Arthur suggested. "If he prefers not to participate financially, we can adjust the arrangement accordingly."

Watson smiled gratefully. "That's perfect, Arthur. I'll discuss it with him and let you know his decision."

Arthur's grin was confident as he reached for his pen again. "James, I have a strong feeling that anonymity will prove the least of our concerns. If your Mr. Holmes is half as remarkable as these notes suggest, we may find ourselves struggling to keep pace with public demand for his adventures—regardless of whose name appears on the title page."

Watson gathered his papers, excitement evident despite his insistence on remaining hidden. "I have just the case in mind for our first attempt. 'A Study in Scarlet'—a murder most mysterious, with international intrigue and a solution that stretches back decades. The deductive work required was extraordinary."

Arthur's eyes lit up with interest. "It sounds perfect. When can you provide me with your notes for this case?"

Watson smiled and reached into his satchel, withdrawing a thick folder bound with string. "Actually, Arthur, I brought them with me today. I hoped this meeting might go well enough to warrant a practical demonstration." He placed the folder on Arthur's desk. "These are my complete notes on the Study in Scarlet case—every detail, every conversation, every step of Holmes's reasoning. Consider it our test case."

Arthur accepted the folder with obvious reverence, untying the string to reveal pages of Watson's meticulous handwriting interspersed with sketches and diagrams. "My word, James, this is remarkably comprehensive. How long did this investigation take?"

"Several weeks from start to finish, though the actual crimes occurred decades apart. The case involved murders in London that were connected to events in the American frontier—a tale of love, revenge, and religious persecution that spans two continents."

Arthur began scanning the opening pages, his expression growing more animated with each line. "This is extraordinary material. The mysterious word 'RACHE' written in blood, the locked room, the pill that proves to be poison..." He looked up with genuine excitement. "James, this has everything a reader could want—mystery, international intrigue, and a detective whose methods are clearly superior to conventional police work."

"And every word of it true," Watson confirmed. "That's what makes these cases so compelling—they demonstrate that reality can be far more ingenious than fiction."

Arthur carefully retied the folder and set it aside with obvious anticipation. "I shall begin working on this immediately. Give me a fortnight to craft the opening chapters, then we can discuss how well the collaboration is proceeding."

Watson stood and moved toward the door, then paused. "Arthur, I want you to know how much I appreciate your willingness to work within these unusual parameters. I wasn't certain anyone would accept such an arrangement."

Arthur was already reaching for a fresh sheet of paper, his mind clearly engaged with the literary possibilities ahead. "James, I have a strong suspicion that these 'unusual parameters' may prove to be the foundation for something quite extraordinary. If your documentation is as thorough as this sample suggests, and if Holmes's methods are as brilliant as you claim, we may be about to introduce the reading public to an entirely new form of detective fiction."

As Watson's footsteps faded down the garden path, Arthur opened the folder once more, already envisioning the story that might emerge from this unlikely collaboration. Outside his study window, the winter fog pressed against the glass, but inside the warm room, the future of detective literature was beginning to take shape—with Arthur Conan Doyle destined to receive all the public credit for bringing the extraordinary Sherlock Holmes to the world.

He smiled as he dipped his pen in ink and began to write: "Meeting with Dr. James Watson - January 25, 1886. Most promising collaboration proposed. Subject: transformation of authentic criminal investigations into publishable fiction. Material received: 'A Study in Scarlet' case notes. Financial arrangements: Three-way split pending Holmes's approval. Potential: extraordinary."

The partnership that would make Sherlock Holmes the most famous detective in literature had officially begun.

Doyle Tells Touie about Watson

January 25, 1886

Arthur Conan Doyle sat transfixed at his desk, the folder of Watson's case notes spread before him like pieces of an intricate puzzle waiting to be assembled. The winter afternoon had grown darker outside his study windows, but he barely noticed as he became absorbed in the extraordinary tale unfolding through Watson's meticulous documentation.

"The murdered man lay in the front room," Arthur read aloud to himself, his voice barely above a whisper. "There had been no robbery, nor is there any evidence as to how he met his death. There are bloodstains on the floor, but no wound upon his person..."

He turned the page eagerly, his medical training allowing him to appreciate both the clinical precision of Watson's observations and the dramatic potential of the mystery itself. The locked room, the mysterious word "RACHE" scrawled in blood, the peculiar circumstances that had baffled Scotland Yard completely—all of it documented with the eye of someone who understood that truth could indeed be stranger than fiction.

The case notes revealed layer upon layer of complexity: the second murder, the connection to events decades past in the American frontier, and most remarkably, the systematic way Holmes had unraveled the entire conspiracy through careful observation and logical deduction. Arthur found himself making notes in the margins, already envisioning how the various elements might be structured into a compelling narrative.

"Remarkable," he murmured, scanning Watson's account of Holmes's analysis of the victims' backgrounds. "The man doesn't just solve crimes—he reconstructs entire histories from the smallest evidence..."

Arthur was so engrossed in the material that he didn't hear the soft footsteps in the hallway outside his study. Only when the door opened with a gentle creak did he look up to find his wife Louisa standing in the doorway, her face showing the patient amusement of a woman accustomed to her husband's literary enthusiasms.

"Arthur," she said gently, "you've been in here for nearly three hours. I was beginning to wonder if Dr. Watson's visit had somehow spirited you away entirely."

Arthur blinked, suddenly aware that the room had grown quite dim around him. At twenty-seven, Louisa retained the gentle beauty that had first caught his attention, though now there was a comfortable domesticity to her presence that spoke of their six months of marriage. She moved into the room with quiet grace, lighting the gas lamp beside his desk before settling into the small chair he kept for visitors.

"Forgive me, my dear," Arthur said, carefully closing the folder while his mind continued to race with the possibilities it contained. "Dr. Watson's material has proven to be... quite extraordinary."

Louisa noted the careful way he handled the papers, recognizing the signs of a project that had captured her husband's complete attention. In their months of marriage, she had learned to distinguish between Arthur's various enthusiasms—his passion for medicine, his love of literature, and most particularly, his burning ambition to establish himself as a professional writer.

"Tell me about it," she said simply, settling back in her chair with the expression of someone prepared to listen to whatever had so thoroughly captivated her husband's imagination.

Arthur leaned back in his chair, organizing his thoughts with the same methodical approach he applied to his medical diagnoses. "Touie, I believe I may have stumbled upon the most remarkable opportunity of my literary career."

Louisa set aside the needlework she had been carrying, recognizing the excitement in her husband's voice. "What sort of opportunity?"

"Dr. Watson has been sharing lodgings with the most extraordinary individual—a consulting detective named Sherlock Holmes. Have you ever heard of such a profession?"

"I can't say that I have."

"Neither had I. But according to Watson, this Holmes fellow possesses remarkable powers of observation and deduction. He solves cases that baffle the official police through pure logical reasoning." Arthur's enthusiasm grew as he spoke. "Watson has been documenting these investigations in detail—cases involving murder, theft, international intrigue—all solved through scientific methods."

Louisa watched her husband's animated expression with fond familiarity. "And he wants you to help him write about them?"

"More than that. He wants me to transform his case notes into publishable stories. Real detective work, Touie, presented as engaging literature." Arthur stood and began pacing, as was his habit when excited. "Think of it—detective fiction based on actual investigative techniques rather than the melodramatic nonsense currently filling the magazines."

"It does sound promising," Louisa agreed. "What sort of man is this Dr. Watson?"

Arthur considered the question carefully. "Intelligent, certainly. A military doctor—served in Afghanistan, I believe. There's a steadiness about him, a reliability that speaks well of his character. But more importantly, he writes with genuine skill. His case notes read like literature already; they simply need proper structure and refinement."

"And you believe you can provide that?"

"I do." Arthur's confidence was evident. "Remember, Touie, I've been preparing for this sort of work my entire writing career. That first story I wrote as a lad—'The Story of a Bengal Tiger'—was crude, certainly, but it showed I could craft adventure and mystery. 'The Mystery of Sasassa Valley' proved I could write for publication."

Louisa nodded. She remembered well Arthur's excitement when that first short story had been published in 1879, and his subsequent frustration as other submissions met with rejection after rejection.

"The medical practice provides our bread and butter," Arthur continued, "but writing—this is where my true ambitions lie. Watson's cases could provide the foundation for an entirely new approach to detective fiction."

"What are the financial arrangements?" Louisa asked practically.

Arthur smiled at his wife's sensible question. "Watson insists on equal division of any profits, though he must remain anonymous for professional reasons. All published works would bear my name alone."

"That seems generous of him."

"Indeed. Though there are... unusual aspects to the arrangement." Arthur paused in his pacing. "Watson was quite specific that I must never publicly acknowledge his contribution. These stories must appear to be entirely my own creation."

Louisa raised an eyebrow. "Why such secrecy?"

"Professional concerns. He's a practicing physician and believes association with sensational fiction could damage his medical reputation. More importantly, his detective friend values privacy above all else."

"This Mr. Holmes—what did you make of him from Watson's descriptions?"

Arthur resumed his seat, his expression growing thoughtful. "Fascinating. Brilliant, certainly, but also eccentric to the point of peculiarity. He plays violin at all hours, conducts chemical experiments in their sitting room, and apparently shoots holes in the wall when bored."

"Good heavens!"

"But his methods, Touie—Watson's descriptions of Holmes's deductive processes are remarkable. The man can apparently deduce a person's entire history from the smallest details—tobacco ash, boot prints, the wear pattern on a coat sleeve."

Louisa picked up her needlework again, her hands working automatically as she considered her husband's words. "And you believe readers would find such stories appealing?"

"I believe there's a hunger for intelligent fiction that respects its audience. The current crop of detective stories relies on coincidence and melodrama. Stories based on actual logical investigation could set an entirely new standard."

"When will you begin?"

"Watson has already provided me with a complete case study— something called 'A Study in Scarlet.' A murder investigation with international connections and a solution that stretches back decades." Arthur's eyes gleamed with anticipation. "If I can successfully transform that first case into publishable form, we may have the beginning of a very profitable series."

Louisa looks carefully at her husband's face in the lamplight. Since opening his medical practice in Southsea four years ago, she had watched Arthur balance his professional obligations with his literary ambitions. The practice provided steady income, but she knew his heart lay with his writing.

"Arthur," she said gently, "you speak of this opportunity with more excitement than I've seen since our wedding day. Do you truly believe it could lead to the writing career you've always wanted?"

Arthur was quiet for a moment, considering her question seriously. "Touie, I've written steadily for years—stories, articles, even attempted novels. Some have found publication, but none have brought the recognition or income I've hoped for. This collaboration with Watson feels different. The source material is authentic, the character of Holmes is genuinely fascinating, and the approach to detective fiction would be unprecedented."

He leaned forward, taking her hands in his. "If these stories succeed, they could establish my reputation as a serious writer. And if they fail..." He shrugged. "I'll still have my medical practice. But I must try, Touie. This may be exactly the opportunity I've been waiting for."

Louisa squeezed his hands affectionately. "Then you must pursue it with all your energy. I have faith in your abilities, Arthur. If anyone can transform Dr. Watson's case notes into compelling literature, it's you."

Arthur felt a surge of gratitude for his wife's unwavering support. "Thank you, my dear. I confess I'm more excited about this project than I've been about any writing endeavor in years."

"When will you see Dr. Watson again?"

"I shall contact him once I have a draft ready for his review," Arthur replied, his gaze drifting back to the precious folder of case notes. "I want to show him how his remarkable material can be transformed into a proper story. If my first attempt meets with his approval..." Arthur smiled. "Then we shall see if we can create something worthy of both his extraordinary detective friend and the reading public."

As they prepared for bed that evening, Arthur found his mind already working on the possibilities that lay ahead. Real cases, solved through genuine scientific methods, transformed into engaging literature. If he could succeed in this collaboration, it might finally provide the path to the professional writing career he had dreamed of since boyhood.

Tomorrow, he thought as he extinguished the lamp, I begin planning how to bring Mr. Sherlock Holmes to the world.

A Study in Scarlet Draft

February 22, 1886

Four weeks had passed since that first meeting, and Dr. James Watson found himself once again walking down the familiar street in Southsea, though this time his satchel contained only a brief but enthusiastic note from Arthur requesting this second meeting to discuss the manuscript he had completed. Watson's pulse quickened with anticipation as he approached the modest Victorian terrace house, knowing that inside awaited either the successful transformation of his carefully documented case notes or confirmation that his literary ambitions had been overly optimistic.

Watson knocked on the door with considerably more confidence than he had felt a month prior, his nervousness tempered by genuine curiosity about what Arthur had accomplished with the raw material of Holmes's most complex investigation.

"James! Come in, come in." Arthur Conan Doyle greeted him with obvious excitement, ushering him into the same cozy study where their collaboration had begun. The writing desk was now dominated by a neat stack of manuscript pages, clearly the product of intensive literary labor, while Watson's original case notes lay organized in careful piles nearby.

"Arthur," Watson said, settling into his familiar chair and noting the energy radiating from his friend, "your message suggested considerable progress. I confess myself eager to see what you've accomplished."

Arthur poured tea from the same battered pot, his movements quick and animated. "James, before we discuss the manuscript itself, I must tell you how impressed I am with the quality of your documentation. Your note-taking ability is extraordinary—every conversation recorded with precision, every piece of evidence catalogued systematically, every deduction of Holmes's captured in exact detail."

Watson felt a flush of pride at the unexpected praise. "I've always believed that accurate records are essential to proper analysis, whether medical or investigative."

"Indeed, and your organizational methods are equally impressive," Arthur continued, gesturing toward the neatly arranged piles of original notes. "You've structured the case chronologically, cross-referenced the various characters and their relationships, even included detailed sketches of the crime scenes. It's the work of a trained observer with genuine literary instincts."

Arthur moved to his desk and lifted the completed manuscript with obvious satisfaction. "However, James, I hope you'll understand when I say that I can see precisely why these notes, remarkable as they are, might not immediately captivate the average reader."

Watson leaned forward with interest rather than offense. "How so?"

Arthur settled into his chair, holding the manuscript like a professor preparing to deliver a lecture. "Your approach—quite properly, given your medical and investigative training—is methodical and comprehensive. You begin with background, proceed through the investigation systematically, and conclude with Holmes's complete explanation of his solution. It's scientifically sound and intellectually satisfying."

"But?" Watson sensed there was more to come.

"But successful fiction requires different considerations than successful documentation," Arthur explained, his voice taking on the enthusiasm of someone discussing a subject close to his heart. "Readers don't simply want information—they want to be engaged, surprised, emotionally invested in the outcome."

Arthur opened his manuscript to the first page. "Consider how you began your account: 'On March 3rd, 1881, I was residing at 111 Baker Street with my friend and colleague, Mr. Sherlock Holmes, when

Inspector Gregson of Scotland Yard called upon us with a most perplexing case.' Perfectly clear, entirely accurate, but..."

"But not particularly gripping," Watson finished, beginning to understand Arthur's point.

"Precisely. Now listen to how I've chosen to open the story." Arthur cleared his throat and read: "In the year 1878 I took my degree of Doctor of Medicine of the University of London, and proceeded to Netley to go through the course prescribed for surgeons in the army. Having completed my studies there, I was duly attached to the Fifth Northumberland Fusiliers as Assistant Surgeon."

Watson blinked in surprise. "You've begun with my personal history rather than the case itself?"

"Because readers need to care about the narrator before they can fully invest in his story," Arthur explained. "By establishing your background—your military service, your wound at Maiwand, your return to London—I create a character the reader can sympathize with before introducing the mystery itself."

Arthur turned several pages, his excitement growing as he warmed to his explanation. "Your notes document the investigation brilliantly, but they assume the reader shares Holmes's analytical detachment. Fiction requires emotional engagement. Readers must feel the frustration of the baffled police, the tension of the pursuit, the satisfaction of the solution."

"And how do you create that engagement?"

"Through structure, pacing, and what I might call strategic revelation of information." Arthur's eyes gleamed with the satisfaction of a craftsman explaining his techniques. "For instance, your notes present Holmes's deductions in the order he made them, which is logical but not necessarily dramatic. I've rearranged some elements to maximize their impact on the reader."

Watson studied his friend's animated features, recognizing the passion of someone who had found their true calling. "Give me a specific example."

Arthur flipped through the manuscript until he found the passage he wanted. "In your notes, Holmes explains early in the investigation how he determined the height and writing habits of the murderer from examining the word 'RACHE' on the wall. Fascinating deduction, clearly presented. But I've moved that revelation to later in the story, allowing readers to puzzle over the mysterious word just as the police did."

"Creating suspense rather than immediate enlightenment," Watson observed.

"Exactly. The reader experiences the mystery as participants rather than as students receiving a lecture." Arthur's enthusiasm was infectious. "Your documentation provides all the elements necessary for compelling fiction—remarkable characters, ingenious plot, authentic investigative methods. What I've attempted to do is arrange those elements for maximum dramatic effect."

Arthur set down the manuscript and fixed Watson with a more serious expression. "James, I want you to understand that every liberty I've taken with the structure serves the purpose of making Holmes's methods more accessible and engaging to general readers. I've changed nothing about his actual deductions or investigative techniques."

Watson felt his excitement building as he grasped the full scope of what Arthur had accomplished. "You've transformed documentation into literature while preserving scientific accuracy."

"That's precisely what I've attempted," Arthur confirmed. "Because ultimately, both of us want the same thing—to present Holmes's extraordinary methods to the reading public in a way that both entertains and educates."

Arthur handed Watson the manuscript with obvious pride. "I believe what I've created honors both your meticulous documentation and the remarkable man whose work you've recorded. But the final judgment, of course, must be yours."

As Watson accepted the manuscript, feeling its weight in his hands, he realized that Arthur had solved a problem he hadn't even fully understood. His notes were comprehensive and accurate, but they were written for someone who already appreciated Holmes's brilliance. Arthur had found a way to make that brilliance accessible to readers who had never witnessed such methods in action.

"Arthur," Watson said, looking up from the neat pages with genuine admiration, "I believe you may have accomplished something remarkable here. You've taken the raw material of actual detective work and transformed it into something that could genuinely captivate the reading public."

"That's been my goal from the beginning," Arthur replied. "To create detective fiction that respects both the intelligence of its readers and the authenticity of its source material. Whether I've succeeded..." He gestured toward the manuscript. "That remains to be seen."

Watson settled back in his chair, ready to discover how Arthur Conan Doyle had transformed the extraordinary case of "A Study in Scarlet" from his careful medical documentation into what might become the foundation of an entirely new approach to detective literature.

Doyle's Private Thoughts

February 22, 1886

Arthur Conan Doyle sat alone in his study, the empty teacups and scattered papers bearing witness to Watson's departed presence. The afternoon had gone well—better than Arthur had dared hope. Watson's enthusiasm for the manuscript had been genuine, his praise for Arthur's literary transformation both generous and insightful. But now, in the quiet aftermath of their meeting, Arthur felt a different kind of anxiety settling over him like evening fog.

Watson had departed with the manuscript tucked carefully under his arm, promising to read it thoroughly once more before taking the next crucial step. And that step, Arthur knew, would determine everything.

He'll show it to Holmes, Arthur thought, staring at the chair Watson had occupied just an hour before. That will be the real test.

During their discussion, Watson had been encouraging about Holmes's likely reception of the work. "Holmes insisted on accuracy above all else," Watson had said, "and you've preserved every essential element of his investigative process." But Arthur detected the careful phrasing of a man who understood his friend's exacting standards and wasn't entirely certain how those standards would apply to literary adaptation.

Arthur rose and moved to the window, watching the late afternoon light fade across the Southsea rooftops. Watson's approval had been gratifying, but Watson was, by his own admission, not a literary man. His praise focused on accuracy, on the faithful preservation of facts and methods. Holmes, from Watson's descriptions, was something else entirely—a brilliant, uncompromising intellect who suffered fools poorly and had little patience for anything that didn't meet his exacting standards.

What if he hates it?

The thought struck Arthur with unexpected force. He had written the story with such care, balancing dramatic effect with scientific accuracy, crafting engaging prose while preserving every crucial deduction. But Holmes hadn't asked for engaging prose. Holmes had reluctantly agreed to allow documentation of his methods, provided they were presented with complete accuracy. Would he view Arthur's literary embellishments as improvements or as unwelcome distortions?

Arthur returned to his desk and picked up Watson's original case notes, now seeming strangely bare after his intensive work with them. Every conversation, every observation, every logical step had been preserved in Watson's meticulous handwriting. But Arthur had rearranged elements for dramatic effect, enhanced details, and crafted dialogue that captured the spirit of conversations without claiming to reproduce them verbatim.

"Holmes darted about the room like a pure-bred foxhound drawing a cover," Arthur murmured, recalling one of his descriptive passages. Would Holmes appreciate being compared to a hunting dog, even in the service of vivid prose? Arthur realized he had been writing about a real person as if he were a fictional character, imposing literary flourishes on someone who might have very different ideas about how his work should be presented.

The consulting detective remained a mystery to Arthur. Watson's descriptions painted a fascinating portrait—brilliant beyond measure, but also moody, eccentric, sometimes difficult. A man who conducted chemical experiments in his sitting room, played violin at all hours, and could deduce a person's entire history from examining their collar or boot heels. How would such a person react to seeing his life's work filtered through a stranger's literary sensibilities?

Arthur began pacing, a habit that helped him think through complex problems. The irony of his situation wasn't lost on him—his entire literary future might depend on the approval of a man he had never met, whose very existence he was committed to concealing from the public. Yet Holmes's reaction mattered more than any editor's, because without

Holmes's continued cooperation, there would be no more stories to write.

Watson will read it again tonight, Arthur calculated, then arrange a meeting with Holmes. Perhaps tomorrow, perhaps the day after. And then...

Arthur's medical training had taught him to examine evidence objectively, but now he found himself second-guessing every choice he had made. Had he accurately portrayed Holmes's deductive methods? The chemical analysis of the pills found at the crime scene, the interpretation of bloodstain patterns, the logical progression from scattered clues to complete solution—all of it would be scrutinized by the man who had actually performed the work.

One error in scientific procedure, one misrepresentation of investigative technique, and Holmes would lose all confidence in Arthur's ability to present his methods properly. Watson had made clear that Holmes's cooperation was reluctant at best, granted only with strict conditions about accuracy and discretion.

The locked room analysis, Arthur worried, mentally reviewing that crucial section. Watson's notes had been precise about Holmes's examination of the blood evidence, his interpretation of the mysterious word "RACHE," his reconstruction of the murderer's actions. Arthur had preserved all the essential elements while making them more accessible to general readers. But would Holmes consider such accessibility a virtue or a compromise of scientific rigor?

Arthur paused at his bookshelf, noting the medical texts that had helped him understand the forensic elements of Watson's documentation. He had researched carefully, consulting additional sources to ensure his understanding was complete. But Holmes's knowledge was clearly extensive and specialized. What if Arthur had misunderstood some crucial aspect of the detective's methodology?

The social dynamics posed another concern. Watson's notes revealed that Holmes often solved cases through psychological insight as much as physical evidence. Arthur had tried to capture this human dimension, but writing convincingly about criminal motivation required delicate handling. Too much speculation and Holmes might consider it unscientific; too little and the story would lose its compelling human element.

I'm writing about a man who solves puzzles that baffle Scotland Yard, Arthur reflected, and he'll judge whether I'm intelligent enough to understand and accurately present his work.

The pressure was extraordinary. Arthur had essentially claimed to comprehend methods that had confounded London's finest detectives. If his portrayal seemed naive or inaccurate to Holmes, the detective would have every reason to end their association immediately.

Arthur moved to his desk and withdrew a sheet of paper, beginning to compose a letter to Watson:

My dear James,

I hope you found the completed manuscript satisfactory upon further review. As you prepare to share it with Mr. Holmes, I want you to know that I understand completely the importance of his approval. Please assure him that every scientific detail has been researched thoroughly, and that any literary embellishments serve only to make his remarkable methods more accessible to general readers.

I should be grateful to receive his honest assessment, including any corrections or suggestions he might offer. Above all, please convey my deep respect for his work and my commitment to presenting it with complete accuracy should he approve our proceeding with publication.

Arthur paused, pen hovering over the paper. What else could he say? How did one address, through an intermediary, a brilliant stranger whose approval could make or break one's literary aspirations?

Finally, he continued:

I confess myself anxious to learn whether my adaptation meets his exacting standards. The quality of the source material is extraordinary, and I hope my treatment proves worthy of both the original investigation and the remarkable man who conducted it.

Arthur

Arthur sealed the letter, knowing it would accompany Watson's copy of the manuscript when he met with Holmes. Soon—perhaps within days—Arthur would learn whether his literary future included the continuing collaboration that could establish his reputation, or whether his first attempt would also be his last.

The real test begins now, Arthur thought as he prepared for bed. Watson's approval had been encouraging, but Holmes's verdict would be definitive. Either Arthur had successfully transformed authentic detective work into compelling literature, or he had failed to understand the very methods he had attempted to present.

Holmes' Concerns

February 25, 1886

The February afternoon had brought a welcome respite from London's perpetual winter gloom, and pale sunlight filtered through the tall windows of 111 Baker Street, illuminating the comfortable chaos that characterized the sitting room shared by Dr. James Watson and Mr. Sherlock Holmes. Mrs. Hudson had outdone herself with the luncheon service, providing a substantial meal of roasted beef and Yorkshire pudding that filled the room with appetizing aromas and temporarily displaced the usual mixture of tobacco smoke and chemical vapors.

Watson sat at the small dining table they had positioned near the window, methodically working through his portion while stealing occasional glances at his friend. Holmes had been unusually subdued for the past three days, ever since Watson had presented him with Arthur Conan Doyle's completed manuscript of "A Study in Scarlet." The great detective had accepted the pages with his characteristic analytical expression and immediately retreated to his bedroom for what Watson assumed would be a thorough review.

Since then, Holmes had emerged only for meals and his morning ablutions, spending his time either reading in absolute silence or conducting what appeared to be correspondence with parties unknown. Watson had learned not to press his friend when Holmes was engaged in intensive mental work, but the suspense was becoming difficult to bear.

"Holmes," Watson ventured as he carved another slice of beef, "Mrs. Hudson has certainly provided us with an exceptional meal today. The beef is particularly fine."

Holmes looked up from his plate with the slightly unfocused expression of someone whose mind had been elsewhere entirely. "Indeed, Watson. Though I confess I've been somewhat... preoccupied with other matters to fully appreciate Mrs. Hudson's culinary efforts."

Watson felt his pulse quicken at this opening. "Ah, yes. I imagine you've had time to review the manuscript I provided earlier this week?"

Holmes set down his fork with deliberate precision and leaned back in his chair, his keen gray eyes fixing upon Watson with renewed attention. "I have indeed completed my analysis of Mr. Doyle's literary effort. Most thorough analysis, actually."

"And your conclusion?" Watson asked, attempting to keep his voice casual despite the anxiety that had been building for days.

Holmes was quiet for a moment, his steepled fingers pressed against his lips in the pose Watson recognized as indicating serious contemplation. "Watson, I must confess that I approached Mr. Doyle's work with considerable skepticism. My experience with popular literature has not predisposed me to expect either accuracy or intelligence from writers who attempt to dramatize actual investigative work."

Watson felt his heart sink slightly at this ominous beginning. "But?"

"But Mr. Doyle has surprised me considerably," Holmes continued, his expression growing more animated. "The man possesses a remarkable ability to present complex investigative methodology in terms that would be accessible to general readers without sacrificing essential accuracy."

Watson leaned forward with renewed hope. "You found the story scientifically sound?"

"Substantially so, yes. Doyle clearly took considerable care to understand the forensic principles underlying my examination of the crime scene. His description of the blood evidence analysis, the interpretation of the mysterious word 'RACHE,' the logical progression from scattered clues to complete solution—all presented with accuracy that suggests genuine comprehension rather than mere copying."

Holmes rose and moved to the mantelpiece, where Watson's manuscript lay precisely where he had placed it three days earlier. "More importantly,

Watson, Doyle has demonstrated something I had not expected to find in a professional writer."

"What's that?"

"Respect for the scientific method," Holmes replied, turning back to face Watson. "He hasn't sensationalized the investigative process or attributed my conclusions to supernatural intuition. Every deduction is presented as the logical result of careful observation and systematic analysis."

Watson felt relief flooding through him like warm brandy. "Then you approve of his approach?"

Holmes returned to his chair, his movements reflecting the satisfaction of a man who had reached a favorable conclusion after intensive consideration. "I am inclined to approve, yes. Though there are several minor corrections that will need to be made."

"What sort of corrections?"

Holmes withdrew a small notebook from his waistcoat pocket and consulted it with characteristic precision. "Nothing fundamental, merely details that require adjustment to ensure complete accuracy. For instance, Doyle has me examining the tobacco ash with a common magnifying glass, when in fact I used my specialized German lens apparatus. Small matter, but such details contribute to the overall authenticity."

"And the characterization? Your portrayal as a fictional detective?"

Holmes's expression grew more thoughtful. "That aspect required the most careful consideration, Watson. Doyle has taken certain liberties with my dialogue and mannerisms, making them rather more... eloquent than my actual speech patterns might warrant. Initially, I found this concerning."

"But upon reflection?"

"Upon reflection, I recognize that effective communication often requires translation between different audiences," Holmes replied. "What matters is that the essential character—my commitment to logical analysis, my impatience with conventional thinking, my methods of approaching criminal investigation—all of this has been preserved accurately."

Watson felt his excitement building as he realized the full implications of Holmes's assessment. "Then you're willing to proceed with publication?"

"I am willing to proceed, provided Mr. Doyle incorporates the minor corrections I've identified." Holmes's voice carried a note of decision that Watson recognized as final. "More than that, Watson—I find myself curious to meet this literary gentleman who has demonstrated such understanding of investigative methodology."

Watson's eyebrows rose with surprise. "You want to meet Arthur personally?"

Holmes nodded with obvious interest. "Indeed. Any man who can accurately present my methods to general readers clearly possesses intelligence worth encountering directly. I should like to take his measure in person before we commit ourselves to what may become an ongoing professional relationship."

Watson set down his napkin, his mind already working through the practical arrangements such a meeting would require. "I'm certain Arthur would be delighted to meet you, Holmes. His respect for your work has been evident throughout our correspondence."

"Excellent. Then perhaps you could arrange for him to call upon us here at Baker Street? I prefer to meet new acquaintances in familiar surroundings, where I can observe them without distraction."

"Of course. When would be convenient for you?"

Holmes consulted his pocket diary briefly. "I have no pressing cases at present. Any afternoon this coming week would be suitable, provided he can spare the time for the journey from Portsmouth."

Watson felt a surge of satisfaction as he contemplated the successful resolution of what had been weeks of careful planning and anxious anticipation. "Holmes, I cannot adequately express how pleased I am by your approval. Arthur has invested considerable effort in this adaptation, and your endorsement means everything to the project's future."

Holmes waved a dismissive hand. "Watson, the man has done excellent work. His literary skills combined with your documentation and my investigative methods could indeed produce something unprecedented in detective fiction."

Mrs. Hudson appeared at that moment to clear away their luncheon dishes, her weathered face showing the satisfaction of someone whose culinary efforts had been properly appreciated. "Will there be anything else, gentlemen?"

"Actually, Mrs. Hudson," Watson said, "we may be receiving a visitor from Portsmouth sometime this week. Dr. Arthur Conan Doyle—a professional colleague of mine. I trust that would present no inconvenience?"

"None whatsoever, Dr. Watson. Any friend of yours is always welcome." Mrs. Hudson gathered the dishes with practiced efficiency. "Shall I prepare the spare room in case the gentleman wishes to stay overnight?"

Holmes looked up with interest. "An excellent suggestion, Mrs. Hudson. If Dr. Doyle is traveling from Portsmouth specifically for this meeting, we should certainly offer him proper hospitality."

"Holmes," Watson said as he prepared to compose his invitation to Arthur, "I believe this meeting may mark the beginning of something quite remarkable."

Holmes had already returned to his chemical apparatus, but he paused to look back at Watson with one of his rare smiles. "Watson, if Mr. Doyle proves as intelligent in person as he has demonstrated on paper, I believe you may be quite right. The reading public may soon discover what actual detective work looks like when properly presented."

As Watson settled at his writing desk to compose the invitation that would bring Arthur Conan Doyle to Baker Street, he felt the deep satisfaction of a man who had successfully navigated complex negotiations to achieve exactly the outcome he had hoped for.

Doyle meets Sherlock Holmes

March 3, 1886

The morning train from Portsmouth to London departed at precisely seven o'clock, and Dr. Arthur Conan Doyle found himself settling into a second-class compartment with a mixture of anticipation and nervous energy that made concentration on his medical journal nearly impossible. The railway carriage was comfortable enough, with red plush seats and adequate heating against the March chill, but Arthur's mind remained fixed on the manuscript that rested in his leather satchel and the crucial meeting that lay ahead.

Three days had passed since Watson had collected the completed draft of "A Study in Scarlet," and yesterday's telegram had been characteristically brief:

HOLMES APPROVES MEETING TUESDAY 3RD MARCH 2 PM BAKER STREET. JOURNEY WARRANTED. J.W.

The sparse phrasing had revealed nothing of Holmes's reaction to the literary adaptation, leaving Arthur to wonder whether he was traveling to London to receive praise or criticism.

As the train gathered speed through the Hampshire countryside, Arthur watched the familiar landscapes roll past the carriage windows. Portsmouth's naval yards gave way to rolling green fields dotted with early spring lambs, then modest market towns where the train paused briefly to collect mail and passengers. The journey to London typically required just over two hours, but today each mile seemed to stretch endlessly as Arthur contemplated the meeting ahead.

Near Guildford, the countryside began to show signs of London's influence—more substantial houses, busier roads paralleling the railway, the occasional factory chimney rising above the trees. Arthur found himself rehearsing potential conversations, imagining how he might respond to various criticisms or questions about his literary choices.

Holmes, from Watson's descriptions, was not a man who minced words or offered empty politeness.

By the time the train reached the London outskirts, Arthur was observing a different world entirely. The suburban villages gave way to increasingly dense development—rows of terraced houses stretching toward the horizon, commercial buildings clustered around local railway stations, and the perpetual haze of coal smoke that marked the approaches to the capital. The rhythmic clacking of wheels on rails provided a steady accompaniment to Arthur's thoughts as he prepared for what might prove to be the most important literary discussion of his career.

Waterloo Station presented its usual chaos of arrival—porters shouting directions, passengers hurrying toward the street, vendors hawking newspapers and refreshments. Arthur made his way through the crowds with the purposeful stride of someone who had visited London often enough to navigate confidently, though never before with such momentous business awaiting him.

The hansom cab journey from Waterloo to Baker Street took him through the heart of London, past the familiar landmarks that never failed to impress a provincial visitor. The Thames reflected the pale March sunlight as they crossed Westminster Bridge, while the Houses of Parliament and Westminster Abbey provided their usual dramatic backdrop. The cab continued north through the busy commercial districts, where shop windows displayed the latest fashions and street vendors competed with the general din of London traffic.

Baker Street, when they finally reached it, proved to be a respectable thoroughfare lined with Georgian townhouses that spoke of solid middle-class prosperity without ostentation. Number 111 stood indistinguishable from its neighbors—a modest four-story building with clean windows and a freshly painted front door that suggested careful maintenance despite modest means.

Arthur paid the cabman and stood for a moment on the pavement, gathering his courage while observing the house that had become so central to Watson's documented adventures. The building showed no external signs of housing London's most extraordinary consulting detective, but Arthur supposed that anonymity was precisely what Holmes would prefer.

At exactly two o'clock, Arthur knocked firmly on the front door. It opened almost immediately to reveal a pleasant-faced woman of middle years whose weathered features spoke of long experience managing a London lodging house.

"Dr. Doyle, I presume?" she said with obvious recognition. "I'm Mrs. Hudson. Dr. Watson said to expect you at two o'clock precisely. Punctuality is much appreciated in this household."

Arthur removed his hat as he stepped into the narrow hallway, noting the comfortable but unremarkable furnishings that characterized a well-run boarding establishment. "Thank you, Mrs. Hudson. I trust I'm not inconveniencing anyone with this visit?"

"Not at all, sir. Mr. Holmes has been quite looking forward to meeting you." Mrs. Hudson gestured toward the staircase with obvious familiarity. "If you'll follow me, please. It's seventeen steps up to their sitting room—I always tell visitors to count them, as the number seems to stick in people's minds."

Arthur followed his hostess up the narrow staircase, indeed counting the steps as suggested. The walls were lined with modest prints and photographs that spoke of residents with diverse interests, while the banister showed the wear of frequent use. At the top of the stairs, Mrs. Hudson knocked gently on a door before opening it with the practiced efficiency of someone who managed such introductions regularly.

"Dr. Doyle to see you, gentlemen," she announced, stepping aside to allow Arthur entry into what was clearly the heart of the establishment.

The sitting room was larger than Arthur had expected, with tall windows providing excellent natural light and comfortable furnishings arranged for both individual reading and social conversation. Books lined two walls from floor to ceiling, while a third wall displayed what appeared to be charts, maps, and scientific instruments. The overall impression was of organized intellectual chaos—the refuge of minds that valued information and analysis above conventional tidiness.

Dr. James Watson rose from a chair beside the fireplace, his familiar face showing obvious pleasure at Arthur's arrival. "Arthur! Welcome to Baker Street. How was the journey from Portsmouth?"

"Quite comfortable, thank you," Arthur replied, shaking Watson's extended hand while his attention was inevitably drawn to the room's other occupant.

Sherlock Holmes stood near the mantelpiece with the composed stillness that Arthur had learned to associate with men accustomed to being observed. At thirty-two, he was taller than Arthur had expected—well over six feet—with the lean build of someone who rarely remained sedentary for extended periods. His sharp gray eyes immediately fixed upon Arthur with an intensity that suggested rapid and comprehensive assessment, while his angular features conveyed an intelligence that was both formidable and slightly unsettling.

"Mr. Holmes," Arthur said, moving forward to offer his hand. "Dr. Watson has spoken of you with such admiration that I confess myself honored by this opportunity to meet."

Holmes accepted the handshake with a firm grip, his keen gaze never wavering from Arthur's face. "Dr. Doyle. Thank you for making the journey from Southsea. I believe we have matters of considerable mutual interest to discuss."

Holmes gestured toward the chairs arranged near the fireplace, his movements economical and precise. "Please, be seated. Mrs. Hudson has provided tea, and I find that important conversations proceed more smoothly when conducted in comfortable circumstances."

As Arthur settled into the offered chair, he noted that Holmes's manner, while courteous, carried an authority that immediately established him as the dominant presence in the room. Watson had described his friend's force of personality, but experiencing it directly was quite different from reading about it in case notes.

"Dr. Doyle," Holmes began without preamble, "I have read your literary adaptation of the Jefferson Hope case with considerable interest. Before we proceed to specific details, I want you to know that I found your work both competent and respectful of the source material."

Arthur felt a surge of relief at these opening words, though Holmes's tone suggested that more complex observations would follow.

"Your medical training is evident in your approach to the forensic elements," Holmes continued, settling into his own chair with characteristic precision. "The blood analysis, the interpretation of the scene evidence, the logical progression from observation to conclusion— all handled with appropriate scientific rigor."

Holmes paused to pour tea with the same methodical attention he apparently applied to all activities. "More importantly, you have managed to present complex investigative reasoning in terms accessible to general readers without sacrificing essential accuracy. That is no mean literary achievement."

Watson leaned forward with obvious satisfaction. "I told you Arthur had genuine literary talent, Holmes."

"Indeed you did, and you were correct in that assessment." Holmes handed Arthur a cup of tea before continuing. "However, Dr. Doyle, there are aspects of your manuscript that require discussion and, in some cases, modification."

Arthur set down his teacup, his attention immediately sharpening. "I'm grateful for any suggestions you might offer, Mr. Holmes. Accuracy was my primary concern throughout the writing process."

Holmes moved to a side table where Arthur's manuscript lay open, marked with numerous annotations in precise handwriting. "The technical corrections are minor—a clarification regarding the chemical analysis of the pills, an adjustment to the timeline of certain deductions. Nothing that affects the fundamental narrative structure."

Holmes returned to his chair with several pages of notes. "However, there are matters of discretion that require more substantial attention."

Arthur nodded, having anticipated this discussion. "Watson mentioned your concerns about privacy and confidentiality."

"Precisely." Holmes's tone became more serious. "Dr. Doyle, your story presents these events as fiction, which provides excellent protection for all parties involved. However, certain details could potentially compromise that protection if they too closely resembled actual circumstances, including the date when the case took place."

Holmes consulted his notes with characteristic precision. "For instance, you have correctly used the address 111 Baker Street throughout the narrative. While this serves the story well, it happens to be our actual address. I would prefer that any published version use a different number on Baker Street—the specific number is immaterial to me, but it should not direct curious readers to our actual door."

Arthur reached for his own notebook, making careful annotations. "That's easily corrected. Any particular number you would prefer?"

"None whatsoever. Choose any fictional number you like—184, 267, whatever strikes your fancy."

Holmes moved to the next item on his list. "More significantly, you have used Watson's actual first name throughout the story. While 'Dr. Watson' provides adequate disguise for casual readers, the combination of 'James Watson' with accurate medical and military background details might prove identifiable to someone with specific knowledge."

Watson looked up with interest. "You're suggesting a different first name for the literary version?"

"I am." Holmes turned to face Watson directly. "James, what would you think of 'John Watson' for publication purposes? It maintains the authenticity of the character while providing additional protection for your professional identity."

Watson considered this proposal thoughtfully. "John Watson... yes, I think that would serve admirably. It preserves the essential character while creating appropriate distance from my actual circumstances."

Arthur made additional notes, recognizing the wisdom of these precautions. "Any other modifications you would recommend, Mr. Holmes?"

Holmes consulted his list once more. "Aside from the date references for each case, those are the primary concerns. The remaining annotations address minor points of investigative procedure—details that only someone with extensive criminal experience would notice, but which should be corrected for complete accuracy."

"Mr. Holmes, James and I have already agreed that I would change the dates surrounding each case, in order to further protect the anonymity of all involved."

"Very well," Holmes replied. Then, he set aside his notes and fixed Arthur with a direct gaze. "Dr. Doyle, I want you to understand that these suggestions reflect my approval of your work rather than criticism of it. You have successfully transformed Watson's case documentation into literature that could genuinely educate readers about proper investigative methods."

Arthur felt a profound sense of relief mixed with professional pride. "Mr. Holmes, I cannot adequately express how gratifying it is to receive your approval. The source material was so extraordinary that I was determined to do it justice."

"And you have done so," Holmes replied with obvious sincerity. "More importantly, you have demonstrated that authentic detective work can be presented as engaging entertainment without compromising scientific integrity. That combination is precisely what the reading public requires."

Holmes stood and moved to the window, looking out at the busy Baker Street afternoon. "Dr. Doyle, if this story finds successful publication, would you be interested in adapting additional cases from Watson's documentation?"

Arthur exchanged glances with Watson, recognizing the significance of this question. "Mr. Holmes, nothing would please me more than the opportunity to continue such collaboration. Watson's case notes reveal investigation after investigation of remarkable complexity and ingenuity."

"Excellent." Holmes turned back to face them both. "Then I believe we have the foundation for what might prove to be an ongoing literary partnership. Provided, of course, that you can maintain the standards of accuracy and discretion we have established today."

Watson smiled with obvious satisfaction. "Holmes, I believe this collaboration could bring your methods to the attention of readers who might never otherwise appreciate the possibilities of scientific investigation."

"That possibility, Watson, is precisely why I have agreed to this venture despite my usual preference for privacy." Holmes returned to his chair with the air of a man who had reached important decisions. "Dr. Doyle, if you can incorporate the modifications we have discussed, I believe 'A Study in Scarlet' will be ready for submission to publishers."

Arthur gathered his materials with a sense of completion mixed with anticipation for the work ahead. "Mr. Holmes, I shall implement every suggestion you've offered. And I want you to know that this meeting has exceeded my most optimistic expectations."

As Arthur prepared to leave 111 Baker Street, he felt the profound satisfaction of having successfully passed the most important literary test of his career. Holmes's approval meant more than any editor's acceptance, because it confirmed that Arthur could transform authentic detective work into compelling literature while maintaining the scientific integrity that made such work valuable.

The journey back to Southsea proved to be far more pleasant than the morning's anxious trip to London. As the hansom cab carried him back toward Waterloo Station, Arthur reflected on the remarkable character he had just met. Holmes was everything Watson had described and more— brilliant, exacting, but also surprisingly generous in his assessment of Arthur's literary efforts.

The Baker Street Address

March 4, 1886

Arthur Conan Doyle sat in his study that evening, Holmes's annotated manuscript spread before him. The detective's request to change their actual Baker Street address from 111 to some fictional number seemed simple enough, yet Arthur found himself strangely hesitant to simply choose any random digits.

"Choose any fictional number you like—184, 267, whatever strikes your fancy," Holmes had said with characteristic indifference to what he clearly considered a trivial detail. And Watson would undoubtedly accept whatever number Arthur selected without question. But something about this decision felt significant to Arthur—this would be the address that readers would forever associate with the great detective.

He set down his pen and leaned back in his chair, his mind wandering as it often did when faced with creative decisions. For some reason, his thoughts drifted back to his boyhood days at Stonyhurst St Mary's Hall, when he was just nine years old and the world seemed full of mysteries waiting to be unraveled.

Those had been formative years, filled with rigorous study under the Jesuit fathers. Mathematics, Latin, literature—and, of course, extensive Biblical studies that had made him intimately familiar with Scripture. Even now, decades later and despite having turned agnostic in his adult years, he could recall passages with startling clarity, the words etched into his memory by countless hours of recitation and study.

The Bible, Arthur mused. So many stories of wisdom and revelation. He had always been particularly drawn to the Old Testament tales of prophets and wise men who could discern hidden truths. As a boy, he had been especially fond of the Book of Daniel—not for its prophecies, which often seemed too abstract for a young mind, but for Daniel himself, the remarkable man who could interpret dreams and reveal the meanings of mysterious signs. Most memorable was Daniel's interpretation of King Nebuchadnezzar's troubling dream, which had baffled all the court's wise men until Daniel revealed its meaning through divine insight.

Arthur smiled, remembering how he had envied Daniel's ability to look at seemingly incomprehensible visions and extract clear, logical explanations. Rather like Holmes, he thought suddenly. The way he examines evidence that baffles everyone else and reveals the truth hidden within.

The comparison struck him as more than coincidental. Daniel's gift had been to take the confused, fragmentary images of dreams and divine their meaning through wisdom and insight. Holmes's gift was remarkably similar—taking the scattered, seemingly meaningless clues of a crime scene and deducing from them a complete understanding of what had transpired.

Arthur leaned forward, the parallel becoming even clearer in his mind. Like the prophet Daniel, Holmes possessed the unique ability to convert raw information—what he called "data"—into true knowledge by understanding and recognizing its significance and meaning. Where others saw only disconnected facts, both men could perceive the underlying patterns that revealed the complete truth.

A particular verse began to form in Arthur's memory, one that had always resonated with him even as a child. Daniel, chapter two, verse twenty-one. Like many Biblical verses, it was divided into two parts—in standard Biblical notation, the first half was designated 2:21a and the second half 2:21b.

It was the second part that had always struck him most powerfully: "giveth wisdom to the wise, and knowledge to them that have understanding."

Arthur had always loved that passage because it seemed to suggest that wisdom was not just a divine gift, but something that came to those who already possessed the capacity for it. Holmes certainly fit that description—a man whose natural intellect had been sharpened through study and observation until he could perceive truths that escaped ordinary minds.

Arthur sat up straighter, an idea beginning to form. The verse reference—Daniel 2:21b, using the standard Biblical notation for the second half of the verse. The numbers seemed to arrange themselves before his eyes: 2... 21... B.

221B.

The more he considered it, the more perfect it seemed. A subtle tribute to the Biblical figure whose gift for interpretation so closely paralleled Holmes's own abilities. It was meaningful without being obvious, scholarly without being pretentious.

He picked up his pen and wrote carefully in the margin of the manuscript: "Change all references from '111 Baker Street' to '221B Baker Street.'"

Arthur leaned back, satisfied with his choice. Holmes would never know the significance of the numbers—the detective had made it clear he cared nothing for such details. Watson would assume it was simply a random selection. But Arthur would know, and somehow that felt appropriate. In a story that celebrated the power of observation and deduction, it seemed fitting that the detective's address should carry its own hidden meaning, visible only to those who possessed the knowledge to discern it.

Daniel the interpreter of dreams, Arthur thought with a small smile, and Sherlock Holmes the interpreter of crimes. Both men blessed with the ability to find truth in mystery.

He gathered the manuscript pages, ready to make the final corrections. Tomorrow he would incorporate Holmes's other minor changes, but the address was now settled. 221B Baker Street would become one of the most famous addresses in literature, though its true significance would remain Arthur's secret.

As he locked the manuscript away for the evening, Arthur reflected on how the smallest details sometimes carried the greatest meaning. Holmes might dismiss the choice of house number as irrelevant, but Arthur understood that in the world of literature, every element served a purpose. The detective who could deduce a man's entire history from the ash on his cigarette would now reside at an address that honored the ancient tradition of using wisdom to unlock hidden truths. Perfect, Arthur thought as he extinguished the lamp. Absolutely perfect.

A Study in Scarlet is Completed

March 27, 1886

The March morning had brought unseasonably warm weather to Southsea, and Dr. Arthur Conan Doyle found himself opening the windows of his study to welcome the fresh air that seemed to promise new beginnings. On his desk lay the completed manuscript of "A Study in Scarlet"—sixty-three pages of careful handwriting that represented five weeks of intensive literary labor and, he hoped, the foundation of his professional writing career.

Arthur lifted the manuscript with the reverence typically reserved for precious artifacts, feeling its satisfying weight in his hands. Every page had been written and rewritten, each sentence crafted to balance dramatic effect with scientific accuracy, every dialogue exchange polished to capture both authentic speech patterns and compelling narrative flow. The transformation from Watson's meticulous case notes to publishable literature was complete.

But before the manuscript could be considered truly finished, Arthur knew he needed to make the final protective changes that would ensure the privacy of those involved. He opened to the first page and carefully made the necessary alterations—changing every reference from "Dr. James H. Watson" to "Dr. John H. Watson," and replacing "111 Baker Street" with "221B Baker Street" throughout the text.

With these final changes complete, Arthur knew he needed one last confirmation that his work met the exacting standards established by their unusual collaboration.

He moved to his writing desk and withdrew a sheet of his finest letterhead, composing a message that would accompany the manuscript on its journey to London:

Arthur sealed the letter and carefully wrapped the manuscript in brown paper, addressing the package to Dr. James Watson at 111 Baker Street,

London. The messenger service he had engaged promised delivery by early afternoon, allowing Watson time for thorough review while the manuscript could still be returned within a reasonable timeframe.

As Arthur watched the messenger disappear down the street with his precious cargo, he felt the familiar mixture of excitement and anxiety that accompanied all his most important literary submissions. But this time was different—this time he wasn't simply hoping that editors would recognize his talent, but trusting that his collaboration with Watson had produced something that transcended conventional fiction entirely.

The next three days passed with excruciating slowness. Arthur attempted to occupy himself with his medical practice, but found his concentration scattered between patient consultations and mental rehearsals of his submission strategy. He had identified four publishers who seemed most likely to appreciate innovative detective fiction: Ward, Lock & Co., Blackwood's Magazine, The Cornhill Magazine, and Cassell & Company. Each had published successful mystery stories, though none had attempted anything quite like what he and Watson had created.

March 30, 1886 - Southsea

The telegram arrived during Arthur's afternoon office hours, delivered by a breathless messenger boy who had clearly been instructed that the message required immediate attention. Arthur opened the yellow envelope with trembling hands, knowing that Watson's verdict would determine whether their collaboration could proceed to the crucial next phase.

MANUSCRIPT EXCELLENT STOP HOLMES THOROUGHLY APPROVES SCIENTIFIC ACCURACY STOP PROCEED WITH SUBMISSIONS IMMEDIATELY STOP CONFIDENT IN SUCCESS STOP WATSON

Arthur read the telegram three times, relief flooding through him with such intensity that he had to sit down to steady himself. Holmes's approval—the one judgment that truly mattered—had been secured. The great detective himself had pronounced the work scientifically sound, meaning that Arthur's literary adaptation had successfully preserved the authentic investigative methods that made their collaboration valuable.

Within an hour, Arthur had prepared four identical packages, each containing a carefully transcribed copy of the complete manuscript along with a cover letter tailored to the specific publisher's interests and previous publications. His hands moved with mechanical efficiency, but his mind raced with possibilities for the future.

My dear Editor,

I have the honor to submit for your consideration a detective story of a new type—one based on authentic investigative methodology rather than mere sensational effect. 'A Study in Scarlet' demonstrates how actual criminal cases are solved through systematic observation and logical deduction, presenting these methods in an engaging narrative that respects both scientific accuracy and reader entertainment.

The protagonist, Mr. Sherlock Holmes of 221B Baker Street, employs techniques of analysis and reasoning that represent the most advanced approaches to criminal investigation currently available. Rather than relying on coincidence or inspiration, he solves complex mysteries through careful examination of physical evidence, psychological insight, and methodical logical reasoning.

His associate, Dr. John Watson, serves as both chronicler and participant in these investigations, providing the medical expertise often crucial to forensic analysis while documenting Holmes's remarkable methods for the benefit of readers.

I believe this story represents a significant advancement in detective fiction, offering readers both compelling entertainment and genuine education in scientific investigative methods. The market appears ready for more sophisticated detective literature, and this work combines authentic methodology with dramatic storytelling in ways that have not been attempted previously.

I should be grateful for your consideration of this manuscript and remain available to discuss any questions you might have regarding the work or its potential for serial publication.

Similar letters accompanied the manuscripts dispatched to the other three publishers, each emphasizing different aspects likely to appeal to that publication's editorial preferences. Blackwood's received emphasis on the story's literary merit and psychological complexity, The Cornhill heard about its educational value and authentic methodology, while Cassell got focus on its commercial potential and innovative approach to popular fiction.

As Arthur watched the four packages depart for London on the afternoon post, he felt a profound sense of completion mixed with anticipation. Everything possible had been done—the story was as perfect as his abilities could make it, Watson's documentation had been transformed with care and respect, Holmes's exacting standards had been satisfied, and the necessary privacy protections had been implemented.

Now came the waiting.

"Touie," Arthur called to his wife as he returned to the house, "I've just sent 'A Study in Scarlet' to four different publishers. Within a month, we should know whether our detective story finds a receptive audience."

Louisa appeared in the doorway of their sitting room, her face showing the patient interest that had sustained her through Arthur's various literary enthusiasms. "How do you feel about it, Arthur? Do you believe one of them will accept it?"

Arthur considered her question carefully, weighing his genuine optimism against his experience of editorial rejection. "I believe we've created something unprecedented, Touie. Whether publishers will recognize its potential..." He shrugged. "That remains to be seen. But I'm confident that if any detective story deserves acceptance, it's this one."

"And if they all reject it?"

Arthur smiled with more confidence than he entirely felt. "Then we'll try other publishers. The story is too good, the character of Holmes too compelling, and the authentic methodology too valuable to remain unpublished indefinitely. Someone will recognize what we've accomplished."

An Offer for A Study in Scarlet

August 28, 1886

The first month after Arthur had sent out the manuscript to various publishers passed with relative calm. Watson tried to occupy himself with his medical practice, but found his thoughts frequently drifting to the stack of identical packages that had departed for publishing houses across London. Arthur had been optimistic about receiving replies within days—surely such an innovative approach to detective fiction would generate immediate interest.

It was in the fourth month that Arthur received a thick envelope bearing the letterhead of Ward, Lock & Co. With trembling hands, he broke the seal, expecting yet another polite rejection. Instead, he found himself reading:

Dear Sir,

We have read your story and are pleased with it. We could not publish it this year as the market is flooded at present with cheap fiction, but if you do not object to its being held over till next year, we will give you £25 for the copyright.

Yours faithfully,

Ward, Lock & Co.

Arthur read the letter three times before its full meaning sank in. Not a rejection—an offer! Modest though it was, someone actually wanted to publish their work.

He immediately sent an urgent message to Watson:

JAMES - WARD, LOCK & CO. HAS MADE AN OFFER! CAN YOU TRAVEL TO SOUTHSEA TOMORROW? WE MUST DISCUSS THIS IMMEDIATELY. BRING OPTIMISM - WE MAY ACTUALLY BECOME PUBLISHED AUTHORS. - ARTHUR.

The following day found Watson sitting in Arthur's study, the letter from Ward, Lock & Co. spread between them like a precious document. Arthur looked both excited and conflicted.

"Twenty-five pounds," Watson mused, reading the offer again. "And they want the complete copyright."

"It's not a fortune," Arthur admitted, "but it's acceptance, James. After all those rejections, someone actually wants to publish our work."

"What does it mean that they want the copyright?"

Arthur leaned back in his chair. "It means they own the story completely once they pay us. All future profits, any subsequent editions, even rights to other countries—everything belongs to them."

Watson frowned. "That seems rather... comprehensive."

"It's not unusual for a first-time author," Arthur assured him. "And frankly, after the responses we've received, I'm not certain we're in a position to negotiate more favorable terms."

"What about the delay? They want to wait until next year."

"Disappointing, but understandable. They claim the market is flooded with cheap fiction—apparently our more thoughtful approach needs time to find its proper audience."

Watson stood and moved to the window, considering their options. "What do you think Holmes will say about this offer?"

"I suspect he'll be more interested in seeing the work published than in the financial arrangements," Arthur replied. "His primary concern has always been accuracy and scientific credibility, not profit."

Watson felt his own excitement building. "Then we'll be published authors."

"We will indeed. And more importantly, the world will meet Sherlock Holmes." Arthur smiled for the first time in weeks. "I suspect that once readers discover our consulting detective, twenty-five pounds will prove to have been quite a bargain."

"When will you respond to Ward, Lock & Co.?"

"Tomorrow. I'll accept their terms and begin preparing for publication next year." Arthur gathered the letter carefully. "James, whatever happens after this, we've accomplished something remarkable. We've taken Holmes's actual casework and transformed it into literature without compromising its scientific integrity."

Arthur was quiet for a long moment, staring at the letter. "James, four months ago I was convinced we had created something revolutionary, something that would immediately capture publishers' attention. The reality has been... humbling."

"But you still believe in the work?"

"Absolutely. I believe we've created something genuinely innovative. But I also recognize that innovation often takes time to find acceptance." Arthur looked up with renewed determination. "Yes, I think we should accept. Twenty-five pounds may be modest, but publication with an established house is invaluable. It gets our work before readers, establishes our credibility, and opens doors for future projects."

As Watson prepared to leave, he felt a profound sense of satisfaction mixed with anticipation. Their literary venture was about to become reality. In just over a year, readers across Britain would be introduced to the logical methods of Sherlock Holmes through the pages of "A Study in Scarlet."

"Arthur," Watson said as he reached the door, "I believe this is just the beginning."

"I believe you're right, James. I believe you're right."

The following morning, Arthur Doyle penned his acceptance to Ward, Lock & Co., officially launching what would become one of the most successful partnerships in literary history. Neither he nor Watson could have imagined that their modest £25 story would someday make Sherlock Holmes the most famous fictional detective in the world.

Watson Visits Arthur & Touie

December 27, 1886

Arthur Conan Doyle settled into the comfortable quiet that follows Christmas celebrations, reviewing patient notes from his morning rounds, while the lingering scents of yesterday's feast still perfumed the house. Louisa was in the sitting room, arranging the last of their Christmas flowers and humming softly to herself.

The sound of the front door knocker interrupted the peaceful domestic scene. Arthur looked up from his papers, wondering who might be calling so late in the afternoon yet before the dinner hour. It was an unusual time for visits, particularly so soon after Christmas when most families were still enjoying their holiday respite.

"I'll see who it is," Arthur called to his wife, setting aside his medical notes and making his way to the front hall. When he opened the door, he was surprised to find Dr. James Watson standing on his doorstep, a wrapped fruit basket in one hand and what appeared to be a Christmas card in the other.

"James! What a pleasant surprise," Arthur exclaimed, genuine warmth in his voice. "What brings you to Southsea on this cold winter afternoon?"

Watson smiled, looking slightly abashed at his unannounced arrival. "I hope you'll forgive the impropriety of calling without notice, Arthur. I found myself with some free time today and thought I might take the liberty of delivering my Christmas greetings in person." He extended the card and basket. "A small token of the season, and my continued appreciation for our friendship."

"How thoughtful of you! Please, come in out of the cold." Arthur stepped aside, welcoming Watson into the warmth of the house. "Touie will be delighted to see you again."

As they entered the sitting room, Louisa looked up with surprise and pleasure. "Dr. Watson! How lovely to see you. Arthur, do take his coat. James, you must warm yourself by the fire."

"Mrs. Doyle, you're very kind." Watson allowed Arthur to take his overcoat and settled gratefully into the chair by the fireplace. "I hope I'm not intruding on your family time."

"Not at all," Louisa assured him. "Christmas is a time for friends, and we consider you very much a friend of this household. And please, call me Touie—all our friends do. Can I offer you some tea? Or perhaps something stronger to ward off the winter chill?"

"Tea would be perfect, thank you."

As Louisa busied herself preparing refreshments, Arthur opened Watson's Christmas card—a tasteful design featuring winter holly—and read the inscription aloud: "To Arthur and Louisa, with sincere gratitude for friendship and partnership. May 1887 bring success to all our endeavors. —James Watson."

"Very thoughtful indeed," Arthur said, setting the card on the mantelpiece. "And this fruit basket is magnificent—wherever did you find such excellent oranges in December?"

Watson chuckled. "A patient of mine imports citrus from Spain. He was generous enough to spare some of his finest specimens."

"Your medical practice is thriving, then?" Arthur asked, settling into his own chair as Louisa brought the tea service.

"Quite well, thank you. The winter months always bring an increase in respiratory complaints, which keeps me busy from dawn until well after dark." Watson accepted his cup gratefully. "Though I must say, the work has been rewarding. There's something satisfying about helping people through the worst of the winter ailments."

"I know exactly what you mean," Arthur agreed. "My own practice has been similarly demanding. Just this morning I had three cases of bronchitis and a rather stubborn case of influenza. But as you say, there's genuine satisfaction in the work."

"And how was your Christmas?" Watson inquired. "I hope you were able to set aside medical concerns for at least a day or two."

Louisa laughed softly. "I practically had to hide Arthur's medical bag to keep him from making rounds on Christmas Day. But we managed a lovely quiet celebration—just the two of us and a magnificent goose."

"And you, James?" Arthur asked. "I hope you found time to celebrate properly."

Watson's expression grew thoughtful. "A quiet day, much like yours. Mr. Holmes was absorbed in some chemical experiment or another, so I spent the afternoon reading by the fire. There's something peaceful about a solitary Christmas when one has had quite enough excitement throughout the year."

"Speaking of Mr. Holmes," Louisa said with gentle curiosity, "how is he faring? Arthur has often wondered about such an unusual gentleman."

"Much the same as always, I'm afraid," Watson replied with a slight smile. "Brilliant one moment, impossible the next. He spent much of Christmas Day testing various tobacco ashes with his magnifying lens, muttering about the distinguishing characteristics of different pipe tobaccos."

Arthur shook his head in amazement. "Even on Christmas Day he pursues his scientific interests?"

"Crime doesn't observe holidays, as Holmes often reminds me. Though I must say, the past few weeks have been relatively quiet on that front, which has allowed me to catch up on my medical reading."

They settled into comfortable conversation about their respective practices, the unusually harsh winter weather, and the small pleasures of domestic life. Watson proved to be an engaging conversationalist, with a dry wit that complemented Arthur's more enthusiastic nature perfectly.

"You know," Arthur said at one point, refilling Watson's teacup, "I've often thought that physicians develop some of the finest conversation skills of any profession. We spend so much time listening to patients, learning to put them at ease."

"That's very true," Watson agreed. "Though I sometimes think we also develop a tendency toward discretion that can make us rather reserved in social situations."

Louisa smiled at both men. "Well, you needn't be reserved here. This is one household where both of you are always welcome to speak freely."

As the afternoon progressed, Watson proved himself to be not only intelligent but genuinely interested in their lives. He asked thoughtful questions about Arthur's writing ambitions beyond their collaboration, showed genuine curiosity about Louisa's charitable work with the local parish, and shared amusing anecdotes from his own medical practice.

"I had a patient last week," Watson said with a chuckle, "who was convinced that his recurring headaches were caused by his neighbor's cat staring at him through the window. Took considerable persuasion to convince him that the cure lay not in avoiding feline gazes, but in moderating his consumption of gin."

"The remedies people invent for themselves!" Arthur laughed. "Just yesterday I had a woman who insisted that wearing her late husband's socks was the only thing preventing her rheumatism from worsening."

"And did you discourage this treatment?" Louisa asked with twinkling eyes.

"Not at all. If it provides comfort and does no harm, I see no reason to interfere with harmless superstitions. Sometimes healing involves more than medicine."

Watson nodded approvingly. "Precisely my philosophy. We treat the whole person, not merely the symptoms."

The winter light was beginning to fade outside the windows, and Watson glanced toward them with the air of a man conscious of time passing.

"I should take my leave soon," he said. "I don't wish to impose on your evening, and I have promised to look in on an elderly patient this evening."

"Must you go so soon?" Arthur protested. "We've barely had time to catch up properly."

"I'm afraid so. But this has been exactly what I hoped for—a chance to see you both, to exchange season's greetings, and to enjoy the company of true friends." Watson stood, and Arthur rose with him.

"You must promise not to be such a stranger," Louisa said warmly. "Our door is always open to you, James."

"You're very kind, Touie. Perhaps when the spring weather arrives, I might impose upon your hospitality again."

As Arthur helped Watson with his coat, the doctor paused in the front hall. "Arthur, I want you to thank you both for such a pleasant afternoon. It's not often that a bachelor finds himself welcomed so warmly into a family home."

"The pleasure has been entirely ours, James. You've brightened what might otherwise have been a rather quiet post-Christmas day."

Watson smiled and extended his hand. "Then I wish you both a prosperous and healthy 1887."

"And to you as well," Arthur agreed, shaking his friend's hand warmly.

As Watson's figure disappeared into the winter evening, Arthur closed the door and returned to the sitting room, where Louisa was arranging Watson's fruit basket on the side table.

"He's a good man," she observed quietly.

"Indeed he is. It's rare to find someone who combines professional competence with such genuine warmth of character."

"He seems rather lonely, though," Louisa added thoughtfully. "Living with that eccentric Mr. Holmes, maintaining such a busy practice. I hope he finds time for friendship and pleasure in his life."

Arthur settled back into his chair, reflecting on the visit. "I think today may have provided him with both. It certainly brought us pleasure to see him again."

Outside, snow began to fall softly against the windows, but inside the warmth of his study, Arthur Conan Doyle felt the contentment that comes from unexpected friendship and the simple pleasures of hospitality shared on a winter afternoon.

A Study in Scarlet is Published

November 2, 1887

Dr. James Watson hurried through the familiar streets of Southsea on a crisp November morning, his breath visible in the cold air. Arthur's urgent message had arrived the previous evening:

JAMES - IT HAS ARRIVED! THE ADVANCE COPY FROM BEETON'S. COME AT YOUR EARLIEST CONVENIENCE TOMORROW. HISTORY AWAITS! - ARTHUR

Watson's heart had been racing since receiving the note. After more than a year and a half since their first meeting, their literary venture was about to become reality. "A Study in Scarlet" would soon be available to readers across Britain.

Arthur answered the door before Watson could knock, his face beaming with excitement. "James! Come in, come in quickly. Wait until you see it!"

Watson followed his friend into the familiar study, where Louisa sat in her chair with an expression of quiet pride. On Arthur's desk, positioned like a precious artifact, lay a copy of Beeton's Christmas Annual for 1887.

"There it is," Arthur said, his voice filled with wonder. "Our story. In print."

Watson approached the desk with something approaching reverence. The annual was an attractive volume, bound in red covers with gilt lettering. And there, prominently displayed on the cover, were the words that made his pulse quicken: "A STUDY IN SCARLET" by A. CONAN DOYLE.

"May I?" Watson asked, reaching toward the publication.

"Of course! It's as much yours as mine, even if the world will never know it."

Watson carefully lifted the annual and opened it to the story's beginning. There it was—the opening he and Arthur had labored over, the careful introduction of John Watson's background, the methodical explanation of Holmes's methods, exactly as Holmes had demanded.

"In the year 1878 I took my degree of Doctor of Medicine of the University of London, and proceeded to Netley to go through the course prescribed for surgeons in the army." Watson read aloud, his voice thick with emotion.

"Look at this," Arthur said, pointing to an illustration on one of the pages. "They've included drawings. That's meant to be Holmes examining the scene at Lauriston Gardens."

Watson studied the image—a tall, thin figure with a magnifying glass, every inch the brilliant detective he knew so well. "He looks exactly as I imagined he would appear to readers. Though perhaps a bit more dramatic than the real Holmes."

Touie laughed softly. "I suspect most readers will prefer the dramatic version, James."

"The typography is excellent," Arthur observed, running his finger along the printed lines. "Clean, readable. And they've given us prominent placement—right after the leading story."

Watson continued turning pages, seeing his careful case notes transformed into literature, his observations of Holmes's methods now preserved for posterity. "Arthur, when I first approached you with this idea, I never truly believed it would come to this. To see it actually published, to know that readers will soon discover Holmes..."

"What do you think he'll make of it?" Arthur asked. "Holmes, I mean, when he sees the published version?"

Watson smiled. "I suspect he'll approve of the scientific accuracy while deploring any dramatic flourishes. Though he may be secretly pleased to see his methods properly documented." He paused, studying a passage about Holmes's deductive reasoning. "This is exactly what he wanted—education disguised as entertainment."

"The question now," Arthur said, settling into his chair, "is whether readers will appreciate such an approach. We've created something quite different from the usual detective fiction."

"Different, yes, but better," Watson replied firmly. "This shows detection as it actually works—through observation, logic, and scientific method. Not through lucky guesses or supernatural insight."

Touie looked up from her needlework. "I have a good feeling about this story, gentlemen. There's something special about it, something that will capture readers' imaginations."

Arthur picked up the advance copy again, handling it with obvious satisfaction. "To think that this time next month, people all over Britain will be reading about Sherlock Holmes for the first time. Families gathered around their Christmas fires, discovering our consulting detective."

"Will you tell Holmes?" Watson asked. "About the publication?"

"I thought you might want to do that yourself. After all, he's your friend and partner. This story belongs to both of you, even if the world will only know my name."

Watson nodded thoughtfully. "I'll show him a copy when they become available. I suspect he'll be more interested in whether we've accurately portrayed his methods than in any commercial success.

Watson's Paddington Practice
September 1, 1888

The September morning sun streamed through the tall windows of the modest Georgian building at 14 Queen Anne Street, Paddington, casting long rectangles of light across the freshly painted walls that would serve as Dr. James Watson's new medical consulting rooms.

At thirty-six, Watson felt the profound significance of this moment—the establishment of his first independent practice, the foundation upon which he would build his married life with Mary Morstan in just two months' time.

He remembered how surprised everyone was when he announced that he had proposed marriage to Mary, and that she had agreed to become the future Mrs. Watson. If someone had told him that he would meet his wife while helping his friend Sherlock Holmes solve a difficult case, he would have immediately dismissed the thought. But it had happened, and he would soon be joined in holy matrimony to the woman he now loved more than life itself.

Watson stood in what would become his examination room, surveying the careful arrangements he had spent the past week perfecting. The ground floor had been transformed into a proper medical facility, with his examination table positioned to take advantage of the excellent natural light, his medical instruments arranged in precise order on a purpose-built cabinet, and his diplomas mounted prominently on the wall where patients could observe his credentials.

The morning post had brought a letter of encouragement from his old friend Stamford, who had helped him locate this property:

My dear Watson,

Paddington is an excellent choice for establishing practice. The area attracts exactly the sort of respectable middle-class clientele who appreciate thorough medical attention and

Watson moved to the window overlooking the quiet street, noting the well-maintained homes and modest commercial establishments that characterized this part of Paddington. The location offered several advantages: close enough to central London to attract patients who valued accessibility, yet far enough from the West End to avoid the highest rental costs. Most importantly, it was a neighborhood where a young married couple could establish themselves respectably without straining their initial finances.

The sound of footsteps on the front steps interrupted his contemplation, and Watson opened the door to find Sherlock Holmes approaching with his characteristic purposeful stride. Holmes carried a wrapped package under his arm and wore the expression of someone bearing both congratulations and carefully concealed melancholy.

"Holmes," Watson said warmly, stepping aside to admit his friend. "How good of you to come. I wasn't certain you'd approve of my abandoning our lodgings for such bourgeois domesticity."

Holmes entered the consulting room with his usual sharp-eyed assessment of new surroundings, taking in every detail from the arrangement of medical instruments to the quality of the window light. "Watson, anyone who has witnessed your methodical approach to medical documentation would have predicted your ability to organize an efficient medical practice."

Holmes set his package on Watson's desk with obvious ceremony. "I've brought you something for the establishment of your new enterprise—though I confess I'm not entirely certain of the appropriate protocol for congratulating a friend on both professional independence and impending matrimony."

Watson unwrapped the package to reveal an elegant leather-bound appointment book, its cover embossed with "Dr. James H. Watson, M.D." in gold lettering. Inside, the first page bore an inscription in Holmes's precise handwriting: "For the documentation of healing as methodical as your attention to detail in all endeavors. May your patients prove as appreciative of your skills as your friends have been. —S.H."

Watson felt genuinely moved by the thoughtful gift. "Holmes, this is perfect. And the inscription... I'm touched by your confidence in this venture."

"Confidence is hardly the appropriate word," Holmes replied, moving to examine Watson's medical instruments with professional interest. "Certainty would be more accurate. Your diagnostic abilities, your attention to detail, your manner with people—all essential qualities for successful medical practice."

Holmes paused at the window, looking out at the Paddington street with the distant expression Watson had learned to associate with his friend's consideration of complex emotional matters. "Watson, I hope you understand that while I may occasionally express skepticism about the institution of marriage, I have nothing but admiration for your choice of bride. Miss Morstan demonstrated remarkable courage and intelligence during our recent investigation."

Watson felt a surge of gratitude for Holmes's support, knowing how difficult such personal observations were for his friend. "Thank you, Holmes. Mary has proven herself worthy of any man's respect, and I consider myself extraordinarily fortunate."

"Indeed. And the practical arrangements? You're confident this location will provide adequate income to support married life?"

Watson gestured toward his carefully organized consulting room. "Stamford's advice has been invaluable in selecting this location. Paddington offers access to exactly the sort of clientele I need—

prosperous enough to pay promptly, conservative enough to prefer established medical methods over experimental treatments."

Holmes nodded approvingly. "And the domestic arrangements? Living above the practice should prove convenient."

"Come, let me show you," Watson said, leading Holmes toward the narrow staircase that connected the consulting room to the residential quarters above.

The upper floor had been arranged as a comfortable flat suitable for a young married couple. The sitting room was modest but well-proportioned, with space for Watson's books and Mary's feminine touches when she became his wife. The bedroom was adequate for their needs, and a small kitchen would allow Mary to manage their domestic arrangements economically until the practice generated sufficient income for household staff.

"It's not Baker Street," Watson said, settling into one of the two chairs positioned by the sitting room's fireplace, "but it will serve our needs while the practice becomes established."

Holmes examined the quarters with the same methodical attention he applied to crime scenes, noting the quality of the furnishings and the practical arrangements Watson had made. "Watson, this represents exactly the sort of sensible planning that should ensure both professional and domestic success."

"I hope so. The rent is manageable, the location should attract steady patients, and Mary seems pleased with the domestic arrangements." Watson paused, his expression growing more serious. "Holmes, I want you to know that establishing this practice doesn't mean abandoning our friendship or our occasional collaborations."

Holmes raised an eyebrow with interest. "Indeed?"

"The distance from Baker Street to Paddington is hardly insurmountable. Should you require medical assistance with your cases, or should you encounter investigations that might benefit from my presence..." Watson smiled. "A married man still needs intellectual stimulation beyond the routine of medical practice."

Holmes moved to the window, his relief evident despite his attempt to maintain casual composure. "Watson, I confess I had wondered whether domestic responsibilities might eliminate your availability for occasional adventures."

"Not eliminate—perhaps reduce the frequency. But Holmes, the work we've done together, the methods you've shared with me, the remarkable cases we've solved—they've become too important a part of my life to abandon entirely."

Watson joined Holmes at the window, both men looking out at the Paddington afternoon. "Besides, Mary has expressed genuine interest in your investigative work. I believe she understands that our friendship extends beyond mere professional collaboration."

"Miss Morstan struck me as remarkably perceptive during our recent case," Holmes observed. "I suspect she recognizes that marriage need not preclude other meaningful relationships."

"Precisely. She appreciates that my association with you has provided intellectual fulfillment that enhanced rather than diminished my other pursuits." Watson's voice grew warmer as he spoke of his fiancée. "Mary understands that a man can be devoted to his wife while maintaining friendships that enrich his professional and intellectual life."

Holmes was quiet for a moment, clearly processing this reassurance about the continuation of their partnership. "Then you anticipate maintaining some involvement in criminal investigation after your marriage?"

"When circumstances permit and when my medical practice allows," Watson confirmed. "Perhaps not the extended cases that required several days away from home, but certainly the sort of investigations that could be concluded within reasonable time frames."

Holmes smiled slightly at Watson's obvious commitment to balancing his various responsibilities. "Watson, I believe your domestic arrangements may prove beneficial to our work rather than limiting it. A settled man with professional standing often finds his credibility enhanced in the eyes of both clients and officials."

Watson moved to his desk and adjusted the position of Holmes's gift, imagining the appointment book filled with the names of patients who would soon depend on his medical expertise. "I've been considering the advantages marriage might bring to both my medical practice and our occasional collaborations. Respectability has its uses in both endeavors."

"Indeed. And a physician with his own established practice commands greater authority than one who merely assists another's work," Holmes observed. "Your independence should enhance rather than diminish your value as a colleague."

As the afternoon progressed toward evening, both men felt the satisfaction of having successfully navigated the transition that Watson's marriage would bring to their relationship. The Paddington practice would provide Watson with the independence and income necessary for married life, while maintaining sufficient flexibility for continued collaboration on Holmes's most interesting cases.

"Holmes," Watson said as they prepared tea in his small kitchen, "I hope you'll consider this flat a second home. Mary and I would be delighted to have you visit regularly, and the guest room will always be available should you need accommodation away from Baker Street."

"That's remarkably generous, Watson. Though I suspect domestic tranquility might not survive regular visits from someone of my irregular habits."

Watson laughed. "Mary has heard enough about your violin playing and chemical experiments to be prepared for occasional disruptions. Besides, she's eager to know you better as a friend rather than simply as the brilliant detective who solved her case."

"Your Miss Morstan demonstrated considerable tolerance for unconventional circumstances during our investigation," Holmes replied. "I suspect she possesses the flexibility necessary to accommodate the occasional demands of criminal investigation."

Watson felt a warmth of satisfaction at Holmes's growing acceptance of his impending marriage. "Mary understands that a man's friendships and professional interests need not diminish with marriage—they simply require more thoughtful management."

As Holmes prepared to return to Baker Street, both men felt the warm satisfaction of friendship that had adapted successfully to changing circumstances. Watson's marriage would bring new responsibilities and new opportunities, but it would not diminish the partnership that had brought them both such professional and personal fulfillment.

"Watson," Holmes said as he gathered his coat, "I believe your Miss Morstan is gaining not only a devoted husband but a man whose experiences with criminal investigation have enhanced his capacity for logical thinking and careful observation."

"And you, Holmes, are gaining not only a married friend but a medical colleague whose domestic stability may enhance rather than limit his availability for collaborative work."

As Holmes's footsteps faded down Queen Anne Street, Watson returned to his consulting room and opened the appointment book Holmes had given him. On the first page, beneath Holmes's inscription, he wrote: "September 1, 1888 - Practice established. Marriage pending. Friendship confirmed. The future appears most promising indeed."

The Night Before the Alter

November 29, 1888

The gray stone walls of St. Marks in London seemed to absorb the late autumn light filtering through the stained glass windows, casting colored shadows across the ancient nave. Dr. James Watson stood at the altar rail, his hands clasped behind his back as he gazed up at the soaring Gothic arches. Tomorrow, November 30th, he would stand in this same spot and marry Mary Morstan, but today he found himself seeking a moment of quiet reflection before the ceremony that would change his life forever.

The soft echo of footsteps on stone drew his attention. Watson turned to see Arthur Conan Doyle approaching down the center aisle, his familiar figure looking somewhat formal in his best traveling suit. The two men had arranged to meet here, away from the bustle of wedding preparations and the curious eyes of London society.

"James," Arthur called softly, his voice respectful of the church's sacred atmosphere. "I hope I'm not disturbing your contemplation."

"Not at all, Arthur. In fact, I was hoping you might arrive early." Watson extended his hand warmly. "Thank you for making the journey from Portsmouth. I know it's been a busy time for your practice."

"I wouldn't have missed it for the world," Arthur replied, gripping Watson's hand firmly. "Besides, it's not every day that one's literary collaborator takes such a momentous step. How are you feeling about tomorrow?"

Watson smiled, a mixture of nervousness and joy playing across his features. "Rather like a man standing at the edge of a precipice, wondering if he's about to fly or fall. But Mary... Arthur, she's remarkable. Patient, intelligent, brave—everything a man could hope for in a wife."

"I'm delighted for you, James. From what little I've observed of Miss Morstan, she seems perfectly suited to you." Arthur paused, glancing around the magnificent church. "And what does Holmes make of your impending nuptials?"

Watson chuckled, though there was a hint of sadness in his expression. "Holmes has been... characteristically enigmatic about the entire affair. He congratulated me, of course, but I sense he views marriage as something of an inconvenience to our partnership. He's already begun making inquiries about new lodgings."

"Ah. I suppose a consulting detective and a newly married couple would find sharing quarters rather... impractical."

"Indeed. Though I've assured him that my marriage won't interfere with my documentation of his cases. Mary understands the importance of the work—she was, after all, intimately involved in the Sign of Four case."

Arthur's eyes brightened with interest. "Speaking of which, I've been meaning to ask about your notes on that investigation. The treasure, the Andaman Islander, the remarkable chase down the Thames—it has all the elements of a thrilling sequel to our first publication."

Watson nodded enthusiastically. "My documentation is complete, and I believe it showcases Holmes's methods even more dramatically than the Study in Scarlet case. The deductive reasoning involved in tracking down Jonathan Small was quite extraordinary."

"Excellent. Though I confess, James, I'm curious about how our first venture has been received by the reading public. I've heard whispers of interest, but nothing definitive."

Watson's expression grew thoughtful as he moved to sit in one of the front pews, Arthur joining him. "The reception has been... intriguing. Several colleagues have mentioned reading the story, though none have connected it to my actual experiences, of course. Dr. Anstruther from my club was particularly enthusiastic—said it was the most realistic detective fiction he'd ever encountered."

"That's precisely what we hoped for," Arthur said with satisfaction. "Authenticity masquerading as fiction."

"Indeed. Though I must admit, I sometimes wonder if we've been too successful in our deception. There are moments when I read our published account and feel as though I'm reading about someone else's life." Watson paused, his voice growing softer. "It's strange, seeing one's own experiences transformed into literature. Liberating, in a way, but also... melancholy."

Arthur studied his friend's profile in the colored light. "Melancholy? How so?"

"The published Watson—'John Watson'—gets to claim his adventures openly. He's recognized as Holmes's partner, his methods are appreciated, his loyalty acknowledged." Watson's smile was wistful. "While I, the real Watson, must remain in the shadows, known only to you and Holmes as the true chronicler of these events."

"Do you regret our arrangement, James? The anonymity we've maintained?"

Watson considered the question carefully. "No, not regret. The work itself has been reward enough—seeing Holmes's methods properly documented, knowing that we've elevated the standard of detective fiction. But sometimes..." He trailed off, then continued with renewed conviction. "But tomorrow changes everything, doesn't it? I'll have Mary to share my thoughts with, someone who knows the truth of my involvement in Holmes's cases."

"She knows about your collaboration with me?"

"She knows I've been documenting Holmes's investigations for publication, though she doesn't know the full extent of our partnership. I thought it best to respect your privacy as well as Holmes's." Watson turned to face Arthur. "She's promised to help me maintain the discretion we've established."

Arthur felt a surge of gratitude for his friend's continued thoughtfulness. "You're remarkably considerate, James. Many men would have revealed everything to their betrothed."

"Mary earned my trust during the Sign of Four case. She proved herself capable of remarkable discretion under extraordinary circumstances." Watson's expression grew warm with affection. "Besides, she's expressed genuine interest in my literary work. I believe she may prove a valuable advisor as we continue our collaboration."

"About that collaboration," Arthur said, his tone growing more serious. "I've been approached by several publishers since the success of 'A Study in Scarlet.' They're eager for more stories featuring Sherlock Holmes. The demand appears to be quite strong."

Watson's eyebrows rose with interest. "Stronger than we anticipated?"

"Much stronger. Ward, Lock & Co. has hinted at more favorable terms for future publications, and I've received inquiries from both Blackwood's and The Strand Magazine." Arthur paused, studying Watson's reaction. "I believe we may have underestimated the public's appetite for authentic detective fiction."

"Holmes will be pleased to hear that his methods are gaining recognition, even if indirectly."

"Indeed. Though I suspect he'll be less pleased with the attention it might bring to his actual practice." Arthur's expression grew concerned. "Have you noticed any increase in unusual clients seeking him out?"

Watson smiled ruefully. "Nothing I can attribute directly to our publication, but Holmes has mentioned receiving several letters from people who claim to have read about 'similar methods' in recent fiction.

He's been rather pointed in his observations about the inconvenience of literary fame."

"We may need to be even more careful about protecting his privacy in future stories."

"Agreed. Though I believe the benefits still outweigh the risks. Holmes's reputation for scientific detection has never been stronger." Watson stood and moved back toward the altar, Arthur following. "And speaking of future stories, I should mention that Holmes has been involved in several remarkable cases since our last publication. The Red-Headed League, the Blue Carbuncle, the Speckled Band—each one more fascinating than the last."

"All documented in your careful style, I assume?"

"Naturally. Though I confess, marriage may require some adjustments to my note-taking routine. Mary has already suggested that I might benefit from a more organized approach to my files."

Arthur laughed. "A wife's influence on a bachelor's habits—I remember those early adjustments well. Touie transformed my study from chaos to order within a month of our wedding."

"I'm rather looking forward to such domestic improvements," Watson admitted. "Though I hope they won't interfere with the quality of my documentation."

"I suspect they'll improve it. Nothing sharpens a man's observations like having someone to share them with." Arthur glanced around the church once more. "James, I hope you know how grateful I am for this partnership. The success of 'A Study in Scarlet' has opened doors I never expected. Literary doors that may lead to the writing career I've always dreamed of."

"The success belongs to all three of us," Watson replied. "Your literary skill, Holmes's extraordinary methods, and perhaps my modest contribution in bridging the gap between them."

"Modest? James, without your careful documentation and your insight into Holmes's character, there would be no stories at all. Don't diminish your role in this collaboration."

Watson felt a flush of pride at his friend's words. "Thank you, Arthur. That means more to me than you know."

The two men stood in comfortable silence for a moment, surrounded by the ancient stones that had witnessed countless ceremonies, celebrations, and solemn occasions. Finally, Arthur spoke again.

"What does the future hold for our partnership, do you think? Will marriage change your perspective on our work?"

Watson considered the question carefully. "I believe it will enhance it, actually. Mary has already shown remarkable insight into human nature. Her observations during the Sign of Four case were invaluable. I suspect she'll prove an excellent advisor as we continue to transform Holmes's investigations into literature."

"And Holmes? How does he view the prospect of your marriage affecting his work?"

"Holmes is... Holmes," Watson replied with a slight smile. "He claims that sentiment is the enemy of logic, but I've seen him demonstrate remarkable loyalty and even affection when circumstances demand it. I believe he'll adjust to the new arrangements, especially if it means continued documentation of his methods."

Arthur nodded. "Then we proceed as planned? The Sign of Four case as our next publication?"

"Absolutely. Though I suspect Holmes will insist on reviewing every detail, just as he did with our first story."

"Of course. His standards for scientific accuracy remain non-negotiable." Arthur paused, then continued with a more personal tone. "James, I want you to know that this collaboration has been one of the most rewarding experiences of my professional life. Working with authentic material, with characters of such depth and intelligence—it's everything a writer hopes for."

"The feeling is entirely mutual, Arthur. You've given Holmes's work the literary treatment it deserves. More than that, you've become a true friend."

The afternoon light had begun to fade, casting longer shadows across the church floor. Arthur glanced toward the entrance, aware that their private moment would soon need to end.

"I should let you return to your wedding preparations," he said. "Though I hope you'll allow me to say one more thing."

"Of course."

"Mary Morstan is a fortunate woman, James. She's gaining not only a devoted husband but a partner in one of the most extraordinary literary ventures of our time." Arthur's expression grew serious. "I hope she understands what a remarkable man she's marrying."

Watson felt a surge of emotion at his friend's words. "Thank you, Arthur. Your friendship and support have meant more to me than I can express."

"The pleasure has been entirely mine." Arthur extended his hand once more. "Until tomorrow, then. I'll see you at the ceremony."

"Until tomorrow."

The Birth of Mary Louise Doyle

January 30, 1889

The winter afternoon light filtered through the lace curtains of the Watson residence in Paddington, casting gentle patterns across the sitting room where Dr. James Watson and his wife Mary had been enjoying the quiet pleasure of organizing their new household. Two months had passed since their wedding at St. Marks, followed by a blissful honeymoon in the Lake District, and they had settled into married life with the comfortable contentment of two people who had found their perfect complement in each other.

Mary sat in her favorite chair near the window, mending one of James's shirts with the careful attention that characterized all her domestic activities. At twenty-seven, she had embraced her role as a married woman with the same quiet competence she had demonstrated during the treacherous Sign of Four case that had brought them together. The Paddington residence, while modest compared to the grand homes of Kensington, had been transformed under her gentle influence into a haven of warmth and domestic harmony.

James lounged in his chair across from her, ostensibly reading the medical journal that lay open in his lap, but in truth simply enjoying the peaceful domesticity of the scene. The demands of his practice had settled into a comfortable routine, and he found himself marveling daily at how marriage had enriched rather than complicated his life. Mary's presence brought a stability and joy that made even the most mundane activities feel blessed.

The afternoon tranquility was interrupted by Mrs. Morrison, their housekeeper, who appeared in the doorway with a telegram in her hand and an expression of barely contained excitement.

"Dr. Watson, Mrs. Watson," she said, her voice carrying the particular inflection that suggested important news. "A telegram has arrived from Portsmouth. From Dr. Doyle."

James and Mary exchanged glances, both immediately alert. Telegrams typically indicated either urgent business or significant news, and given the time of year, they both hoped it was the latter.

"Thank you, Mrs. Morrison," James said, accepting the yellow envelope with anticipation. He opened it carefully and read the brief message aloud:

MY DEAR JAMES AND MARY - DELIGHTED TO INFORM YOU THAT LOUISA SAFELY DELIVERED OUR DAUGHTER ON JANUARY 28TH. MOTHER AND CHILD ARE BOTH WELL. LITTLE MARY LOUISE IS PERFECT. YOUR FRIENDSHIP HAS MEANT SO MUCH DURING THIS TIME. WITH GRATITUDE AND JOY - ARTHUR AND TOUIE.

Mary's face lit up with immediate delight. "Oh, James! They've had their baby! A daughter!"

Mary set aside her mending and moved to stand beside her husband's chair, reading the telegram again with obvious joy. "They named her Mary! James, I'm so touched. To think that Arthur and Touie would choose to honor our friendship in such a way..."

"It speaks to how much our relationship has meant to them," James agreed, his voice warm with affection for the friends who had become so central to their lives. "Arthur once told me that our collaboration had brought him not just professional success but genuine friendship. This gesture suggests the feeling is entirely mutual."

Mary moved to her writing desk, already composing their response in her mind. "We must send our congratulations immediately. And James, we should plan to visit them as soon as Touie is well enough to receive guests."

"Absolutely," James agreed, joining his wife at the desk. "Though we should be mindful of the customs surrounding new mothers. Perhaps mid-February would be appropriate? That would give Touie time to recover while still allowing us to welcome little Mary Louise properly."

Mary began composing their reply with the careful attention she brought to all correspondence. "What should we say? I want to convey our joy without being overwhelming."

James considered this, understanding his wife's desire to strike exactly the right tone. "Perhaps something simple but heartfelt? Our congratulations, our excitement about meeting the baby, and our intention to visit when convenient for them?"

Mary nodded and began writing with her characteristic neat handwriting:

Dearest Arthur and Touie,

Your wonderful news has filled our home with joy. We are absolutely delighted to hear of little Mary Louise's safe arrival and send our warmest congratulations to you both. To know that you have chosen to honor our friendship through your daughter's name touches us more deeply than words can express. We hope Touie is recovering well and that you are all enjoying these precious first days as a family of three. We would be honored to call upon you in mid-February, if that timing would be convenient, to welcome little Mary Louise properly and to celebrate this joyous occasion with our dearest friends. With our love and very best wishes.

James and Mary Watson.

James read over his wife's shoulder, nodding approvingly. "Perfect, my dear. Warm but respectful of their need for privacy during these early days."

As Mary addressed the telegram for immediate dispatch, both felt the particular happiness that comes from sharing in the joy of beloved friends. The news of the baby's arrival seemed to complete something in their own domestic contentment—the knowledge that the couple whose friendship had enriched their courtship and marriage was now experiencing the same blessed expansion of their family circle.

"James," Mary said as she sealed their response, "I confess I'm already imagining what gift we should bring when we visit. Something special for the baby, certainly, but also something to acknowledge Touie's accomplishment."

"What did you have in mind?"

Mary's eyes sparkled with the planning enthusiasm that James had learned to appreciate. "For the baby, perhaps a beautiful christening gown? I could commission something from Mrs. Hartwell—she does the most exquisite needlework. And for Touie, maybe a piece of jewelry to commemorate the occasion? A locket, perhaps, where she could keep a small photograph of the baby?"

James smiled at his wife's thoughtful consideration. "Both excellent ideas. And Mary, we should also consider something for Arthur. Becoming a father is a momentous occasion for a man, and he's been such a good friend to us."

"What would be appropriate for a new father?"

James considered this carefully. "Perhaps a fine bottle of champagne to mark the occasion? Or a book—something meaningful that he could give to his daughter when she's older. A first edition of poetry, perhaps, or a beautifully bound collection of fairy tales."

Mary clapped her hands together with delight. "Oh, a book she could treasure throughout her life! James, you have such wonderful instincts for these things."

"You know," Mary said as they settled back into their chairs, the telegram safely dispatched, "this makes me think about our own future. Someday, perhaps, Arthur and Touie will be receiving similar news from us."

James looked at his wife with tender affection. "Someday, indeed, my dear. Though for now, I'm perfectly content with our happiness as it stands."

"As am I," Mary agreed, returning to her mending with a smile that spoke of complete contentment. "But it's lovely to think that little Mary Louise will grow up knowing Uncle James and Aunt Mary, and that our friendship with her parents will be part of her childhood memories."

The February visit to Portsmouth was already taking shape in their minds—the excitement of meeting the new baby, the pleasure of seeing Arthur and Touie in their new roles as parents, the opportunity to celebrate this milestone in the lives of friends who had become so essential to their own happiness.

Mary Watson Joins the Team

March 15, 1889

The modest drawing room of the Watson residence in Paddington bore the comfortable marks of a marriage now four months old. Afternoon sunlight streamed through lace curtains, illuminating the careful blend of masculine and feminine touches that spoke of two lives thoughtfully merged into one. Dr. James Watson's medical journals shared shelf space with his wife's collection of poetry, while her delicate watercolors hung alongside his more austere anatomical prints.

Mary Watson moved gracefully about the room, arranging tea service on the mahogany table while her husband paced near the window, occasionally glancing toward the street. At twenty-seven, Mary had settled into married life with the same quiet competence she had demonstrated during the treacherous Sign of Four case that had brought them together. Her golden hair was pinned in the fashionable style of a respectable married woman, and her blue dress spoke of modest prosperity rather than ostentation.

"Arthur should arrive shortly," James said, consulting his pocket watch for the third time in as many minutes. "I do hope this meeting won't prove too overwhelming for you, my dear. Our collaboration can be rather... intense."

Mary smiled, her eyes holding the gentle humor that had first captivated her husband. "James, I witnessed you and Mr. Holmes track down a murderous pygmy through the London sewers. I believe I can manage a discussion about literature with Dr. Doyle."

"Of course, forgive me. I simply want everything to go smoothly. This meeting feels rather momentous—our first collaboration as a married couple, and with such promising material."

The sound of the front door knocker interrupted their conversation. James straightened his waistcoat and moved toward the hallway, while Mary made final adjustments to the tea arrangement.

"That will be Arthur," James called back. "Punctual as always."

Arthur Conan Doyle's familiar voice carried from the entrance hall as James welcomed him, their conversation animated but too distant for Mary to distinguish words. She had met Arthur only briefly at the wedding ceremony, but James had spoken of him with such warmth and respect that she felt she knew him well through her husband's accounts.

The two men entered the drawing room together, Arthur carrying his customary leather satchel and wearing the expression of barely contained enthusiasm that Mary had learned to associate with literary discussions.

"Mrs. Watson," Arthur said, bowing slightly as he approached. "How delightful to see you again, and in such charming circumstances. Marriage clearly agrees with you both."

"Dr. Doyle, welcome to our home," Mary replied, extending her hand. "James has been eagerly anticipating this meeting. Please, do sit down. I've prepared tea, though I can offer something stronger if you prefer."

"Tea would be perfect, thank you." Arthur settled into the chair James indicated, his keen eyes taking in the domestic details with the same observational skills that had made him an ideal collaborator. "I must say, James, you've created a lovely home here. Far more civilized than those Baker Street lodgings you described."

James laughed, taking his place beside Mary on the small sofa. "Mary's influence, I'm afraid. She's transformed my bachelor chaos into something approaching respectability."

"The chaos was rather charming," Mary said, pouring tea with practiced grace. "Though I confess I've enjoyed organizing James's files. His documentation of Mr. Holmes's cases is remarkably detailed, but the filing system was... creative."

Arthur accepted his cup with interest. "You've been reviewing James's case notes?"

"With his permission, of course. As someone who was personally involved in the Sign of Four investigation, I found it fascinating to read James's professional account of events I experienced firsthand." Mary's expression grew more serious. "It's given me tremendous appreciation for the quality of his work—and for the importance of your collaboration."

James felt a surge of pride at his wife's words. "Mary has proven remarkably insightful about the literary potential of Holmes's cases. I believe her perspective will be invaluable as we develop our next publication."

"Indeed?" Arthur leaned forward, his interest clearly piqued. "What are your thoughts on the Sign of Four case, Mrs. Watson?"

Mary considered her response carefully. "From a literary standpoint, it has everything readers could want—mystery, adventure, exotic locations, romance, and of course, Mr. Holmes's brilliant deductions. But more than that, it showcases the human cost of crime in a way that 'A Study in Scarlet' perhaps did not."

Arthur nodded approvingly. "Elaborate on that, if you would."

"The treasure brought nothing but misery to everyone it touched," Mary continued, warming to her subject. "Major Sholto died of fear, his sons were driven to desperation, Jonathan Small lost his freedom and ultimately his life pursuing it. Even I, as the supposed beneficiary, found it brought more terror than joy."

"That's a remarkably sophisticated analysis," Arthur said, making notes in his ever-present notebook. "James, you mentioned in your message that you believe this case demonstrates Holmes's methods even more dramatically than our first publication?"

James nodded eagerly. "The deductive reasoning involved in tracking down Small was extraordinary. Holmes's analysis of the wooden leg prints, his insights into the psychology of both Small and his companion, the logical progression from the locked room mystery to the final chase—it's a masterpiece of criminal investigation."

"And the exotic elements?" Arthur inquired. "The Andaman Islander, the Indian treasure, the historical background—they're rather more sensational than the American frontier setting of our first story."

Mary interjected thoughtfully, "But they're also completely authentic. I lived through those events, and I can attest that James's account captures not only the facts but the atmosphere of genuine terror and mystery. Dr. Doyle, if we're to work together regularly, I hope you'll call me Mary rather than Mrs. Watson. Such formality seems unnecessary among collaborators."

Arthur smiled warmly. "I would be honored to call you Mary. And please, call me Arthur. We're partners in this endeavor now, after all."

"Arthur it is," Mary said with a pleased smile. "Now, as I was saying about the authenticity of the exotic elements..."

Arthur made a note in his book, clearly pleased with the more informal arrangement. "The authentic nature of these elements is precisely what will set our work apart from other detective fiction. Most writers invent their exotic backgrounds from whole cloth, but you actually lived through these events."

"Exactly," James agreed. "Mary can provide details about the emotional reality of the situation that my clinical notes might miss. The fear, the uncertainty, the way ordinary people react to extraordinary circumstances."

Mary nodded. "For instance, Arthur, when I first entered that room where poor Mr. Sholto lay dead, James's notes describe the physical evidence accurately—the locked door, the unusual circumstances, the thorny stick. But they don't capture the wave of terror that swept over me, the way the very air seemed poisoned with menace."

Arthur looked up from his notes, his eyes bright with interest. "That's exactly the sort of detail that will transform this from a mere puzzle into a true story. The human element that makes readers care about the outcome."

"Which brings me to an important question," Arthur continued, his expression growing more serious. "Mary, James has indicated that you're willing to be involved in our collaboration, but I want to ensure you understand what that means."

Mary looked inquiringly at her husband, who nodded encouragingly.

"Our work requires absolute discretion," Arthur explained. "The public must never know that these stories are based on real cases, or that James is anything more than a fictional character in my imagination. Can you maintain that level of secrecy?"

"Arthur," Mary said with a slight smile, "I kept silent about a murderous treasure hunt, a vengeful convict, and a pygmy with poison darts. I believe I can manage to keep quiet about literary collaboration."

Arthur chuckled. "Point taken. Then you understand the stakes involved?"

"I understand that you three have created something unprecedented— detective fiction based on actual scientific investigation. I also understand that this work has the potential to influence public perception of criminal investigation for years to come." Mary's voice grew more passionate. "That's not a responsibility I take lightly."

James reached for his wife's hand, squeezing it affectionately. "Mary has already made several suggestions about how to present the Sign of Four case that I believe will strengthen the narrative considerably."

"Such as?" Arthur prompted.

Mary consulted a small notebook of her own. "The story should begin with my visit to Mr. Holmes, rather than with background exposition. Readers will be drawn into the mystery immediately through my personal stake in the outcome."

Arthur made rapid notes. "Excellent. What else?"

"The relationship between the Sholto brothers needs more development. James's notes focus primarily on Bartholomew, but Thaddeus's neurotic behavior and family guilt provide important context for understanding how the treasure corrupted everyone it touched."

"Very astute," Arthur agreed. "And the romantic element?"

Mary colored slightly but continued steadily. "James has been rather... modest in his account of our courtship. But I believe readers will appreciate seeing Holmes's brilliant friend find happiness, even if Holmes himself remains a bachelor."

James looked embarrassed. "Mary, I hardly think—"

"Nonsense," Arthur interrupted. "Mary is absolutely right. The romantic subplot provides emotional weight that will balance Holmes's intellectual achievements. It also demonstrates that scientific method and human feeling can coexist—something our first story perhaps didn't emphasize enough."

Mary smiled gratefully at Arthur's support. "Precisely. The story shows that logic and emotion aren't opposites—they're complementary aspects of complete human experience."

Arthur set down his pen and leaned back in his chair. "Mary, I'm impressed. You have genuine literary instincts. James, you've chosen your collaborator well—in marriage as well as in literature."

"I'm beginning to think Mary may be the most valuable member of our partnership," James said with obvious pride.

"Now you're both being silly," Mary protested, though she looked pleased. "I simply have the advantage of having lived through the events in question. I can provide the feminine perspective that you gentlemen might overlook."

Arthur nodded seriously. "That perspective will be invaluable. Detective fiction has traditionally been written by men for men, but I suspect our audience includes many women readers who would appreciate more sophisticated character development."

"Speaking of our audience," James interjected, "what news do you have about the reception of 'A Study in Scarlet'?"

Arthur's expression brightened considerably. "Excellent news, actually. Ward, Lock & Co. reports that the Beeton's Christmas Annual sold exceptionally well, largely due to our story. They're eager to publish more Holmes adventures, and they're offering much more favorable terms."

"How much more favorable?" Mary asked practically.

Arthur consulted his notes. "They're proposing a proper book publication of the Sign of Four case, with significantly better financial arrangements. Instead of selling the copyright outright, we'd retain rights and receive royalties on future sales."

James whistled softly. "That's a substantial improvement."

"Indeed. And there's more—I've been approached by The Strand Magazine about serializing Holmes stories. They're willing to pay premium rates for monthly installments."

Mary's eyes widened. "Monthly installments? That would mean regular income rather than single payments."

"Precisely. The magazine format would also allow us to publish shorter cases—those single-day investigations that might not justify a full book." Arthur turned to James. "Do you have documentation of such cases?"

"Dozens of them. The Blue Carbuncle, the Red-Headed League, the Speckled Band—each one a complete investigation that could stand alone as a magazine story."

"Wonderful. Mary, what do you think of this serialization approach?"

Mary considered carefully. "It would allow you to build a regular readership, people who eagerly await each new Holmes adventure. Like the sensation novels that appear in monthly parts, but with the advantage of scientific authenticity."

"Exactly what I was thinking," Arthur agreed. "We could create a literary phenomenon—readers who follow Holmes's cases as if they were real events happening in their own time."

James looked thoughtful. "Holmes might appreciate the regular documentation of his methods. He's often complained that his techniques aren't properly understood by the public."

"Speaking of Holmes," Arthur said, "how has he responded to the success of our first publication?"

James smiled wryly. "With characteristic ambivalence. He's pleased that his methods are gaining recognition, but concerned about the attention it might bring to his actual practice. He's already noticed an increase in unusual correspondence from people who've read the story."

"Nothing problematic, I hope?"

"Not yet. But Holmes has made it clear that he expects even greater care with privacy protection in future publications."

Mary nodded. "Which brings us to a practical question about the Sign of Four case. How do we handle the fact that I'm a real person who might be recognized?"

Arthur had clearly anticipated this concern. "We'll change your name, of course, and modify some personal details. Perhaps make you a governess rather than a governess's daughter, alter your physical description slightly. The essential character remains the same, but with enough changes to protect your privacy."

"That seems sensible," Mary agreed. "Though I admit it will be strange to read about myself as a fictional character."

"No stranger than it is for James to read about 'John Watson,'" Arthur pointed out. "In fact, that raises another question. Should we maintain the name 'John Watson' for consistency, or would you prefer a different fictional identity for this story?"

James considered this. "I think consistency is important. Readers who enjoyed 'A Study in Scarlet' will want to follow the continued adventures of John Watson. Besides, I've grown rather fond of my literary alter ego."

Mary laughed. "Just don't let success go to your head, darling. You're still the same James Watson who leaves his medical bag in three different rooms and forgets to wind his watch."

Arthur chuckled at the domestic observation. "Marriage certainly provides its own form of scientific observation, doesn't it?"

"Indeed," James agreed. "Mary has already improved my note-taking habits considerably. She's suggested a more systematic approach to organizing case files."

"Which will be essential if we're going to maintain the quality of our work while increasing our output," Arthur noted. "The magazine serialization will require more regular production than our current approach."

Mary leaned forward, her expression growing more businesslike. "That brings us to the practical arrangements for our collaboration. How do you envision this working on a day-to-day basis?"

Arthur consulted his notebook. "I propose that James continue his current practice of documenting cases as they occur. When we identify a suitable case for publication, he'll prepare a detailed account which I'll then adapt for literary presentation. The three of us will review the result before submission."

"And the financial arrangements?" Mary inquired.

"I suggest we maintain the equal split between James and myself, with the understanding that your contributions to the collaboration are part of James's involvement," Arthur replied. "Unless you'd prefer a different arrangement?"

James looked at his wife questioningly. Mary shook her head. "That seems fair. I'm not looking for separate compensation—I'm interested in the work itself."

"Excellent. Then we're agreed on the basic structure of our partnership?" Arthur looked at both Watsons for confirmation.

"We are," James said firmly. "When would you like to begin work on the Sign of Four case?"

Arthur smiled. "If I may, I'd like to begin today. I've brought writing materials, and with Mary's firsthand perspective available, we could make significant progress on the opening chapters."

Mary clapped her hands together. "How exciting! I've never participated in the creation of literature before."

"Then let's begin," Arthur said, opening his satchel and withdrawing paper and pens. "Mary, would you be willing to describe your initial visit to Baker Street? The emotional state you were in, your first impressions of Holmes, the atmosphere of the meeting?"

As Mary began to speak, her voice taking on the cadence of someone reliving a vivid memory, James watched with satisfaction. This was even better than he had hoped—not only was his wife supporting their literary venture, she was enhancing it with insights and perspectives that neither he nor Arthur could have provided alone.

The Sign of Four Draft

July 2, 1889

The study in Arthur Conan Doyle's Portsmouth home had taken on the appearance of a battlefield. Papers covered every available surface—James Watson's meticulous case notes spread across the main desk, Mary's handwritten observations scattered among them, and Arthur's own draft pages stacked in neat piles according to chapter. The afternoon heat made the room stuffy despite the open windows, and Arthur's shirt sleeves were rolled up as he bent over the final pages of his manuscript.

Three and a half months had passed since that productive afternoon meeting in the Watson drawing room, and Arthur had thrown himself into the work with an intensity that surprised even him. The Sign of Four had proven to be a more complex narrative challenge than A Study in Scarlet—the exotic elements, the romantic subplot, and Mary's personal involvement had required careful balance to maintain both authenticity and literary appeal.

Arthur set down his pen and rubbed his tired eyes. The final chapter lay before him, still damp with ink, completing what he believed to be his finest work yet. Where their first collaboration had established Holmes's methods and Watson's reliability, this new story showcased the full range of the detective's capabilities while adding the human warmth that Mary's involvement had brought to the narrative.

"Finished at last," he murmured to himself, then called out to his wife. "Touie! Could you bring some tea? I believe I've completed the draft."

Louisa appeared in the doorway, her expression mixing pride with concern. Over the past months, she had watched her husband pour himself into this work with an dedication that bordered on obsession.

"Really finished, Arthur? Or finished until you decide to rewrite the opening again?"

Arthur chuckled, acknowledging the accuracy of her observation. "Truly finished this time. I've incorporated all of Mary's suggestions about the romantic elements, used James's technical notes for the detective work, and I believe I've found the right balance between adventure and authenticity."

Louisa moved into the study, carefully navigating the paper-strewn floor. "It's certainly been a more complex undertaking than your first Holmes story. All those letters back and forth with the Watsons, the revisions based on Mary's memories..."

"Worth every hour of effort," Arthur replied, gathering the scattered pages into a neat stack. "Mary's contributions have been invaluable. She's provided insights into the emotional reality of the case that neither James nor I could have imagined. The scene where she first enters the Sholto house, the terror she felt when confronting the locked room mystery— those details transform the story from a mere puzzle into genuine human drama."

"And James's documentation?"

"As meticulous as ever. But this case showcased Holmes's abilities even more dramatically than the first. The deductive reasoning involved in tracking down Jonathan Small, the psychological insights into both the criminal and his exotic companion, the spectacular chase down the Thames—it's a masterpiece of criminal investigation."

Arthur stood and moved to the window, looking out at the garden where the July roses were in full bloom. "I believe we've created something unprecedented, Touie. A detective story that combines intellectual rigor with genuine emotion, authentic investigative methods with romantic adventure."

"What happens next?"

"I'll send copies to both James and Holmes for their review. James will want to verify the accuracy of the investigative details, and Holmes..."

Arthur paused, remembering the detective's exacting standards. "Holmes will scrutinize every word to ensure his methods are presented correctly."

"You're not concerned about his reaction?"

Arthur considered this. "Less than I was with our first story. I've learned to anticipate his concerns and address them preemptively. Besides, this case demonstrates his capabilities so clearly that I believe even Holmes will be pleased with the portrayal."

"And the romantic elements? The marriage between James and Mary?"

"Handled with appropriate restraint, I believe. The romance serves the story without overwhelming it. More importantly, it demonstrates that Holmes's brilliant friend can find personal happiness without abandoning his commitment to scientific investigation."

Louisa smiled at her husband's enthusiasm. "You've grown quite fond of these fictional characters, haven't you?"

"They're not fictional to me anymore, Touie. James and Mary are dear friends, and Holmes..." Arthur paused, searching for the right words. "Holmes has become almost real through James's documentation. I can hear his voice when I write his dialogue, anticipate his reactions to various situations. It's the strangest sensation—writing about people who exist, but presenting them as creations of my imagination."

"It must be difficult to maintain such deception."

"Necessary, though. The arrangement protects everyone involved— James's medical practice, Holmes's privacy, Mary's reputation. And it allows us to present authentic investigative methods without compromising actual criminal cases."

Arthur returned to his desk and began organizing the various drafts and notes. "I believe I'll send the manuscript to Holmes first. His approval is essential, and any changes he requires can be incorporated before James sees the final version."

"When will you contact him?"

"Today, if possible. I'll prepare a clean copy of the manuscript and send it by messenger to Baker Street." Arthur's expression grew more serious. "Holmes's standards are exacting, but they're also what make our work authentic. Without his insistence on accuracy, we'd be producing mere fiction instead of something that could genuinely educate readers about scientific investigation."

The Sign of Four represented more than just their second literary collaboration. It was proof that their partnership could evolve and improve, that authentic detective work could be presented in increasingly sophisticated ways, and that the reading public's appetite for scientific investigation was even stronger than they had originally hoped.

Arthur worked steadily through the afternoon, transcribing his handwritten draft into clean, legible pages suitable for Holmes's review. As he worked, he found himself anticipating the detective's response. Would Holmes appreciate the more complex narrative structure? Would he approve of the romantic subplot, or would he find it unnecessarily sentimental? Most importantly, would he find the portrayal of his investigative methods accurate and instructive?

By early evening, Arthur had completed the clean copy. He wrapped the manuscript carefully in brown paper and addressed it to "Mr. Sherlock Holmes, 111 Baker Street, London." Along with the package, he included a brief note:

Dear Mr. Holmes,

I have completed the literary adaptation of the Sign of Four case, incorporating both Dr. Watson's detailed documentation and Mrs. Watson's firsthand observations. I believe this narrative demonstrates your investigative capabilities even more dramatically than our first collaboration, while maintaining the scientific accuracy you

As Arthur sealed the package, he felt the familiar mixture of anticipation and anxiety that accompanied each stage of their collaboration. Holmes's approval was never guaranteed, and the detective's standards seemed to grow more exacting with each success.

"The manuscript is ready," Arthur announced to Louisa, who had been reading quietly in the sitting room. "Tomorrow it will be on its way to London for Holmes's review."

"How long before you expect to hear back?"

"With Holmes, one never knows. He might respond immediately if something displeases him, or he might deliberate for weeks if the matter requires careful consideration." Arthur settled into his chair, suddenly feeling the exhaustion of months of intensive work. "But I'm confident in the quality of what we've produced. The story combines everything readers want—mystery, adventure, romance, and authentic detective work."

"And if Holmes approves?"

"Then we'll have our second Sherlock Holmes adventure ready for publication. Ward, Lock & Co. is eager to publish it as a proper book, and The Strand Magazine has expressed interest in serializing future cases." Arthur's eyes gleamed with the possibility. "We may be on the verge of creating something truly significant in detective fiction."

The Sign of Four Approved

July 3, 1889

The following afternoon, Mrs. Hudson knocked on the door of Holmes's study with unusual formality. "Mr. Holmes, there's a package arrived for you by special messenger. From Portsmouth."

Holmes looked up from his chemical apparatus, his sharp eyes immediately focusing with interest. "Ah, from our literary collaborator, no doubt. The timing suggests he's completed his work on the Sign of Four case."

Watson, who had been reviewing medical journals in his chair by the window, set aside his reading. "The manuscript is finished already? Arthur has been working with remarkable efficiency."

"Efficiency motivated by enthusiasm," Holmes observed, accepting the wrapped package from Mrs. Hudson. "And, I suspect, by his wife's editorial suggestions and Mary's firsthand contributions."

Holmes examined the package with the same attention he typically reserved for criminal evidence, noting the paper, the handwriting, even the way the string had been tied. "Methodical wrapping, careful addressing, quality paper—all consistent with a man who takes his literary work seriously."

"Will you read it immediately?" Watson asked.

"I shall begin this evening," Holmes replied, setting the package aside. "A work of this complexity requires careful attention. I want to review not only the accuracy of my methods as presented, but also the overall narrative structure and character development."

Watson looked surprised. "Character development? That's rather more literary consideration than you typically apply."

"Our first collaboration succeeded because it balanced scientific accuracy with narrative appeal," Holmes explained. "If this partnership is to continue and expand, as Arthur suggests it might, each story must meet increasingly sophisticated standards."

Holmes moved to his desk and began clearing space for the manuscript. "Besides, Watson, Mary's involvement adds a new dimension to these stories. Her perspective as someone who actually lived through the events in question could provide insights that neither you nor Arthur might have considered."

"You approve of her participation?"

"I approve of authenticity in all its forms," Holmes replied. "If Mary Watson can enhance the accuracy and emotional truth of these accounts, then her contributions are not only welcome but essential."

Watson smiled at his friend's pragmatic acceptance. "I'll be curious to hear your thoughts on Arthur's treatment of the romantic elements."

Holmes paused in his preparations, a slight smile playing about his lips. "Watson, even I recognize that human emotion is a significant factor in criminal investigation. The Sign of Four case was driven by greed, revenge, and ultimately love—all powerful motivations that influenced every aspect of the mystery."

"Still, it will be interesting to see how you respond to reading about your own friend's courtship and marriage."

"Indeed," Holmes agreed. "Though I suspect Arthur has handled those elements with appropriate restraint. His literary instincts seem sound, and his understanding of our collaborative goals appears to be complete."

Holmes moved to the window, looking out at the busy street below. "Watson, I confess myself curious about something. How do you find this process of seeing your own experiences transformed into literature? Is it unsettling to read about your fictional alter ego?"

Watson considered the question carefully. "It's strange, certainly. Sometimes I read Arthur's accounts and feel as though I'm observing my own life from the outside. But it's also... liberating, in a way."

"How so?"

"The fictional John Watson gets to be recognized as your partner, Holmes. His contributions are acknowledged, his methods appreciated, his loyalty celebrated." Watson's voice grew softer. "While I, the real Watson, must remain in the shadows of our collaboration."

Holmes turned from the window, his expression unusually thoughtful. "Watson, I hope you understand that your contributions to my work have never been undervalued, regardless of public recognition."

"I do understand that, Holmes. And I find compensation in knowing that our collaboration is genuinely advancing the cause of scientific investigation." Watson gestured toward the manuscript package. "Each story we publish educates readers about proper detective methods, potentially influencing a new generation of investigators."

"Precisely. The work itself is the reward, not the public credit." Holmes returned to his desk. "Now, I believe I'll spend the remainder of the afternoon preparing to give Arthur's manuscript the attention it deserves."

"How long do you expect your review to take?"

"Several days, at minimum. I want to examine every detail of the investigative methods, verify the accuracy of the criminal psychology, and ensure that the exotic elements are presented authentically without becoming sensational."

Holmes picked up the package, weighing it in his hands. "This represents months of collaborative effort between three intelligent people. It deserves a thorough and respectful review."

"And if you find problems with the manuscript?"

"Then I'll identify them clearly and suggest specific remedies. Arthur has proven himself capable of incorporating feedback constructively." Holmes set the package down again. "But I suspect I'll find this work superior to our first collaboration. The additional perspectives, the more complex case material, the growing sophistication of our partnership—all suggest that this story will represent a significant advancement in detective fiction."

Watson rose from his chair, gathering his medical journals. "I'll leave you to your preparations, then. When you're ready to discuss the manuscript, you know where to find me."

"Actually, Watson, I believe I'll contact you once I've completed my review. The manuscript represents a collaborative effort, and my response should be collaborative as well."

As Watson prepared to leave, Holmes called after him. "Watson, you might let Mary know that I'm particularly interested in her contributions to this work. Her firsthand perspective on the events in question could provide valuable insights into the accuracy of Arthur's emotional and psychological elements."

"I'll tell her. She'll be pleased to know her contributions are valued."

After Watson's departure, Holmes remained in his study, contemplating the package that contained their second literary collaboration. The success of A Study in Scarlet had exceeded all expectations, but it had also raised the stakes for future stories. Readers would expect each new Holmes adventure to meet or exceed the standards established by their first publication.

Holmes opened the package carefully, revealing the neat stack of manuscript pages. Arthur's handwriting was clear and professional, with careful attention to paragraph structure and margin notes indicating his editorial considerations.

"The Sign of Four," Holmes read aloud from the title page. "A Further Adventure of Sherlock Holmes. By A. Conan Doyle."

Holmes settled into his chair and began to read, his analytical mind immediately engaging with both the literary presentation and the investigative accuracy.

The Sign of Four Completed

July 6, 1889

For three days, Sherlock Holmes had been immersed in Arthur Conan Doyle's manuscript of "The Sign of Four," and the neat stack of pages now bore the evidence of his meticulous review—marginal notes in his precise handwriting, small check marks indicating approval, and surprisingly few corrections scattered throughout the text.

Holmes set down his pen and leaned back in his chair, his sharp features reflecting the kind of intellectual contentment that typically followed the successful conclusion of a particularly challenging case. The manuscript had proven to be everything he had hoped for and more—a sophisticated blend of authentic investigative method and compelling narrative that surpassed even their successful first collaboration.

Mrs. Hudson's voice carried up from the entrance hall, announcing Dr. Watson's arrival for their scheduled afternoon meeting. Holmes had sent a brief message that morning requesting Watson's presence to discuss the completed review, and he noted with satisfaction that his friend was precisely punctual.

"Watson," Holmes called as footsteps approached the study door. "Please, come in. I have excellent news regarding our literary venture."

Dr. Watson entered with an expression of barely contained anticipation. Over the past three days, he had found it increasingly difficult to concentrate on his medical practice, his thoughts repeatedly returning to Holmes's review of Arthur's work. The success or failure of their second collaboration would largely determine the future of their literary partnership.

"Holmes," Watson said, settling into his familiar chair. "Your message suggested you've completed your review of Arthur's manuscript?"

"Indeed I have." Holmes gestured toward the manuscript with evident satisfaction. "Watson, I am pleased to report that Mr. Doyle has not only met but exceeded my expectations. This work represents a significant advancement in both literary sophistication and investigative authenticity."

Watson felt a surge of relief so powerful it left him momentarily speechless. "Then you approve? Without major revisions?"

"I approve with only minor suggestions—a clarification here and there regarding specific deductive techniques, a small adjustment to the timeline of the Thames chase, nothing that would require substantial rewriting." Holmes picked up the manuscript, handling it with the same care he typically reserved for valuable evidence. "More importantly, Watson, this story demonstrates the evolution of our collaborative method in ways that bode well for future projects."

"In what way?"

Holmes began his characteristic pacing, his movements reflecting the intellectual excitement that accompanied his most successful deductions. "Arthur has achieved something remarkable—he has maintained complete scientific accuracy while creating a narrative that is significantly more sophisticated than our first effort. The characterization is deeper, the emotional resonance more authentic, and the investigative methodology more clearly presented."

Watson leaned forward with interest. "And Mary's contributions?"

"Invaluable," Holmes replied without hesitation. "Her firsthand perspective has added layers of authenticity that neither you nor Arthur could have provided alone. The scenes depicting her emotional state during the investigation, her reactions to the various revelations, the psychological reality of being drawn into such extraordinary circumstances—all ring absolutely true because they are true."

Holmes paused in his pacing, fixing Watson with an intent gaze. "Moreover, the romantic subplot has been handled with remarkable restraint and effectiveness. Rather than overwhelming the investigative elements, it enhances them by demonstrating the human stakes involved in criminal activity."

"You don't find the marriage plot overly sentimental?"

"On the contrary, I find it essential to the story's impact." Holmes resumed his pacing. "Watson, crime is not merely an intellectual puzzle—it is a disruption of human relationships, a violation of social bonds, a source of genuine suffering for real people. Mary's presence in the narrative reminds readers that detective work exists to protect and restore human happiness."

Watson smiled at his friend's unexpectedly philosophical observation. "I hadn't considered the sociological implications."

"Because you were too close to the events in question. Arthur's literary perspective allows him to see the broader significance of individual cases." Holmes returned to his desk and gathered his notes. "Which brings me to my primary conclusion about this manuscript."

"Yes?"

"It represents proof that our collaborative method can produce work of lasting literary value while maintaining absolute investigative integrity." Holmes's voice carried a note of satisfaction that Watson rarely heard. "If we can maintain this standard of quality while expanding our output, we may well establish an entirely new genre of detective fiction."

Watson felt his excitement building. "Then you believe we should proceed with publication?"

"I believe we must proceed. The reading public deserves access to authentic detective methodology, and this manuscript provides that access in the most engaging form possible." Holmes handed Watson a sheet of paper covered with his neat handwriting. "These are my suggested revisions—minor adjustments that will enhance the scientific accuracy without compromising the narrative flow."

Watson scanned the list quickly, noting that most of Holmes's suggestions involved small clarifications of investigative technique or slight modifications to preserve client confidentiality. "These seem quite manageable. Arthur should be able to incorporate them easily."

"Precisely my intention. I have no desire to impede the publication process with unnecessary revisions." Holmes moved to the window, looking out at the busy street below. "Watson, you may inform Arthur that he has my complete approval to proceed with finding a publisher for this work."

"He'll be delighted to hear it. I believe he's already identified potential publishers who might be interested."

Holmes nodded approvingly. "Excellent. Though I trust he'll exercise the same discretion in selecting a publisher that he's shown in crafting the narrative itself."

Watson rose from his chair, eager to share the good news with Arthur. "I'll send a message to Portsmouth immediately. This represents months of collaborative effort, and Arthur will be tremendously relieved to have your approval."

"And Watson," Holmes called as his friend reached the door. "You might also convey my particular appreciation for Mary's contributions. Her insights have elevated this work beyond mere detective fiction into something approaching literature."

"I'll be sure to tell her. She's invested considerable time and emotional energy in ensuring the accuracy of the narrative."

As Watson prepared to leave, Holmes returned to his desk and picked up the manuscript once more. "Watson, I find myself curious about the future of our collaboration. Arthur has mentioned the possibility of magazine serialization, shorter cases published monthly rather than as complete books."

"Yes, The Strand Magazine has expressed interest in such an arrangement."

"That format might suit our purposes admirably. It would allow for regular documentation of my methods while building a consistent readership." Holmes considered the implications. "Do you have sufficient material for such an approach?"

Watson smiled. "Holmes, you've been involved in dozens of fascinating cases since we began this collaboration. The Red-Headed League, the Blue Carbuncle, the Speckled Band—each one demonstrates your methods in different ways. I could provide Arthur with material for years to come."

"Excellent. Then our literary partnership may prove even more productive than we originally anticipated."

After Watson's departure, Holmes remained in his study, reflecting on the manuscript that lay before him. The Sign of Four represented more than just their second collaboration—it was evidence that authentic detective work could be transformed into compelling literature without sacrificing either accuracy or appeal.

Watson's Good News

July 7, 1889

Dr. Watson's arrival at his Paddington home that evening brought an atmosphere of celebration that Mary immediately detected. She had been arranging flowers in the front parlor when she heard her husband's key in the lock, followed by footsteps that seemed unusually buoyant.

"James?" she called. "You sound remarkably pleased about something."

Watson appeared in the parlor doorway, his face beaming with the kind of satisfaction that typically followed his most successful medical cases. "My dear Mary, I have the most wonderful news about our literary collaboration."

Mary set down her flowers, immediately giving her husband her complete attention. "Holmes has finished reviewing Arthur's manuscript?"

"Not only finished, but approved it completely. He described it as superior to our first publication in every respect." Watson moved to his wife and took her hands in his. "Mary, he specifically praised your contributions as invaluable to the story's authenticity and emotional impact."

Mary's eyes widened with pleased surprise. "Really? Mr. Holmes appreciated my involvement?"

"More than appreciated—he considers it essential. He said your firsthand perspective provided layers of authenticity that neither Arthur nor I could have achieved alone." Watson's voice grew more animated. "He believes we've created something that transcends mere detective fiction and approaches genuine literature."

Mary felt a flush of pride at the great detective's approval. "And the romantic elements? I was concerned he might find them overly sentimental."

"Quite the opposite. Holmes believes the romantic subplot enhances the investigative elements by demonstrating the human stakes involved in criminal activity." Watson paused, still marveling at his friend's unexpectedly philosophical response. "He said that Mary's presence in the narrative reminds readers that detective work exists to protect and restore human happiness."

"How remarkably thoughtful of him," Mary said softly. "I confess I wasn't certain how he would respond to having his brilliant friend's courtship documented for public consumption."

Watson chuckled. "Holmes continues to surprise me with his capacity for emotional insight when the situation demands it. But the important thing is that we have his complete approval to proceed with publication."

"Then you'll contact Arthur immediately?"

"I've already sent a messenger to Portsmouth with the excellent news and Holmes's minor revision suggestions." Watson's expression grew more serious. "Mary, I want you to understand what this approval means. Holmes's standards are extraordinarily high, and his praise for this work suggests that our collaboration may achieve something far more significant than we originally anticipated."

Mary moved to the window, looking out at the evening light filtering through their small garden. "James, when I first became involved in this project, I thought I was simply helping with an interesting literary venture. But I'm beginning to understand that we're creating something that might influence how people think about crime and investigation for years to come."

"Precisely. And your contributions have been essential to that achievement." Watson joined his wife at the window. "Holmes specifically requested that I convey his appreciation for your insights."

"I'm honored by his confidence. Though I must admit, it feels strange to think that our personal experiences will soon be available for public consumption, even in disguised form."

Watson nodded understandingly. "It is peculiar to see one's own life transformed into literature. But Arthur has handled the personal elements with such discretion and artistry that I believe we can be proud of the result."

"What happens next?"

"Arthur will incorporate Holmes's minor suggestions and begin approaching publishers. He mentioned previously that Ward, Lock & Co. might be interested in our next work, and several other publishers have apparently expressed curiosity about additional Holmes stories."

Mary turned from the window, her expression thoughtful. "The financial arrangements should be much more favorable this time, shouldn't they? Given the success of your first publication?"

"Arthur seems to think so. He's mentioned the possibility of retaining rights rather than selling them outright, which could provide ongoing income rather than a single payment." Watson paused, considering the implications. "Mary, if this collaboration continues to succeed, it might eventually provide sufficient income to reduce my dependence on medical practice."

"You're thinking of becoming a full-time writer?"

Watson considered this carefully. "Not exactly. But the possibility of combining medical practice with regular literary income is certainly appealing. It would allow me to be more selective about my patients while continuing to document Holmes's cases."

Mary smiled at her husband's evident enthusiasm. "Then we should hope that Arthur finds an enthusiastic publisher quickly."

"I suspect he will. The demand for detective fiction seems to be growing, and authentic detective fiction is still quite rare." Watson moved to his desk and began composing a letter. "I want to send Arthur a more detailed account of Holmes's response while the conversation is still fresh in my memory."

As Watson wrote, Mary reflected on the remarkable journey that had brought them to this point. Less than a year ago, she had been a governess struggling with mysterious letters and threatening messages. Now she was a married woman contributing to a literary collaboration that might influence popular understanding of criminal investigation.

"James," she said eventually, "do you think readers will believe in Holmes? Will they accept such extraordinary deductive abilities as credible?"

Watson looked up from his writing. "I think readers are ready for a detective who uses logic rather than luck. People are becoming more scientific in their thinking—they'll appreciate Holmes's methodical approach to investigation."

"And they'll never know it's all completely authentic?"

"That's the genius of our arrangement. Readers get to experience genuine detective work presented as entertainment, while Holmes maintains his privacy and we avoid the complications of public recognition."

Mary nodded, understanding once again the careful balance their collaboration required. "Then we must hope that Arthur finds a publisher who appreciates what we've created."

A Welcome Invitation

December 14, 1889

The winter afternoon had settled into that peculiar London twilight that seemed to arrive almost before tea time, and the gas lamps along the Paddington streets cast warm circles of light against the gathering gloom. Dr. James Watson made his way wearily up the front steps of his modest home, his medical bag heavy with the implements of a particularly challenging house call. Mrs. Henderson's bronchitis had proven more stubborn than expected, requiring a longer consultation than he had anticipated.

Before Watson could retrieve his key, the front door swung open to reveal his wife Mary, her face bright with an excitement that immediately banished his fatigue. She had clearly been watching for his arrival from the front parlor window—a habit she had developed during their ten months of marriage that never failed to warm his heart.

"James!" Mary exclaimed, reaching for his medical bag as he stepped into the warmth of their entry hall. "You're later than expected. I was beginning to worry that Mrs. Henderson had taken a turn for the worse."

Watson allowed his wife to relieve him of his bag, grateful as always for her practical assistance. "Nothing quite so dramatic, my dear. The old lady simply required more time than usual—her condition is improving, but slowly. At her age, these winter ailments require patience from both doctor and patient."

Mary helped him with his coat, her movements quick and efficient despite her obvious eagerness to share some news. "I'm glad she's recovering. But James, the most wonderful thing has happened while you were out!"

Watson paused in the process of hanging his coat on the familiar peg, noting the barely contained excitement in his wife's voice. "Oh? What sort of wonderful thing?"

Instead of answering immediately, Mary took his arm and led him toward their sitting room, where the afternoon tea service waited beside a crackling fire. On the mantelpiece, propped against the clock in a position of obvious importance, stood an elegant envelope bearing Arthur Conan Doyle's distinctive handwriting.

"A letter from Arthur arrived by special messenger about an hour ago," Mary announced, settling beside her husband on their small sofa. "Not just any letter, James—an invitation!"

Watson reached for the envelope, recognizing immediately the quality of the paper and the care with which it had been addressed. "An invitation? To what occasion?"

"Read it aloud," Mary urged, pouring tea with hands that trembled slightly with excitement. "I've already read it three times, but I want to hear your reaction."

Watson broke the seal carefully and unfolded the single sheet of Arthur's finest letterhead. He cleared his throat and began to read:

Dear James and Mary,

Touie and I would be delighted if you would join us for dinner at Simpson's in the Strand on Saturday, December 28th, at seven o'clock. We have much to celebrate, and no one's company would give us greater pleasure than yours. Please let us know at your earliest convenience if this arrangement suits your schedules. With warmest regards and anticipation.

Arthur Conan Doyle

Watson set down the letter, his own excitement beginning to match his wife's. "Simpson's! Mary, that's quite an elegant venue. Arthur must have something particularly significant in mind."

"That's exactly what I was thinking!" Mary leaned forward eagerly. "He doesn't specify what they're celebrating, but given the formality of the invitation and the choice of restaurant..."

"It must be connected to our literary collaboration," Watson agreed. "Perhaps The Sign of Four has found a publisher, or the terms have proven even more favorable than Arthur anticipated."

Mary nodded enthusiastically. "Or perhaps both! James, this could represent a genuine triumph for your partnership with Arthur."

Watson felt a familiar surge of pride at the thought of their collaborative success. The months following Holmes's approval of Arthur's manuscript had been filled with anticipation, but Arthur had kept the details of his publisher negotiations largely to himself, sharing only that "progress was being made" and that "the terms look quite promising."

"Whatever the occasion," Watson said, taking Mary's hand, "I'm delighted that Arthur wants to share it with us. The friendship we've developed with the Doyles has become one of the great pleasures of our married life."

"Indeed," Mary agreed warmly. "Touie has become such a dear friend, and Arthur... well, Arthur has proven himself not only a gifted collaborator but a genuinely good man."

Watson stood and moved to their writing desk in the corner of the room. "I should reply immediately. An invitation to Simpson's deserves prompt acceptance."

"Of course we'll accept," Mary said, then paused thoughtfully. "But James, what should we bring? If they're celebrating something significant, surely we should acknowledge the occasion appropriately."

Watson paused in the process of selecting paper and pen. "What sort of acknowledgment did you have in mind?"

Mary rose and joined him at the desk, her expression growing more thoughtful. "Well, given that it's just before Christmas, and considering how close we've all become, perhaps Christmas gifts would be appropriate? Something to mark both the holiday season and whatever success they're celebrating."

"Christmas gifts for Arthur and Touie?" Watson considered this. "That's a lovely idea, Mary. What did you have in mind?"

Mary began pacing the small sitting room, her mind clearly working through possibilities. "For Touie, perhaps something personal but not overly intimate—we've become good friends, but we've only known each other for a year. A beautiful book of poetry? Or perhaps some fine stationery?"

"Both excellent ideas," Watson agreed. "And for Arthur?"

Mary paused in her pacing, her expression growing more complex. "That's more challenging, isn't it? Arthur has become such an important part of our lives—your literary partner, but also a genuine friend. The gift should acknowledge both relationships without seeming either too professional or too personal."

Watson nodded, understanding the delicate balance his wife was considering. "Perhaps something related to his writing, but with a personal touch?"

"Exactly what I was thinking. A fine pen set, perhaps? Or a leather-bound notebook of the sort writers use?" Mary's eyes brightened with possibility. "Or what about books? Arthur has such wide-ranging interests—medicine, literature, history. We could select something that acknowledges his intellectual curiosity."

Watson began composing his acceptance letter while considering their gift options. "Whatever we choose, it should reflect our appreciation for his friendship as much as our professional collaboration."

"Precisely." Mary resumed her pacing, clearly energized by the planning process. "James, I'm so looking forward to this dinner. It feels like a milestone of sorts—not just for your literary work, but for the friendships we've built through this collaboration."

Watson paused in his writing, struck by his wife's observation. "You're absolutely right, Mary. When I first approached Arthur with those case notes over three years ago, I never imagined it would lead to such genuine friendships."

"Or to such personal happiness," Mary added softly. "After all, if not for the literary collaboration, we might never have met. The Sign of Four case brought us together, and now Arthur's literary treatment of that case may be bringing us all together to celebrate its success."

Watson set down his pen and turned to face his wife fully. "Mary, I hope you know how grateful I am for your involvement in this partnership. Your contributions to the manuscript, your insights into the emotional elements of the story, your friendship with Touie—all of it has enriched both the work and our lives immeasurably."

Mary felt a flush of warmth at her husband's words. "The pleasure has been entirely mine, James. To be part of something so significant, to help bring authentic detective work to the reading public, to contribute to the advancement of scientific investigation..." She paused, her voice growing softer. "It's given me a sense of purpose I never expected to find."

Watson completed his acceptance letter and sealed it carefully. "Then we're agreed? We'll accept Arthur's invitation with enthusiasm, and we'll bring Christmas gifts to acknowledge both the holiday and whatever success we're celebrating?"

"Absolutely. And James?" Mary's eyes held a hint of mischief. "I think we should dress particularly well for this dinner. If Arthur has chosen Simpson's, he clearly intends this to be a memorable occasion."

Watson chuckled at his wife's practical consideration. "Then I'll have my best suit pressed, and you can wear that beautiful blue dress you've been saving for special occasions."

"Perfect. This feels like exactly the sort of occasion that dress was meant for." Mary moved to the window, looking out at the gaslit street. "James, I have such a good feeling about this dinner. Whatever Arthur has to celebrate, I suspect it's going to exceed all our expectations."

Watson joined his wife at the window, his arm settling naturally around her waist. "I suspect you're right, my dear. Arthur's enthusiasm in that invitation suggests something quite significant indeed."

Celebration at Simpson's

December 28, 1889

The grand dining room of Simpson's in the Strand hummed with the elegant conversation of London's most prosperous citizens, the soft clink of crystal and silver providing a refined percussion to the evening's festivities. Gas lamps cast a warm glow over the mahogany paneling and crisp white tablecloths, while the aroma of perfectly roasted beef wafted from the famous carving stations that made the restaurant a destination for discerning diners throughout the city.

Dr. James Watson and his wife Mary arrived precisely at seven o'clock, their best winter coats checked with the attendant as they were led to their reserved table near one of the tall windows overlooking the Strand. Mary's blue silk dress, saved for just such an occasion, rustled softly as she settled into her chair, while James's finest evening suit lent him an air of prosperity that his modest medical practice didn't quite support.

"How elegant this is," Mary whispered, her eyes taking in the restaurant's refined atmosphere. "Arthur has certainly chosen well for whatever celebration he has in mind."

Watson nodded, adjusting his collar with the slight nervousness of a man unaccustomed to such formal dining. "I confess myself curious about the occasion. Arthur's letter suggested something quite significant, but he's been remarkably circumspect about the details."

The maitre d' approached with practiced discretion. "Dr. Watson, I presume? Dr. Doyle requested that I inform you he and Mrs. Doyle should arrive within the next few minutes. Would you care to order beverages while you wait?"

"Thank you, yes. A sherry for my wife, and I'll have a brandy, if you please."

As their drinks arrived, Watson found himself reflecting on the journey that had brought them to this moment. From his first tentative approach to Arthur with those case notes, through the challenges of their collaboration, to this elegant celebration of what appeared to be genuine success—each step had strengthened both their professional partnership and personal friendship.

"James, look," Mary said softly, gesturing toward the entrance. "There they are."

Arthur Conan Doyle entered the dining room with his characteristic confident stride, his arm proudly supporting his wife Louisa, who looked radiant in a deep green velvet dress that complemented her auburn hair. Even from across the room, Watson could see the barely contained excitement in Arthur's expression—the look of a man bursting with good news.

"James! Mary!" Arthur called out as they approached the table, his voice carrying just enough to be heard without disturbing other diners. "How wonderful to see you both. You look absolutely splendid."

The men shook hands warmly while the women exchanged affectionate embraces, their friendship having deepened considerably over the months of collaboration. Louisa's eyes sparkled with the same excitement that animated her husband's features.

"Arthur, Touie," Mary said as they settled into their chairs, "you both look positively glowing. Whatever you're celebrating has clearly agreed with you."

Arthur exchanged a meaningful glance with his wife before turning back to their guests. "Indeed we are celebrating, though I confess I'm finding it difficult to contain my enthusiasm until a more appropriate moment in the evening."

The waiter appeared at Arthur's elbow with practiced timing. "Good evening, Dr. Doyle. Your usual table, I see. What may I bring you and Mrs. Doyle to drink?"

"A bottle of your finest champagne," Arthur replied without hesitation. "We have something quite special to celebrate this evening."

Watson's eyebrows rose with interest. "Champagne? Arthur, you're making us positively breathless with anticipation."

"And well you should be," Arthur replied, his eyes twinkling with mischief. "But first, let us order our dinner. I believe you'll find the evening's offerings quite exceptional."

The waiter presented menus with flourish, though Watson noticed that Arthur barely glanced at his before setting it aside. "Actually, I have a recommendation, if you're amenable. Simpson's is famous for their carving cart, and tonight they're featuring Beef Wellington. It's prepared tableside with considerable ceremony—rather fitting for our celebration."

Mary clapped her hands together with delight. "How wonderful! I've heard of Simpson's carving cart but never experienced it myself."

"Then we're agreed?" Arthur looked around the table, receiving enthusiastic nods from all parties. "Excellent. Waiter, Beef Wellington for four, and please ensure we have your most theatrical carver for the presentation."

As the waiter departed to arrange their meal, Arthur could no longer contain his excitement. He reached across the table to clasp Watson's hand with both of his own.

"James, my dear friend, I can wait no longer. The most marvelous thing has happened—Lippincott's Monthly Magazine has not only agreed to publish 'The Sign of Four,' but they've offered terms that exceed our most optimistic expectations!"

Watson felt his pulse quicken. "Arthur! That's wonderful news! What sort of terms?"

"They're publishing it as a proper book, not just in an annual," Arthur continued, his voice growing more animated. "More importantly, we retain the copyright and will receive royalties on all sales. They've also expressed interest in a long-term partnership for future Holmes stories."

Mary leaned forward eagerly. "A long-term partnership? What does that mean exactly?"

Louisa spoke for the first time since sitting down, her voice warm with pride. "It means they want to establish Arthur as their premier detective fiction author. They're proposing a series of Holmes stories, both as books and for magazine serialization."

Watson felt a surge of excitement so powerful it left him momentarily speechless. "Arthur, this is extraordinary. Beyond anything we could have hoped for when we began this collaboration."

"But there's more," Arthur continued, his grin widening. "They've also made an offer for the rights to republish 'A Study in Scarlet' as a standalone book, with much more favorable terms than our original agreement."

The champagne arrived at that moment, the cork popping with a satisfying sound that seemed to punctuate Arthur's announcement. As the golden liquid fizzed in their glasses, Watson found himself contemplating the magnitude of what his friend had just revealed.

"A toast," Arthur said, raising his glass. "To authentic detective fiction, to the scientific method, and to the friendships that have made this remarkable journey possible."

They drank deeply, the champagne's effervescence matching the bubbling excitement at their table. Watson set down his glass with a trembling hand, still processing the implications of Arthur's news.

"Arthur, I must ask—what does Holmes make of these developments?"

Arthur's expression grew more serious. "I've informed him of the basic arrangement, of course. He's pleased that his methods will receive wider dissemination, though he's also concerned about maintaining the privacy protections we've established."

"And the financial arrangements?" Mary inquired practically.

"Unchanged. James and I continue to split the proceeds equally, with the understanding that your contributions, Mary, are part of James's involvement in the collaboration." Arthur paused, his expression growing more thoughtful. "Though I must say, given the magnitude of these new opportunities, we may need to discuss more formal arrangements for future projects."

Before Watson could respond, a magnificent spectacle approached their table. The carving cart, laden with a golden-brown Beef Wellington that seemed to glow in the gaslight, was wheeled ceremoniously to their table by a chef in pristine whites. The theatrical presentation that followed— the careful slicing of the pastry, the revelation of the perfectly pink beef within, the artistic arrangement on their plates—provided a welcome interlude that allowed the full impact of Arthur's news to settle in their minds.

As they savored the exceptional meal, conversation flowed between the professional implications of their success and the personal pleasure of sharing such a moment with dear friends. Watson found himself marveling at how their literary partnership had evolved into something far richer than he had ever imagined possible.

"You know," Mary said as their plates were cleared away, "when James first told me about his collaboration with you, Arthur, I never imagined it would lead to anything quite so... momentous."

Arthur smiled warmly. "Nor did I, Mary. What began as a simple desire to transform James's case notes into publishable fiction has become something that may well influence the future of detective literature."

"Speaking of which," Louisa interjected with a knowing smile, "I believe this might be an appropriate moment for gift exchanges. After all, Christmas was just three days ago, and we have much to celebrate."

Mary's eyes brightened with anticipation. "Oh yes! James and I brought something for both of you."

Watson reached beneath the table and withdrew two elegantly wrapped packages. "These are small tokens of our appreciation—for Christmas, and for the friendship that has grown from our collaboration."

Arthur accepted his gift with obvious pleasure, carefully removing the wrapping to reveal a leather-bound notebook of the finest quality, its cover embossed with his initials in gold. "James, Mary—this is exquisite. Perfect for a writer's thoughts and observations."

Louisa's gift proved to be a beautifully illustrated volume of poetry, selected with care to reflect both her literary interests and the season of celebration. "How thoughtful of you both. I shall treasure this."

"And we have something for you as well," Arthur said, producing packages of his own. For Watson, a elegant fountain pen set in a polished wooden box. For Mary, a delicate silver locket engraved with her initials.

As the gifts were admired and thanks exchanged, Watson felt a profound sense of completion. The evening had begun with anticipation and was ending with the kind of warm satisfaction that comes from success shared with true friends.

"Arthur," Watson said as they prepared to leave, "I want you to know how grateful I am—not just for your literary skill, but for your friendship. What we've accomplished together has exceeded my wildest expectations."

Arthur gripped his friend's hand warmly. "The gratitude is mutual, James. And Mary, your contributions have been invaluable. We've created something remarkable together."

As they stepped out into the crisp December evening, their breath visible in the cold air, Watson felt the weight of the future settling pleasantly on his shoulders.

Shorter Stories Requested

May 5, 1890

Arthur Conan Doyle opened all the windows of his study to welcome the fresh air that carried the scent of blooming lilacs from his garden. His writing desk, usually cluttered with manuscripts and correspondence, had been cleared in anticipation of Dr. James Watson's visit—a meeting that promised to address both personal and professional developments in their ongoing collaboration.

Arthur paced near the window, occasionally glancing toward the street, his mind occupied with the various matters they would need to discuss. The success of "The Sign of Four" had exceeded even their optimistic projections, and The Strand Magazine and other publishers had been pressing for more Holmes stories with an urgency that was both gratifying and challenging. More immediately, James's letter requesting this meeting had hinted at changes in his personal circumstances that might affect their partnership.

The sound of the front gate announced Watson's arrival, and Arthur moved to the hallway to greet his friend personally. Through the etched glass of the front door, he could see Watson's familiar figure approaching with the steady gait that had characterized him since their first meeting over four years ago.

"James!" Arthur called out, opening the door before his friend could knock. "How good to see you. The journey from London wasn't too taxing, I hope?"

Watson clasped Arthur's extended hand warmly, his weathered face showing the satisfaction of a man who had left his medical responsibilities in capable hands for the afternoon. "Not at all, Arthur. The spring weather made it quite pleasant, actually. Thank you for agreeing to meet on such short notice."

"Nonsense. Your letter suggested matters of some importance, and besides, I've been eager to discuss our next publishing ventures." Arthur led Watson into his study, where tea service waited on a small table near the open windows. "Please, sit down. Touie sends her regards, by the way—she's visiting her sister in London, or she would have insisted on joining us."

Watson settled into his familiar chair, accepting the offered cup gratefully. "Give her my best when you write. And Mary sends her warmest regards to you both." He paused, his expression growing more serious. "Arthur, I appreciate you making time for this meeting. I have some news that may affect our collaboration, and I wanted to discuss it with you in person."

Arthur leaned forward with interest. "Nothing problematic, I hope?"

"Quite the opposite, actually." Watson's face brightened. "I've been offered an opportunity to relocate my medical practice from Paddington to Kensington. It's only about two miles distance, but it represents a significant advancement in both clientele and professional standing."

Arthur set down his teacup, immediately understanding the implications. "Kensington! James, that's excellent news. A much more prestigious location for a medical practice."

"Indeed. The opportunity arose through a colleague who's retiring—Dr. Pemberton, whom you may remember me mentioning. He's offered to transfer several of his long-established patients to my care, along with the lease on his consulting rooms." Watson's enthusiasm was evident. "The curious thing is, I already have quite a number of patients in Kensington from my current practice. The move would actually consolidate my clientele geographically."

"That sounds like an ideal arrangement. What reservations do you have?"

Watson hesitated slightly. "Well, the financial commitment is substantial—higher rent, the cost of relocation, establishing new arrangements with local pharmacists and hospitals. But more importantly for our purposes, I wanted to ensure the move wouldn't interfere with our literary collaboration."

Arthur waved a dismissive hand. "James, you mustn't let our partnership influence such an important professional decision. If this move advances your medical career, you have my complete support."

"That's generous of you, Arthur. But practically speaking, the relocation will require considerable attention over the next few months. I'll have less time available for extensive case documentation, at least initially."

Arthur considered this, then smiled. "Actually, James, your timing may be remarkably fortuitous. I was hoping to discuss a significant change in our publishing approach that might actually work better with your reduced availability."

Watson raised an eyebrow with interest. "What sort of change?"

Arthur moved to his desk and withdrew a folder containing correspondence from various publishers. "We've been approached by several magazines about serializing Holmes stories on a monthly basis. The Strand Magazine, in particular, has made quite an attractive offer."

"Monthly serialization? That's intriguing, but how would it work practically?"

"Here's the key point," Arthur said, settling back into his chair with obvious excitement. "Both 'A Study in Scarlet' and 'The Sign of Four' contain approximately forty thousand words each. That length is perfect for book publication, but far too extensive for monthly magazine stories."

Watson nodded thoughtfully. "I see the challenge. What solution do you propose?"

"Shorter, self-contained stories of roughly ten thousand words each. Complete investigations that can be told efficiently without the extensive background and character development we've included in the longer works." Arthur's eyes gleamed with possibility. "Think of Holmes's single-day cases—the Blue Carbuncle, the Red-Headed League, the Speckled Band. Each demonstrates his methods clearly while providing a complete narrative arc."

Watson frowned slightly. "Ten thousand words? Arthur, I'm not certain that's sufficient to properly document Holmes's investigative process. My case notes alone often exceed that length."

"Ah, but that's where editorial skill becomes essential," Arthur replied confidently. "The key is to focus on the most dramatic and instructive elements of each case while maintaining scientific accuracy. We compress the timeline, eliminate extraneous details, and concentrate on showcasing Holmes's deductive methods in their most impressive form."

Watson considered this carefully. "You believe ten thousand words can adequately present a complete criminal investigation?"

"I'm certain of it. Remember, James, our goal isn't to provide exhaustive documentation—it's to educate readers about scientific detection while entertaining them with compelling mysteries." Arthur leaned forward earnestly. "Besides, monthly publication would establish regular income rather than the occasional payments we receive from book sales. It could provide you with financial security while you're establishing your new practice."

The practical implications of Arthur's observation struck Watson immediately. "Regular monthly income would indeed be helpful during the transition to Kensington. But would Holmes approve of such abbreviated accounts of his work?"

"I believe he'll appreciate the wider dissemination of his methods," Arthur replied. "Monthly magazine publication reaches far more readers than our books alone. Besides, the shorter format will require us to focus on the intellectual content rather than details—exactly what Holmes has always preferred."

Watson set down his teacup and moved to the window, looking out at Arthur's garden while contemplating the proposal. "It's certainly an intriguing approach. And you're right that many of Holmes's cases could be effectively presented in shorter form."

"Precisely. In fact, I've already identified the case I'd like to adapt first, if you're agreeable." Arthur consulted his notes. "A Scandal in Bohemia— the investigation involving the photograph and the remarkable Irene Adler."

Watson turned back with obvious interest. "An excellent choice. That case demonstrates Holmes's methods while involving genuinely high stakes and fascinating characters."

"My thinking exactly. The royal connections provide drama, Irene Adler represents one of the few people to outwit Holmes, and the investigation showcases multiple deductive techniques." Arthur's enthusiasm was building. "I believe I can craft a ten-thousand-word version that captures all the essential elements while maintaining the pace necessary for magazine publication."

"And you want to proceed with this approach for the monthly series?"

"If you're willing. I would write the initial draft based on your case notes, then submit it for your review before approaching Holmes for his approval." Arthur paused, studying his friend's expression. "James, this format could allow us to publish a new Holmes story every month for years to come, assuming your documentation continues to provide suitable material."

Watson felt his excitement growing as he considered the possibilities. "The reading public would have regular access to Holmes's methods, presented consistently and authentically. It could genuinely influence public understanding of criminal investigation."

"Exactly what we've hoped to achieve from the beginning." Arthur stood and began his characteristic pacing. "Moreover, the monthly format would allow us to present a wider variety of cases than we could manage with book-length publications. Different types of crimes, various social classes, diverse investigative challenges—all demonstrating the universal applicability of scientific detection."

Watson returned to his chair, his mind working through the practical implications. "When would you begin work on the Scandal in Bohemia adaptation?"

"Immediately, if you approve the approach. I could have a draft ready for your review within two weeks." Arthur's tone grew more serious. "But James, I want to ensure you're comfortable with this significant change in our collaborative method."

Watson considered carefully, weighing the professional opportunities against his personal circumstances. "Arthur, I believe this monthly serialization approach may be exactly what our partnership needs. It provides regular income, reaches more readers, and allows for more efficient use of the extensive case material I've documented."

"Then we're agreed? I'll proceed with adapting the Scandal in Bohemia case for magazine publication?"

"We are indeed." Watson stood and extended his hand. "I look forward to seeing how you condense my rather lengthy notes into an engaging ten-thousand-word story."

Arthur gripped Watson's hand firmly. "I'm confident you'll be pleased with the result. And James—congratulations on the Kensington opportunity. It represents a significant advancement in your medical career."

"Thank you, Arthur. Though I suspect our literary collaboration may soon prove as professionally significant as my medical practice."

As Watson prepared to leave for his return journey to London, both men felt the satisfaction of having successfully navigated another evolution in their partnership. The move to Kensington would advance Watson's medical career, while the shift to monthly magazine publication promised to expand their literary success beyond anything they had previously imagined.

Sherlock Leaves the Writing Team

July 4, 1890

Dr. James Watson climbed the familiar stairs to 111 Baker Street with a leather portfolio tucked under his arm, its contents representing what he hoped would be the next evolution of their literary partnership with Arthur Conan Doyle.

Holmes sat by the open window, his sharp profile etched against the gauze curtains that fluttered in the occasional breeze. His shirt sleeves were rolled up, and a glass of iced water sat untouched on the table beside him. Even the great detective, it seemed, was not immune to the oppressive July weather.

"Watson," Holmes said without turning from the window, "I trust your relocation to Kensington proceeds satisfactorily? Your footsteps suggest the satisfaction of a man whose professional circumstances have improved considerably."

Watson smiled, setting down his portfolio and settling into his usual chair. "Your powers of observation remain as sharp as ever, Holmes. Yes, the new practice is exceeding my expectations. The clientele is more established, the consulting rooms are excellent, and Mary has taken to the improved neighborhood with considerable enthusiasm."

"Excellent. And our literary collaborator? How does Arthur fare with his writing endeavors?"

Watson leaned forward, his expression growing more animated. "That's precisely what I wanted to discuss with you today, Holmes. Arthur has developed an approach to magazine serialization that I believe will revolutionize how detective fiction is presented to the public."

Holmes finally turned from the window, his keen gray eyes focusing on Watson with renewed interest. "Indeed? What sort of approach?"

"Shorter stories—much shorter. Where 'A Study in Scarlet' and 'The Sign of Four' each contained roughly forty thousand words, Arthur proposes magazine stories of approximately ten thousand words." Watson opened his portfolio and withdrew a manuscript. "Complete investigations, but focused on the most essential elements of your methods."

Holmes raised an eyebrow. "Ten thousand words? Watson, that's barely a quarter of the length of our previous collaborations. Can such abbreviated accounts adequately present the complexities of criminal investigation?"

"Arthur believes they can, and I'm beginning to share his confidence." Watson held up the manuscript. "I've brought an example—his adaptation of the Irene Adler case. 'A Scandal in Bohemia,' he's calling it."

Holmes's expression sharpened with interest. "The photograph affair? An excellent choice—it certainly demonstrates the limitations of pure logic when confronted with superior intellect."

"Precisely. Arthur has crafted a version that captures all the essential deductive elements while maintaining the dramatic tension and character development that made the case so memorable." Watson set the manuscript on the table between them. "I believe you'll find that the shorter format actually enhances the impact of your methods by focusing attention on the most instructive moments."

Holmes glanced at the manuscript but made no move to reach for it. "The concept has merit, certainly. Monthly publication would provide regular dissemination of proper investigative techniques. But Watson, I'm afraid I must decline to review this particular example."

Watson looked up with surprise. "Decline? But Holmes, surely you want to ensure the accuracy—"

"Watson," Holmes interrupted, moving to his chemical apparatus, "consider this—you've been documenting my cases for over four years now. Arthur has successfully adapted two complex investigations with minimal revision required. Both of you understand my methods and standards intimately."

Holmes's manner became more formal as he turned back to face Watson. "The time has come for you to proceed without my direct oversight. I have complete confidence in your ability to ensure investigative accuracy, just as I trust Arthur's literary judgment to present the material effectively."

Watson felt a flutter of uncertainty. "Holmes, surely your review remains essential? Your standards for accuracy—"

"Have been thoroughly internalized by both you and Arthur," Holmes replied firmly. "Moreover, Watson, I find myself increasingly occupied with current casework. The demands of active investigation leave little time for reviewing literary adaptations of past cases."

Holmes moved to the window again, looking out at the heat-shimmered street below. "I simply cannot spare the time to review every short story you and Arthur propose to publish. My caseload has grown considerably, and I must focus my attention on current investigations rather than literary retrospectives."

Watson studied his friend's profile, recognizing the signs of a decision already made. "You're saying you won't review any of the magazine stories?"

"I'm saying that our collaboration has reached a point where my direct involvement is no longer necessary," Holmes replied. "You and Arthur have proven yourselves capable of producing authentic, instructive, and engaging accounts of detective work. The review process has served its purpose."

Watson gathered the manuscript, his mind working through the implications of Holmes's complete withdrawal. "And if we have questions about specific cases or techniques?"

"Then you may certainly consult me on matters of investigative detail. But the routine review and approval process for these shorter stories? Watson, I'm far too occupied with active cases to devote time to such oversight." Holmes's voice carried a note of finality. "I have complete confidence in your partnership with Arthur."

Holmes returned to his desk and began organizing papers with characteristic efficiency. "Watson, you must understand—I have three major cases currently demanding my attention, correspondence from potential clients accumulating daily, and chemical experiments that require precise timing. I simply cannot allocate hours to reviewing literary manuscripts when my investigative work requires immediate focus."

As Watson prepared to leave, Holmes called after him. "Watson, take the manuscript with you. Read it yourself, apply the standards we've established together, and trust your judgment. I'm confident you'll find Arthur's work entirely satisfactory without requiring my approval."

Watson paused at the door, manuscript in hand. "Then this represents the end of your involvement in our literary ventures?"

"It represents the beginning of your independence," Holmes replied, already turning back to his papers. "Which is, after all, the natural evolution of any successful collaboration. I'm simply too busy with actual detective work to continue serving as literary editor."

The 1st Group of Short Stories

July 18, 1890

The afternoon train from London had arrived precisely on time, and Dr. James Watson found himself walking the familiar path to Arthur Conan Doyle's Portsmouth residence with a sense of anticipation mixed with slight apprehension. The leather portfolio under his arm contained not only the approved manuscript of "A Scandal in Bohemia" but also news that would fundamentally alter their collaborative process.

Arthur answered the door before Watson could knock, his face bright with the eager expression that had become characteristic whenever their literary partnership was the subject of discussion.

"James! Excellent timing. I was just reviewing some correspondence from The Strand Magazine." Arthur relieved Watson of his hat and coat with practiced efficiency. "They're even more enthusiastic about our proposed monthly series than I had dared hope. Come, let's settle in the study—I have tea ready and several matters to discuss."

Watson followed his friend into the familiar book-lined room, noting the careful organization that had replaced Arthur's earlier creative chaos. Success, it seemed, had brought with it a more systematic approach to the writing craft.

"Arthur, before we discuss The Strand's enthusiasm, I have some rather significant news about Holmes's involvement in our future collaborations." Watson settled into his usual chair and accepted the offered teacup. "News that may surprise you considerably."

Arthur paused in the act of pouring his own tea, his attention immediately focused. "Nothing problematic, I hope? Holmes hasn't developed concerns about the magazine serialization approach?"

"Quite the contrary. Holmes has expressed complete confidence in our partnership." Watson opened his portfolio and withdrew the "Scandal in

Bohemia" manuscript. "So much confidence, in fact, that he's declined to review this adaptation."

Arthur's eyebrows rose with surprise. "Declined to review it? But surely he wants to ensure the accuracy of his methods as presented?"

"That's exactly what I thought," Watson replied, settling back in his chair. "But Holmes made a rather compelling argument. He pointed out that after four years of collaboration, both you and I have thoroughly internalized his standards and methods. More importantly, he's finding himself increasingly occupied with active casework."

Arthur set down his teacup, his expression growing more thoughtful. "You mean he's too busy with actual detective work to spare time for literary review?"

"Precisely. Holmes was quite direct about it—he has three major cases currently demanding his attention, correspondence from potential clients accumulating daily, and various experiments requiring his focus." Watson smiled at the memory. "He said, and I quote, 'I simply cannot allocate hours to reviewing literary manuscripts when my investigative work requires immediate attention.'"

Arthur stood and began his characteristic pacing, his mind clearly working through the implications. "So Holmes is effectively withdrawing from our editorial process entirely?"

"He prefers to call it 'the beginning of our independence,'" Watson replied. "Holmes expressed complete confidence that we can maintain the quality and authenticity of our work without his direct oversight."

Arthur paused in his pacing, a slow smile spreading across his features. "James, do you realize what this means? We can proceed from your case notes directly to publication without the weeks of waiting for Holmes's review and potential revisions."

"Exactly what I was thinking. The process becomes considerably more efficient." Watson leaned forward with growing enthusiasm. "Arthur, I reviewed your 'Scandal in Bohemia' adaptation myself, applying the standards Holmes has taught us over these years. The work is not only accurate but genuinely superior to our previous efforts in terms of narrative pace and reader engagement."

Arthur returned to his chair, his excitement now matching Watson's. "Then we can proceed with The Strand Magazine's offer immediately? Though I should mention their specific timeline requirements—and my own preparations."

Watson raised an eyebrow with interest. "Your own preparations?"

Arthur moved to his desk and withdrew a carefully organized folder. "James, I confess I've been anticipating this development. Knowing how methodical Holmes is, and how thorough your documentation has become, I suspected we might eventually reach this point of independence." He opened the folder with obvious satisfaction. "I've already prepared a comprehensive plan for The Strand series."

Watson leaned forward with curiosity. "What sort of plan?"

"A complete schedule," Arthur replied, consulting his notes. "The Strand cannot begin publishing our Holmes stories until their July 1891 issue— nearly a full year from now. They propose to run twelve consecutive monthly stories from July 1891 through June 1892, with 'A Scandal in Bohemia' as the inaugural story."

"July 1891 through June 1892," Watson mused. "That's a full year of monthly Holmes adventures."

"Precisely. And James, I've spent considerable time reviewing all your case documentation to select the most suitable investigations for magazine serialization." Arthur's eyes gleamed with pride in his methodical approach. "I believe I've identified the perfect twelve cases, arranged in optimal order for maximum reader engagement."

Watson felt his excitement building. "You've already selected all twelve cases?"

Arthur consulted his detailed notes. "Indeed. Let me share my proposed schedule with you." He cleared his throat and began reading from his carefully prepared list:

"July 1891 - 'A Scandal in Bohemia' as our inaugural story, introducing readers to Holmes's methods through the memorable Irene Adler case.

August 1891 - 'The Red-Headed League,' demonstrating how Holmes can deduce elaborate criminal schemes from seemingly absurd circumstances.

September 1891 - 'A Case of Identity,' showing Holmes's ability to solve crimes that others dismiss as mere domestic troubles.

October 1891 - 'The Boscombe Valley Mystery,' providing a rural setting and demonstrating that Holmes's methods work equally well outside London.

November 1891 - 'The Five Orange Pips,' an international conspiracy that shows the global reach of criminal activity.

December 1891 - 'The Man with the Twisted Lip,' perfect for the Christmas season as it involves themes of redemption and hidden identity.

January 1892 - 'The Adventure of the Blue Carbuncle,' a Christmas-themed case that shows Holmes's capacity for mercy and seasonal goodwill.

February 1892 - 'The Adventure of the Speckled Band,' one of Holmes's most dramatic cases involving apparent supernatural elements with logical solutions.

March 1892 - 'The Adventure of the Engineer's Thumb,' demonstrating how industrial crime can be as complex as any drawing-room mystery.

April 1892 - 'The Adventure of the Noble Bachelor,' taking us into aristocratic society and international complications.

May 1892 - 'The Adventure of the Beryl Coronet,' showing how family secrets can lead to apparent theft and public disgrace.

June 1892 - 'The Adventure of the Copper Beeches,' concluding our series with a case that showcases both Holmes's protective instincts and his most brilliant deductions."

Watson stared at Arthur in amazement. "You've planned the entire year's worth of stories? Arthur, this is remarkable. The variety, the seasonal elements, the progression from simpler to more complex cases..."

"I wanted to ensure we had a coherent series that would build readership while demonstrating the full range of Holmes's capabilities," Arthur explained with evident satisfaction. "Each case serves a specific purpose in the overall sequence, while providing the variety necessary to maintain reader interest across twelve consecutive months."

Watson reviewed the list with growing admiration. "The Christmas stories perfectly positioned for December and January, the dramatic cases spaced throughout to maintain excitement, the international elements balanced with domestic mysteries..." He looked up at Arthur with genuine respect. "This is masterful planning."

"And with nearly a year until publication begins, I can adapt each case systematically, working from your documented notes without the pressure of monthly deadlines." Arthur consulted his calendar. "I estimate I can complete one adaptation every three weeks, which would give us the entire series finished by next spring, well in advance of publication."

Watson stood and moved to the window, contemplating the magnitude of what Arthur had planned. "Twelve consecutive months of authentic detective stories in The Strand Magazine. By the time we reach the Copper Beeches conclusion in June 1892, Holmes will be a household name throughout Britain."

"That's precisely the goal," Arthur agreed, joining Watson at the window. "Regular monthly publication will establish Holmes as a permanent fixture in popular literature, while authentic investigative methods reach thousands of readers who might never otherwise encounter scientific detection."

Watson turned back to his friend with obvious gratitude. "Arthur, I'm impressed by the thoroughness of your planning. You've clearly given this series the systematic attention it deserves."

"James, this represents the culmination of everything we've worked toward," Arthur replied earnestly. "Our partnership has evolved from experimental collaboration to a professional enterprise capable of sustained excellence. This twelve-month series will prove that authentic detective fiction can achieve both literary merit and commercial success."

Arthur returned to his desk and gathered his detailed notes. "Then we're agreed? This schedule represents our commitment to The Strand Magazine for the year-long series?"

"Completely agreed," Watson said, extending his hand. "Arthur, I believe you've created a plan that will establish Sherlock Holmes as the most famous detective in literature while maintaining the scientific authenticity that makes our work valuable."

As they shook hands, both men felt the satisfaction of having successfully planned their most ambitious literary venture.

The Christmas Goose

December 24, 1890

The December afternoon had brought a light snowfall to London, and the cozy sitting room of the Watson residence in Paddington glowed with the warm light of the gas lamps and the small Christmas tree that Mary had decorated with particular care. Dr. James Watson sat in his comfortable chair by the fire, reviewing his latest case notes while Mary worked on her embroidery nearby, both enjoying the peaceful domesticity of Christmas Eve.

The sound of an unusual commotion at their front door drew their attention—voices conferring in urgent whispers, followed by what appeared to be careful maneuvering of something substantial. Before either could investigate, their housekeeper Mrs. Morrison appeared in the doorway, her face bright with curiosity and barely contained excitement.

"Dr. and Mrs. Watson," she announced with obvious pleasure, "there's been a delivery. A most extraordinary delivery, if I may say so."

Watson looked up from his notes with interest. "What sort of delivery, Mrs. Morrison?"

"A gentleman from Harrods, sir, with a large hamper and instructions that it must be presented to you immediately. He said it was sent with the compliments of Dr. Arthur Conan Doyle of Portsmouth, and that particular care had been taken to ensure its arrival today."

Mary set down her embroidery, her eyes sparkling with delighted surprise. "Arthur sent us something from Harrods? James, what could it possibly be?"

Mrs. Morrison stepped aside to reveal two uniformed delivery men carrying an elegant wicker hamper of considerable size, its contents carefully packed and bearing the distinctive Harrods label that spoke of quality and expense. A cream-colored envelope was attached to the hamper's handle with a red ribbon.

"Where would you like this placed, sir?" the senior delivery man inquired respectfully.

"The dining table, I think," Watson replied, rising to assist with the arrangements. As the men carefully positioned the hamper and departed with appropriate thanks and a generous gratuity, Watson and Mary found themselves staring at their unexpected gift with mounting anticipation.

"The envelope first, I think," Mary suggested, carefully untying the ribbon with the reverence such an elegant presentation deserved.

Watson opened the envelope to reveal a beautiful Christmas card featuring a winter scene reminiscent of the Devonshire countryside, and inside, a letter written in Arthur's familiar hand:

My Dear James and Mary,

Touie and I wanted to ensure that your Christmas dinner would be something truly special, so we have taken the liberty of sending you what Harrods assures us is their finest Christmas goose, fully prepared and ready for your table tomorrow. Please consider this a small token of our gratitude for the friendship and collaboration that have enriched our lives so immeasurably this year.

We know that the past months have been intensive as we prepared our twelve adventures for The Strand Magazine, and we wanted to mark the season with something that would allow you both to enjoy Christmas Day without the burden of extensive preparation.

I must also share some exciting news about our plans for the new year. Touie and I have decided to undertake a rather extensive Continental tour, beginning with Vienna in late January of next year, where I hope to research some historical material for my next non-Holmes project. In March, we plan to continue to Venice, Milan, and Paris, returning to London on March 24th.

Mary looked up from the letter with tears of gratitude glistening in her eyes. "James, this is the most thoughtful gesture imaginable. Arthur has arranged our entire Christmas dinner!"

Watson felt deeply moved by his friend's generosity. "And such expense! A fully prepared goose from Harrods, delivered on Christmas Eve... Arthur has gone to extraordinary lengths to ensure this would arrive exactly when needed."

Mary moved to examine the hamper more closely, carefully lifting the lid to reveal not just the promised goose but an array of accompaniments that spoke of meticulous planning. "James, look at this—there's stuffing, cranberry sauce, roasted vegetables, even what appears to be Christmas pudding. It's a complete feast!"

Watson joined his wife in examining Arthur's magnificent gift, noting the careful packing and the detailed instructions that would make Christmas dinner effortless. "Mary, I'm almost overwhelmed by Arthur's thoughtfulness. To arrange all this, to ensure it arrived on Christmas Eve..."

"It shows how much our friendship means to him," Mary replied softly. "And James, what exciting news about their Continental tour! Vienna, Venice, Milan, Paris—what a wonderful opportunity for them both."

Watson nodded, though he felt a moment of concern about the timing. "I hope Arthur isn't over committing himself. The twelve stories for The Strand represent a substantial workload, and if he's traveling extensively..."

Mary picked up the letter again, rereading Arthur's assurances about his writing schedule. "But he says he's already completed six stories and is confident about finishing the rest. Arthur has always been remarkably disciplined about his writing commitments."

"True," Watson agreed. "And he's right that travel often stimulates creativity. The Continental tour might well enhance rather than hinder his work on our remaining stories."

Mary began making mental plans for their Christmas dinner, her excitement growing as she realized how perfectly Arthur had arranged everything. "James, we must write to thank them immediately. And perhaps we should send something to Portsmouth—it's too late for Christmas delivery, but we could arrange something special for New Year's."

Watson moved to his writing desk, already composing his response in his mind. "I'll write this evening. Arthur and Touie deserve to know how much their generosity means to us."

As evening settled over their Paddington home, Watson and Mary found themselves reflecting on the remarkable friendship that had developed from their literary collaboration. Arthur's Christmas gift represented far more than mere generosity—it demonstrated the deep affection and consideration that characterized their relationship.

"James," Mary said as they prepared their own letter of thanks, "I'm so grateful that your work brought us into friendship with Arthur and

Touie. They've enriched our lives in ways that extend far beyond the professional collaboration."

Watson nodded, feeling the same gratitude. "When I first approached Arthur with those case notes over three years ago, I never imagined it would lead to such genuine friendship. Arthur has proven himself not only a gifted collaborator but a truly good man."

"And Touie has become such a dear friend," Mary added. "I shall miss them terribly during their Continental tour, though I'm excited to hear about their adventures."

As Watson completed his letter of thanks, expressing their gratitude for Arthur's thoughtfulness and wishing the Doyles safe and inspiring travels, both he and Mary felt the warm satisfaction that comes from being remembered and cherished by true friends.

The Doyle's move to South Norwood
June 15, 1891

The June afternoon had brought the first real warmth of summer to London, and Dr. James Watson found himself grateful for the cross-ventilation in his Kensington consulting rooms as he completed his notes from the morning's patient consultations. At his desk, Mary sat arranging correspondence with the efficient grace that had made her such an invaluable partner in both his medical practice and their ongoing literary collaboration with Arthur Conan Doyle.

The past year had been remarkably productive. The success of "The Sign of Four" had exceeded all their expectations, and Arthur's systematic preparation of twelve monthly stories for The Strand Magazine represented the most ambitious publishing venture any of them had ever attempted. With "A Scandal in Bohemia" scheduled to launch the series in just two weeks, anticipation had reached fever pitch in their household.

"James," Mary said, looking up from a letter she had been reading with obvious pleasure, "the most wonderful news has arrived from Arthur and Touie."

Watson set aside his medical notes, immediately giving his wife his full attention. Correspondence from Southsea had become increasingly frequent as the launch date for their Strand series approached, but Mary's tone suggested something particularly significant.

"They're moving!" Mary announced, her face bright with excitement. "Listen to this:

My dear Mary and James,

Touie and I are delighted to share our most exciting news. We have purchased a house at 12 Tennison Road, South Norwood, and will be relocating from Southsea by the end of this month. The house is charming, with excellent railway connections to

Watson felt his eyebrows rise with interest. "South Norwood? That's considerably closer to London than Southsea."

"Exactly what I was thinking," Mary replied, continuing to read from Arthur's letter. "'The timing could not be better, as our collaboration with The Strand Magazine will require more frequent communication with London publishers. Being within easy reach of the city will allow me to attend editorial meetings without the lengthy journey from Southsea.'"

Watson leaned back in his chair, immediately grasping the practical advantages of Arthur's decision. "It makes perfect sense, actually. With monthly deadlines beginning in July, proximity to The Strand's offices could prove invaluable."

Mary nodded enthusiastically. "But James, listen to this part: 'Most importantly, the new location will allow us to entertain friends more easily, as South Norwood is accessible from central London by a pleasant train journey of less than an hour. We very much hope that you and Mary will be among our first visitors to 12 Tennison Road.'"

Watson felt a surge of warmth at Arthur's thoughtful inclusion of their friendship in his practical planning. "That's remarkably considerate of him. And Mary, it will mean we can see them much more frequently."

"My thoughts exactly!" Mary's enthusiasm was unmistakable. "James, we could visit for an afternoon and return the same evening, or they could come to us just as easily. After years of Southsea being such a journey, this feels like a wonderful development."

Watson moved to the window, looking out at the busy Kensington street while contemplating the implications of Arthur's relocation. "The timing is indeed perfect. With the Strand series launching next month, Arthur will need to be more available for editorial consultations, promotional activities, whatever business arrangements such success might require."

"And Touie mentioned her charitable work," Mary added, scanning the letter for additional details. "She's become quite involved with children's welfare organizations, hasn't she? London would offer many more opportunities for such activities."

Watson returned to his chair with obvious satisfaction. "Mary, I believe this represents exactly the sort of strategic thinking that will ensure our collaboration's continued success. Arthur is positioning himself to take full advantage of the opportunities our Strand partnership will create."

Mary set down the letter and looked at her husband with the expression of someone who had been considering an important proposal. "James, what would you think of our attending their housewarming celebration? Arthur mentions they're planning to host a gathering in early July to christen their new home."

"A housewarming in South Norwood?" Watson considered this prospect with genuine interest. "Mary, that sounds delightful. And the timing would be perfect—just after 'A Scandal in Bohemia' appears in The Strand. We could celebrate both their new home and the launch of our monthly series."

Mary's eyes sparkled with anticipation. "Oh, James, I can already imagine how wonderful it will be. A proper celebration with dear friends, marking both a new home and the beginning of what promises to be our most successful publishing venture yet."

Watson picked up Arthur's letter and read through it again, noting the careful balance between practical explanations and personal warmth that characterized all his friend's correspondence. "Mary, there's something else significant about this move. South Norwood suggests Arthur is committed to establishing himself permanently as a London literary figure rather than a provincial author who occasionally publishes in the capital."

"You think the move represents increased professional ambition?"

Watson considered this carefully. "I think it represents confidence in our collaboration's future. Arthur is investing in proximity to London because he believes our partnership with The Strand will create opportunities that justify such a commitment."

Mary rose and moved to their writing desk, already beginning to compose their response. "Then we should reply immediately, expressing our delight at their news and our enthusiasm for visiting their new home."

"Absolutely. And Mary, we should also mention how perfect the timing is for the Strand series launch. Arthur will want to know that we appreciate the strategic advantages of his relocation."

As Mary began writing their congratulatory response, Watson reflected on how perfectly this development complemented their other recent successes. The Kensington medical practice was thriving, their marriage was bringing them both deep satisfaction, and their literary collaboration was about to achieve unprecedented visibility through The Strand Magazine's monthly publication.

Now, with Arthur and Touie relocating to South Norwood, even their friendship would benefit from increased accessibility and regular contact. The careful planning that had characterized every aspect of their literary partnership was extending into their personal relationships, creating a social framework that could support whatever successes lay ahead.

"James," Mary said, looking up from her writing, "shall I mention that we're eager to see how Arthur has organized his new study? I'm curious whether proximity to London will change his working methods."

Watson smiled at his wife's perceptive observation. "Excellent idea. Arthur will appreciate our interest in the practical aspects of his writing arrangements. And Mary, perhaps we should mention our own excitement about the Strand series beginning next month."

"Of course! I'll write that we can hardly wait to see 'A Scandal in Bohemia' in print, and that we're confident the monthly format will be even more successful than our previous book publications."

Mary Watson is with Child

July 5, 1892

James Watson's move from Paddington had proven even more beneficial than anticipated, bringing both a more distinguished clientele and the financial security that had allowed him to be more selective about his cases while continuing his documentation of Holmes's investigations.

On his desk lay a stack of The Strand Magazine issues from the past year, the topmost being the June 1892 edition containing "The Adventure of the Copper Beeches"—the twelfth and final story in their remarkably successful monthly series. It had been exactly one year since "A Scandal in Bohemia" launched their collaboration with The Strand Magazine in July 1891, and the success had exceeded even Arthur's most optimistic projections.

Mary Watson sat in the comfortable chair beside her husband's desk, her hands folded carefully in her lap as she waited for him to complete his examination notes from his previous patient. At thirty, she had grown more confident and poised during their three and a half years of marriage, her role as an advisor in James's literary collaboration having given her a sense of purpose that extended well beyond domestic concerns.

"James," she said quietly, her voice carrying an unusual note of nervous anticipation. "When you have a moment, I'd like to speak with you about something rather important."

Watson looked up from his notes, immediately detecting the carefully controlled excitement in his wife's manner. In their years of marriage, he had learned to recognize the subtle signs that indicated Mary had something significant to share—the way she sat particularly straight, the careful modulation of her voice, the slight flush in her cheeks that suggested barely contained emotion.

"Of course, my dear," Watson said, setting aside his pen and giving his wife his complete attention. "You have that look about you that suggests news of some consequence."

Mary smiled at her husband's perceptive observation. "You're quite right. James, I've been waiting for the appropriate moment to share this with you, and I believe that moment has arrived." She paused, her hands moving unconsciously to rest on her abdomen. "I'm with child."

Watson felt the words register with a shock of pure joy that left him momentarily speechless. He rose from his chair and moved to kneel beside Mary's seat, taking her hands in his own with gentle reverence.

"Mary," he said, his voice thick with emotion. "Are you certain? When did you... how long have you suspected?"

"I've been fairly certain for the past two weeks, but I wanted to be completely sure before telling you." Mary's eyes sparkled with happiness as she watched her husband's reaction. "Dr. Morrison confirmed it yesterday afternoon. Based on all the signs, I should expect our child to arrive around the middle of April next year—April 12th, to be precise."

Watson calculated quickly in his mind. "April 12th, 1893. Mary, that's wonderful news! The most wonderful news possible." He leaned forward to embrace his wife carefully, his medical training making him acutely aware of the precious new life she carried.

Mary laughed softly at her husband's sudden gentleness. "James, I'm pregnant, not made of porcelain. Dr. Morrison assures me that everything appears completely normal and healthy. This is a natural pregnancy with every indication of proceeding smoothly."

"Of course, forgive me," Watson said, though his protective instincts remained clearly evident. "It's just that the idea of becoming a father... Mary, I can hardly believe it."

"Nor can I, entirely. But James, I'm so very happy." Mary's expression grew more thoughtful. "This will change things for us, of course. Our involvement in the literary collaboration, our social activities, our entire way of life will need to adapt to accommodate a child."

Watson nodded thoughtfully, his gaze briefly falling on the stack of Strand Magazine issues. "Indeed it will. But Mary, these are the most wonderful changes imaginable. Our child will grow up in a household where scientific inquiry and literary achievement are valued, where authentic detective work is documented and shared with the world."

He picked up the June issue, showing her the cover featuring "The Adventure of the Copper Beeches." "Just look at this—our twelfth consecutive monthly story, completing exactly one year since Arthur and I began the series with 'A Scandal in Bohemia' in July 1891. The success has been extraordinary, and now we'll have a child to witness this remarkable journey."

Mary smiled at the sight of the familiar publication. "It's amazing to think that for an entire year, thousands of readers have been following Holmes's adventures every month. And James, the financial security it provides will be especially valuable with a child on the way."

"Speaking of which," Mary continued, "I believe we should share our news with Arthur and Touie. They've become such dear friends, and I know they'll be delighted. After all, they've been part of this incredible year of success since 'A Scandal in Bohemia' first appeared."

Watson considered this suggestion with obvious pleasure. "Absolutely. Though I think such momentous news deserves to be shared in person rather than through correspondence. What would you say to inviting them to London, or perhaps we could travel to Portsmouth?"

Mary's face brightened considerably. "Oh, James, what a wonderful idea! It's been far too long since we've all been together, and announcing this news in person would make it feel so much more special. Besides, Arthur will want to discuss what comes next after completing our first full year with The Strand Magazine."

"Then it's settled. I'll send a message to Arthur today, suggesting we arrange a meeting at the earliest mutual convenience." Watson moved to his writing desk, already composing the invitation in his mind. "Perhaps we could invite them to dine with us here in Kensington? Our dining room may be modest compared to Simpson's, but the intimacy would be perfect for sharing such personal news."

"Perfect," Mary agreed. "And James, when we tell them, I hope they'll understand how much their friendship has meant to us. Arthur's collaboration has been such an important part of our lives, especially this past year with the monthly publications reaching their successful conclusion. And Touie has become like a sister to me."

The Watsons Share Their News

July 18, 1892

The Watson's dining room had been transformed for the occasion, with Mary's finest china set upon their mahogany table and arrangements of summer flowers brightening every corner. Prominently displayed in the sitting room was the complete collection of their twelve Strand Magazine issues, from "A Scandal in Bohemia" in July 1891 through "The Adventure of the Copper Beeches" in June 1892—a testament to their remarkably successful year-long collaboration.

Arthur and Louisa Doyle had arrived on the afternoon train, their faces showing the pleasure of renewed friendship and curiosity about the "important matter" that James had mentioned in his invitation. Both couples had dressed with particular care for the occasion, sensing that this meeting held special significance beyond their usual social gatherings.

"Mary, you look absolutely radiant," Louisa observed as they settled in the sitting room before dinner. "London life continues to agree with you both, I see. And James, congratulations on the completion of your first full year with The Strand Magazine. What a remarkable achievement— twelve consecutive monthly stories!"

Arthur nodded with obvious satisfaction. "It's extraordinary to think that when we published 'A Scandal in Bohemia' last July, we weren't certain whether the monthly format would sustain reader interest. Now The Strand can hardly keep up with the demand for back issues of the entire series."

Watson smiled at his friend's enthusiasm. "The success has been gratifying, certainly. 'A Scandal in Bohemia' proved to be the perfect inaugural story for the series. But actually, Arthur, our Holmes collaboration isn't the only reason we asked you both here today."

Mary exchanged a meaningful glance with her husband. "Thank you, James. Touie, Arthur, there's a particular reason for the glow you mentioned, which we're eager to share with you both."

Arthur leaned forward with interest, his writer's instincts detecting the undertone of barely contained excitement in both his hosts. "It sounds as though congratulations may be in order for more than just our literary success."

Watson stood, moving to place his hand affectionately on Mary's shoulder. "Arthur, Touie, we've asked you here because you're our dearest friends, and we wanted you to be among the first to know our wonderful news." He paused, his face beaming with joy. "Mary is expecting our first child."

The reaction was immediate and joyous. Louisa sprang from her chair to embrace Mary, while Arthur clasped Watson's hand with genuine enthusiasm.

"Mary! James! How absolutely wonderful!" Louisa exclaimed, tears of happiness glistening in her eyes. "When? How are you feeling? Oh, I'm so thrilled for you both!"

Arthur's congratulations were equally heartfelt. "James, my dear fellow, this is the most splendid news possible. You'll make excellent parents, both of you. And what perfect timing—just as our year-long series reaches its triumphant conclusion."

Mary accepted Louisa's embrace gratefully. "Thank you both. We're due in April—April 12th, if Dr. Morrison's calculations are correct. Everything appears to be proceeding normally, and I'm feeling quite well."

"April!" Louisa said, her mind already working through possibilities. "That gives us plenty of time to plan properly. Mary, my dear, this calls for a proper celebration—something special to mark such a momentous occasion."

Watson looked puzzled. "What sort of celebration did you have in mind, Touie?"

Louisa's eyes began to sparkle with the same enthusiasm she brought to her charity work. "A baby shower, of course! It's becoming quite fashionable among society ladies—a gathering to celebrate the expectant mother and provide gifts for the coming child."

Mary looked intrigued but uncertain. "A baby shower? I've heard the term mentioned, but I'm not entirely familiar with the custom."

"Oh, it's perfectly lovely," Louisa continued, her excitement building. "The expectant mother's friends gather to offer congratulations, share advice about motherhood, and present gifts for the baby. I could organize something quite special here in London—perhaps at one of the better hotels."

Arthur smiled at his wife's immediate enthusiasm. "Touie has become quite the social organizer through her charity work. If she sets her mind to planning a baby shower, I guarantee it will be an event to remember."

"The guest list alone could be quite distinguished," Louisa mused, her mind already working through possibilities. "Through my charity connections, I've become acquainted with several quite prominent ladies. Mrs. Catherine Gladstone, for instance—the Prime Minister's wife. She's been tremendously supportive of our children's welfare projects."

Mary's eyes widened with surprise. "Mrs. Gladstone? Touie, surely someone of her standing wouldn't attend a baby shower for someone she's never met?"

"Nonsense," Louisa replied firmly. "Catherine is remarkably gracious, and she's always interested in supporting worthy causes. Besides, once I mention that you're the wife of the medical gentleman who collaborates with the author of those Sherlock Holmes stories she and the Prime Minister enjoy so much, I'm certain she'll be intrigued."

Arthur chuckled at this observation. "Indeed, the Prime Minister has become quite devoted to our monthly publications. I heard from our publisher that he specifically requests each new issue and has the complete set from 'A Scandal in Bohemia' onward."

Watson felt a moment of concern about their carefully maintained privacy. "Touie, you'll be discreet about the true nature of our collaboration, won't you?"

Louisa waved a dismissive hand. "Of course, James. I'll simply mention that you provide medical consultation for Arthur's detective fiction. Which is perfectly true, even if it's not the complete story."

Arthur nodded approvingly. "That's exactly the right approach. It acknowledges James's involvement without compromising our privacy arrangements."

Mary found herself caught up in Louisa's enthusiasm. "Touie, if you're truly willing to organize such an event, I would be absolutely delighted. Though I confess, the prospect of meeting Mrs. Gladstone and other such distinguished ladies is rather intimidating."

"You'll be perfect, my dear," Louisa assured her. "You have such natural grace and intelligence. Besides, most of these women are mothers themselves—they'll understand exactly what you're experiencing."

As the evening progressed over an excellent dinner, the conversation flowed between practical planning for the baby shower and warm personal reflections on the changes that parenthood would bring. Arthur and James found themselves discussing how fatherhood might affect their literary collaboration, while Mary and Louisa delved into the details of social arrangements and guest lists.

"The timing couldn't be better," Arthur observed, raising his wine glass. "Our year-long series with The Strand Magazine, from 'A Scandal in Bohemia' through 'The Copper Beeches,' has established our reputation and provided regular income. Now you'll have a child to share in our continued success."

"I'm thinking the Langham Hotel would be perfect," Louisa said as they enjoyed their dessert. "It's elegant but not ostentatious, and their private dining rooms are ideal for intimate gatherings."

"When were you thinking of holding this celebration?" Mary asked.

"Late August, perhaps? That would give me time to organize properly while ensuring you're still comfortable enough to fully enjoy the occasion." Louisa's organizational skills were clearly in full display. "We'll want to allow time for proper invitations, menu planning, and of course, coordinating with everyone's social calendars."

Arthur raised his glass in a toast. "To new beginnings—the expansion of the Watson family and the continued success of our literary partnership. May our future endeavors prove as remarkable as this past year has been."

As they drank to the future, all four friends felt the deep satisfaction of sharing momentous news with those who mattered most. The baby shower would be merely the beginning of the celebrations that would mark this new chapter in their lives, but the foundation of friendship and mutual support that made such celebrations possible was already firmly established.

When the Doyles prepared to return to their hotel that evening, the parting was filled with excitement about the plans ahead rather than the usual sadness of separation. Louisa was already composing invitation lists in her mind, while Arthur was considering how this development might influence future Holmes stories.

"Mary," Louisa said as they embraced goodbye, "I want you to know how honored I am that you've allowed me to organize this celebration. It will be one of the most meaningful events I've ever planned."

"Touie, your friendship means the world to us," Mary replied. "I can't imagine anyone I'd rather have orchestrating such an important occasion."

As the Doyles' carriage disappeared into the London evening, James and Mary stood together in their doorway, reflecting on how perfectly the evening had unfolded.

Mary Watson's Baby Shower

August 15, 1892

The private dining room at the Langham Hotel had been turned into an elegant feminine sanctuary, with arrangements of summer flowers adorning every surface and delicate china tea service set for a dozen distinguished ladies. Louisa Doyle had spared no effort in organizing what promised to be one of London's most memorable baby showers, her extensive social connections having produced a guest list that represented the very pinnacle of British society.

Mary Watson sat in the place of honor, radiant in a dress of pale blue silk that accommodated her now-visible pregnancy while maintaining the elegance appropriate to such a distinguished gathering. At ten weeks since her announcement to the Doyles, her condition was showing enough to make the celebration feel perfectly timed, though she remained comfortable enough to fully enjoy the occasion.

Louisa moved gracefully between the assembled guests, her own condition now unmistakable at six months along, though she carried herself with the dignified poise that pregnancy had only enhanced. Her dress of deep rose silk had been carefully chosen to accommodate her expanding figure while maintaining the sophisticated appearance befitting the hostess of such a distinguished gathering.

"Mary, my dear, you look absolutely glowing," said Mrs. Catherine Gladstone, the Prime Minister's wife, as she settled into the chair beside the guest of honor. At sixty, Catherine retained the dignified bearing that had made her one of London's most respected society hostesses, and her presence at the shower had elevated the entire event's social significance.

"Mrs. Gladstone, you're too kind," Mary replied, still somewhat amazed to find herself in such exalted company. "I'm so grateful that you could join us. Touie mentioned that you know each other through charity work?"

"Indeed," Catherine replied warmly. "Louisa and I have collaborated on several projects supporting the welfare of children in the East End. She's a remarkably dedicated woman, and when she mentioned your special occasion—along with her own wonderful news, of course—I couldn't resist the opportunity to meet the wife of the gentleman who provides medical consultation for those fascinating detective stories."

Catherine leaned forward conspiratorially. "I must tell you, my husband has become quite devoted to the monthly Holmes adventures in The Strand Magazine. He was particularly impressed with 'A Scandal in Bohemia'—the story that began the series last July. William said it demonstrated the kind of methodical thinking that's needed in political analysis as well as criminal investigation."

Mary felt a moment of careful relief at Catherine's discretely phrased understanding of James's role. "Arthur's Holmes stories have certainly found a devoted readership. James enjoys contributing his medical expertise to ensure the authenticity of the investigative methods."

"And what a success the year-long series has been!" Catherine continued. "William tells me that The Strand Magazine has had to increase their print run substantially to meet demand. From 'A Scandal in Bohemia' through that final story last month—what was it called?"

"'The Adventure of the Copper Beeches,'" Mary supplied. "Yes, the entire twelve-month series exceeded all expectations."

"You must be quite proud of your husband's contribution to such a literary phenomenon," Catherine observed.

Across the room, Louisa was regaling a small group of ladies with the story of how she had insisted on organizing this celebration, one hand resting unconsciously on her rounded abdomen as she spoke. "When James and Mary shared their wonderful news with us last month, I immediately knew we must do something special. After all, they've become such dear friends, and this child will be welcomed into a household where both intellectual achievement and domestic happiness are equally valued."

Mrs. Elizabeth Fawcett, wife of the renowned political economist Henry Fawcett, leaned forward with interest. "Mrs. Doyle, I understand your husband is not only a successful author but also a practicing physician. How remarkable to have such diverse talents contributing to the Holmes stories. And how wonderful that you're both expecting at the same time—you and Mrs. Watson will be able to share this extraordinary experience together."

"Indeed," Louisa replied, her face brightening at the observation. "When Mary told us her news, I confess I was delighted to discover we would be going through this journey together, albeit a few months apart. It's given our friendship an even deeper dimension—we can truly understand what each other is experiencing."

As the afternoon progressed, Mary found herself the center of attention from women whose husbands represented the pinnacle of British achievement in politics, academia, and the arts. The conversation flowed effortlessly between practical advice about motherhood, intellectual discussion of the Holmes stories, and warm personal observations about the joys of family life.

"Mrs. Watson," said Mrs. Joan Tennyson, the Poet Laureate's wife, "I hope you'll allow me to present you with something rather special." She withdrew from her reticule a small, leather-bound volume. "This is a collection of verses about motherhood and childhood, compiled from various sources. I thought you might enjoy having something literary to mark this special time."

Mary accepted the gift with genuine gratitude. "Mrs. Tennyson, how thoughtful! I shall treasure this always."

"And Mrs. Doyle," Mrs. Tennyson continued, turning to Louisa with a warm smile, "I have something for you as well." She produced another small volume. "A collection of lullabies from various traditions—I thought it might be useful in a few months' time."

Louisa's eyes filled with pleased surprise. "How incredibly thoughtful of you. I hadn't expected... that is, this gathering was meant to celebrate Mary."

"Nonsense," Mrs. Tennyson replied firmly. "When two such accomplished ladies are both blessed with coming motherhood, it deserves double celebration."

The presentation of gifts continued throughout the afternoon, with several ladies offering dual presentations for both expectant mothers. Baby clothes of the finest materials, silver rattles from established jewelers, handmade blankets created specifically for the occasion—each gift reflected both the givers' social position and their genuine affection for both women.

Catherine Gladstone's gift proved particularly touching—two small silver lockets, each containing a blessing written in her own hand. "For both children," she explained, "to remind them always that they are welcomed into households where truth, justice, and intellectual honesty are valued above all material concerns."

Meanwhile, several streets away at the Criterion Bar, Arthur Conan Doyle and James Watson had settled into comfortable leather chairs with their brandies, having been diplomatically excluded from the feminine celebration.

"I must say, James, this exile to the public house is far more pleasant than I anticipated," Arthur observed, raising his glass in a toast. "To fatherhood—may it prove as rewarding as our literary partnership has been this past year."

Watson clinked his glass against Arthur's, his face showing the contentment of a man whose personal and professional lives were both proceeding excellently. "Arthur, I can't adequately express how grateful I am for Touie's efforts in organizing this celebration. The guest list she assembled is remarkable—and it's gratifying to know that our Holmes stories have reached such distinguished readers."

"Indeed. Mrs. Gladstone's presence alone makes this one of the most distinguished social events Mary will ever attend." Arthur leaned back in his chair, clearly pleased with his wife's social achievements. "Though I confess, I'm rather curious about how much these distinguished ladies understand about our true collaborative arrangements."

Watson considered this carefully. "I believe Touie has handled that perfectly—presenting me as your medical consultant for the Holmes stories. Which is technically accurate, even if it doesn't reveal the full extent of my involvement."

"Precisely. It acknowledges your contribution without compromising our privacy arrangements." Arthur gestured toward the busy street visible through the bar's windows. "James, do you realize how remarkable this past year has been? From 'A Scandal in Bohemia' in July 1891 through 'The Copper Beeches' last month—twelve consecutive stories, each one reaching thousands of readers. And now, with children on the way for both our families, we're entering an entirely new phase of our success."

Watson followed his friend's gaze, reflecting on the remarkable turn of events. "It's extraordinary, isn't it? When we began the monthly series with 'A Scandal in Bohemia,' I never imagined it would lead to such social recognition. And now, exactly one year after our inaugural publication, we're celebrating the expansion of both our families."

"How do you think fatherhood will affect your involvement in our collaboration?"

Watson had clearly given this question considerable thought. "I believe it will enhance rather than diminish my contributions. The perspective of parenthood should provide new insights into the human motivations that drive so many criminal cases. Besides, the financial security our partnership provides will be especially valuable with a child to support."

Arthur nodded approvingly. "My thoughts exactly. The success of our first year-long series has established us firmly with The Strand Magazine, and the regular monthly income becomes even more significant when one has family responsibilities. And for Touie and me, having a child at the same time as you and Mary—it creates a bond that goes beyond professional partnership."

"Yes," Watson agreed warmly. "Our children will grow up knowing each other, perhaps as friends, certainly as part of this extended family we've created through our work together."

As the afternoon wore on, both men found themselves looking forward to the reunion with their wives and the detailed accounts they would undoubtedly receive of the distinguished company and memorable conversations that had characterized the baby shower.

The celebration at the Langham Hotel concluded with expressions of mutual affection and promises of continued friendship from women who had welcomed both Mary and Louisa into their exclusive social circle. As the guests departed, many extending invitations for future gatherings, both expectant mothers felt the deep satisfaction of knowing that their children would be born into a world where intellectual achievement and authentic accomplishment were recognized and celebrated.

When James and Arthur rejoined their wives that evening, they found both women glowing with the success of an afternoon that had exceeded all expectations. The baby shower had accomplished far more than simply celebrating Mary's pregnancy—it had confirmed both families' position in London society and strengthened the social connections that would benefit their personal lives and continued literary collaboration.

"Mary," Louisa said as they prepared to part, "I cannot express how meaningful this afternoon has been. To share this experience with such a dear friend, to see our friendship celebrated by such distinguished ladies..."

"Touie," Mary replied, taking her friend's hands, "organizing this celebration while expecting yourself—I can never thank you enough. To know that our children will grow up as part of this circle, that they'll witness the remarkable work their fathers have accomplished together..."

Arthur placed an affectionate hand on his wife's shoulder. "Touie's enthusiasm for this event has been remarkable. I think having her own experience to anticipate made Mary's celebration even more meaningful to her."

"Indeed," James agreed, helping Mary with her wrap. "And the timing couldn't be more perfect. Our Holmes stories complete their first triumphant year, our families are expanding, and the friendships that have sustained our collaboration continue to deepen."

The 2nd Group of Short Stories

August 21, 1892

The late summer afternoon had brought an oppressive humidity to London, and Dr. James Watson found himself grateful for the high ceilings and cross-ventilation of his Kensington consulting rooms. He had closed his practice early, having cleared his schedule specifically for Arthur Conan Doyle's urgent visit. The telegram that had arrived three days prior had been unusually terse even by Arthur's economical standards:

MUST MEET IMMEDIATELY. STRAND PROPOSAL BOTH THRILLING AND TERRIFYING. CAN YOU RECEIVE ME SUNDAY AFTERNOON? CRITICAL DECISIONS REQUIRED - ARTHUR.

Watson paced near the tall windows overlooking the quiet street, occasionally glancing at the clock on his mantelpiece. Arthur's message had suggested a level of agitation that was quite unlike his usually composed friend, and Watson found himself growing increasingly curious about what proposition from The Strand Magazine could provoke such a reaction.

The sound of rapid footsteps on the front steps announced Arthur's arrival, and Watson moved quickly to admit his friend before he could knock. Arthur Conan Doyle stood on the threshold, his usually immaculate appearance slightly disheveled, his traveling coat showing evidence of a hurried journey from Portsmouth, and his face bearing the expression of a man grappling with momentous decisions.

"James," Arthur said without preamble, stepping into the cool hallway with obvious relief. "Thank you for agreeing to meet on such short notice. I'm afraid the situation requires immediate attention, and your counsel is absolutely essential."

Watson helped his friend with his coat, noting the tension in Arthur's movements. "Of course, Arthur. Come, let's settle in the study where we can speak privately. Mary has taken tea with Mrs. Pemberton next door, so we'll have complete privacy for our discussion."

Arthur followed Watson into the comfortable study, but instead of settling into his usual chair, he immediately began pacing with the agitated energy that Watson had learned to associate with his friend's most complex literary challenges.

"James, The Strand Magazine has made us an offer that is simultaneously the answer to our prayers and a potential disaster," Arthur began, his voice carrying an undertone of barely controlled anxiety. "They want twelve more Holmes stories, starting with the December 1892 issue."

Watson settled into his chair, immediately grasping the implications. "December 1892? Arthur, that's less than four months away. How much advance preparation time are they allowing?"

"That's precisely the problem," Arthur replied, pausing in his pacing to fix Watson with an intense stare. "They need the first story by mid-October to meet their publication schedule. For our previous series, I had nearly a full year to prepare all twelve stories in advance. This time, I'll be working practically from month to month."

Arthur moved to Watson's desk and withdrew a letter from his coat pocket. "But James, the financial terms they're offering... I simply cannot refuse them, despite the impossible timeline."

Watson accepted the letter, scanning its contents with growing amazement. "Arthur, these figures... they're offering nearly double what we received for the entire previous series, and this is just for the first story alone."

"Precisely. The success of our year-long series, from 'A Scandal in Bohemia' through 'The Copper Beeches,' has exceeded their most optimistic projections. They're prepared to pay premium rates to ensure we commit to another full year of monthly publications." Arthur resumed his agitated pacing. "But James, I'm terrified that I won't be able to maintain the quality standards we've established while working under such pressure."

Watson set down the letter, his mind immediately moving to practical solutions. "Arthur, what specific concerns do you have about the timeline?"

Arthur paused, organizing his thoughts with characteristic precision. "Several major issues. First, I won't have the luxury of completing all twelve stories in advance, which means I can't ensure consistent quality across the entire series. Second, I'll need to select cases much more rapidly than our previous methodical process. Third, each story will need to be adapted from your case notes with minimal time for revision and refinement."

"And fourth," Watson added, understanding his friend's predicament completely, "you'll be under constant deadline pressure, which could affect both the literary quality and the investigative authenticity of the stories."

"Exactly." Arthur collapsed into his chair with evident exhaustion. "James, when we began this collaboration over six years ago, we had the luxury of unlimited time to perfect our approach. Now, commercial success has created expectations that may be impossible to meet."

Watson leaned forward, his expression growing more determined. "Arthur, I believe we can meet this challenge, but it will require a different approach to our collaboration."

Arthur looked up with renewed attention. "What sort of different approach?"

Watson moved to his filing cabinet and withdrew several thick folders. "I've been thinking about this since receiving your telegram. The solution lies in better organization of our source material."

He spread the folders across his desk, revealing meticulously organized case documentation. "Arthur, over the past six years, I've documented nearly sixty of Holmes's investigations in varying degrees of detail. Some are complete narratives, others are partial notes, but all contain the essential elements necessary for literary adaptation."

Arthur examined the files with growing interest. "This is remarkably systematic, James. You've organized them by... what criteria?"

"Multiple categories," Watson explained, his enthusiasm building. "Length of investigation, complexity of deductive reasoning, dramatic potential, seasonal appropriateness, and—most importantly for our current situation—the completeness of my documentation."

Watson opened one of the folders, revealing pages of neat handwriting interspersed with sketches and diagrams. "For instance, this is my complete account of 'The Adventure of Silver Blaze'—the case involving the missing racehorse and the peculiar circumstances surrounding its trainer's death. Every detail is documented, every conversation recorded, every deduction explained."

Arthur's eyes widened as he scanned the material. "James, this is extraordinary. With documentation this complete, I could adapt it into a story with minimal additional research."

"Precisely my thinking. And here," Watson opened another folder, "is 'The Adventure of the Cardboard Box'—a case involving severed ears and a tale of jealousy that demonstrates Holmes's ability to deduce entire family histories from the smallest evidence. Again, completely documented and ready for adaptation."

Arthur began examining additional files, his anxiety visibly decreasing as he realized the wealth of prepared material at his disposal. "James, you've essentially created a complete library of Holmes's cases, organized for maximum efficiency."

"And here's my proposed solution to The Strand's timeline pressure," Watson continued, pulling out a carefully prepared list. "I've identified fifteen cases with the most complete documentation, arranged in order of adaptation difficulty. The simplest could be turned into stories within a week, while the more complex might require two weeks."

Arthur studied the list with growing admiration. "This is brilliant organizational work, James. But even with this preparation, the timeline remains challenging."

Watson nodded, his expression growing more serious. "Which brings me to my second proposal. Arthur, I believe I need to become more actively involved in the actual writing process."

Arthur looked up with surprise. "What do you mean?"

"I mean that instead of simply providing you with case notes for adaptation, I could prepare detailed story outlines—essentially first drafts that focus on the investigative elements while leaving the literary refinement to you." Watson's voice gained conviction as he explained his thinking. "It would divide the work more efficiently while maintaining our established quality standards."

Arthur considered this proposal carefully. "James, that's an intriguing idea, but would it compromise the literary quality we've established?"

"Not if we approach it systematically," Watson replied. "I would prepare the basic narrative structure, ensuring investigative accuracy and including all essential plot elements. You would then apply your literary skills to refine the dialogue, enhance the details, and polish the prose to publication standards."

Arthur stood and began pacing again, but this time his movements showed excitement rather than anxiety. "It could work, James. It could actually work quite well. Your medical and investigative expertise combined with my literary experience, but with a more collaborative writing process."

"Exactly. And with the documentation I've already prepared, we could maintain consistent quality even under deadline pressure." Watson gestured toward his organized files. "I estimate that with this approach, we could produce a polished story every three weeks instead of the month-to-month schedule The Strand requires."

Arthur paused in his pacing, a slow smile spreading across his features. "James, I believe you've solved our dilemma. But are you certain you can spare the additional time required? With your medical practice and Mary's pregnancy..."

Watson waved a dismissive hand. "Arthur, the financial terms The Strand is offering would allow me to reduce my patient load if necessary. Besides, Mary has been encouraging me to become more actively involved in our collaboration. She believes my investigative insights could enhance the stories' authenticity."

"Then we're agreed? We'll accept The Strand's offer and implement this new collaborative approach?"

Watson extended his hand with a confident smile. "We are indeed. Arthur, I believe this challenge may actually improve our partnership by forcing us to work more closely together."

Arthur gripped his friend's hand firmly, his earlier anxiety now completely replaced by determination. "Then let's begin immediately. Which case would you recommend for our December publication?"

Watson moved to his organized files, consulting his prepared list. "I believe 'Silver Blaze' would be perfect for our opening story. It's a compelling mystery involving a famous racehorse, demonstrates Holmes's most brilliant deductive work, and my documentation is so complete that you could begin adaptation immediately."

Arthur examined Watson's notes on the case, his excitement growing as he read. "This is perfect, James. The missing racehorse, the murdered trainer, the mysterious circumstances—it has everything readers could want in an engaging mystery."

"And here's our complete schedule," Watson said, producing another carefully prepared document. "If we begin with 'Silver Blaze' for December, I recommend 'The Adventure of the Cardboard Box' for January, 'The Adventure of the Yellow Face' for February, and so on through the series, concluding with 'The Adventure of the Final Problem' in November 1893."

Arthur studied the proposed schedule with growing appreciation, pausing when he reached the final entry. "The Final Problem? James, that's quite a dramatic title for our concluding story."

"Indeed it is," Watson replied, his expression growing more serious. "It involves Holmes's confrontation with Professor Moriarty—his most dangerous adversary. The case culminates in Holmes finally eliminating the criminal mastermind who has been the source of so much trouble. I believe it will provide a fitting climax to our second series."

Arthur nodded approvingly. "A twelve-month arc from 'Silver Blaze' through 'The Final Problem'—it has a satisfying narrative structure. Each case positioned for maximum impact while building toward the ultimate confrontation with Moriarty."

As the afternoon progressed, both men found themselves energized by the challenge ahead rather than daunted by it. The new collaborative approach would require more intensive work from both partners, but it also promised to strengthen their partnership while meeting The Strand's demanding expectations.

"Arthur," Watson said as they concluded their planning session, "I want you to know how much I appreciate your confidence in expanding my role in our collaboration. This feels like the natural evolution of our partnership."

"The confidence is entirely justified, James. Your investigative expertise and organizational skills are exactly what we need to meet this challenge successfully." Arthur gathered his materials with obvious satisfaction. "I'll return to Portsmouth and begin work on 'Silver Blaze' immediately. With your detailed documentation and our new collaborative approach, I'm confident we can maintain the quality standards that made our first series so successful."

The Birth of Kingsley Doyle

November 15, 1892

The telegram arrived at the Watson residence in Paddington at half past ten on the morning of November 15th, delivered with the urgency that marked truly significant news. Dr. James Watson was reviewing patient notes in his consulting room when Mary burst through the door, her face radiant with excitement despite the early hour.

"James!" she exclaimed, her hand resting protectively on her rounded abdomen where their own child grew steadily toward the April birth they eagerly anticipated. "The most wonderful news from Arthur and Touie!"

Watson immediately set aside his papers, recognizing the barely contained joy in his wife's voice. At six months along in her pregnancy, Mary had developed an even deeper appreciation for the miracle of new life, and her enthusiasm for any birth news had become infectious.

"Good news, I hope?" Watson said, though Mary's expression had already provided the answer.

Mary handed him the telegram, her eyes sparkling with delight. "Read it aloud, darling. I want to hear it again."

Watson unfolded the brief message, noting the characteristically economical but heartfelt words:

KINGSLEY ARTHUR DOYLE ARRIVED SAFELY 3:47 AM NOVEMBER 15TH. LOUISA AND SON BOTH WELL. MARYS HOSPITAL PADDINGTON. VISITING HOURS 2-4 PM DAILY. YOUR PRESENCE WOULD BRING GREAT JOY - ARTHUR.

Watson looked up to find Mary already reaching for her coat, her movements quick with purpose despite her condition. "Mary, my dear, surely you don't intend to travel across London to the hospital today? In your condition—"

"James Watson," Mary interrupted with gentle firmness, "Touie has just given birth to her second child, and she's barely two miles from our own doorstep. Of course we're going to see her today. This afternoon, in fact."

Watson felt his protective instincts warring with his understanding of female friendship. "But the journey, the hospital environment, the strain on you and our child..."

Mary moved to him and took his hands in hers, her expression growing more serious. "James, when I was terrified about our own child's birth, Touie organized that beautiful baby shower and surrounded me with the most distinguished women in London. She made me feel celebrated and supported when I needed it most."

She paused, her voice growing softer. "Now she's lying in a hospital bed with her newborn son, probably exhausted and overwhelmed, and we're debating whether it's convenient to visit? No, darling. Some things matter more than convenience."

Watson studied his wife's determined expression, recognizing the strength of character that had first attracted him to her during the Sign of Four case. "You're absolutely right, of course. Friendship requires presence, not just sentiment."

"Exactly." Mary's smile returned full force. "Besides, I want to see this little Kingsley for myself. And I want Touie to know that when our turn comes in April, she'll have friends who understand the joy and terror of bringing new life into the world."

The November afternoon had brought a crisp clarity to London, and the Watsons made their way through the familiar Paddington streets with careful efficiency. Mary had insisted on walking despite James's offer to hire a cab, claiming that the exercise was beneficial for both her and their unborn child. She carried a carefully wrapped bouquet of hothouse flowers and a small gift she had selected from their finest baby linens.

St. Mary's Hospital presented the reassuring facade of modern medical competence, its clean windows and well-maintained entrance speaking of an institution that took seriously its responsibility for London's mothers and children. The porter who directed them to the maternity ward showed the practiced courtesy of someone accustomed to excited visitors bearing flowers and good wishes.

They found Arthur in the corridor outside the ward, pacing with the restless energy of a new father whose joy was tempered by the exhaustion that accompanied sleepless nights of anticipation. His face lit up immediately upon seeing the Watsons approach, and he moved quickly to greet them.

"James! Mary!" Arthur exclaimed, clasping Watson's hand warmly before turning to embrace Mary with careful attention to her condition. "How good of you to come so quickly. Touie will be absolutely delighted to see you both."

Mary studied Arthur's face with the observant eye of someone who had recently learned to recognize the signs of new parenthood. "Arthur, you look wonderfully happy but absolutely exhausted. How long has Louisa been in labor?"

"Since yesterday evening," Arthur replied, running a hand through his disheveled hair. "Nearly eighteen hours, though the doctor assures me that's quite normal for a second child. But Mary, when I finally heard that first cry at quarter to four this morning..." He paused, his voice thick with emotion. "There's simply nothing that prepares you for that moment."

Watson felt his own anticipation for fatherhood intensify at Arthur's words. "And Louisa? She's recovering well?"

"Remarkably well, considering the ordeal. She's tired, naturally, but alert and already completely devoted to young Kingsley." Arthur's eyes sparkled with pride. "James, he's magnificent. Perfect in every detail, with the strongest lungs in all of London."

A nurse approached with the efficient manner that characterized hospital staff. "Dr. Doyle? Your wife is awake and asking for her visitors."

Arthur turned to the Watsons with obvious pleasure. "Shall we? Though I should warn you—Touie has been quite emotional since the birth. Happy tears, but tears nonetheless."

They followed Arthur through the clean, well-lit corridor to a private room that spoke of the comfortable accommodations available to families of means. Sunshine streamed through tall windows, and the room was filled with floral arrangements that testified to the many friends who had already heard the joyful news.

Louisa lay propped against clean white pillows, her auburn hair arranged carefully around a face that glowed with the particular radiance that follows successful childbirth. In her arms lay a small bundle wrapped in soft blue blankets, and her expression as she looked down at her son held the wonder that never quite fades from a mother's first contemplation of her child.

"Mary! James!" Louisa exclaimed, her voice carrying a joy that immediately filled the room. "How wonderful that you're here. Come, you must meet Kingsley Arthur Doyle."

Mary moved immediately to the bedside, her own maternal instincts fully engaged as she leaned carefully forward to examine the newest member of the Doyle family. "Oh, Touie, he's absolutely beautiful. Look at those perfect little features!"

Watson approached more cautiously, his medical training making him automatically assess both mother and child for signs of health and well-being. What he saw reassured him completely—Louisa showed every sign of normal post-birth recovery, while the infant displayed the alert awareness that marked a healthy newborn.

"May I?" Mary asked, extending her arms with the confidence of someone who had spent considerable time recently contemplating the mechanics of holding babies.

Louisa carefully transferred her son to Mary's waiting arms, watching with obvious pleasure as Mary cradled the infant with natural skill. "He's been remarkably calm since birth," Louisa said. "The doctor says it's a good sign when they're alert but peaceful."

Mary gazed down at the baby with an expression that mixed joy with anticipation. "Kingsley," she said softly, "what a distinguished name. He looks like he'll grow up to be quite the gentleman."

Arthur moved to stand beside his wife's bed, his hand resting gently on her shoulder. "We chose Kingsley for its strength, and Arthur for the family connection. Though Touie insists he has the Doyle temperament already—very determined about what he wants and when he wants it."

Watson watched his wife holding the newborn and felt a complex surge of emotions—joy for their friends, anticipation for their own child, and a profound gratitude for the domestic happiness that had become possible through their literary success. The regular income from The Strand Magazine had provided the security that made such family expansions financially feasible.

"Touie," Mary said, carefully returning the baby to his mother's arms, "I want you to know how grateful I am that you organized that beautiful baby shower. Being surrounded by such distinguished women, feeling celebrated and supported—it meant more to me than I can express."

Louisa's eyes filled with tears at Mary's words. "My dear Mary, it was my absolute pleasure. And when your time comes in April, you'll have friends who understand exactly what you're experiencing."

Arthur moved to the window, looking out at the London afternoon with obvious satisfaction. "It's remarkable, isn't it? Here we are, celebrating the birth of our son during what has been the most successful year of our literary collaboration. The Holmes stories bringing joy to thousands of readers, our friendships deepening, our families growing..."

Watson nodded, understanding perfectly the sense of completion Arthur was expressing. "It does feel like everything is aligning as it should. The success of our work providing the foundation for these personal celebrations."

Mary settled into the chair beside Louisa's bed, clearly prepared for an extended visit despite her own condition. "Now, Touie, you must tell me everything. The labor, the birth, how you're feeling—I want to understand what I should expect in the spring."

Arthur and Watson exchanged glances of masculine understanding, recognizing that the conversation was about to enter territory where their presence was welcome but not essential.

"Perhaps," Arthur suggested, "James and I might take a brief walk while you ladies discuss the mysteries of motherhood?"

"Excellent idea," Watson agreed. "We can visit the hospital's café and allow Mary and Touie to share whatever confidences new mothers need to exchange."

As the men prepared to leave, Louisa called after them. "Arthur, don't forget to tell James about the letter from The Strand Magazine. "

Arthur's face brightened with professional excitement. "James, Herbert Greenhough Smith wrote that our stories have achieved the highest circulation in The Strand's history. They've had to order additional print runs to meet demand."

Watson felt a surge of satisfaction at this news. "The public response continues to exceed all expectations?"

"By considerable margins. Smith believes the serial format has created exactly the kind of sustained reader engagement that makes magazines financially successful." Arthur's enthusiasm was evident. "James, our collaboration is not only serving the cause of authentic detective fiction—it's demonstrating that the reading public has a genuine appetite for intelligent entertainment."

As they left the women to their intimate conversation and made their way toward the hospital's café, both men felt the profound satisfaction that comes from witnessing the successful intersection of personal and professional achievement. Arthur's second son had arrived safely, Mary's pregnancy continued to progress normally, and their literary collaboration was reaching unprecedented heights of public success.

The hospital's modest café provided a quiet refuge where new fathers and visiting relatives could gather their thoughts while medical matters proceeded in the capable hands of professional staff. Arthur and Watson settled at a table near the window, where the November light provided adequate illumination for conversation without the formal atmosphere that might inhibit personal reflection.

"James," Arthur said, stirring sugar into his tea with obvious satisfaction, "I confess that holding my son for the first time this morning gave me an entirely new perspective on our collaborative work."

Watson raised an eyebrow with interest. "How so?"

"When I looked down at Kingsley—perfect, helpless, completely dependent on Touie and me for everything—I realized that our Holmes stories aren't just entertainment for the current generation of readers." Arthur's voice grew more thoughtful. "They're contributions to the world our children will inherit."

The baby's first day of life had been marked not only by his parents' joy but by the recognition that he was inheriting a world slightly improved by the collaborative efforts of friends who had discovered that authentic achievement required both individual talent and mutual support.

Tragedy Strikes the Watsons

May 10, 1893

The morning had begun with promise. Dr. James Watson had awakened in his Kensington home to find his wife Mary stirring restlessly beside him, her hand pressed to her rounded abdomen with the familiar expression of late pregnancy discomfort. At eight months, she was still four weeks from her expected delivery date, but the child had been active throughout the night, and Mary had commented with gentle humor that their son or daughter seemed eager to make an early appearance.

"Perhaps the baby has inherited your impatience," Mary had said, smiling at her husband over their morning tea. "Though I confess, I'm rather looking forward to meeting this little one, even if it means enduring the ordeal of childbirth."

Watson had kissed his wife's forehead and departed for his morning rounds with the comfortable assumption that he would return to find Mary resting peacefully, perhaps working on the baby clothes she had been embroidering with such careful attention to detail. The nursery had been completed weeks ago, with a cradle Arthur had helped him select and blankets that Louisa had insisted on purchasing during their last visit to London.

But shortly after noon, as Watson was examining a patient with chronic bronchitis, his housekeeper Mrs. Morrison had appeared at his consulting room door with an expression of urgent concern.

"Doctor Watson, you must come home immediately," she said, her voice tight with anxiety. "Mrs. Watson has taken poorly, and I've sent for Dr. Thornton as you instructed, but the pains have come on very suddenly and very strong."

Watson's medical training immediately recognized the signs of premature labor, and he abandoned his patient with hurried apologies, racing through the London streets with a growing sense of dread. Mary was strong and healthy, but childbirth was always dangerous, and early delivery increased the risks considerably.

He arrived at their Kensington home to find Dr. Thornton, one of London's most respected obstetricians, already in attendance. The older physician's grave expression told Watson everything he needed to know even before a word was spoken.

"James," Dr. Thornton said, drawing him aside as the sounds of Mary's labor echoed from the bedroom above. "The situation is complicated. The child is presenting awkwardly, and Mary is losing considerable blood. I've done everything possible, but..."

The afternoon became a nightmare of waiting, punctuated by Mary's cries of pain and the hushed conferences between Dr. Thornton and the midwife he had summoned. Watson found himself relegated to the role of helpless observer, his medical knowledge sufficient to understand the gravity of the situation but powerless to intervene in the specialist's domain.

As evening approached, the sounds from the bedroom grew weaker, and Watson knew with terrible certainty that he was losing both his wife and their unborn child. When Dr. Thornton finally emerged from the bedroom, his face was that of a man who had fought a battle against death and lost.

"James," he said simply, placing a hand on Watson's shoulder. "I'm sorry. There was nothing more that could be done."

Watson climbed the stairs to their bedroom with leaden feet, knowing that he would find his world forever changed. Mary lay still and pale against the white sheets, her face peaceful in death, while beside her lay the tiny form of their son—for it had been a son—who had never drawn breath in this world.

The next hours passed in a blur of necessary arrangements and sympathetic visitors. The rector arrived to offer consolation, the undertaker came to discuss funeral arrangements, and neighbors appeared with food and awkward expressions of condolence. But Watson moved through it all like a man in a trance, his mind unable to fully process the magnitude of his loss.

As night fell, Watson found himself alone in the house that had been filled with such happiness and expectation just that morning. The nursery door stood open, revealing the cradle and baby clothes that would never be used. Mary's sewing basket sat beside her chair, the tiny garments she had been embroidering still bearing the marks of her last stitches.

He could not bear it. The weight of grief was suffocating him in these rooms where every object held memories of their life together. Without conscious decision, Watson gathered a few essential belongings and fled into the London night, his feet carrying him toward the only sanctuary he could imagine.

The next day, James arrived at Baker Street and rang the bell.

Mrs. Hudson answered the door at 111 Baker Street in her nightgown and robe, her weathered face immediately showing concern at the sight of Dr. Watson standing on the threshold in the early morning darkness. He looked haggard and broken, his usually neat appearance disheveled, his eyes holding the terrible emptiness of a man who had lost everything that mattered.

"Dr. Watson," she said softly, drawing him into the familiar hallway. "My dear man, what's happened?"

Watson could not speak. The words would not come. He simply stood in the entrance hall, his small bag in his hand, looking lost and defeated.

Holmes appeared at the top of the stairs, his sharp eyes immediately taking in the scene below. He descended quickly, his usual analytical demeanor replaced by genuine concern for his friend's obvious distress.

"Watson," Holmes said quietly, approaching with careful steps. "What brings you here at this hour?"

Still Watson could not speak. Instead, he simply looked at Holmes with eyes that held such pain that even the great detective's composure faltered.

"Mary," Holmes said, understanding immediately. "And the child?"

Watson nodded once, the simple gesture seeming to drain the last of his strength. He swayed slightly, and Holmes stepped forward to steady him.

"Mrs. Hudson," Holmes said, his voice carrying an authority that brooked no argument. "Please prepare Dr. Watson's old room immediately. He'll be staying with us."

Mrs. Hudson nodded, her maternal instincts immediately engaged. "Of course, Mr. Holmes. I'll have it ready directly." She looked at Watson with the gentle concern of a woman who had seen much sorrow in her years. "You come along now, Doctor. You need rest and care."

Holmes guided Watson to his old chair by the fireplace, where so many evenings had been spent in comfortable companionship. The familiar surroundings seemed to provide some small comfort, though Watson remained silent, staring into the flames with unseeing eyes.

"Hudson," Holmes said quietly, "perhaps some tea with a measure of brandy. And send word to Dr. Thornton that Dr. Watson is in our care."

As Mrs. Hudson bustled away to fulfill these instructions, Holmes settled into his own chair, maintaining the companionable silence that had always been one of their friendship's greatest strengths. He did not attempt to offer words of comfort—what words could possibly address such loss?—but simply provided the steady presence of unwavering friendship.

Watson finally spoke, his voice barely above a whisper. "They're both gone, Holmes. Mary and our son. Both gone."

Holmes closed his eyes briefly, feeling the weight of his friend's grief. "I'm sorry, Watson. Deeply sorry."

"I couldn't stay in the house," Watson continued, his voice hollow. "Everything there... her things, the nursery we prepared... I couldn't bear it."

"Of course you couldn't," Holmes replied gently. "This is your home too, Watson. It always has been."

Mrs. Hudson returned with the tea and brandy, her movements careful and quiet. She had lived long enough to understand grief, and she moved about the sitting room with the practiced discretion of someone who knew when to help and when to simply be present.

"Your room is ready, Doctor," she said softly. "The bed is made up fresh, and I've put a warming pan between the sheets. You'll be comfortable there."

Watson looked up at her with gratitude he could not express. "Thank you, Mrs. Hudson. You're very kind."

"Nonsense," she replied briskly, though her eyes were gentle. "You're family here. You'll stay as long as you need, and we'll take proper care of you."

The following days passed in a fog of grief and necessary arrangements. Holmes took charge of the practical matters, corresponding with the undertaker and the rector, while Mrs. Hudson ensured that Watson ate and rested. The funeral was held on May 14th, a simple but dignified service that brought together the friends who had shared in James and Mary's happiness.

Arthur and Louisa Doyle traveled from Portsmouth immediately upon receiving Holmes's telegram, their faces showing the shock and sorrow of friends who had so recently celebrated the pregnancy that was to bring such joy. Arthur said little, but his presence was a comfort, and Louisa wept openly for the friend she had grown to love.

"If there's anything we can do," Arthur said quietly to Holmes after the service. "Anything at all."

"Time," Holmes replied. "Time and friendship. That's all anyone can offer."

In the weeks that followed, Watson retreated into himself. He made no mention of his medical practice, showed no interest in the literary collaboration that had brought him such satisfaction, and seemed to find purpose in nothing. He would sit for hours in his old chair, staring into the fire or out the window, lost in memories of the life that had been so cruelly taken from him.

Holmes watched his friend with growing concern, but he knew that grief could not be rushed or reasoned away. He maintained his own routines, solved his cases, and conducted his experiments, but always with careful attention to Watson's needs. When Watson showed signs of appetite, Holmes ensured food was available. When Watson seemed restless, Holmes suggested walks in the fresh air. When Watson wanted only silence, Holmes provided it.

Mrs. Hudson proved to be a source of quiet strength. She had seen many sorrows in her years, and she understood the particular emptiness that followed the loss of a child. She made sure Watson's room was always comfortable, that his clothes were clean, and that he knew himself to be welcomed and cared for.

"You mustn't worry about imposing," she told Watson one evening when he attempted to apologize for his prolonged presence. "This is your home, and you'll stay as long as you need. Mr. Holmes and I, we understand grief. It takes its own time."

Watson could only nod, too overwhelmed by her kindness to speak.

The letters from publishers went unanswered. The medical practice remained closed. The world that had once seemed so full of purpose and meaning had collapsed into nothing more than the simple effort of surviving each day.

But slowly, imperceptibly, the presence of faithful friends began to work its healing power. Holmes's steady companionship, Mrs. Hudson's maternal care, and the familiar routines of Baker Street provided a foundation upon which Watson could begin the long process of rebuilding his shattered life.

The Death of Sherlock Holmes

June 22, 1893

Dr. James Watson sat in his old chair by the fireplace at 111 Baker Street, a chair that had once been merely a comfortable seat but had now become something approaching a refuge from a world that felt alien and hostile. Six weeks had passed since the terrible morning when his life had been torn apart, and while the sharp edge of grief had dulled slightly, it had been replaced by a profound emptiness that seemed to drain color from everything around him.

Holmes had gone out on a case that morning, tactfully providing privacy for the meeting Watson had finally agreed to after weeks of gentle persistence from Arthur Conan Doyle. The correspondence from Portsmouth had been patient and understanding, never pressing, but maintaining the thread of connection that bound their literary partnership. Today, for the first time since Mary's death, Watson had felt strong enough to face the practical realities of their professional obligations.

Mrs. Hudson announced Arthur's arrival with the subdued courtesy she had maintained throughout Watson's residence. "Dr. Doyle to see you, Doctor Watson," she said softly, her weathered face showing the maternal concern that had never wavered during these difficult weeks.

Arthur entered the sitting room with careful steps, his usual confident bearing tempered by obvious concern for his friend's emotional state. He had aged noticeably since Watson had last seen him, the weight of sympathetic sorrow adding lines around his eyes and a gravity to his expression that spoke of shared grief.

"James," Arthur said simply, settling into Holmes's vacant chair with the hesitant manner of a man uncertain of his welcome. "Thank you for agreeing to see me. I hope you understand that I wouldn't have pressed for this meeting if it weren't necessary."

Watson looked up from his contemplation of the empty fireplace, his eyes showing a recognition that seemed to require considerable effort. "Arthur. Of course. I know you've been patient with my... absence from our obligations. I'm grateful for your understanding."

"There's no need for gratitude, James. Grief takes its own time, and friendship means accepting that." Arthur leaned forward slightly, his voice carrying the gentle concern of someone who genuinely cared. "But I'm afraid I do need to discuss our current situation with The Strand Magazine. Not to pressure you, but simply to understand how you wish to proceed."

Watson nodded slowly, forcing his mind to engage with practical matters that seemed to belong to someone else's life. "Yes, I suppose we must face that eventually. Where do we stand with our commitments?"

Arthur consulted a small notebook, his movements careful and deliberate. "We've published seven stories in our second series, from 'Silver Blaze' in December through 'The Adventure of the Resident Patient' in August. The readers have responded enthusiastically, and The Strand continues to be pleased with our work."

"Seven stories," Watson repeated, the numbers seeming to register slowly. "That leaves five more to complete the promised twelve, ending with..." He paused, his expression growing more focused. "Ending with 'The Final Problem' in November."

"Exactly. 'The Adventure of the Crooked Man' is scheduled for July, 'The Adventure of the Greek Interpreter' for September, 'The Adventure of the Naval Treaty' for October, and then..." Arthur hesitated, watching Watson's face carefully. "Then 'The Final Problem' for November, completing our twelve-story series."

Watson was quiet for a long moment, staring out the window at the London street where ordinary life continued its relentless pace. When he finally spoke, his voice carried a quality of decision that hadn't been present since his return to Baker Street.

"Arthur, I want to complete our obligations to The Strand. The work has been too important, too successful, to abandon because of my personal circumstances." He turned back to face his friend directly. "I can provide you with the case material for the remaining stories. My documentation is complete, and you've proven yourself more than capable of adapting them independently."

Arthur felt a mixture of relief and concern at Watson's words. "James, I appreciate your sense of responsibility, but please don't feel obligated to—"

"It's not obligation," Watson interrupted, his voice carrying a firmness that recalled his former self. "It's... purpose, I suppose. The work we've done together has brought authentic detective methods to thousands of readers. That achievement shouldn't be abandoned because I lack the strength to continue."

Arthur studied his friend's face, recognizing both the genuine commitment and the underlying fragility. "Then we can complete the series as planned? You're certain you're strong enough to provide the necessary case documentation?"

Watson managed a slight smile, the first Arthur had seen since arriving. "Arthur, I may be broken, but I'm not useless. I can certainly review my notes and provide you with the material you need. Holmes has been characteristically understanding about my... withdrawal from active collaboration."

"And after we complete the series in November? The Strand will undoubtedly want to discuss future projects."

Here Watson's expression grew more serious, and Arthur sensed they were approaching the real purpose of this meeting. Watson rose from his chair and moved to the window, looking out at the busy street with unseeing eyes.

"Arthur, there's something I need to ask of you. Something that may seem strange, but which I believe is necessary." Watson's voice carried a weight that made Arthur immediately attentive. "When you write 'The Final Problem'—the story of Holmes's confrontation with Professor Moriarty—I want you to end it with Holmes's death."

Arthur started in his chair, certain he had misunderstood. "I'm sorry, James. Did you say Holmes's death?"

Watson turned back to face him, his expression resolute despite the pain that still shadowed his features. "I want Holmes to go over the Reichenbach Falls with Moriarty. I want the reading public to believe that both men died in their final confrontation."

Arthur stared at his friend in amazement. "James, you can't be serious. Kill off Holmes? After all the success we've achieved, all the readers who have come to love the character?"

"I am entirely serious," Watson replied, returning to his chair with the careful movements of a man still weak from grief. "Arthur, I cannot commit to more stories after November. I don't know when—if—I'll be strong enough to resume active collaboration. And I won't have Holmes simply disappear from literature because his chronicler is too broken to continue."

Arthur leaned forward, his mind working through the implications. "But surely, in time, when you've recovered from your loss..."

"Arthur," Watson said gently, "you're assuming I will recover. That the man who could document Holmes's cases with enthusiasm and dedication will somehow return." He shook his head slowly. "I don't know if that man exists anymore. I don't know if I'll ever again find purpose in anything beyond the simple act of surviving each day."

The sitting room fell silent except for the familiar sounds of London traffic filtering through the windows. Arthur felt the weight of his friend's despair and recognized that this was not merely the temporary darkness of fresh grief, but something deeper and more permanent.

"James," Arthur said finally, "I understand what you're asking, but are you certain this is what you want? To end Holmes's career at the height of his popularity?"

Watson nodded slowly. "Better to end it with dignity and drama than to let it simply fade away because I lack the strength to continue. 'The Final Problem' provides the perfect opportunity—Holmes dies heroically, eliminating his greatest enemy at the cost of his own life. It's the kind of ending that befits a great detective."

Arthur was quiet for several minutes, contemplating not only the literary implications but the personal cost to his friend. Finally, he spoke with the gravity the moment demanded.

"If that's truly what you want, James, then I'll write it that way. Holmes and Moriarty will both perish at the Reichenbach Falls, and the world will believe that the great detective died as he lived—in service to justice."

Watson felt a wave of gratitude so profound it nearly overwhelmed him. "Thank you, Arthur. I know it seems like a terrible waste of everything we've built together, but I simply cannot continue indefinitely. This way, Holmes gets the ending he deserves rather than simply disappearing."

Arthur rose and moved to stand beside his friend's chair. "James, I want you to know that I understand completely. Grief changes us in ways we can't predict, and you shouldn't feel obligated to maintain commitments made when your life was entirely different."

"The irony isn't lost on me," Watson said with a bitter smile. "The real Holmes continues his work, solving cases and applying his methods with the same brilliance as always. But the fictional Holmes—the one the public knows and loves—will die because his chronicler lost the will to continue."

Arthur placed a hand on Watson's shoulder. "Perhaps that's fitting, in a way. The fictional Holmes exists because of your partnership with me, your documentation of the real Holmes's methods. If that partnership must end, perhaps the fictional character should end as well."

Watson looked up at his friend with genuine appreciation. "You understand perfectly. That's exactly what I was thinking, though I couldn't have expressed it so clearly."

"Then it's settled," Arthur said, returning to his chair. "We'll complete the remaining five stories as planned, ending with Holmes's death in 'The Final Problem.' And James... if someday you find yourself ready to return to this work, if you discover that documenting Holmes's cases brings you purpose again, we can always find a way to explain his survival."

Watson shook his head. "Arthur, don't plan for that possibility. Write 'The Final Problem' as a true ending. Let Holmes die with honor, and let that be sufficient."

After Arthur's departure, Watson remained in his chair as the afternoon light faded into evening. For the first time since Mary's death, he felt something approaching peace. The future remained uncertain and painful, but at least one burden had been lifted. Holmes would have a fitting end, their professional obligations would be met, and Watson could retreat into whatever healing time might bring without leaving unfinished business behind.

When Holmes returned from his case that evening, he found Watson still sitting by the empty fireplace, but there was something different in his posture—a sense of resolution that hadn't been present for weeks.

"Watson," Holmes said quietly, settling into his own chair. "You seem... lighter somehow. I trust your meeting with Arthur went well?"

Watson looked at his friend with something that might have been the beginning of a smile. "Yes, Holmes. We've made the necessary arrangements. Arthur will complete our remaining obligations to The

Strand Magazine, ending with a story in November called 'The Final Problem.'"

Holmes raised an eyebrow with interest. "The Final Problem? That suggests rather dramatic conclusion."

"Indeed it does," Watson replied, and for the first time in weeks, there was a note of something approaching satisfaction in his voice. "Indeed it does."

The sitting room settled into its familiar evening quiet, with the two friends sharing the comfortable silence that had sustained their friendship through so many years. Outside, London continued its ceaseless activity, but inside 111 Baker Street, two men contemplated endings—one fictional, one all too real—and found in that contemplation a kind of peace that neither had expected.

Watson Sells His Practice

November 15, 1893

The November afternoon had brought the first real chill of winter to London, and Dr. James Watson found himself staring out the window of 111 Baker Street at the gray sky that seemed to mirror his own internal landscape. Six months had passed since the tragedy that had shattered his world, and while the acute pain of grief had settled into something more manageable, it had been replaced by a profound listlessness that seemed to drain purpose from even the most mundane activities.

Watson turned from the window and settled into his familiar chair, the movement accompanied by the soft rustle of unopened correspondence that had been accumulating on the side table for weeks. Bills from his medical suppliers, inquiries from former patients, professional journals—all the detritus of a practice that had been abandoned but not formally closed.

Holmes sat at his chemical apparatus, ostensibly absorbed in some experiment involving the analysis of tobacco ash, but Watson had learned to recognize the signs of his friend's tactful observation. The great detective had been remarkably patient during these months of recovery, never pressing Watson to resume normal activities, never commenting on his prolonged absence from medical practice.

"Holmes," Watson said quietly, his voice carrying the careful tone of a man broaching a difficult subject. "I believe the time has come for me to face certain practical realities."

Holmes looked up from his apparatus, his sharp gray eyes immediately focusing with the attention Watson's rare voluntary conversations had come to deserve. "What sort of realities, Watson?"

Watson gestured toward the pile of correspondence with a mixture of resignation and distaste. "My medical practice. I cannot continue to simply ignore it indefinitely. The patients deserve better than an absent physician, and the financial obligations require attention."

Holmes set down his test tube with deliberate care, recognizing the significance of this first acknowledgment of practical responsibilities since Mary's death. "Have you given thought to when you might feel ready to resume your consultations?"

Watson was quiet for a long moment, his gaze returning to the gray sky outside. When he finally spoke, his voice carried a finality that caught Holmes's attention immediately.

"I don't believe I shall ever feel ready, Holmes. I don't believe I can return to medical practice at all."

Holmes leaned back in his chair, studying his friend's profile with the careful attention he typically reserved for complex criminal puzzles. "Watson, surely such feelings are natural after what you've endured. In time—"

"No," Watson interrupted, turning to face Holmes directly. "It's not simply a matter of time or healing, Holmes. When I think of returning to my consulting rooms, of examining patients, of dealing with the ordinary complaints and concerns of medical practice..." He paused, searching for words to express something that felt fundamental and unchangeable. "The will is simply gone. Completely gone."

Holmes absorbed this information with the same methodical consideration he applied to all significant evidence. "You're saying you wish to abandon medicine entirely?"

Watson nodded slowly. "I know it seems wasteful—the years of training, the established practice, the reputation I built in Kensington. But Holmes, I cannot summon even the slightest interest in returning to that life. The very thought of it feels... impossible."

"Then what do you propose to do with the practice? It represents a considerable investment, both financial and professional."

Watson's expression grew more troubled. "That's precisely the problem. I know I should sell it, find someone suitable to take over the patient relationships I've neglected. But the thought of dealing with solicitors, interviewing potential buyers, negotiating terms..." He shook his head helplessly. "I simply lack the energy for such arrangements."

Holmes stood and moved to the window, his mind already working through possibilities with characteristic efficiency. "Watson, you mustn't let such practical concerns add to your burden. These matters can be handled."

"By whom? I can hardly ask you to manage the sale of a medical practice."

Holmes was quiet for several minutes, his sharp profile etched against the gray light as he contemplated the problem. Finally, he turned back to Watson with the expression of a man who had reached a decision.

"Watson, leave the matter with me. I may know of someone who would be interested in acquiring an established Kensington practice."

Watson looked up with the first spark of hope he had shown in weeks. "Really? Someone suitable?"

"Possibly. Let me make some inquiries." Holmes returned to his chair, his manner becoming more businesslike. "In the meantime, you should gather whatever financial records and patient information would be necessary for a proper transfer."
"Holmes, I cannot adequately express how grateful—"

Holmes waved a dismissive hand. "Watson, after everything you've endured, the least I can do is spare you the additional burden of complex business arrangements."

Three weeks later, Watson was surprised by the arrival of a gentleman whose card identified him as Dr. Verner, recently returned from establishing medical practices in various international locations. He was a man of middle years with the confident bearing of someone who had achieved considerable success in his profession, and his manner toward Watson was both respectful and understanding.

"Dr. Watson," Dr. Verner said as he settled into the chair Holmes had provided for the meeting, "Mr. Holmes has spoken to me about your Kensington practice. I understand you're considering making it available for purchase?"

Watson felt immediately at ease with the stranger's direct but sympathetic approach. "Yes, that's correct. Personal circumstances have made it impossible for me to continue, and I believe my patients would be better served by someone who can give them proper attention."

Dr. Verner nodded with the understanding of a medical man who recognized the demands of the profession. "Mr. Holmes mentioned that you've built an excellent reputation in Kensington, with a distinguished clientele and well-appointed consulting rooms. Such an established practice would be of considerable interest to someone looking to settle in London."

"The practice has been successful," Watson agreed, "though I confess I've neglected it rather badly these past months."

"Understandable under the circumstances," Dr. Verner replied with professional discretion. "Dr. Watson, if you're genuinely interested in selling, I believe I could make an offer that would be satisfactory to both parties."

Watson leaned forward with interest. "What sort of arrangement did you have in mind?"

Dr. Verner consulted a small notebook, his manner becoming more businesslike. "Based on Mr. Holmes's description of your practice—the location, the established patient base, the quality of the consulting rooms and equipment—I would be prepared to offer twelve hundred pounds for the complete transfer of ownership."

Watson blinked in surprise. "Twelve hundred pounds? Dr. Verner, that's remarkably generous. The practice is valuable, certainly, but given its recent neglect..."

"Dr. Watson, an established practice in Kensington with your professional reputation is worth precisely that amount to someone who appreciates its potential," Dr. Verner replied firmly. "Besides, I'm in a position to proceed quickly and with minimal complications, which I understand would be preferable given your circumstances."

Watson felt a wave of relief so profound it nearly overwhelmed him. "Dr. Verner, if you're serious about such an offer, I would be delighted to accept. The speed and simplicity you mention would indeed be tremendously valuable."

"Excellent. I propose we arrange the transfer for March 1st, 1894. That would give me time to complete my current arrangements while allowing you adequate time to organize any personal effects you wish to retain." Dr. Verner smiled warmly. "I believe this arrangement will serve both our needs admirably."

As Dr. Verner departed with promises to have proper legal documents prepared, Watson found himself experiencing something approaching happiness for the first time since Mary's death. The burden of the abandoned practice, which had weighed on his conscience for months, would be lifted completely, and the generous price would provide financial security for whatever uncertain future lay ahead.

Holmes, who had remained tactfully absent during the negotiation, returned to find Watson actually smiling—a sight that had been notably absent from Baker Street for far too long.

"I take it Dr. Verner's offer was satisfactory?" Holmes inquired with carefully controlled pleasure.

"More than satisfactory—extraordinarily generous," Watson replied, his voice carrying a lightness that had been missing for months. "Holmes, I cannot thank you enough for arranging this introduction. Dr. Verner seems ideally suited to take over the practice, and his offer removes every financial concern I might have had."

Holmes settled into his chair with obvious satisfaction. "I'm delighted the arrangement suits you both, Watson. Dr. Verner struck me as exactly the sort of conscientious physician who would appreciate what you've built in Kensington."

Watson studied his friend's face, recognizing something in Holmes's expression that suggested deeper involvement than he wished to acknowledge. "Holmes, I realize I never asked how you came to know Dr. Verner. He seemed remarkably well-informed about my circumstances, and his offer was extraordinarily generous—far more than the practice was worth in its current neglected state."

Holmes looked up from his apparatus with the slight smile that often accompanied his most successful deductions. "Watson, there are times when the specific details of an introduction matter less than the successful outcome it produces."

"Holmes," Watson said quietly, "Dr. Verner wouldn't happen to be related to you, would he?"

Holmes returned to his experiment with the satisfied air of a man whose plans had achieved their intended result. "Watson, sometimes fortune requires a little assistance to find its proper direction."

Watson is Back at Baker Street

March 1, 1894

On the evening of March 1st, after the legal documents had been signed and his medical career officially ended, Watson sat in his familiar chair at Baker Street, watching Holmes conduct one of his chemical experiments with the absorbed attention that marked all his scientific endeavors. The financial security provided by Dr. Verner's purchase meant that Watson could remain at Baker Street indefinitely, without the pressure of professional obligations he no longer felt capable of meeting.

As Watson sat in the familiar quiet of that March evening, his gaze wandered to the corner where Holmes kept his violin case, and suddenly his mind was carried back across the years to another time, another beginning. The memory came with startling clarity—that January morning in 1882 when young Stamford had led him through the chemical laboratory at Bart's Hospital, chattering nervously about the "queer fellow" who might be willing to share lodgings.

"Dr. Watson, Mr. Sherlock Holmes," Stamford had said with obvious relief at having completed his awkward introduction. And Holmes had looked up from his test tube with those penetrating gray eyes and declared, "You have been in Afghanistan, I perceive."

Watson smiled at the memory. How astonished he had been by that casual demonstration of deductive reasoning! How impossible it had seemed that this lean, intense young man could read his entire military history from a glance. He had been a broken man then too, in his own way—invalided out of the Army, uncertain of his future, searching for purpose and companionship in a city that seemed vast and indifferent.

"You don't know Sherlock Holmes yet," Stamford had warned him. "Perhaps you would not care for him as a constant companion." But how wrong that assessment had proven to be. Holmes had offered exactly what Watson needed most—intellectual stimulation, genuine friendship, and a sense of purpose that had sustained him through more than a decade of remarkable adventures.

And now, twelve years later, here he was again—a broken man seeking refuge in the same rooms, with the same friend who had welcomed him without question or condition. The circumstances were different, but the fundamental need was the same—the need for a place where friendship mattered more than convention, where loyalty was given freely and without condition.

Holmes had aged, of course, as they both had. The sharp features were perhaps a bit more lined, the hair showing traces of gray, but the essential character remained unchanged. Still the same penetrating intelligence, still the same capacity for both brilliant deduction and surprising kindness, still the same willingness to offer sanctuary to a friend in need.

"Watson," Holmes said quietly, looking up from his experiment, "you seem lost in thought."

"I was remembering," Watson replied, "how we first met. How young we both were, how uncertain the future seemed."

Holmes set down his apparatus and leaned back in his chair. "And yet here we are, more than a decade later, still sharing these same rooms."

"Yes," Watson said, feeling something that might have been the beginning of peace. "Here we are."

The gas lamps flickered gently in their familiar sconces, casting the same warm light that had illuminated their first conversations, their early cases, their gradual recognition that they had found in each other something rare and valuable—a friendship that could survive any test.

Watson realized that in losing everything else, he had rediscovered something he had perhaps taken for granted during his years of marriage and professional success. The simple, enduring comfort of true companionship. The knowledge that whatever challenges lay ahead, he would not face them alone.

They had come full circle, these two men who had found each other by chance in a hospital laboratory twelve years ago. The young Army doctor and the eccentric consulting detective had become something neither had expected—brothers in all but blood, united by shared experiences that had tested and strengthened their bond beyond any ordinary friendship.

The future remained uncertain. Watson might never again find the enthusiasm for documentation that had made their literary collaboration so successful. But he had this—the familiar sitting room, the comfortable chairs, the presence of a friend who asked nothing but offered everything.

It was enough. More than enough. It was home.

A Chance Encounter

December 10, 1899

The London fog hung thick and yellowed in the December air as Arthur Conan Doyle emerged from the narrow townhouse on Montague Street, his medical bag weighing heavy in his gloved hand. Mrs. Smith's consumption was worsening, and despite his best efforts with the latest treatments, he feared the winter would be her last. The lamplighters had already begun their evening rounds, casting wavering pools of gaslight through the murk that seemed to swallow the city whole.

Doyle pulled his overcoat tighter against the bitter wind and set off toward the main thoroughfare, his breath forming small clouds that dissipated quickly in the damp air. The familiar weight of melancholy that often accompanied his medical visits was upon him—the reminder that for all his literary success, there remained suffering he could not cure with mere words.

As he turned onto Baker Street, a movement in the amber glow of a shop window caught his attention. Two figures stood before Harrisons & Sons, the antiquarian shop, their forms rendered indistinct by the fog but somehow achingly familiar. Doyle slowed his pace, squinting through the gloom. The taller figure—lean, angular, with that distinctive silhouette— stood with his back to the street, pointing at something within the window display. His companion, shorter and more robust, nodded vigorously at whatever observation was being made.

A chill that had nothing to do with the December evening ran down Doyle's spine. It could not be, and yet...

As if responding to some unspoken signal, the two men stepped away from the window. The shorter figure turned in Doyle's direction while his companion strode purposefully in the opposite direction, his distinctive deerstalker hat disappearing into the fog like a specter returning to the netherworld from whence it came.

"Good Lord," Doyle muttered under his breath, quickening his step.

The approaching figure resolved itself into unmistakable clarity: the sturdy frame, the familiar military bearing, the dependable countenance that Doyle had described in such detail that he could have drawn it from memory. Dr. James Watson walked toward him with the same steady gait Doyle had imagined through countless stories.

"Arthur!" Watson called out, his voice carrying the warmth and reliability that had endeared him to readers across the Empire. "What an unexpected pleasure."

"James," Doyle replied, removing his hat briefly despite the cold. "Indeed, quite unexpected. I was just visiting a patient in the area. And you? I couldn't help but notice you were with—" He glanced toward the fog where the other figure had vanished.

"Ah, yes." Watson's expression grew slightly guarded, though his smile remained genuine. "Just concluded a bit of business, actually. Nothing too pressing, I assure you."

They fell into step together, their footfalls echoing off the wet cobblestones. Doyle found himself studying Watson's face in the gaslight, marveling at the lines around his eyes, the slight graying at his temples— details he had never specified in his writing yet which seemed perfectly natural, as if Watson had been aging in real time alongside the stories.

"You must have been working on a case with Holmes," Doyle ventured, unable to keep the curiosity from his voice.

Watson glanced at him sideways, then nodded slowly. "Yes, as a matter of fact. Though I'm pleased to say the case is now over—settled completely, thankfully."

"Successfully resolved, I hope?"

"Oh, quite successfully. Holmes was, as always, rather brilliant in his deductions." Watson paused, seeming to weigh his words. "I'm afraid I cannot go into the particulars, you understand. Client confidentiality and all that. But I can say it concerned Charles Augustus Howell—the art dealer."

Doyle's eyebrows rose. "Howell? The man they call the master blackmailer? Good heavens, Watson. I've read about him in the papers. A most unsavory character, by all accounts. He's been preying upon people for years, using their secrets against them."

"The very same," Watson confirmed, his voice carrying a note of satisfaction. "Though I doubt we shall be hearing much more from Mr. Howell's schemes in the future."

They walked in comfortable silence for a moment, the fog swirling around them like the ghosts of unwritten stories. Doyle found himself studying his companion's profile, struck by the strange sensation of conversing with his own creation made flesh.

"You know, James," he said finally, "this case of yours—it might make for quite an interesting story. That is, if we were ever to decide to continue those tales again."

Watson's step faltered almost imperceptibly, and when he looked at Doyle, there was something unreadable in his expression—perhaps wariness, perhaps sadness.

"The weather has turned quite bitter, hasn't it?" Watson said, adjusting his scarf with deliberate care. "I do believe we're in for snow before the week is out. Mrs. Hudson was saying just this morning that she could feel it in her bones. She's remarkably accurate about such things, you know. Something about the way the wind shifts from the Thames."

Doyle recognized the deflection for what it was and chose not to press the matter. Some conversations, he had learned, were best left for another time—or perhaps for another world entirely.

"Indeed," he replied simply. "London winters can be quite unforgiving."

As they reached the corner where their paths would diverge, Watson extended his hand. "It has been a genuine pleasure, Arthur. Do take care of yourself in this weather."

"And you as well, James. Give my regards to—" Doyle paused, then smiled. "Well, give my regards."

Watson's eyes crinkled with understanding. "I shall indeed."

As Doyle watched the doctor disappear into the fog, he stood for a long moment in the lamplight, wondering if he had truly seen what he believed he had seen, or if the London mist played tricks on more than just the eyes. In the distance, a church bell tolled the hour, and somewhere in the fog, he could have sworn he heard the faint sound of a violin playing a melancholy air.

Pulling his coat closer against the night, Arthur Conan Doyle set off for home, carrying with him the strangest consultation of his medical career—and perhaps the most extraordinary literary review he would never write.

The Hound of the Baskervilles

June 1, 1900

The late afternoon sun streamed through the tall windows of Arthur Conan Doyle's study at Undershaw, illuminating the comfortable disorder that had become characteristic of a successful author's working space. At forty-one, Arthur had found in this Surrey home exactly what Louisa had needed—clean air that rivaled Switzerland's beneficial climate, but with the comfort of remaining in England among family and friends. The house, which he had designed specifically for her recovery from tuberculosis, had become a sanctuary where both health and literary productivity could flourish.

Arthur leaned back in his leather chair, surveying the evidence of eight years of remarkably diverse literary achievement spread across his desk. Since November 1893, when "The Final Problem" had sent Sherlock Holmes tumbling over the Reichenbach Falls, he had published historical novels, military analyses, medical treatises, and works on spiritualism. Each had found its audience, each had enhanced his reputation as a serious man of letters, and each had proven that Arthur Conan Doyle was far more than merely the creator of a fictional detective.

His latest work, "The Great Boer War," lay before him in completed manuscript form—a serious analysis of the South African conflict that had earned him considerable respect among critics and military historians. Beside it sat correspondence from publishers eager to discuss his next historical romance, and a letter from the War Office thanking him for his contributions to public understanding of modern warfare.

And yet, as Arthur contemplated this evidence of his literary evolution, he found his thoughts returning with persistent frequency to those earlier years of collaboration with Dr. James Watson. The Holmes stories had possessed a vitality and authenticity that his other works, however accomplished, somehow lacked. The partnership with James had produced something genuinely unique—detective fiction that educated readers about actual investigative methods while entertaining them with compelling mysteries.

Arthur rose and moved to the tall bookcase that dominated one wall of his study. Behind the published volumes of his various works, carefully preserved in their original folders, lay the case documentation that James had provided during their years of collaboration. He had kept them all, unable to bring himself to destroy what represented not only potential stories but also the record of an extraordinary friendship.

It had been over six years since he had last examined these files, but today something drew him to revisit the material that had once brought him such professional satisfaction. His fingers traced along the folders until they found one that was thicker than most of the others, filled with James's characteristically meticulous documentation of a case that had captured Arthur's imagination even during their period of active collaboration.

He withdrew the folder and opened it carefully, revealing pages of neat handwriting interspersed with sketches and diagrams. "The Hound of the Baskervilles," Arthur read aloud from the folder's label, and immediately felt the familiar excitement that had always accompanied their most promising material.

The case had occurred in the autumn of 1888, during the height of their productive partnership, and James had documented it with exceptional thoroughness. Arthur remembered being struck by the gothic atmosphere, the complex family history, and the brilliant way Holmes had unraveled what appeared to be a supernatural mystery through pure logical analysis. It had always seemed destined for literary adaptation, but the complexity of the material had made it appear better suited for a full-length book rather than their monthly magazine commitments.

Then had come the pressure of their regular publications to The Strand, followed by the tragedy that had ended their collaboration entirely. The Baskerville case had remained in this folder, documented but never transformed into the literature it deserved to become.

Arthur settled back into his chair and began reading James's account from the beginning. The opening was immediately compelling—the mysterious death of Sir Charles Baskerville, the ancient family curse, the spectral hound that was said to haunt the Devonshire moors. As he read, Arthur found himself once again impressed by the quality of James's documentation. Every conversation was recorded verbatim, every deduction carefully explained, every detail preserved with the eye of someone who understood that truth could be more compelling than any fiction.

The case was substantial enough for a proper book—perhaps 60,000 words when fully developed. More importantly, it was complete in itself, requiring no reference to Holmes's supposed death at the Reichenbach Falls. If presented as an adventure that had occurred before those tragic events, it could be published without any need to explain Holmes's resurrection or compromise the finality they had established.

Arthur paused in his reading, struck by the elegant simplicity of this solution. For eight years, publishers had pleaded for new Holmes stories, but he had been trapped by his own declaration of the detective's death. A story set in the past would solve that problem completely. Readers could have their beloved detective back, at least temporarily, without any need for complex explanations or resurrections.

But such a project would require James's cooperation, and Arthur had seen little of his old friend in recent years. Their correspondence had continued sporadically—brief notes marking holidays or significant events—but he knew little about James's current state of mind or whether the passage of time had brought any healing to his grief-shattered spirit. The last Arthur had heard, James had never returned to medical practice after the tragedy of 1893, and continued to reside at 111 Baker Street with Holmes.

Arthur moved to his writing desk and withdrew a sheet of his finest letterhead, now bearing the address "Undershaw, Hindhead, Surrey." Perhaps it was time to test whether the friendship that had once brought them such mutual satisfaction might be capable of limited revival. Not a return to their intensive collaborative relationship—Arthur understood that such a thing might be impossible—but perhaps a single project that could benefit them both while bringing Holmes back to the public that had never stopped mourning his loss.

He began to write, his pen moving carefully as he sought exactly the right tone:

My dear James,

I hope this letter finds you in good health and reasonable spirits as we enter this new century. As you can see from the letterhead, Louisa and I have made our permanent home here at Undershaw in Hindhead, where the Surrey air has proven as beneficial to her health as the physicians promised. The house has become a sanctuary for both her recovery and my continued literary work.

I write not to disturb your peace or to press for any commitments you might find burdensome, but to share a possibility that has occurred to me and to seek your thoughts on whether it might have merit.

This morning, while reviewing old papers in my study, I came across your documentation of the Baskerville case—the spectral hound on the Devonshire moors that so fascinated us both in 1888. Reading through your meticulous notes again after all these years, I am struck anew by the extraordinary quality of the material and the compelling nature of the investigation itself.

The thought occurred to me that this case might represent a unique opportunity. The story could be presented as occurring before the events at Reichenbach Falls, requiring no resurrection or explanation—simply a 'lost' adventure that had somehow not been published previously. The material is sufficiently substantial to support a full-length book, and the gothic atmosphere combined with Holmes's brilliant deductive work could create something truly memorable.

I do not propose this lightly, nor do I wish to impose upon your current circumstances. I understand completely the personal costs our collaboration once required, and I would never presume to suggest a return to the intensive partnership of our earlier years.

However, if you felt able to provide guidance on adapting this single case—perhaps reviewing a manuscript to ensure accuracy—it might serve multiple purposes. The public would have their beloved detective back, at least temporarily. The financial rewards could be substantial. Most importantly, it would allow us to honor the memory of our collaboration while bringing one of Holmes's finest investigations to the literary recognition it deserves.

Please understand that I ask nothing hasty or burdensome. If the idea has any appeal, we could proceed slowly and carefully, with no pressure and no obligations beyond what you feel comfortable undertaking. If you prefer that Sherlock Holmes remain definitively buried, I will respect that decision completely and mention the matter no further.

I simply felt that the possibility should be offered, in case time has brought you to a place where such a project might provide satisfaction rather than pain.

If you would be willing to discuss this further, I would be happy to travel to London at your convenience, or you would be most welcome here at Undershaw. Louisa often speaks of you with continued affection and would be delighted to see you again.

Whatever you decide, please know that I think of our friendship with continued gratitude. You gave me the opportunity to bring authentic detective work to the world, and that gift can never be diminished by time or circumstance.

With warmest regards and hopes for your continued well-being,

Arthur

P.S. The railway connection from London to Hindhead is quite convenient, should you find yourself inclined to visit. Undershaw sits on a hill with magnificent views, and I believe you would find the atmosphere conducive to quiet reflection on whatever decision seems best to you.

Arthur read through the letter twice, adjusting a phrase here and there to ensure it struck exactly the right note—hopeful but not pressing, enthusiastic but respectful of James's situation. He sealed it carefully and rang for his housekeeper to arrange its posting to London.

As evening approached and the Surrey countryside settled into peaceful quiet around Undershaw, Arthur returned to the Baskerville documentation, reading through James's meticulous account with growing excitement. The story had everything—mystery, atmosphere, brilliant deduction, and a satisfying resolution that vindicated scientific method over superstition.

Louisa appeared in the doorway of his study, her health much improved from their early years of struggle with tuberculosis, though she still moved with the careful grace of someone who had learned not to take physical well-being for granted.

"Arthur," she said gently, "you seem quite absorbed this evening. What has captured your attention so completely?"

Arthur looked up at his wife with the expression of a man who had rediscovered something valuable he had thought permanently lost. "I've been reading through old case notes from my collaboration with James Watson. There's a story here, Touie—perhaps the finest Holmes adventure never published."

Louisa moved into the study, her interest immediately engaged. "And you're thinking of proposing collaboration with Dr. Watson again?"

"I've already written to him," Arthur replied, indicating the sealed letter on his desk. "Though I've tried to make it clear that I'm suggesting only a single project, with no pressure for anything beyond what he feels capable of providing."

Louisa settled into the chair beside Arthur's desk, her expression thoughtful. "Do you think enough time has passed for him to consider such work without pain?"

Arthur considered the question carefully. "I don't know, honestly. But Touie, the Baskerville case represents some of the finest detective work Holmes ever accomplished, and James's documentation is extraordinarily complete. If he felt able to guide the adaptation, we could create something worthy of both the original investigation and the literary standards we once maintained."

"And if he declines?"

Arthur smiled, though his expression carried a hint of wistfulness. "Then at least I will have offered him the opportunity to see this remarkable case receive the recognition it deserves. Sometimes, Touie, the important thing is not the outcome but the gesture itself."

Louisa nodded, understanding her husband's complex motivations. "Then we shall wait to see what Dr. Watson's response brings. But Arthur, I hope you're prepared for whatever answer he provides— whether it brings renewed collaboration or confirms that some chapters of our lives must remain closed."

Watson is Invited to Undershaw

June 15, 1900

Five days had passed since Dr. James Watson had posted his cautious reply to Portsmouth, expressing interest in Arthur's Baskerville proposal while carefully avoiding any firm commitment to the collaboration itself. The morning post brought Arthur's prompt response, though Watson noted immediately that the return address was not Portsmouth but Hindhead, Surrey—a location that stirred his memory of correspondence mentioning Arthur's move to a new residence for his wife's health.

Watson opened the envelope to find Arthur's familiar handwriting, though the letterhead now bore the elegant inscription "Undershaw, Hindhead, Surrey":

My dear James,

Your letter expressing interest in discussing the Baskerville project has brought Touie and me considerable hope. I understand completely your reluctance to commit to such an undertaking without careful consideration, and I believe I may have a suggestion that would allow you to evaluate the project properly.

Rather than asking you to make any decisions based on correspondence alone, would you be willing to visit us here at Undershaw for a few days? Such a visit would allow you to review the complete case documentation without obligation, while giving us the opportunity to discuss whether this collaboration might be feasible under terms that would be comfortable for you.

Our home is situated in the healthful air of Hindhead, which has proven beneficial for Touie's constitution. We have a comfortable guest room that looks out over the Sussex countryside, and the quiet atmosphere would be ideal for the kind of thoughtful consideration this project deserves. Most importantly, seeing each other again after so many years might help us determine whether our old collaborative spirit could be successfully renewed.

I want to emphasize that this invitation carries no expectations beyond friendly discussion. You would be under no obligation to proceed with any publication, and if after reviewing the material you decide the project isn't suitable, that decision would be entirely respected.

If you could spare the time for such a visit—perhaps three or four days—we could explore the possibilities together without pressure or commitment from either party.

Please let me know if such an arrangement appeals to you. The train service from London is excellent, and I would of course meet you at the station.

With hopes for renewed friendship, regardless of any professional considerations.

Arthur

Watson read the letter twice, appreciating Arthur's careful respect for the boundaries he had established. The invitation was clearly designed to allow him to evaluate the project thoroughly without feeling trapped by premature commitments—exactly the approach he needed to feel comfortable moving forward.

Holmes emerged from his bedroom at that moment, already dressed for what appeared to be a day of investigation, and Watson handed him Arthur's invitation without comment.

"Undershaw," Holmes observed after reading the letter thoughtfully. "Arthur's new residence in Surrey. I understand the move was necessitated by his wife's health concerns."

Watson nodded, remembering fragments of information from their correspondence. "Touie has been struggling with respiratory ailments for several years. The Hindhead location was specifically chosen for its beneficial air."

Holmes studied the invitation with his characteristic attention to detail. "Watson, I believe Arthur has approached this matter with considerable wisdom. Rather than pressing for commitment, he's offering you the opportunity to make an informed decision."

"You think I should accept the invitation?"

Holmes moved to the window, looking out at the busy Baker Street morning with the thoughtful expression Watson had learned to associate with his friend's consideration of complex situations. "Watson, this represents exactly the sort of careful approach you need. No commitments, no obligations—simply the chance to see old friends and evaluate whether this project might provide satisfaction rather than burden."

Watson felt the appeal of Arthur's cautious proposal. "The prospect of reviewing the case material without pressure does seem... manageable."

"Moreover," Holmes continued, "the change of scene might prove beneficial regardless of any professional considerations. You've spent considerable time within these walls, Watson. A few days in the Surrey countryside with valued friends could provide renewal whether or not it leads to literary collaboration."

Watson stood and moved to his writing desk, though his movements carried more deliberation than decisive commitment. "I believe I shall accept the invitation—not to commit to the project, but to explore whether such commitment might be possible."

"An excellent distinction," Holmes approved. "When will you reply?"

Watson reached for his pen, already composing his careful response. "Today. But I want to be absolutely clear that this visit represents consideration, not agreement."

As Watson began writing his reply, he felt something between interest and apprehension—not the excitement of commitment, but the cautious hope that perhaps, in the quiet atmosphere of Undershaw, surrounded by complete case documentation and the friendship of people who understood both his capabilities and his limitations, he might discover whether the collaboration Arthur proposed could provide purpose without overwhelming the careful equilibrium he had achieved.

My dear Arthur,

Your invitation is both generous and thoughtfully presented. I would indeed be interested in visiting Undershaw to review the Baskerville material and discuss whether such a collaboration might be feasible. However, I want to be entirely clear that I am accepting your invitation to explore the possibility, not to commit to the project itself.

If, after reviewing the documentation and considering the scope of work involved, I find the project beyond my current capabilities, I hope you will understand that such a decision would reflect my limitations rather than any lack of appreciation for your proposal.

With these understandings clearly established, I would be delighted to visit for three or four days at your convenience. Please let me know what dates would suit your schedule.

With gratitude for your patience and continued friendship.

James

Watson sealed the letter, feeling the careful satisfaction that comes from taking a measured step forward without abandoning the protective boundaries that had become essential to his emotional stability.

"Holmes," Watson said as he prepared the letter for posting, "I find myself genuinely curious about this project, though I remain uncertain whether I'm capable of the sustained collaboration it would require."

Holmes smiled with obvious approval. "Watson, curiosity is precisely the right foundation for such exploration. Whether it leads to collaboration or simply to a pleasant visit with old friends, you're taking exactly the right approach."

Watson Visits Undershaw

July 8, 1900

The morning train from Waterloo Station had been punctual, and Dr. James Watson found himself settling into a first-class compartment with something approaching anticipation rather than the dutiful resignation that had characterized most of his social engagements during the past seven years. The countryside rolling past the carriage windows seemed particularly verdant in the July sunshine, and Watson allowed himself to acknowledge that the prospect of seeing Arthur and Louisa again—and perhaps engaging with serious literary work for the first time since Mary's death—held genuine appeal.

As the train gathered speed through the Surrey hills, Watson reflected on the correspondence that had brought him to this journey. Arthur's initial proposal regarding The Hound of the Baskervilles had arrived at exactly the right moment—not too soon after his period of acute grief, but not so late that the idea of collaborative work had become impossible to contemplate. The careful boundaries Arthur had suggested, the respect for Watson's emotional limitations, and most importantly, the extraordinary quality of the case material itself had combined to make this venture seem not just possible but potentially rewarding.

The conductor's announcement of their approach to Haslemere station interrupted Watson's contemplation, and he gathered his modest traveling bag with the methodical efficiency that had characterized his military service and subsequent professional life. Arthur had arranged for a carriage to meet the train, explaining in his most recent letter that Undershaw was situated on the Surrey hills above Hindhead, requiring a drive of perhaps twenty minutes through countryside that Louisa had described as "remarkably beneficial to both lungs and spirits."

The carriage waiting outside Haslemere station proved to be well-appointed and comfortable, driven by a middle-aged man whose weathered face and practical manner suggested long familiarity with the local roads. As they departed the station and began climbing into the

Surrey hills, Watson found himself genuinely impressed by the landscape—rolling green hills dotted with stands of pine and birch, the air noticeably cleaner and fresher than London's perpetual haze of coal smoke and urban industry.

"First time visiting Undershaw, sir?" the driver inquired as they navigated a particularly scenic stretch of road.

"Indeed it is," Watson replied, settling back to enjoy the views. "I understand it's quite a remarkable house."

"That it is, sir. Dr. Doyle had it built special for Mrs. Doyle's health—the air up here on the Surrey hills is said to be near as good as Switzerland for lung troubles. Modern as anything, too—electric lighting throughout, and one of those new hot water systems for the bathrooms."

Watson nodded with interest, remembering Arthur's letters describing the careful planning that had gone into Undershaw's construction. Louisa's tuberculosis diagnosis in 1893 had prompted their experimental residence in Switzerland, but Arthur's research had convinced him that the Surrey air could provide similar benefits while allowing them to remain in England near family and friends.

As they crested a particular rise in the road, the driver gestured ahead with obvious pride in his local knowledge. "There she is, sir— Undershaw. Quite something to see, isn't it?"

Watson followed the man's gesture and felt his breath catch slightly at his first glimpse of Arthur's architectural achievement. Undershaw sat prominently on a rise overlooking the Surrey countryside, its red brick facade and distinctive gables creating an impression of both substantial comfort and thoughtful design. The house was clearly modern, built with the latest conveniences, but its proportions and setting gave it a timeless quality that spoke of a home designed for both family life and serious work.

"Dr. Doyle designed much of it himself," the driver continued as they approached the curved drive that led to the main entrance. "Wanted to ensure every room would have proper ventilation and natural light. They say his study on the upper floor has windows facing three directions, giving him views clear across to the South Downs on a clear day."

As their carriage drew up before Undershaw's main entrance, Watson noted the careful landscaping that complemented the house's architecture—mature trees providing both shade and privacy, gardens that suggested Louisa's influence in their arrangement, and everywhere the sense of a property designed not just for impressive appearance but for the practical needs of a family that valued both health and intellectual work.

The front door opened before Watson could gather his traveling bag, revealing Arthur Conan Doyle approaching with the confident stride and warm smile that had characterized their friendship from its earliest days. At forty-one, Arthur had grown more distinguished in appearance, his frame carrying the slight fullness that spoke of prosperity and success, but his enthusiasm remained as infectious as ever.

"James!" Arthur called out, reaching the carriage with obvious pleasure. "How splendid to see you again, and what perfect weather you've brought for your first visit to Undershaw."

Watson accepted Arthur's firm handshake gratefully, feeling immediately welcomed despite the years that had passed since their last meeting. "Arthur, the house is magnificent. Even more impressive than your letters suggested."

"Wait until you see it properly," Arthur replied, relieving Watson of his bag with characteristic efficiency. "But first, come and greet Louisa. She's been looking forward to your visit with tremendous anticipation."

As they approached Undershaw's entrance, Watson noted the quality of the construction—solid brick work, carefully crafted woodwork around windows and doorframes, and the subtle architectural details that spoke of a house built without regard to economy but with considerable attention to both beauty and functionality. Everything about the property suggested success, thoughtful planning, and the kind of domestic stability that Watson had once known but had thought might be forever beyond his reach.

Louisa Doyle appeared in the doorway with the grace and warmth that Watson remembered from their previous meetings, though he noted immediately that she looked stronger and healthier than during her London visits of recent years. The Surrey air had clearly agreed with her, and her manner suggested the contentment of a woman whose domestic arrangements provided both comfort and the support necessary for her husband's literary work.

"James," she said, stepping forward to embrace him with genuine affection, "how wonderful to have you here at last. Arthur has been talking of little else since receiving your letter agreeing to visit."

Watson found himself genuinely moved by the warmth of his reception, feeling for the first time in years the pleasure of being welcomed into a happy household as a valued friend rather than an object of sympathy. "Louisa, you look wonderfully well. The Surrey climate clearly agrees with you."

"Indeed it does. After those difficult years when my health was so uncertain, to find ourselves in a place that provides both the medical benefits I require and the comfort of remaining in England..." She gestured toward the house with obvious satisfaction. "Arthur designed Undershaw specifically with my needs in mind, but it has proven beneficial for his work as well."

Arthur led them into the entrance hall, which Watson immediately recognized as representing the best of modern domestic architecture—high ceilings providing excellent ventilation, carefully positioned windows ensuring abundant natural light, and the kind of practical arrangements that spoke of a house designed by someone who understood both literary work and family life.

"James, let me show you to your room first," Arthur said, beginning to ascend a staircase that curved gracefully toward the upper floors. "You'll be staying in what we call the garden room—it overlooks the South Downs and catches the morning sun beautifully."

As they climbed the stairs, Watson noted the electric lighting that the carriage driver had mentioned, along with the quality of the woodwork and the careful attention to detail that characterized every aspect of the house's construction. Clearly, Arthur's literary success had provided the means for creating exactly the kind of home environment that could support both serious work and domestic happiness.

The guest room proved to be spacious and comfortable, with tall windows that did indeed provide remarkable views across the Surrey countryside toward the distant South Downs. The furnishings were elegant but not ostentatious, and Watson noted immediately the thoughtful touches—a writing desk positioned to take advantage of the natural light, bookshelves stocked with volumes that suggested consideration for a literary visitor's interests, and the kind of comfortable chair that invited either reading or quiet contemplation.

"This is magnificent, Arthur," Watson said, setting his bag beside the wardrobe. "You've created something remarkable here."

Arthur's face showed obvious pleasure at his friend's approval. "After those years of uncertainty about Louisa's health, of traveling between Switzerland and England seeking the right climate, it feels wonderful to have found a place that provides both the medical benefits she requires and the stability we need for family life."

"And for your work?"

"Ah, wait until you see the study. But first, let's settle you properly and perhaps have some tea. Louisa has prepared quite a spread in your honor, and I'm eager to discuss the Baskerville project with you in detail."

As they descended the stairs toward what Arthur described as the morning room, Watson felt a growing sense of anticipation for the conversations that lay ahead. The house itself suggested that Arthur's literary career had reached a level of success that provided genuine security, while Louisa's obvious good health and the family's domestic happiness created an atmosphere conducive to serious collaborative work.

The morning room proved to be another example of Undershaw's thoughtful design—large windows providing excellent views of the gardens, comfortable seating arranged to encourage conversation, and the kind of practical elegance that spoke of a house designed for both family use and entertaining literary guests. Louisa had indeed prepared an impressive tea service, with delicate sandwiches and cakes that suggested both her recovery of strength and her pleasure in welcoming a valued friend.

"James," Louisa said as they settled into comfortable chairs, "I know you are here primarily to discuss the Baskerville Case, but before we get into that, tell me... what have you been up to these past 6 years?"

"Touie," exclaimed Arthur, "don't be so direct! Poor James has just arrived, and we must give him time to settle in."

Watson sensed that Touie was a little uncomfortable with her husband's remarks. "It's fine, Arthur, I must face the music that I have not been the best correspondent since my dear Mary passed. Touie, I owe you and Arthur both some explanation of my activities."

"Thanks to my fellow lodger on Baker Street, I have been quite distracted from my feelings," James continued. "Holmes has allowed me to immerse myself into his cases, and it's been quite like the old days for me. Believe when I tell you that helping Holmes solve cases has been my saving grace. If I didn't have that, I don't know what would have become of me!"

"Well, I think I speak for both Touie and myself when I say how happy we are that you were under such good care, and that you have now returned to discuss a project that may have significant benefit to all concerned."

"Yes, the Baskerville case. It was indeed a case that I will never forget. The Devonshire moors, the family history stretching back generations, the apparent supernatural elements that Holmes had to unravel through pure logical analysis—it represented detective work at its most challenging."

Arthur leaned forward with obvious interest. "James, I've read through your case notes multiple times since our correspondence began, and I'm struck by the completeness of your documentation. Not just the investigative details, but the elements, the psychological insights into the various characters involved."

"It was a case that demanded such thoroughness," Watson replied, his voice growing stronger as he engaged with the material that had once brought him such professional satisfaction. "The family curse, the apparent supernatural manifestations, the complex relationships between the various suspects—Holmes's solution required understanding not just the physical evidence but the human motivations that had shaped events over decades."

Louisa set down her teacup with the careful attention of someone genuinely interested in the conversation. "Arthur mentioned that you played a particularly active role in this investigation—more collaborative than in some of your other cases?"

Watson nodded, feeling a stirring of the old professional pride. "Holmes allowed me to conduct independent research into the Baskerville family history while he focused on the more immediate aspects of the mystery. My conclusions about the family relationships proved essential to understanding Stapleton's motivations and methods."

Arthur's excitement was becoming increasingly evident. "That's precisely what makes this case so perfect for literary adaptation. It's not simply a matter of Holmes demonstrating his deductive abilities—it's a genuine partnership between two intelligent men approaching a complex problem from complementary directions."

"And the elements," Louisa added, "from what Arthur has described, the Devonshire setting provides exactly the kind of Gothic backdrop that makes detective fiction so compelling to readers."

Watson found himself smiling as he recalled the dramatic landscape that had provided the stage for one of Holmes's most brilliant investigations. "The Grimpen Mire, the ancient stone huts scattered across the moor, the Baskerville Hall with its family portraits and tragic history—all authentic details that enhanced rather than distracted from the logical progression of the investigation."

Arthur stood and moved to a side table where he had arranged several folders and notebooks. "James, I've been preparing extensively for this collaboration. Not just reviewing your case notes, but researching the historical background, the geographical details, even the natural history of Dartmoor to ensure complete accuracy."

He opened one of the folders, revealing maps, botanical illustrations, and what appeared to be genealogical charts. "If we're going to present this as authentic detective work—even disguised as fiction—then every detail must be absolutely correct."

Watson examined Arthur's research materials with growing appreciation for his friend's thoroughness. "This is impressive work, Arthur. You've clearly taken the project seriously."

"How could I not? James, this represents the opportunity to bring one of Holmes's finest investigations to the reading public, using source material that exceeds anything available to other detective fiction writers." Arthur's voice carried the enthusiasm that had always characterized his most successful literary ventures. "With your guidance on the investigative details and my literary experience, we could create something unprecedented."

Louisa watched both men with obvious satisfaction, recognizing the signs of a creative collaboration beginning to form. "James, what would you need from Arthur to feel confident about proceeding with this project?"

Watson considered the question carefully, understanding its importance for his own peace of mind as well as for the practical success of their venture. "Complete control over the investigative accuracy. Any literary embellishments Arthur wishes to make are acceptable, but the deductive methods, the evidence analysis, the logical progression of Holmes's reasoning—all of that must remain precisely as it occurred."

"Absolutely agreed," Arthur replied without hesitation. "The authenticity of the investigative content is what will set this story apart from conventional detective fiction."

"And the emotional elements?" Watson continued. "My own role in the investigation, the relationship between Holmes and myself, the human drama underlying the mystery—all of that must be handled with appropriate restraint."

Arthur nodded seriously. "James, I remember well how skillfully you and Mary contributed to the emotional authenticity of our earlier collaborations. I would want to honor that tradition while respecting the boundaries you've established."

"Mary would have been fascinated by this case. The family psychology, the way past events shaped present crimes, the Gothic atmosphere that enhanced rather than obscured the logical elements."

"Then you're willing to proceed?" Arthur asked, his voice carrying both hope and careful respect for Watson's emotional state.

Watson looked around the comfortable morning room, noting the evidence of domestic stability and creative success that Undershaw represented, feeling the warmth of friendship that had sustained their relationship through triumph and tragedy alike. For the first time in seven years, the prospect of serious literary work seemed not just bearable but genuinely appealing.

"Yes, Arthur," Watson said with growing conviction. "I believe I am ready to help bring the Hound of the Baskervilles to the reading public. It's a story that deserves to be told, and if anyone can tell it properly, it's you."

Arthur's face lit up with genuine joy, while Louisa clasped her hands together with obvious delight. "James, this is wonderful news. Arthur has been hoping for this opportunity since he first proposed it."

"And I have been hoping for the return of purpose to my professional life," Watson replied, surprised by his own emotional response to making this commitment. "The Baskerville case represented detective work at its finest. If we can present it properly, it might educate readers about authentic investigative methods while honoring the memory of what Holmes and I achieved together."

Arthur moved to the windows overlooking the Surrey countryside, his mind clearly already working on the practical aspects of their collaboration. "James, I propose we begin immediately. I'll prepare a detailed outline based on your case notes, which you can review and correct. Then I'll draft the opening chapters for your approval before proceeding with the complete manuscript."

"That seems an excellent approach," Watson agreed. "And Arthur—I want you to know how much I appreciate the sensitivity you've shown in proposing this project. The careful boundaries, the respect for my emotional limitations, the understanding that this might be our only collaboration."

"James," Arthur replied, turning back from the window with obvious sincerity, "your friendship and professional partnership have been among the greatest privileges of my life. To have the opportunity to work together again, even briefly, feels like an unexpected gift."

Remembering Mary Watson

November 30, 1900

Dr. James Watson stood on the Strand outside the familiar entrance to Simpson's, watching the evening bustle of London flow around him while he gathered the courage for what might prove to be either a significant step forward or a painful mistake. The gas lamps cast their warm glow against the November darkness, and the restaurant's windows beckoned with the same elegant promise they had offered eleven years ago when he and Mary had dined here with Arthur and Louisa in celebration of their literary triumph.

Eleven years. And today would have been his and Mary's twelfth wedding anniversary.

Watson checked his pocket watch—five minutes before seven o'clock, the time he had specified in his invitation to the Doyles. He had chosen this date deliberately, after weeks of careful consideration, understanding that facing this particular anniversary in this particular place might represent either healing or unbearable pain. But the completion of "The Hound of the Baskervilles" just three days prior had filled him with something he hadn't felt since Mary's death—a sense of meaningful accomplishment that seemed to demand acknowledgment.

The maitre d' recognized him immediately, a testament to Simpson's tradition of remembering distinguished guests even after years of absence. "Dr. Watson, how good to see you again. Your table is ready, and I believe your guests have just arrived."

Watson followed the familiar path through the elegant dining room, noting with bittersweet recognition the table where he and Mary had once sat with such happiness and anticipation. As he approached the reserved table near the window, he saw Arthur and Louisa Doyle rising to greet him, their faces showing the careful mixture of joy and sympathy that marked friends who understood the complex emotions of this occasion.

"James," Arthur said, clasping his hand warmly. "Thank you for suggesting this gathering. When I received your letter proposing dinner here tonight, I knew immediately that it was exactly the right thing to do."

Louisa embraced him with the gentle affection that had characterized their friendship for so many years. "My dear James, you look... well. More at peace than I've seen you in years."

Watson settled into his chair, glancing around the dining room where so many memories lingered like friendly ghosts. "I wasn't certain I would be able to go through with this evening until I actually arrived. But seeing you both here, in this place that holds such significance for all of us... it feels right."

Arthur gestured to the waiter for champagne, then paused to look at Watson with obvious concern. "James, if this becomes too difficult at any point, we can leave immediately. No one would think less of you."

"I know," Watson replied, his voice steady despite the emotion clearly visible in his eyes. "But Arthur, I need to do this. I need to honor Mary's memory while also acknowledging what we've accomplished together these past months. This seemed like the only appropriate way to mark both occasions."

The champagne arrived with the same ceremony Watson remembered from their previous celebration, the cork popping with a sound that seemed to bridge the years between past joy and present remembrance. As the golden liquid filled their glasses, all three friends felt the weight of time and change, but also the enduring strength of affection that had sustained them through triumph and tragedy alike.

"To Mary," Arthur said quietly, raising his glass with the solemnity the moment demanded. "To her memory, her love, and the happiness she brought to all who knew her."

They drank in reverent silence, each lost in their own memories of the remarkable woman who had brought such warmth and intelligence to their collaborative work and personal friendships. Watson set down his glass with hands that trembled only slightly, his composure holding despite the profound emotion of the moment.

"Mary would have been pleased that we completed the Baskerville book," Watson said eventually, his voice carrying a mixture of sadness and satisfaction. "She always believed in the importance of our work—the value of bringing authentic detective methods to the reading public."

Louisa leaned forward with gentle interest. "James, I hope you don't mind my asking, but what made you decide to suggest this particular gathering? The anniversary, this location—it must have required considerable courage to face such powerful associations."

Watson was quiet for a moment, gathering his thoughts with the same care he had once applied to documenting Holmes's most complex cases. "Three nights ago, when I read through Arthur's completed manuscript of 'The Hound of the Baskervilles' for the final time, I realized something that surprised me. For the first time since Mary's death, I felt genuinely proud of something I had accomplished."

He paused, looking out the window at the London evening. "Not just satisfied that a task was completed, but proud of the quality of what we had created together. The old feeling of professional fulfillment, of having contributed something valuable to the world—it was still there, waiting to be rediscovered."

Arthur smiled with obvious pleasure. "James, that manuscript represents some of the finest work either of us has ever produced. Your guidance on the investigative details, your insights into Holmes's character, your suggestions for enhancement—all essential to the book's success."

"But more than that," Watson continued, "I realized that working on the Baskerville case had allowed me to honor my memories of collaborating with you while also honoring my memories of Mary. She was so much a part of our literary partnership, so supportive of the work we were doing."

Watson's voice grew stronger as he continued. "This evening—dining here on our anniversary, celebrating the completion of our book—isn't about forgetting Mary or moving beyond her memory. It's about integrating that memory into a life that can still find purpose and meaning."

Louisa felt tears gathering in her eyes at her friend's words. "James, that's perhaps the most beautiful thing I've ever heard you say. Mary would be so proud of the man you've become through this terrible trial."

The waiter approached with menus, but Arthur waved him away with a gentle gesture. "We'll have the Beef Wellington, prepared tableside as before. This evening calls for the same ceremony we enjoyed during our last celebration here."

As their meal was prepared with the theatrical flourish that made Simpson's famous, conversation flowed between memories of Mary and excitement about the book that would soon introduce the world to one of Holmes's most adventures. Watson found himself able to speak of his wife with affection rather than just grief, sharing stories of her insights into their collaborative process and her enthusiasm for the authentic detective methods they were documenting.

"Do you remember," Watson said as they savored the perfectly prepared beef, "how Mary suggested that the Sign of Four story should begin with her visit to Holmes rather than with background exposition? Arthur, that insight transformed the entire structure of the narrative."

"Indeed it did," Arthur agreed warmly. "Mary had remarkable literary instincts. Her contributions to our work were invaluable, even if the world never knew the extent of her involvement."

"She would have been fascinated by the Baskerville case," Watson continued, his voice growing more animated. "The Gothic atmosphere, the family psychology, the way Holmes stripped away layers of superstition to reveal scientific truth. Mary always appreciated stories that honored both rational analysis and human emotion."

As the evening progressed, Watson found himself experiencing something he hadn't felt since that terrible May day seven years ago—the ability to speak of Mary with joy rather than just sorrow, to remember their shared happiness without being overwhelmed by its loss.

"James," Louisa said as they lingered over their dessert, "may I ask what your plans are now? Will you consider future literary projects, or was the Baskerville book truly the single collaboration you originally envisioned?"

Watson considered the question carefully, recognizing its importance for his own future as well as for Arthur's publishing plans. "I'm not ready to commit to regular collaboration—that level of intensive work might still be beyond my emotional capabilities. But if another exceptional case presented itself, if Arthur found material that truly excited his literary imagination..." He smiled slightly. "I think I might be open to the possibility."

Arthur felt a surge of hope at these words, though he was careful not to press for more specific commitments. "James, whatever you decide about future projects, I want you to know that these past months of working together have been among the most satisfying of my literary career. Not just because of the quality of the work we've produced, but because of what it represents—proof that friendship and professional partnership can survive even the most devastating trials."

As the evening drew to a close, Watson felt a profound sense of completion—not the completion that comes from ending something, but the completion that comes from integrating past and present into a sustainable whole. He had honored Mary's memory, celebrated their literary achievement, and discovered that grief and renewed purpose could coexist without diminishing each other.

"Thank you both," Watson said as they prepared to leave Simpson's, "for understanding why this evening was necessary and for helping me mark both an ending and a beginning."

"Thank you," Arthur replied, "for having the courage to suggest it. This has been one of the most meaningful celebrations of my life."

As he walked through the London streets toward Baker Street, Watson felt Mary's presence not as a source of pain but as a blessing that would accompany him whatever paths his life might take.

Meeting with The Strand

March 17, 1901

The afternoon post arrived at the Doyle residence with unusual ceremony, delivered personally by the local postmaster rather than the regular carrier—a distinction reserved for correspondence bearing the most prestigious London addresses. Arthur Conan Doyle looked up from his historical research with mild curiosity as Louisa entered his study carrying an envelope that bore the distinctive letterhead of The Strand Magazine.

"Arthur," she said, her voice carrying the excitement that had characterized all their recent correspondence regarding literary matters, "this appears to be rather more formal than their usual communications."

Arthur accepted the envelope with interest, noting immediately the quality of the paper and the embossed letterhead that spoke of official business rather than routine editorial correspondence. Since submitting the completed manuscript of "The Hound of the Baskervilles" in December, he had received several brief acknowledgments from The Strand's offices, but nothing that suggested the kind of serious negotiation this envelope promised.

He broke the seal carefully and unfolded what proved to be a formal invitation written in the precise handwriting of a professional secretary:

Dr. Arthur Conan Doyle is respectfully requested to attend a meeting with Mr. Herbert Greenhough Smith, Editor of The Strand Magazine, at our offices at 8 Exeter Street, Strand, London, at 2:30 PM on Tuesday, March 19th, 1901, to discuss matters of mutual professional interest regarding the publication of 'The Hound of the Baskervilles.' Luncheon will be provided. Please confirm your attendance at your earliest convenience. —Miss Dorothy Richardson, Secretary to Mr. Smith

Arthur read the invitation twice, his expression growing more thoughtful with each line. "Touie, this is quite formal for a routine editorial meeting.

'Matters of mutual professional interest' suggests they have specific proposals to discuss."

Louisa moved to read over her husband's shoulder, her own experience with literary business making her immediately alert to the implications. "The timing suggests they've made their decision about publication. But Arthur, why request a formal meeting rather than simply sending their offer by post?"

"An excellent question," Arthur replied, already moving to his writing desk to compose an acceptance. "Perhaps the terms are complex enough to require detailed discussion. Or perhaps they want to negotiate additional commitments beyond the single book."

Arthur paused in his writing, struck by a sudden concern. "Touie, I hope they understand that this is meant to be an isolated publication. I was quite clear in my original correspondence that there would be no commitment to future Holmes stories."

"I'm sure you were, dear. But you know how persistent publishers can be when they sense a profitable opportunity." Louisa's tone carried gentle warning. "You'll need to be very firm about the limitations you've established with James."

Arthur completed his acceptance with characteristic efficiency, confirming his attendance while privately hoping that The Strand's invitation represented enthusiasm for the Baskerville story rather than pressure for expanded collaboration. Whatever their intentions, he would need to balance their commercial interests with the careful boundaries he and James had established.

The next day, the morning train from Portsmouth to London had been punctual, and Arthur found himself walking through the familiar streets of the Strand district with time to spare before his scheduled meeting. The March weather was crisp but pleasant, and London seemed to pulse with the energy that had always invigorated him during his visits to the capital.

At precisely 2:30 PM, Arthur presented himself at the offices of The Strand Magazine at 8 Exeter Street, a substantial building that spoke of commercial success and literary prestige. The reception area was elegantly appointed with comfortable furniture and framed covers from notable issues, including several that featured Arthur's original Holmes stories from their first series.

"Dr. Doyle," said the young woman at the reception desk, rising with obvious recognition. "I'm Miss Richardson, Mr. Smith's secretary. He's expecting you and asked me to bring you up immediately."

Arthur followed her through corridors lined with artistic renderings and photographs related to the magazine's most successful publications, noting with satisfaction that the Holmes stories were prominently featured among their showcased achievements. The building hummed with the efficient activity of a thriving publication, and Arthur felt the familiar excitement that accompanied serious literary business.

Herbert Greenhough Smith's office occupied a corner of the building's third floor, its tall windows providing excellent light and a commanding view of the busy Strand below. Smith himself proved to be a man of middle years with the keen, intelligent expression Arthur had come to associate with successful editors—someone capable of balancing commercial considerations with genuine literary appreciation.

"Dr. Doyle!" Smith exclaimed, rising from behind an impressive mahogany desk to greet his visitor. "How good of you to come to London on such short notice. Please, sit down. I trust your journey was comfortable?"

Arthur settled into the offered chair, noting that Smith's desk was dominated by what appeared to be the complete manuscript of "The Hound of the Baskervilles," marked with numerous annotations and editorial notes. "Quite comfortable, thank you. I confess myself curious about the formal nature of this invitation. Your message suggested matters of considerable importance."

Smith's eyes lit up with obvious enthusiasm. "Indeed they are, Dr. Doyle. Indeed they are." He gestured toward the manuscript with the reverence typically reserved for precious artifacts. "I have read your Baskerville story three times since receiving it, and I can state without exaggeration that it represents some of the finest detective fiction ever submitted to this magazine."

Arthur felt a surge of professional pride tempered by curiosity about Smith's specific intentions. "I'm gratified by your response. The story is based on exceptionally detailed source material, which I believe contributes to its authenticity."

"Authenticity is precisely the word," Smith agreed, leaning forward with growing excitement. "Dr. Doyle, this story possesses a quality that sets it apart from all other detective fiction—a depth of investigative detail and conviction that makes the fantastic elements completely believable."

Smith rose and moved to the window, his manner suggesting a man preparing to make a significant proposal. "The question before us is how best to present this remarkable work to the reading public. Initially, we had assumed it would be published as a complete book, but upon reflection, I believe we have a far more exciting opportunity."

Arthur raised an eyebrow with interest. "What sort of opportunity?"

Smith turned back to face him, his expression now showing the calculated enthusiasm of a successful businessman who had identified a particularly profitable venture. "Serial publication, Dr. Doyle. Nine monthly installments, beginning with our August 1901 issue and concluding with April 1902."

Arthur felt a moment of genuine surprise. "Serial publication? I hadn't considered that approach for a work of this length."

"Consider the advantages," Smith continued, warming to his theme. "Rather than a single publication event, we create nine months of sustained reader engagement. Each installment builds anticipation for the next, creating exactly the kind of regular readership that made your original Holmes series so successful."

Smith returned to his desk and withdrew a carefully prepared schedule. "August 1901 through April 1902—nine months of Sherlock Holmes returning to The Strand Magazine. Our circulation figures for those months would undoubtedly exceed anything we've achieved since your original series concluded in 1893."

Arthur studied the proposed schedule, recognizing the commercial logic while feeling slightly overwhelmed by the magnitude of what Smith was suggesting. "Nine months of Holmes stories... that would indeed represent a significant literary event."

"Precisely!" Smith's enthusiasm was now undisguised. "Dr. Doyle, the public has mourned Holmes's death for over seven years. His return, even temporarily, would be the publishing sensation of the decade. But serial publication would maximize both the literary impact and the commercial potential."

Arthur was quiet for a moment, considering the implications not just for the story but for the reading public that had never stopped hoping for Holmes's resurrection. "Mr. Smith, I can see the appeal of your approach. The story is certainly substantial enough to support serial publication, and the format would indeed create sustained reader interest."

"Then you'll agree to the serialization?" Smith asked hopefully.

"I believe I will," Arthur replied, though his tone carried a note of caution. "However, I must emphasize once again that this represents an isolated publication. The Baskerville story can be serialized as you suggest, but there must be no expectation of additional Holmes material."

Smith's expression shifted slightly, and Arthur recognized the look of a man preparing to broach his primary objective. "About that, Dr. Doyle... surely, given the extraordinary public response that this serialization will undoubtedly generate, you might reconsider your position regarding future Holmes stories?"

Arthur felt the familiar tension that accompanied discussions of expanded literary commitments. "Mr. Smith, I was quite explicit in my original correspondence. 'The Hound of the Baskervilles' represents a unique opportunity based on previously unavailable material. There simply isn't comparable documentation for additional stories."

"But surely," Smith pressed, "the success of this publication will demonstrate the continued viability of the Holmes character? The financial rewards alone..."

"Mr. Smith," Arthur interrupted gently but firmly, "I appreciate your commercial enthusiasm, but the circumstances that made the Baskerville story possible are genuinely unique. I cannot commit to future Holmes publications because I lack the source material necessary to maintain the quality standards this story represents."

Smith leaned back in his chair, clearly disappointed but not entirely discouraged. "I understand your position, Dr. Doyle, though I hope you'll keep an open mind. If additional source material should become available—if circumstances should change—I trust you would consider approaching us first?"

Arthur nodded diplomatically. "If such circumstances were to arise, The Strand would certainly receive first consideration. You've been remarkably supportive of my work over the years."

"Excellent. Then shall we proceed with the serialization as outlined? Nine monthly installments, beginning with August 1901?" Smith's manner became more businesslike as he moved toward specific arrangements.

"Yes," Arthur agreed, feeling both excitement and relief at having successfully navigated the discussion of future commitments. "I believe the serial format will serve the story well. Each installment can end with appropriate dramatic tension while building toward the final resolution."

Smith smiled with obvious satisfaction. "Wonderful. I'll have our contracts department prepare the necessary agreements. The terms, as you might expect, will be quite generous—considerably more favorable than your original Holmes series, reflecting both inflation and the extraordinary nature of Holmes's return to print."

As their meeting concluded with handshakes and promises of prompt contract preparation, Arthur felt the complex satisfaction of having achieved his immediate goals while successfully protecting the boundaries he had established with James. The Baskerville story would receive the publication treatment it deserved, reaching thousands of readers hungry for authentic detective fiction, while maintaining the limited scope that made the collaboration possible.

The Hound is a Hit

August 15, 1901

The spacious drawing room of the Langham Hotel had been transformed into an elegant venue for the Ladies' Charitable Society's fundraising afternoon, with tasteful arrangements of late summer flowers adorning the tables where London's most distinguished women had gathered to support the organization's mission of providing meals for the city's homeless population. Louisa Doyle moved gracefully between the groups of volunteers, her organizational skills and genuine compassion having made her a valued member of the society despite her Portsmouth residence requiring periodic travel to London for their events.

At forty-four, Louisa had grown more confident in these social settings, her years as the wife of a successful author having provided her with the poise necessary to navigate conversations with women whose husbands occupied positions of considerable influence in British society. Today's gathering represented one of the charity's most important fundraising efforts, and Louisa had volunteered to help coordinate the silent auction that would provide a significant portion of their annual budget.

"Mrs. Doyle," called a familiar voice from across the room, "might I have a word with you when you have a moment?"

Louisa turned to see Mrs. Catherine Pemberton approaching with obvious purpose, her face bright with an excitement that seemed to transcend the charitable enthusiasm that typically characterized these gatherings. Mrs. Pemberton was the wife of Sir Harold Pemberton, a prominent Member of Parliament whose support for social welfare legislation had made him well-known among charitable organizations, and her presence at these events always lent additional prestige to their endeavors.

"Mrs. Pemberton," Louisa replied warmly, setting aside the auction catalog she had been reviewing. "How lovely to see you again. I hope you're pleased with the turnout for today's event?"

266

"Indeed I am—the response has been most gratifying," Mrs. Pemberton said, then leaned forward with the conspiratorial manner of someone sharing particularly delightful news. "But Mrs. Doyle, I simply must tell you how absolutely thrilled I am about your husband's latest literary achievement!"

Louisa felt a moment of pleasant surprise mixed with curiosity. "Oh? Which achievement did you have in mind?"

Mrs. Pemberton's eyes sparkled with enthusiasm. "Why, the return of Sherlock Holmes, of course! I purchased the August issue of The Strand Magazine yesterday afternoon, and I've already read the first installment of 'The Hound of the Baskervilles' twice. It's absolutely magnificent!"

Louisa felt her pulse quicken with a mixture of pride and careful caution. The first installment of Arthur's serialized story had been published just over a week ago, but she hadn't yet heard any direct public response to Holmes's literary resurrection. "I'm delighted that you enjoyed it, Mrs. Pemberton."

"Enjoyed it? My dear woman, I was completely captivated!" Mrs. Pemberton's voice carried the genuine enthusiasm of a devoted reader. "When I saw the announcement that Sherlock Holmes was returning to The Strand Magazine, I could hardly believe it. After eight years of mourning his death at those dreadful Reichenbach Falls, to have him back again..."

Mrs. Pemberton paused, her expression growing more animated. "And the story itself is extraordinary. The mysterious death of Sir Charles Baskerville, the legend of the spectral hound, that wonderfully opening on the Devonshire moors—it's everything one could hope for in a Holmes adventure."

Louisa found herself genuinely moved by the woman's enthusiasm while simultaneously aware of the complex circumstances that had made the story possible. "Arthur worked very hard to ensure the story would meet readers' expectations."

"Oh, he's exceeded them completely!" Mrs. Pemberton exclaimed. "Mrs. Doyle, you must understand—my husband and I have been devoted readers of the Holmes stories since 'A Study in Scarlet' first appeared. We have the complete collection, and we've read them multiple times. But this new story... there's something special about it, something that feels even more authentic than the earlier adventures."

Louisa felt a moment of pride in James's contribution to the story's authenticity, though she could hardly explain to Mrs. Pemberton the real source of that convincing detail. "I'll be sure to convey your appreciation to Arthur. He'll be tremendously pleased to know the story has found such an enthusiastic reception."

"Mrs. Doyle, I hope you don't mind my saying so, but this story is absolutely the talk of London society," Mrs. Pemberton continued, her voice dropping to a more confidential tone. "At Lady Thornton's dinner party last evening, the conversation was dominated by speculation about how Holmes could have survived the Reichenbach Falls. Several guests had quite elaborate theories!"

Louisa smiled, amused by the irony of readers developing complex explanations for a resurrection that hadn't actually occurred. "And what did you think of their theories?"

"Ingenious but unnecessary," Mrs. Pemberton replied with obvious satisfaction. "I noticed immediately that The Strand's introduction states quite clearly that this is an adventure from before the Reichenbach Falls events. A 'previously undocumented case,' they called it. Quite clever of your husband to find such material after all these years."

"Indeed," Louisa agreed, grateful for Arthur's foresight in establishing that framework for the story's publication.

Mrs. Pemberton leaned closer, her expression becoming more earnest. "Mrs. Doyle, dare I hope that this story represents the beginning of Holmes's permanent return? Surely, if your husband has access to additional undocumented cases..."

Here Louisa felt the weight of the careful boundaries that had made even this single collaboration possible. "I'm afraid Arthur views this as a special, isolated publication rather than the beginning of a new series. The circumstances that made it possible were quite unique."

Mrs. Pemberton's face showed obvious disappointment, though her enthusiasm remained undimmed. "Well, I suppose we must be grateful for what we have. Though I confess, Mrs. Doyle, that if I could convey to your husband the joy his work brings to readers like myself and my husband..."

"I shall certainly tell him about your response," Louisa assured her. "Arthur always appreciates hearing from readers who understand what he's trying to achieve in his detective fiction."

As Mrs. Pemberton was called away to assist with another aspect of the charity event, Louisa found herself reflecting on the remarkable public enthusiasm for Holmes's return. She had known, intellectually, that the character remained popular despite his literary death eight years ago. But hearing Mrs. Pemberton's genuine excitement, learning that the story was "the talk of London society," seeing the authentic delight of a devoted reader—all of this brought home the magnitude of what Arthur and James had accomplished.

The afternoon continued with its charitable focus, but Louisa found herself noticing how many conversations seemed to touch, at least briefly, on the new Holmes story. At the tea service, she overheard two women discussing their plans to purchase the August Strand as soon as they could locate copies. During the silent auction, another volunteer mentioned that her husband had expressed frustration at being unable to find the magazine at his usual vendor, as all copies had sold out by midday.

As the event concluded and Louisa prepared for her journey back to Portsmouth, Mrs. Pemberton approached once more, this time accompanied by two other ladies whose faces showed the same eager excitement.

"Mrs. Doyle," Mrs. Pemberton said, "I've been telling Mrs. Fairfax and Lady Morrison about your husband's new Holmes story. They're both devoted readers who've been hoping for exactly such a development."

"Mrs. Doyle," said Mrs. Fairfax, a distinguished woman with silver hair and keen eyes, "I wonder if you might tell us—when can we expect the next installment? The August issue ends with such dramatic tension that my husband has been quite impossible, demanding to know what happens next!"

Louisa smiled at the woman's obvious frustration with the serial format's built-in suspense. "The September issue should be available within the next week or two. Arthur is quite pleased with how the story develops in the coming chapters."

"Excellent!" Lady Morrison interjected. "My book club has decided to follow the serial month by month—it's become quite the social event, discussing each installment as it appears."

As Louisa finally extracted herself from these enthusiastic conversations and made her way to the railway station, she felt a profound sense of satisfaction mixed with amazement. The public response to Holmes's return was exceeding even Arthur's most optimistic expectations, and the story was clearly resonating with readers in ways that justified all the careful work he and James had invested in its preparation.

August 25, 1901 - Portsmouth (Evening)

The evening train from London had been punctual, and Louisa arrived at the Portsmouth station to find Arthur waiting with the eager expression that had characterized all his recent interactions related to the Baskerville publication. The past week had brought a steady stream of correspondence from The Strand Magazine, sharing circulation figures and reader response that confirmed the story's immediate success.

"Touie!" Arthur called out, approaching with obvious pleasure. "How was the charity event? I trust the fundraising went well?"

"Very well indeed," Louisa replied as Arthur helped her into their carriage. "But Arthur, you'll never guess what dominated the conversation among London's most distinguished ladies."

Arthur raised an eyebrow with interest. "I suspect I can guess, actually. Has the first installment of the Baskerville story reached society circles?"

"Reached them?" Louisa laughed, settling beside her husband as their carriage began the familiar journey home. "Arthur, it's become the sensation of London society. Mrs. Pemberton—Sir Harold's wife—approached me specifically to express her delight with Holmes's return. She's read the first installment twice and can hardly wait for the September issue."

Arthur felt a surge of satisfaction mixed with slight amazement. "Really? She mentioned it specifically?"

"More than mentioned—she was absolutely effusive in her praise. Called it 'magnificent' and said it feels even more authentic than the original Holmes stories." Louisa's eyes sparkled with amusement. "She also mentioned that it was the primary topic of conversation at Lady Thornton's dinner party, with guests developing elaborate theories about how Holmes survived Reichenbach Falls."

Arthur chuckled at this development. "I hope you explained the actual framework—that it's presented as occurring before the Reichenbach events?"

"I did, and she appreciated the elegance of that approach. But Arthur, the enthusiasm was remarkable. Multiple women mentioned having difficulty finding copies of The Strand because they were selling out so quickly. One lady said her book club is following the serial month by month as a social event."

Arthur leaned back in the carriage seat, processing this news with obvious pleasure. "Touie, when I agreed to this collaboration with James,

I hoped the story would find an appreciative audience. But this level of public enthusiasm..."

"It suggests that the public's affection for Holmes has only grown stronger during his eight-year absence," Louisa observed. "Mrs. Pemberton mentioned that she and her husband have been devoted readers since 'A Study in Scarlet' and have read the complete collection multiple times. The character has clearly maintained his hold on readers' imaginations."

Arthur was quiet for a moment, contemplating the implications of such sustained public interest. "The irony is remarkable, isn't it? I killed Holmes to escape what felt like creative imprisonment, and his death only made readers more devoted to his memory."

"And now his return, even temporarily, has created exactly the kind of literary sensation that any author would dream of achieving." Louisa studied her husband's profile in the carriage's dim light. "How do you feel about that, Arthur? Does the public enthusiasm change your perspective on future Holmes stories?"

Arthur considered her question carefully. "It's gratifying, certainly, to know that the work is reaching such an appreciative audience. But Touie, the circumstances that made this story possible remain unique. James agreed to provide guidance for this single collaboration, with very clear boundaries about not committing to regular publication."

"And you respect those boundaries completely?"

"Absolutely. James has been through enough trauma without feeling pressured to resume the intensive collaborative work that our original series required." Arthur's voice grew more serious. "Besides, the authentic quality that readers are responding to comes directly from James's detailed documentation. Without his investigative insights and character understanding, any future Holmes stories would lack exactly what makes the Baskerville story so compelling."

As their carriage approached the familiar streets of Portsmouth, Louisa felt a complex mixture of pride in her husband's success and appreciation for his loyalty to the friendship that had made it possible. The public enthusiasm for Holmes's return was undeniable, and the financial rewards would be substantial. But Arthur's commitment to honoring the boundaries James had established spoke well of both his character and his understanding of what their collaboration truly represented.

"Then you're content with this being Holmes's only return to publication?" Louisa asked.

Arthur smiled, though his expression carried a hint of wistfulness. "Content with giving Holmes the sendoff he deserves—a story worthy of his reputation, reaching an audience that has never stopped appreciating his methods. If this proves to be his final adventure, at least it will be a magnificent one."

The public's delight with Holmes's return vindicated all the careful work Arthur and James had invested in the story, while the story's limited scope honored the boundaries that had made such collaboration possible.

Mycroft's Endorsement

August 28, 1901

Mid-October had brought an unexpected chill to London, and Dr. James Watson found himself grateful for the warmth of the familiar sitting room at 111 Baker Street as he reviewed the morning correspondence. Among the usual collection of bills and professional journals lay an envelope that immediately commanded his attention—heavy cream paper bearing the distinctive letterhead of the Diogenes Club, addressed in the precise handwriting he recognized as belonging to Mycroft Holmes.

Watson opened the envelope with some curiosity, as communication from Sherlock's elder brother was infrequent and typically indicated matters of unusual significance. The message was characteristically brief:

"Dr. Watson—I would be grateful if you and my brother could call upon me at the Diogenes Club this afternoon at three o'clock. A matter has arisen that requires discrete discussion among the three of us. The club's private meeting room has been reserved for our use. —M. Holmes"

Holmes emerged from his bedroom at that moment, already dressed for what appeared to be a day of investigation, and Watson handed him the note without comment. Holmes read it with the same methodical attention he applied to all correspondence, his sharp gray eyes revealing a mixture of curiosity and slight concern.

"Mycroft rarely requests meetings without significant cause," Holmes observed, setting down the letter with obvious thoughtfulness. "And the formal tone suggests official rather than familial business."

Watson nodded, having reached the same conclusion. "Do you have any notion what might prompt such a summons?"

Holmes moved to the window, looking out at the busy Baker Street morning with the distant expression Watson had learned to associate with his friend's consideration of complex possibilities. "Several matters come to mind, though I confess none seem to justify the formal arrangements Mycroft has specified."

"Current cases you're working on?"

"Nothing that would typically interest Mycroft's department. The Whitehall burglary is purely criminal, the missing racehorse involves no government connections..." Holmes paused, turning back to Watson with a more serious expression. "Though there is one development that might have attracted official attention."

Watson raised an eyebrow with interest. "Oh?"

"The public response to the Baskerville story has been rather more... prominent than we anticipated when Arthur first proposed the collaboration." Holmes's tone carried a note of careful consideration. "Mycroft's position requires him to monitor anything that captures significant public attention, particularly matters that might affect public perception of investigative methods."

Watson felt a moment of unease at this observation. "You think the government has concerns about the Holmes stories?"

"Not concerns, necessarily. But awareness, certainly." Holmes returned to his chair with characteristic efficiency. "Watson, when a fictional detective captures the public imagination as thoroughly as these stories have managed, it inevitably affects how people think about real criminal investigation."

"And that would interest Mycroft because...?"

Holmes smiled slightly at his friend's innocence regarding the complexities of government oversight. "Because public opinion influences everything from jury selection to police funding to legislative priorities. When thousands of readers develop expectations about investigative methods based on stories in The Strand Magazine..."

"Those expectations affect actual criminal cases," Watson finished, understanding the implications immediately.

"Precisely. Though whether Mycroft views this as beneficial or problematic remains to be determined."

The afternoon journey to the Diogenes Club on Pall Mall took Watson and Holmes through the heart of London's governmental district, past the imposing facades of buildings where the Empire's most significant decisions were made daily. Watson had visited the club once before, years earlier, and remembered it as an institution dedicated to the pursuit of absolute silence—a place where London's most influential men could read, think, and conduct discrete business without the intrusions of ordinary social interaction.

They were met at the club's entrance by a porter whose manner suggested he had been specifically instructed regarding their arrival. Without a word, he led them through corridors lined with portraits of distinguished members and past reading rooms where middle-aged gentlemen sat in complete silence, absorbed in newspapers and official documents.

The private meeting room to which they were escorted was comfortably appointed with leather chairs arranged around a small table, its tall windows providing both adequate light and sufficient privacy for confidential discussion. Mycroft Holmes was already present, his considerable frame settled into the largest chair with the deliberate composure that characterized all his movements.

At forty-six, Mycroft Holmes had grown even more substantial than Watson remembered, his presence filling the room with the authority of someone accustomed to wielding significant governmental power. His keen gray eyes—so similar to his brother's but somehow more calculating—immediately fixed upon Watson with an intensity that suggested this meeting concerned him specifically.

"Doctor Watson," Mycroft said, rising with the careful courtesy that marked his interactions with those he respected. "Thank you for accepting my invitation. I trust the journey from Baker Street was comfortable?"

Watson accepted Mycroft's offered handshake, noting the firm grip that spoke of a man who had not allowed sedentary work to diminish his essential vitality. "Quite comfortable, thank you, Mr. Holmes. Though I confess myself curious about the occasion for this meeting."

Mycroft gestured for both men to be seated, his movements deliberate and purposeful. When they were settled, he fixed Watson with a direct gaze that seemed to penetrate any pretense or evasion.

"Doctor Watson," Mycroft began, his voice carrying the measured authority of someone accustomed to discussing matters of genuine importance, "I hear of Sherlock everywhere!"

Watson felt his pulse quicken at these words, immediately understanding their implication. Mycroft's emphasis on "Sherlock" rather than "Holmes" suggested specific knowledge rather than general observation, and his direct address to Watson rather than his brother confirmed what Watson had long suspected—that their carefully maintained fiction had not deceived everyone.

"I'm not sure I understand your meaning," Watson replied carefully, though his expression undoubtedly revealed his comprehension of Mycroft's words.

Mycroft smiled slightly, the expression carrying both amusement and respect. "Doctor Watson, my position requires me to monitor developments that might affect public perception of governmental institutions, including law enforcement and criminal investigation. When stories appearing in The Strand Magazine demonstrate investigative techniques of unusual sophistication and authenticity..."

Holmes leaned forward with obvious interest. "Mycroft, are you suggesting that—"

"I am suggesting nothing, Sherlock. I am stating facts." Mycroft's tone carried the precision Watson had learned to associate with men who dealt in sensitive information. "The stories appearing under Arthur Conan Doyle's byline demonstrate knowledge of investigative procedures, criminal psychology, and forensic methodology that far exceeds what any novelist could achieve through research alone."

Watson felt the weight of exposure settling upon him, though Mycroft's manner suggested curiosity rather than disapproval. "And you conclude from this that...?"

"That Dr. Doyle has access to source material of exceptional quality and authenticity," Mycroft replied diplomatically. "Material that could only be provided by someone with extensive firsthand experience of criminal investigation at the highest levels."

Holmes studied his brother's face with the analytical attention he typically reserved for complex evidence. "Mycroft, what exactly are you saying?"

"I am saying that the public's enthusiasm for these stories reflects their recognition—conscious or otherwise—that they are reading accounts of actual investigative work rather than mere fiction." Mycroft leaned forward slightly, his expression growing more serious. "And I am saying that this represents a development of considerable positive value."

Watson looked up with surprise. "Positive value?"

Mycroft nodded emphatically. "Doctor Watson, consider the alternatives. The public's understanding of criminal investigation has historically been shaped by sensational novels that bear no resemblance to actual detective work, by newspaper accounts that emphasize drama over methodology, and by personal experiences with local constables who may lack advanced training."

He paused, allowing this observation to register before continuing. "Now, suddenly, thousands of readers are being exposed to authentic investigative techniques presented as engaging entertainment. They are learning to appreciate logical deduction, scientific methodology, and systematic analysis of evidence."

Holmes raised an eyebrow with growing interest. "And you view this education as beneficial?"

"Enormously beneficial," Mycroft replied without hesitation. "Informed citizens make better jurors, more supportive voters, and more cooperative witnesses. When the public understands and appreciates proper investigative methods, it strengthens every aspect of law enforcement."

Watson felt his understanding of the situation shifting as he grasped the implications of Mycroft's analysis. "You're saying that the Holmes stories serve an educational function that benefits actual criminal investigation?"

"Precisely. Though I suspect that was not their original intention." Mycroft's keen gaze returned to Watson with obvious respect. "Doctor Watson, regardless of how these stories are produced or who provides their source material, they represent the most effective education in investigative methodology that the British public has ever received."

Mycroft stood and moved to the window, his substantial frame silhouetted against the afternoon light as he continued his analysis. "Moreover, the timing could not be more advantageous. Public confidence in law enforcement has been shaken by several highly publicized investigative failures. These stories demonstrate that criminal cases can be solved through intelligent application of scientific principles rather than mere luck or intuition."

"And you believe this strengthens public support for law enforcement?" Watson asked.

"I believe it strengthens public understanding of what effective law enforcement requires," Mycroft replied, turning back to face them. "Educated citizens are more likely to support adequate funding for police training, more willing to provide detailed witness statements, more capable of serving effectively on juries."

Holmes had been listening with growing appreciation for his brother's perspective. "Mycroft, are you suggesting that these stories serve an unofficial educational function that benefits government interests?"

"I am suggesting that they serve an official educational function, whether intended or not." Mycroft's voice carried a note of finality that indicated he had reached the primary purpose of their meeting. "Which brings me to my request."

Watson felt his attention sharpen as Mycroft returned to his chair with obvious purpose.

"Doctor Watson," Mycroft said, addressing him directly, "if there are additional stories that could be shared with the public—additional case material that could be adapted for publication—then I believe you should work with Dr. Doyle and produce them."

Watson stared at Mycroft in amazement. "You're encouraging me to continue the collaboration?"

"I am suggesting that such collaboration serves important public interests," Mycroft replied carefully. "The educational value of authentic detective fiction far outweighs any concerns about... unconventional publishing arrangements."

Holmes leaned forward with obvious curiosity. "Mycroft, are you speaking in an official capacity?"

Mycroft's expression grew more formal. "I am speaking as someone whose responsibilities include monitoring developments that affect public welfare and governmental effectiveness. The Holmes stories represent such a development."

He paused, then continued with the measured authority that characterized his most serious communications. "Doctor Watson, you may consider this conversation as indicating that appropriate governmental authorities view your literary collaboration as serving valuable public purposes. Any concerns you might have about the... irregular nature of your involvement can be set aside."

Watson felt the significance of this statement settling over him like an unexpected benediction. For years, he had wondered whether their deception of the reading public was ethically justified. Now, the highest levels of government were suggesting that it served essential educational functions.

"Mr. Holmes," Watson said carefully, "are you saying that the government approves of our approach to presenting authentic detective work as fiction?"

"I am saying that results matter more than methods," Mycroft replied with diplomatic precision. "If fictional accounts of detective work educate the public more effectively than official reports or academic treatises, then such accounts serve legitimate governmental interests."

Mycroft stood, indicating that their meeting was approaching its conclusion. "Doctor Watson, I hope you will give serious consideration to expanding your collaboration with Dr. Doyle. The public appetite for these stories appears inexhaustible, and the educational benefits are demonstrable."

"And if I agree to additional collaborations?"

"Then you may proceed with confidence that your work serves purposes that extend far beyond mere entertainment." Mycroft's tone carried the weight of official blessing. "The government of Her Majesty appreciates citizens who contribute to public education and law enforcement effectiveness, regardless of the methods they employ."

As Watson and Holmes prepared to leave the Diogenes Club, both felt the profound significance of what they had just experienced. The careful fiction they had maintained for so many years had been penetrated by someone whose position required him to understand such matters, but rather than exposure bringing consequences, it had brought encouragement and official recognition of their work's value.

"Watson," Holmes said as they emerged onto Pall Mall, "I believe Mycroft has just provided you with the most extraordinary endorsement any writer could hope to receive."

Watson nodded, still processing the implications of Mycroft's words. "Holmes, do you think he's right about the educational value of our stories?"

"I think Mycroft understands the relationship between public opinion and governmental effectiveness better than anyone in London," Holmes replied. "If he believes our collaboration serves important public purposes, then it undoubtedly does."

A Letter from Ann Hunter

The September morning had brought the first hint of autumn to the Surrey hills, and Arthur Conan Doyle sat in his study at Undershaw reviewing the morning correspondence with the satisfaction that had become characteristic of his recent days. The second installment of "The Hound of the Baskervilles" had appeared in The Strand Magazine just days earlier, and the letters arriving from readers demonstrated an enthusiasm that exceeded even his most optimistic expectations.

Most of the correspondence followed predictable patterns—expressions of delight at Holmes's return, speculation about how the detective had survived the Reichenbach Falls, and urgent requests for more stories featuring the beloved consulting detective. Arthur had developed efficient responses to such letters, appreciating the readers' enthusiasm while carefully maintaining the boundaries he had established regarding future publications.

But one envelope in the morning's collection immediately commanded his attention. The return address read "Miss A. Hunter, Queen Mary's Grammar School, Walsall," written in the precise handwriting that spoke of someone accustomed to correspondence with educational authorities. Something about the formal presentation and provincial address suggested this might be different from the usual fan correspondence.

Arthur opened the letter with mild curiosity, expecting perhaps an inquiry from an educator about using the Holmes stories in her curriculum. What he found instead made him set down his teacup with hands that trembled slightly:

Dear Dr. Doyle,

I hope you will forgive the presumption of a stranger writing to you, but after reading the first installment of 'The Hound of the Baskervilles' in last month's Strand

Magazine, I find myself compelled to make an inquiry that may seem rather extraordinary.

My name is Ann Hunter, and I am currently Head Mistress at Queen Mary's Grammar School here in Walsall. However, I believe I may be familiar to you under different circumstances, as I am certain you have written about my experiences in one of your Sherlock Holmes stories.

Approximately ten years ago, when I was working as a governess, I found myself in most distressing circumstances involving a peculiar position offered to me by a Mr. Rucastle at a place called the Copper Beeches in Hampshire. The situation became quite dangerous, and I was rescued through the intervention of Mr. Sherlock Holmes and Dr. Watson, who responded to my letter seeking their assistance.

Dr. Doyle, when I read your story 'The Adventure of the Copper Beeches,' which appeared in The Strand some years ago, I recognized my own experiences immediately, though I noticed that certain names and details had been altered for publication. In your story, I appeared as 'Miss Violet Hunter,' and Dr. Watson was referred to as 'Dr. John Watson,' though the gentleman who assisted me introduced himself simply as 'Dr. Watson.'

I perfectly understand the need for such discretionary changes in names and circumstances. However, this presents me with a dilemma: I would very much like to write directly to Mr. Holmes and Dr. Watson to express my gratitude for their intervention during that terrible ordeal, but I am uncertain how to contact them given that the published account uses altered names.

Dr. Watson's kindness during that frightening experience, and Mr. Holmes's brilliant deductions that undoubtedly saved me from considerable danger, have remained in my memory as examples of the finest qualities of human character. I have prospered considerably since those difficult days, having worked my way up from governess to my current position as Head Mistress. Much of my success I attribute to the confidence I gained from surviving that trial, and to the example set by the two gentlemen who came to my aid when I had nowhere else to turn.

Would it be possible for you to assist me in making contact with them? I understand completely if discretion prevents you from providing their direct address, but perhaps *you could forward a letter of thanks from me to them through whatever channels you employed when researching their cases for your stories?*

I remain, with the utmost respect and gratitude for your literary work which has allowed their remarkable methods to reach so many readers,

Miss Ann Hunter Head Mistress
Queen Mary's Grammar School Walsall, Staffordshire

Arthur read the letter twice, feeling a profound mixture of admiration and concern. Here was undeniable proof that their carefully constructed approach to protecting identities had been partially successful—Miss Hunter clearly understood the need for discretionary changes—but also that some participants in actual cases could still recognize their own experiences despite such alterations.

The implications were both reassuring and challenging. On one hand, Miss Hunter's letter demonstrated that intelligent participants understood and appreciated the need for privacy protection. On the other hand, it revealed that people involved in Holmes's actual cases might step forward seeking direct contact, creating exactly the sort of complications that the fictional framework was designed to prevent.

More immediately pressing was the question of how to respond to her entirely reasonable request. Miss Hunter was clearly an intelligent, educated woman who deserved consideration, and her desire to express gratitude to the men who had helped her was entirely appropriate. But providing direct contact information would compromise the careful boundaries that made the collaboration possible.

Arthur rose and moved to the window, looking out at the Surrey countryside while considering various approaches to this delicate correspondence. Miss Hunter's letter suggested someone of good character who had overcome significant challenges to achieve professional success—precisely the sort of person who might be trusted with sensitive information, yet also someone whose inquiry demonstrated how their carefully constructed privacy protections could be penetrated by determined and intelligent participants.

Arthur moved to his writing desk, considering how to balance honesty with discretion:

Dear Miss Hunter,

Your letter of September 2nd has reached me here at my Surrey residence, and I must express both my gratification at learning of your professional success and my appreciation for the thoughtful manner in which you have approached this sensitive matter.

You are quite correct in recognizing your own experiences in 'The Adventure of the Copper Beeches,' and I am pleased that you understand the need for the discretionary changes in names and circumstances that publication requires. Your rise from governess to Head Mistress speaks admirably of your character and determination, and I believe the gentlemen who assisted you would be delighted to learn of your achievements.

Regarding your desire to express your gratitude directly, I find myself in a position that requires careful consideration of competing obligations. The gentlemen to whom you refer have always insisted upon complete discretion regarding their work, and the arrangements under which I have been permitted to adapt their cases for publication include strict assurances about maintaining their privacy.

However, I am moved by the obvious sincerity of your wish to convey your thanks, and I believe I may be able to suggest a solution that serves both your generous intentions and their need for discretion. If you would be willing to entrust me with whatever message you wish to convey, I would be honored to ensure that it reaches them through the appropriate channels I maintain for my research purposes.

I can assure you that both gentlemen remember your case with considerable satisfaction, not only for its successful resolution but particularly for the courage you displayed under quite extraordinary circumstances. Your welfare has been a matter of continuing interest to them, and I am confident they would be gratified to learn of your professional accomplishments.

Please let me know if this arrangement would be acceptable to you. While I understand it is not precisely the direct contact you requested, I hope you will appreciate that it represents the best accommodation possible given the constraints under which all parties must operate.

With sincere respect for your achievements and deep appreciation for your understanding of these delicate matters,

Arthur Conan Doyle

P.S. I should mention that your perceptive observation about the name variations in the published account demonstrates exactly the sort of intelligent discretion that gives me confidence in proposing this arrangement.

Arthur sealed the letter carefully, recognizing that he was establishing a precedent that might prove significant as their collaboration continued. Miss Hunter's inquiry had revealed both the strengths and vulnerabilities of their approach to protecting privacy while maintaining authenticity— she had recognized her story but also understood the need for discretionary changes.

An Urgent Meeting

September 11, 1901

The Criterion Bar on Piccadilly Circus had always been one of London's most convivial meeting places for gentlemen conducting business that required both privacy and comfort, and Dr. James Watson found himself appreciating anew its elegant appointments as he awaited Arthur Conan Doyle's arrival. The September afternoon had brought unseasonable warmth to London, and Watson had secured a table in the bar's quieter corner, where serious conversation could proceed without the intrusions of casual eavesdropping.

Watson consulted his pocket watch—five minutes before two o'clock, the time Arthur had specified in his telegram requesting this meeting. The message had been characteristically brief:

JAMES - MUST DISCUSS FUTURE POSSIBILITIES URGENTLY. CRITERION BAR WEDNESDAY 2PM. EXTRAORDINARY DEVELOPMENTS REQUIRE IMMEDIATE CONSULTATION - ARTHUR.

The "extraordinary developments" presumably referred to the unprecedented public response to "The Hound of the Baskervilles," now in its second month of serialization in The Strand Magazine. Watson had observed the phenomenon himself during his recent walks through London—news vendors struggling to keep copies of The Strand in stock, conversations about Holmes's return overheard in omnibuses and tea shops, and a general excitement among the reading public that exceeded anything their previous collaborations had achieved.

Arthur appeared at the entrance precisely on time, his familiar figure moving through the crowd with the confident bearing that success had brought to his manner. At forty-two, Arthur carried himself with the assurance of a man whose literary achievements had provided both financial security and professional recognition, though Watson noted immediately that his friend's expression held an intensity suggesting matters of genuine importance.

"James!" Arthur called out as he approached the table, extending his hand with obvious pleasure. "Thank you for agreeing to meet on such short notice. How are you managing the London heat?"

Watson rose to greet his friend, noting that Arthur looked well despite the obvious preoccupation that had prompted this urgent meeting. "Quite comfortably, thank you. Though I confess myself curious about these 'extraordinary developments' you mentioned in your telegram."

Arthur settled into the chair across from Watson, his movements suggesting barely contained excitement mixed with careful consideration of complex possibilities. "James, the public response to the Baskerville story has exceeded every projection The Strand made. Their circulation figures for the August and September issues have broken all previous records."

The waiter approached with practiced efficiency, and Arthur ordered brandy while Watson requested his usual whiskey. As they waited for their drinks, Arthur leaned forward with growing animation.

"But it's not just the circulation numbers, James. It's the nature of the response. Letters are arriving daily—not just expressions of enjoyment, but genuine gratitude for Holmes's return. People are describing the stories as if Holmes were a real person they had missed and were delighted to see again."

Watson felt a complex mixture of satisfaction and concern at this development. "And The Strand's reaction to such enthusiasm?"

Arthur's brandy arrived, and he took a careful sip before continuing. "Herbert Greenhough Smith has approached me three times in the past fortnight about additional Holmes stories. The commercial potential has become impossible to ignore."

Watson studied his friend's face, recognizing the signs of a man grappling with significant decisions. "Arthur, when we agreed to the Baskerville collaboration, we established very clear boundaries. A single story, set before the Reichenbach Falls, with no commitment to further publications."

"I know, James. And I've honored those boundaries completely in my discussions with Smith. But..." Arthur paused, his expression growing more serious. "The success of the Baskerville story has made me reconsider whether those boundaries serve our best interests."

Watson felt his attention sharpen immediately. "In what way?"

Arthur set down his glass and fixed Watson with the direct gaze that characterized his most important conversations. "James, what if we brought Holmes back permanently? Not just for occasional stories set in the past, but for ongoing adventures in the present?"

Watson stared at his friend in amazement. "Permanently? Arthur, Holmes died at the Reichenbach Falls. We established that conclusively in 'The Final Problem.' How could we possibly explain his resurrection without compromising the integrity of everything we've written?"

Arthur smiled with the expression of a man who had given considerable thought to exactly such objections. "We don't resurrect him, James. We reveal that he never actually died."

"I don't understand."

Arthur leaned forward, his voice taking on the enthusiastic tone Watson remembered from their most productive collaborative discussions. "What if Holmes escaped from the waterfall? What if his apparent death was a carefully planned deception designed to eliminate Moriarty while allowing Holmes to escape his enemies?"

Watson considered this possibility, his mind immediately working through the logical implications. "You're suggesting that Holmes allowed everyone—including myself—to believe he had died, when in fact he had survived and been living in secret?"

"Precisely. It would explain his absence while preserving the possibility of his return. More importantly, it would allow us to continue documenting his current cases without any need to explain supernatural resurrection."

Watson was quiet for a long moment, weighing the literary possibilities against his own emotional investment in the finality they had established. When he finally spoke, his voice carried careful consideration rather than immediate enthusiasm.

"Arthur, such an approach would certainly solve the practical problems of bringing Holmes back to publication. But it would require me to acknowledge that my own account of his death was either mistaken or deliberately deceptive."

"Not deceptive, James—simply incomplete. You could have believed sincerely that Holmes had died, only to discover later that he had survived through methods too dangerous to reveal at the time."

Arthur's excitement was becoming more evident as he developed his argument. "Think of the dramatic possibilities! Holmes returning after years of secret investigations, revealing that his apparent death allowed him to eliminate criminal networks that could never have been approached openly. The reader sympathy for your grief at his loss, followed by the joy of his unexpected return..."

Watson found himself considering the proposal with growing interest despite his initial skepticism. "And you believe the reading public would accept such an explanation?"

"James, the reading public wants Holmes back more than they want logical consistency. If we present his survival as the result of brilliant planning rather than lucky accident, readers will embrace the explanation gratefully."

Watson took a careful sip of his whiskey, using the pause to organize his thoughts about this unexpected development. "Arthur, there's another consideration beyond reader acceptance. Such a plan would require Holmes's agreement to resume regular collaboration. He withdrew from our literary partnership specifically because he found the review process too time-consuming."

"True, but circumstances have changed significantly since then. Your documentation skills have evolved to the point where you could provide complete case accounts requiring minimal review. Holmes could continue his actual detective work while trusting you to handle the literary presentation."

Arthur's voice grew more persuasive as he continued. "Besides, James, Mycroft's recent endorsement suggests that governmental authorities view our work as serving important educational purposes. Holmes might be more willing to participate knowing that the stories serve legitimate public interests."

Watson felt the appeal of Arthur's reasoning, recognizing both the commercial opportunities and the potential satisfaction of resumed regular collaboration. "The practical arrangements would need careful consideration. Holmes's time constraints, the selection of suitable cases, the maintenance of privacy protections..."

"All manageable, James. We've proven our ability to handle such challenges with the Baskerville story. The only real question is whether you're prepared to commit to regular collaboration rather than the occasional project we've pursued recently."

Watson set down his glass, understanding that Arthur was proposing far more than literary resurrection—he was suggesting a fundamental expansion of their partnership. "Arthur, I confess the prospect is both appealing and daunting. The financial rewards would certainly be substantial, and the opportunity to continue documenting Holmes's methods..."

"Would serve the educational purposes Mycroft identified while providing readers with the authentic detective fiction they've clearly been craving," Arthur finished. "James, this could represent the beginning of the most productive phase of our collaboration."

Watson was quiet for several minutes, contemplating not just the immediate proposal but its implications for his future. Regular collaboration would require sustained creative effort of a kind he hadn't attempted since Mary's death, but it would also provide purpose and intellectual stimulation that had been largely absent from his life.

"If we proceed with such a plan," Watson said finally, "how would you propose to handle Holmes's return? The resurrection scene itself?"

Arthur's eyes lit up with obvious satisfaction at this sign of serious consideration. "I envision a single powerful story revealing his survival—perhaps through your discovery that he had been living secretly in London, continuing his investigations while allowing the world to believe him dead. The emotional reunion, the explanation of his methods, the revelation of what he's accomplished during his 'death'..."

"And then?"

"Then we return to regular publication. Monthly stories, perhaps, or bi-monthly, depending on the availability of suitable case material and our own schedules."

Watson felt himself responding to Arthur's enthusiasm despite his continued reservations about the magnitude of such a commitment. "The idea has considerable merit, Arthur. Though I would need to discuss it thoroughly with Holmes before making any definitive decisions."

"Of course. But James, are you genuinely interested in pursuing this possibility? Not just the single resurrection story, but the ongoing collaboration it would make possible?"

Watson considered the question with the careful attention it deserved, weighing his current satisfaction with quiet retirement against the appeal of renewed purpose and meaningful work. "Arthur, I believe I am interested. The Baskerville collaboration reminded me how much satisfaction I derive from such work, and the public response suggests that our efforts serve purposes beyond mere entertainment."

Arthur's face showed obvious delight at this response. "Then you'll speak with Holmes about the possibility?"

"I will. Though I want to be clear that any commitment would depend entirely on his willingness to participate and the practical arrangements we could establish."

"Understood completely." Arthur raised his glass in an impromptu toast. "James, to the possibility of bringing Sherlock Holmes back to life!"

Watson clinked his glass against Arthur's, feeling the excitement of potential new adventures mixed with careful consideration of the challenges ahead. "To possibilities, Arthur. Though we should perhaps reserve celebration until we know whether Holmes approves of being resurrected."

As their lunch continued with discussion of practical arrangements and potential timelines, both men felt the familiar energy that had characterized their most successful collaborative periods. The conversation ranged from financial considerations to creative possibilities, from privacy protections to reader expectations, building a framework for what might become their most ambitious literary venture yet.

As they prepared to part, Arthur reached into his coat pocket and withdrew a letter. "James, before you leave, there's one other matter that might interest you. I received a rather remarkable piece of correspondence last week."

Watson accepted the envelope, noting immediately the return address: "Miss A. Hunter, Queen Mary's Grammar School, Walsall." As he read through Miss Hunter's carefully composed letter, his expression grew increasingly thoughtful.

"Good Lord," Watson said, looking up at Arthur with obvious amazement. "She recognized herself in 'The Copper Beeches' story."

"Indeed. And she's handled the recognition with exactly the sort of intelligence and discretion one would hope for." Arthur's voice carried genuine admiration for Miss Hunter's approach. "I've responded with an offer to forward any message she wishes to convey to you and Holmes through appropriate channels."

Watson reread portions of the letter, his memory clearly engaged with recollections of the actual case. "I remember her well—remarkably composed under extraordinary circumstances. It's gratifying to learn she's achieved such professional success."

"Will you consider responding to her directly? I believe she deserves acknowledgment from someone who was actually present during her ordeal."

Watson folded the letter carefully, his expression showing both consideration and growing resolution. "Yes, Arthur. I think a direct response would be entirely appropriate. Miss Hunter demonstrated considerable courage during that investigation, and her subsequent achievements speak well of her character."

Watson paused, then continued with obvious decision. "If we do proceed with bringing Holmes back to publication, Miss Hunter's letter suggests we can trust intelligent readers to understand our need for discretionary changes while appreciating the authentic investigative content."

"My thoughts exactly. Her response indicates that our approach to balancing authenticity with privacy protection has been successful."

The afternoon had transformed what Watson had expected to be a routine meeting into a discussion of possibilities that might fundamentally change their literary partnership. Whether Holmes would approve of being brought back from his fictional death remained to be seen, but for the first time since completing "The Final Problem" eight years earlier, both men could envision a future where Sherlock Holmes might return permanently to the pages of The Strand Magazine.

Watson meets with Ann Hunter

October 21, 1901

The autumn afternoon had brought a crisp clarity to London that seemed to sharpen every detail of the familiar cityscape, and Dr. James Watson found himself walking through Piccadilly Circus with a sense of anticipation he hadn't experienced in years. The meeting he was about to undertake represented something entirely new in his experience—a reunion with someone whose life had been dramatically affected by Holmes's intervention, but who now knew the true nature of their literary collaboration.

Watson arrived at the Criterion Bar precisely at twenty-five minutes past two, allowing himself a few moments to secure an appropriate table and prepare for what promised to be a conversation unlike any he had previously experienced. The establishment's elegant appointments provided exactly the right atmosphere for reconnecting with someone who had risen from governess to educational leadership, while its discrete seating arrangements would ensure privacy for discussions that might touch on sensitive matters.

At precisely half past two, Watson observed a woman entering the bar with the confident bearing of someone accustomed to professional responsibilities, and he recognized immediately the composed intelligence that had impressed him during those dangerous days at the Copper Beeches a decade ago. Miss Ann Hunter had clearly prospered in the intervening years, her dress and manner speaking of someone who had achieved genuine success through her own efforts.

Watson rose as she approached, noting that while the years had brought maturity to her features, the essential character he remembered—the careful observation, the quiet determination—remained unchanged.

"Dr. Watson," she said, extending her hand with a warm smile that mixed gratitude with genuine pleasure at this reunion. "How wonderful to see you again after all these years. You look remarkably well."

"Miss Hunter—though I understand congratulations are in order for your promotion to Head Mistress," Watson replied, accepting her handshake and noting the firm confidence that spoke of her professional achievements. "Please, do sit down. How was your conference?"

Miss Hunter settled into the offered chair with obvious satisfaction. "Quite successful, thank you. The National Association of Head Teachers has been discussing reforms to secondary education, particularly regarding opportunities for young women. It's gratifying to be part of such important discussions."

Watson found himself genuinely impressed by the evident success of someone whose courage had been so thoroughly tested during that harrowing investigation. "From what Dr. Doyle shared of your correspondence, your rise to such a position represents remarkable achievement. I confess myself curious about your journey from those difficult days to your current standing."

Miss Hunter's expression grew more thoughtful as she considered how to summarize a decade of determined effort. "The experience at the Copper Beeches was, paradoxically, one of the most formative of my life. Not because of the danger itself, but because of what I learned about my own capabilities when faced with seemingly impossible circumstances."

She paused as the waiter approached, ordering tea while Watson requested his usual whiskey. When they were alone again, she continued with obvious sincerity.

"Dr. Watson, when I found myself trapped in that terrible situation, with no family to support me and very limited resources, I discovered that I could think clearly under pressure, assess complex situations accurately, and take calculated risks when necessary." Her voice carried the quiet confidence of someone who had tested herself thoroughly. "Those skills proved invaluable as I worked my way up through various educational positions."

Watson felt moved by her account, recognizing in it the kind of character development that made their investigative work genuinely meaningful. "Miss Hunter, I'm delighted to hear that such a frightening experience contributed positively to your subsequent success. Holmes always believed that overcoming genuine challenges strengthened rather than diminished people of good character."

"Mr. Holmes was quite right," she replied warmly. "Though I must say, Dr. Watson, that your own kindness during that ordeal was equally important to my eventual recovery. The way you treated my concerns seriously, the respectful manner in which you listened to my account of the strange circumstances—all of that helped me understand that intelligent people would take my observations seriously."

Watson colored slightly at the praise, though he felt genuine satisfaction at learning that their professional approach had provided lasting benefit. "We were simply doing our duty as we understood it. Though I'm gratified to know that our methods were helpful beyond the immediate resolution of the case."

Miss Hunter leaned forward with obvious interest. "Dr. Watson, may I ask about the literary aspect of our case? When I read 'The Adventure of the Copper Beeches' in The Strand Magazine, I was struck by how accurately the essential details had been preserved despite the necessary changes to names and specific circumstances."

Watson felt the familiar complex emotions that accompanied discussions of their collaborative deception. "Miss Hunter, you clearly understand the delicate nature of transforming actual cases into publishable fiction. Your discretion in approaching Dr. Doyle, and your understanding of why such changes were necessary, suggests exactly the sort of intelligence we hoped such stories would attract."

"I confess I was curious about the process," she continued. "How do you and Dr. Doyle manage to balance authenticity with the privacy requirements that publication demands?"

Watson considered how much he could safely reveal to someone who had already demonstrated both intelligence and discretion. "The challenge is considerable, certainly. Dr. Doyle possesses remarkable literary skills, while I provide... consultation regarding the investigative elements. The goal is always to preserve the educational value of authentic detective methods while protecting all involved parties."

Miss Hunter nodded with obvious appreciation for the complexity involved. "The result is quite remarkable. Reading about 'my' case allowed me to understand aspects of Mr. Holmes's reasoning that weren't clear to me at the time. The way he deduced the family relationships, for instance, and his insights into Rucastle's psychological motivations."

Watson felt a surge of professional pride at this observation. "Holmes always insisted that our published accounts should educate readers about proper investigative methodology. Your comment suggests we succeeded in that goal, at least in your case."

As their conversation continued, Watson found himself genuinely enjoying the opportunity to discuss their work with someone who had experienced it firsthand. Miss Hunter proved to be an engaging conversationalist, sharing amusing anecdotes from her educational career while displaying the same keen intelligence that had served her so well during her dangerous ordeal.

"I must say, Dr. Watson, that following the current serialization of 'The Hound of the Baskervilles' has been particularly fascinating," Miss Hunter said as they moved through their second round of refreshments. "The details, the complex family psychology—it represents Mr. Holmes at the height of his analytical powers."

Watson smiled at her enthusiasm. "The Baskerville case was indeed one of Holmes's most challenging investigations. Dr. Doyle has done remarkable work in adapting such complex material for serialization."

"Do you miss it?" Miss Hunter asked suddenly, her tone growing more personal. "The active investigation, the intellectual challenge of working with someone of Mr. Holmes's extraordinary abilities?"

Watson was quiet for a moment, surprised by both the directness of the question and his own emotional response to it. "Actually, Miss Hunter, I am still sharing a flat on Baker Street with Mr. Holmes, and I am still working with him on his cases."

Watson found himself speaking more openly than he had intended. "The collaboration with Holmes represented some of the most intellectually satisfying work of my professional life. Your own experience demonstrates why such work feels meaningful—when investigative success leads to genuine positive outcomes for people of good character, the satisfaction transcends mere intellectual exercise."

As the afternoon progressed toward early evening, their conversation ranged from professional experiences to personal reflections, with Watson finding himself increasingly impressed by Miss Hunter's intelligence and character. She had clearly transformed her early trials into genuine strength, achieving professional success while maintaining the compassionate concern for others that had been evident even during her most desperate circumstances.

"Miss Hunter," Watson said as he noticed the lengthening shadows outside the bar's windows, "I hope you don't mind my asking, but when do you return to Walsall? I trust your travel arrangements are comfortable?"

Miss Hunter glanced at the small watch pinned to her dress. "Actually, Dr. Watson, I'm not traveling back until tomorrow morning. The conference organizers arranged accommodations at a hotel near Russell Square, so I have this evening quite free."

Watson felt a sudden inspiration, recognizing an opportunity to extend what had become one of the most enjoyable conversations he had experienced in years. "Miss Hunter, if you have no other commitments this evening, would you do me the honor of joining me for dinner? I know of an excellent restaurant—Simpson's in the Strand—where we could continue our conversation in more comfortable surroundings."

Miss Hunter's face lit up with obvious pleasure at the invitation. "Dr. Watson, that's extraordinarily kind of you. I would be delighted to accept, if you're certain it wouldn't be an imposition."

"Not an imposition at all—quite the opposite, in fact. Your company has made this afternoon most enjoyable, and I confess myself reluctant to see our reunion end so soon." Watson smiled warmly. "Shall we say seven o'clock at Simpson's? It's quite near here, just a short walk down the Strand."

"Seven o'clock would be perfect," Miss Hunter replied, gathering her gloves and reticule. "Thank you so much for such a thoughtful invitation, Dr. Watson. I'm very much looking forward to continuing our conversation."

"Until seven o'clock then, Miss Hunter," Watson said, rising to escort her to the bar's entrance. "I believe you'll find Simpson's provides exactly the right atmosphere for the continuation of such excellent conversation."

As Watson watched Miss Hunter disappear into the London crowds, making her way back to her hotel to prepare for dinner, he felt a lightness of spirit that had been absent for far too long. The prospect of spending the evening in such agreeable company, continuing discussions that had already proven so engaging, filled him with an anticipation that transcended mere social pleasure.

Dinner at Simpson's

October 21, 1901

The gaslight cast its familiar warm glow across the elegant dining room of Simpson's, and Dr. James Watson felt a profound sense of completion as he guided Miss Ann Hunter to their reserved table near the tall windows overlooking the Strand. The restaurant's theatrical carving service continued its nightly ritual at neighboring tables, the ceremony of perfectly prepared beef providing exactly the right backdrop for what promised to be a memorable evening.

Miss Hunter had changed for dinner into a dress of deep blue silk that spoke of both professional success and refined taste, while Watson had donned his finest evening attire with more care than he had exercised for any social occasion in recent memory. As they settled into their chairs, both felt the pleasant anticipation that accompanies the continuation of unexpectedly rewarding conversation.

"Dr. Watson, this is magnificent," Miss Hunter said, her eyes taking in Simpson's renowned atmosphere with obvious appreciation. "I've heard of this establishment for years, but never had occasion to dine here. Thank you again for such a thoughtful invitation."

Watson smiled as he assisted her with her chair, feeling the satisfaction of having chosen exactly the right venue for their reunion. "The pleasure is entirely mine, Miss Hunter. Simpson's seemed appropriate for celebrating both your professional achievements and our unexpected opportunity to meet again after so many years."

As they reviewed the menu and ordered their dinner—the famous Beef Wellington, prepared tableside with appropriate ceremony—conversation flowed naturally from their afternoon discussions to broader reflections on the changes the past decade had brought to both their lives.

"I must confess," Miss Hunter said as their wine was poured, "that reading the current serialization of 'The Hound of the Baskervilles' has been a most unusual experience. Having personal knowledge of how these stories are created, I find myself appreciating both Dr. Doyle's literary skill and the authentic investigative content in ways I never could have before our correspondence."

Watson felt the familiar complex emotions that accompanied discussions of their collaborative work. "The Baskerville case was indeed one of Holmes's most investigations. Dr. Doyle has managed to capture not only the logical progression of the detection but also the Gothic elements that made the case so memorable."

"The balance between authentic methodology and dramatic storytelling is quite remarkable," Miss Hunter continued. "Though I suppose such balance requires extraordinary collaboration between the literary and investigative elements."

Watson nodded, appreciating her tactful recognition of the partnership's complexity. "Such collaboration certainly presents unique challenges. But Miss Hunter, our afternoon conversation has made me curious about your own remarkable journey since we last met. Rising from governess to Head Mistress represents extraordinary achievement—what path led you to such success?"

Miss Hunter's expression grew more thoughtful as she considered how to summarize a decade of determined effort. "The truth is, Dr. Watson, that the Copper Beeches experience fundamentally changed how I viewed my own capabilities. Before that terrible situation, I had never been tested under such extreme circumstances."

She paused as their soup course arrived, using the moment to organize her thoughts. "When I discovered I could think clearly under genuine danger, assess complex situations accurately, and take necessary risks when circumstances demanded—well, those realizations gave me confidence to pursue opportunities I might never have considered otherwise."

"And your career progression?"

"I left Hampshire immediately after the Rucastle affair," Miss Hunter continued, her voice carrying the matter-of-fact tone of someone who had made difficult but necessary decisions. "The entire situation had become... untenable for personal as well as professional reasons. I secured a position as assistant teacher at a girls' school in Birmingham, then moved to increasingly responsible positions as my experience grew."

Watson detected something in her tone that suggested more complex circumstances than professional ambition alone. "Miss Hunter, if I may ask—were there personal considerations that influenced your departure from Hampshire?"

Miss Hunter was quiet for a moment, her expression showing the careful consideration of someone deciding how much personal information to share. "Dr. Watson, you have been nothing but kind and respectful, both during our original acquaintance and today. I believe I can speak frankly with you about circumstances I've rarely discussed with anyone."

Watson leaned forward slightly, his medical training making him naturally attentive to signs of emotional difficulty. "Please, feel free to share whatever you're comfortable discussing. Though certainly don't feel obligated to reveal anything too personal."

"Actually, there was a gentleman," Miss Hunter said, her voice growing quieter. "Someone I had been... attached to before accepting the Rucastle position. The young man you and Mr. Holmes observed outside the house that evening—he was indeed my fiancé."

Watson felt immediate understanding, remembering Holmes's deduction about the figure they had glimpsed during their surveillance. "Ah, yes. Holmes suspected as much from his behavior and positioning."

"When the full extent of Mr. Rucastle's deception became clear, when the danger I had unknowingly been placed in was revealed..." Miss Hunter paused, her composure remaining steady despite the obvious difficulty of the subject. "My fiancé felt that my judgment in accepting such a position reflected poorly on my character. He believed I should have recognized the suspicious circumstances immediately."

Watson felt a surge of indignation at such unfair criticism. "Miss Hunter, surely any reasonable person would understand that you were deliberately deceived by someone who had considerable practice in such manipulation."

Miss Hunter managed a slight smile at his immediate defense. "You're very kind, Dr. Watson. But Thomas—my former fiancé—came from a family that valued caution above all else. To them, finding oneself in such a situation, regardless of the circumstances, suggested poor judgment that might reflect badly on their family's reputation."

"And so the engagement was dissolved?"

"By mutual agreement, though I confess the decision was more his than mine initially." Miss Hunter's voice carried acceptance rather than bitterness. "In retrospect, Dr. Watson, his reaction revealed aspects of his character that would have made for an unhappy marriage. A husband who would blame his wife for being deceived by criminals is not a husband who would provide the kind of partnership necessary for genuine happiness."

Watson found himself deeply impressed by her philosophical acceptance of what must have been a painful experience. "Miss Hunter, such perspective speaks remarkably well of your character. Many people would have carried resentment about such treatment."

"Perhaps. But the experience taught me valuable lessons about both my own capabilities and the kind of person I wanted to become." Miss Hunter's expression grew more confident. "Since then, I've focused entirely on my professional development. Education provides purpose, intellectual stimulation, and the opportunity to influence young minds— satisfactions that have proven more reliable than romantic attachments."

As their main course arrived with Simpson's characteristic theatrical presentation, Watson found himself reflecting on the parallels between Miss Hunter's experience and his own journey through loss and recovery. When the carving ceremony concluded and they were settled with their perfectly prepared dinner, he felt compelled to share his own more recent trials.

"Miss Hunter, your candor about personal difficulties encourages me to share something of my own circumstances," Watson said, his voice taking on the careful tone he had learned to use when discussing his greatest loss. "When you ask about my life since our original acquaintance, I'm afraid the account includes considerable tragedy."

Miss Hunter immediately set down her fork, her expression showing the compassionate attention of someone who recognized serious revelation approaching. "Dr. Watson, please don't feel obligated to share anything that might be painful. Though if you wish to speak of it, I'm certainly willing to listen."

Watson took a careful sip of wine, gathering strength for a discussion he rarely undertook with anyone outside his closest circle. "Miss Hunter, I was married. To a remarkable woman named Mary, whom I met during another of Holmes's investigations. She was intelligent, kind, and brought more happiness to my life than I had thought possible."

"Was married?" Miss Hunter repeated softly, her tone conveying immediate understanding that tragedy had followed.

"Mary died in May of 1893, during childbirth. We lost both her and our son." Watson's voice remained steady, though the pain of those words had never entirely diminished. "It was... the end of everything I had thought my life would become."

Miss Hunter's eyes filled with tears of genuine sympathy. "Oh, Dr. Watson. I cannot imagine such loss. To lose both your wife and child... how does one possibly recover from such devastation?"

Watson looked out the window at the London evening, marshaling the thoughts that had taken him years to organize. "The honest answer is that one doesn't recover completely. One learns to live with the loss, to find purpose despite it, but the fundamental change is permanent."

"Where did you find the strength to continue?"

"Friends, primarily. Holmes provided sanctuary when I couldn't bear to remain in the house where Mary and I had been so happy. Mrs. Hudson—our landlady—offered the kind of maternal care that kept me functional when I lacked the will to care for myself. And the work—our literary collaboration—eventually provided purpose again."

Miss Hunter reached across the table and briefly touched Watson's hand, a gesture of comfort that transcended the social conventions typically governing such acquaintances. "Dr. Watson, I hope you don't mind my saying that your ability to speak of such loss with composure, to find ways to honor your wife's memory while continuing to live meaningfully—it suggests extraordinary strength of character."

Watson felt moved by her understanding, recognizing in her response the kind of genuine sympathy that came from someone who had faced her own significant trials. "Miss Hunter, your compassion means more to me than you might realize. Few people understand how grief changes but never entirely ends."

"Perhaps those who have faced their own losses are better equipped to understand others' pain," Miss Hunter replied gently. "Though I confess that what you endured far exceeds anything in my own experience."

As their dinner continued, the conversation gradually shifted from their shared sorrows to more hopeful reflections on how such experiences had shaped their current perspectives. Both had discovered inner resources they hadn't known they possessed, both had found ways to transform personal trials into professional purpose, and both had learned to value genuine human connection over conventional social expectations.

"Dr. Watson," Miss Hunter said as they lingered over their dessert and coffee, "I hope you won't think me forward, but this evening has been one of the most meaningful conversations I've had in years. Your willingness to share such personal experiences, your obvious respect for my own journey—it's exactly the kind of interaction I had hoped might be possible but rarely encounter."

Watson felt his own gratitude for the evening's unexpected intimacy. "Miss Hunter, the pleasure has been entirely mutual. To meet someone who understands both the challenges of rebuilding one's life after significant loss and the satisfaction that comes from meaningful work— such understanding is far rarer than it should be."

As they prepared to conclude their dinner, both felt the reluctance that accompanies the end of unexpectedly rewarding time spent together. The gaslight flickered gently in its familiar sconces, and Simpson's continued its evening service around them, but their attention remained focused on the connection they had discovered.

"Miss Hunter," Watson said as he prepared to escort her from the restaurant, "when do you return to Walsall? I confess myself hopeful that this evening represents the beginning of a correspondence, if not the possibility of future meetings when your duties bring you to London."

Miss Hunter's face lit up with obvious pleasure at this suggestion. "I return tomorrow afternoon, but I travel to London regularly for educational conferences and meetings. Dr. Watson, I would be delighted to continue our acquaintance through correspondence, and certainly through personal meetings when circumstances permit."

"Excellent. Then you must consider me at your disposal whenever professional obligations bring you to the capital." Watson's voice carried genuine warmth as he helped her with her wrap. "This evening has reminded me how much I've missed the company of someone who understands both the importance of meaningful work and the value of honest conversation."

As they emerged onto the Strand, where hansoms waited to carry them to their respective accommodations, both felt the satisfaction of time well spent and the anticipation of continued friendship. The October evening was crisp but pleasant, and London seemed to sparkle with possibilities neither had expected when the day began.

"Dr. Watson," Miss Hunter said as he helped her into her cab, "thank you for such a memorable evening. Your friendship, your willingness to share your experiences, your obvious respect for mine—all of it has meant more to me than you might realize."

Watson accepted her extended hand, holding it briefly in farewell. "Miss Hunter, the gratitude is entirely mine. This evening has been a gift I hadn't dared hope for. Please write when you're settled in Walsall, and let me know when your next London visit might be planned."

"I shall write within the week," she promised, her smile visible even in the dim light of the carriage. "And Dr. Watson—I hope you know that meeting someone of your character and understanding gives me great hope for whatever the future might hold."

The walk back to Baker Street took him through familiar London streets that seemed somehow brighter, more welcoming than they had in years.

The 3rd Group of Short Stories
March 17, 1902

The March morning had brought the first genuine warmth of spring to the Surrey hills, and Dr. James Watson found himself appreciating anew the magnificent setting of Undershaw as Arthur Conan Doyle's carriage carried him up the familiar drive. The success of "The Hound of the Baskervilles," now nearing completion of its serialization in The Strand Magazine, had vindicated every aspect of their careful collaboration, and today's meeting would determine whether that success could be transformed into the sustained literary partnership they had discussed at the Criterion Bar six months earlier.

Arthur greeted him at the entrance with obvious enthusiasm, his manner carrying the confident energy of a man whose most ambitious literary venture was proving triumphantly successful. At forty-three, Arthur had grown into his role as one of Britain's most celebrated authors, though Watson noted that success had not diminished his genuine warmth or his careful attention to the collaborative relationships that made such achievement possible.

"James!" Arthur called out, clasping his friend's hand with characteristic vigor. "Perfect timing—Touie has just finished preparing luncheon, and I have our complete case files organized in the study. The response to the final Baskerville installments suggests the public is more than ready for Holmes's permanent return."

Watson followed Arthur into Undershaw's familiar comfort, noting the evidence of prosperity and domestic happiness that filled every corner of the elegantly appointed home. Louisa appeared in the hallway with her gentle smile, looking remarkably well and clearly pleased to welcome their valued friend.

"James," she said warmly, "how wonderful to see you again. Arthur has been absolutely vibrating with excitement about today's planning session.

I believe he's identified enough case material to keep you both busy for the next several years."

"Touie's quite right," Arthur agreed, leading Watson toward his study. "But first, lunch and proper celebration of what we've accomplished with the Baskerville story. The final installment appears next month, and Greenhough Smith tells me the public response has exceeded every previous Strand record."

The study at Undershaw had been transformed since Watson's last visit, with filing cabinets containing carefully organized documentation from their years of collaboration, and Arthur's desk dominated by neat stacks of case files arranged according to some system of his own devising. The room spoke of serious literary business conducted with methodical attention to both creative and practical considerations.

"Arthur," Watson said, settling into his familiar chair, "before we begin planning future stories, I want you to know how deeply satisfying it's been to see Holmes return to such public acclaim. The letters I've received from readers expressing gratitude for his resurrection—quite touching, really."

"The gratitude is entirely mutual, James. Without your willingness to collaborate again, Holmes would have remained permanently buried." Arthur opened one of the files with obvious satisfaction. "But now we have the opportunity to establish his return on a permanent basis, beginning with the explanation of his survival at Reichenbach Falls."

Watson leaned forward with interest. "You've given considerable thought to the resurrection story?"

"Indeed I have. The key is to make his survival seem not only possible but inevitable—the result of careful planning rather than fortunate accident." Arthur consulted his notes with characteristic precision. "I propose a story called 'The Adventure of the Empty House,' which would reveal that Holmes escaped from Moriarty through a combination of athletic skill and strategic deception."

"And the explanation for his prolonged absence?"

Arthur's eyes gleamed with creative enthusiasm. "Holmes allowed everyone—including you—to believe he had died because it provided the perfect opportunity to dismantle Moriarty's remaining network while his enemies thought him dead. Three years of secret investigations, eliminating criminal enterprises that could never have been approached openly."

Watson found himself impressed by the elegance of this solution. "It would explain both his survival and his silence, while providing dramatic material for the resurrection story itself."

"Precisely. And James, I've identified the perfect case to serve as the framework—the murder of Ronald Adair, with the peculiar circumstances that brought you back into contact with Holmes." Arthur handed Watson a thick file. "Your documentation suggests a case perfectly suited for both dramatic revelation and demonstration of Holmes's continued investigative brilliance."

Watson opened the file, immediately recognizing his own careful notes about the mysterious shooting that had puzzled Scotland Yard completely. "The locked room murder, the impossible circumstances, the connection to the card-playing scandal—yes, this would provide exactly the right framework for Holmes's return."

"More importantly," Arthur continued, "it allows for your own emotional journey—the grief of believing Holmes dead, the shock of discovering his survival, the joy of renewed partnership. Readers will experience the resurrection through your eyes."

As they discussed the specific structure of the resurrection story, both men felt the familiar excitement of collaborative planning at its most productive. The story would satisfy every requirement—dramatic revelation, logical explanation, and compelling mystery that showcased Holmes's methods while emotionally engaging readers who had mourned his loss for nine years.

"Arthur," Watson said as they concluded their discussion of the Empty House framework, "assuming this resurrection story succeeds as we hope, what do you envision for the ongoing series? Regular monthly publication?"

Arthur moved to his filing cabinet and withdrew a substantial folder marked "Series Planning." "James, I've been preparing for exactly this conversation. Based on your complete case documentation, I believe we could commit to twelve monthly stories following the resurrection—a full year of Holmes's return."

"Twelve stories?" Watson raised an eyebrow with interest. "That would represent quite an ambitious commitment."

"But entirely feasible, given the wealth of material you've documented over the years." Arthur opened the folder to reveal careful lists and timeline charts. "I've identified twelve cases that would provide ideal variety while maintaining the quality standards our readers have come to expect."

Arthur began reading from his prepared list: "Following 'The Empty House' in October, I propose 'The Adventure of the Norwood Builder' for November—the case involving young McFarlane and the ingenious deception that nearly sent an innocent man to prison. December could feature 'The Adventure of the Dancing Men'—the cipher case with such tragic personal consequences. January might be 'The Adventure of the Solitary Cyclist,' demonstrating Holmes's ability to protect vulnerable clients from sophisticated predators."

Watson listened with growing appreciation for Arthur's methodical approach. "You've clearly given this considerable thought. What about the remaining eight?"

"February could showcase 'The Adventure of the Priory School'—the kidnapping case involving the Duke's son, with its complex family motivations. March might feature 'The Adventure of Black Peter'—the harpooning murder that so perfectly demonstrated Holmes's practical knowledge of maritime affairs." Arthur's enthusiasm was building as he outlined his vision.

"April could present 'The Adventure of Charles Augustus Milverton'—though we'd need to handle that one carefully, given the social sensitivities involved. May might be 'The Adventure of the Six Napoleons,' showing Holmes's ability to find method in apparent madness. June could feature 'The Adventure of the Three Students,' demonstrating that even academic misconduct can involve genuine detective work."

Watson found himself impressed by both the variety and the logical progression Arthur had planned. "And the final three stories?"

"July could present 'The Adventure of the Golden Pince-Nez'—the locked library murder with its ingenious solution. August might feature 'The Adventure of the Missing Three-Quarter'—the rugby mystery that shows Holmes's versatility across social classes. And September could conclude our year with 'The Adventure of the Abbey Grange'—the case that so perfectly demonstrates how apparent domestic tragedy can conceal complex criminal conspiracy."

Arthur set down his list with obvious satisfaction. "Twelve stories that would showcase every aspect of Holmes's abilities while providing readers with consistent monthly entertainment from October 1902 through September 1903."

Watson studied the proposed schedule, his medical training making him automatically assess the practical requirements such a commitment would entail. "Arthur, this represents a substantial undertaking for both of us. Are you confident we can maintain the quality standards while meeting such regular deadlines?"

"With your detailed documentation and our proven collaborative methods, I believe we can," Arthur replied confidently. "Moreover, James, the financial arrangements The Strand is offering for regular

Holmes stories would provide you with income that could support whatever lifestyle choices you might want to make."

Watson felt the appeal of such security, recognizing that sustained literary income could provide options he had never seriously considered. "The financial aspect is certainly attractive. But Arthur, I want to be absolutely certain that Holmes approves of this expanded collaboration before we commit to such an ambitious schedule."

"Of course. Though I suspect Holmes will appreciate the regular documentation of his methods, especially given Mycroft's endorsement of our educational function." Arthur gathered his planning materials with obvious satisfaction. "But James, there's one other matter I wanted to discuss while you're here."

Watson looked up with interest. "Oh?"

Arthur moved to the window, his manner suggesting a shift to more personal concerns. "I've recently become acquainted with a colleague—Dr. Marcus Pemberton, who has built quite a successful practice in Haslemere. Excellent reputation, distinguished clientele, modern facilities."

"And?" Watson sensed there was more to this introduction.

"Pemberton is considering retirement—his health has been troubling him lately, and he's looking for someone qualified to take over his practice. Someone with established credentials who could maintain the high standards his patients expect." Arthur turned back to Watson with obvious purpose. "James, when he mentioned this situation, I immediately thought of you."

Watson felt his pulse quicken at the unexpected possibility. "Arthur, are you suggesting I consider returning to medical practice?"

"I'm suggesting you might want to explore the option. Pemberton's practice represents exactly the sort of professional opportunity that could provide both meaningful work and financial independence." Arthur's voice carried careful enthusiasm. "Moreover, Haslemere is close enough to London for occasional collaboration on Holmes stories, but far enough to provide the quieter lifestyle you might prefer."

Watson found himself genuinely intrigued by this development. "What sort of practice has Dr. Pemberton established?"

"Mixed general practice with particular strength in treating respiratory ailments—the clean Surrey air attracts patients seeking healthful recovery. Well-appointed surgery, excellent equipment, established relationships with London specialists for complex cases." Arthur consulted his notes. "Most importantly, a patient base that appreciates thoroughness over expedience."

Watson was quiet for a moment, contemplating possibilities he hadn't seriously considered since selling his Kensington practice eight years earlier. "Arthur, do you think Dr. Pemberton would be interested in meeting with me? Not necessarily with any commitment, but simply to discuss what such an arrangement might involve?"

"I'm certain he would. In fact, he mentioned that anyone you might recommend would receive his immediate attention." Arthur smiled at his friend's obvious interest. "James, you could explore the possibility without any obligation. If the situation appeals to you, excellent. If not, no harm done."

As their afternoon of planning continued, Watson found himself dividing his attention between the exciting prospects for Holmes's literary return and the unexpected possibility of resuming the medical career he had abandoned in grief and despair. Both opportunities represented forms of renewal he had thought permanently beyond his reach.

"Arthur," Watson said as they concluded their session with a detailed timeline for the next year's publications, "I want to thank you for suggesting the Pemberton opportunity. Whether or not it proves suitable, the very possibility of returning to meaningful medical work feels... liberating."

"The pleasure is mine, James. You've given me the gift of bringing Holmes back to the reading public. If I can help you rediscover professional satisfaction through medicine, it seems a fair exchange."

As Watson prepared for his return journey to London, both men felt the satisfaction of having successfully planned what promised to be their most ambitious collaborative venture. Holmes would be resurrected through "The Empty House," followed by twelve monthly adventures that would establish his permanent return to popular literature. And Watson would explore the possibility of resuming the medical career that had once provided such professional fulfillment.

"James," Arthur said as they waited for the carriage that would take Watson to the station, "whatever decisions you make about the medical practice, I hope you know how much this collaboration has meant to me. Not just professionally, but personally."

Watson clasped his friend's hand warmly. "Arthur, the feeling is entirely mutual. Our partnership has reminded me that life retains the capacity for meaningful work and genuine friendship, even after the greatest losses."

As the carriage carried Watson away from Undershaw and toward whatever decisions lay ahead, he felt the anticipation of possibilities that honored his past while promising renewal for his future.

Watson's Return to Medicine

April 23, 1902

Holmes sat in his familiar chair by the fireplace, his sharp profile illuminated by the dancing flames as he studied the morning news. His fingers, long and delicate as those of a pianist, drummed silently against the arm of his chair—a habit Watson had observed countless times during their years together, invariably indicating that his restless mind was working through some complex problem.

"Holmes," Watson began, settling into his own chair with a slight grunt that reminded him, not unpleasantly, of his advancing years. "I have something of importance to discuss with you."

Holmes looked up from the telegram, his grey eyes sharp and attentive. "Indeed? Your manner suggests this is not merely another case brought to our door by some distressed client."

"No, my dear fellow. This concerns... well, it concerns our partnership."

Holmes set down the newspaper with deliberate care and turned his full attention to Watson. In all their years together, Watson had rarely seen him so immediately focused on his words. "I am listening, Watson."

Watson had rehearsed this conversation countless times during his walk from the publisher's office, yet now, faced with those penetrating eyes, he found himself struggling to find the right words. "Holmes, you must understand how deeply I value our association. The cases we have solved together, the adventures we have shared—they have given my life a new richness and purpose since I lost Mary and our son. I never imagined possible at the time that I would recover, but I did, thanks to you."

"I sense a 'however' approaching," Holmes observed, his voice carefully neutral.

"However," Watson continued, offering him a rueful smile, "I find myself thinking increasingly of my original profession. It has been years since I practiced medicine in any meaningful way, and I confess that I feel... well, that I feel a calling to return to the healing arts."

Holmes was silent for a long moment, his fingers steepled beneath his chin in the gesture Watson knew so well. The fire crackled softly, and from the street below came the muffled sounds of London evening—the clip-clop of horses, the distant cry of a newspaper vendor, the rumble of an omnibus.

"You wish to resume your medical practice," Holmes said finally. It was not a question.

"I do. I have had the opportunity to take over Dr. Pemberton's practice at Queen Anne Street. He is retiring and has offered to transfer his patients to me. The work would be... well, it would be quite different from tracking down criminals and solving mysteries."

"Different, indeed." Holmes reached for his pipe, a gesture Watson recognized as his way of buying time to think. "And what of our work together? What of the cases that come to this very door because they require not just my methods, but your steady hand and practical mind?"

The question Watson had been dreading. "Holmes, you managed quite well before we met. Your reputation was already established. I have no doubt that you could continue to do so."

"Could, perhaps. But would I wish to?" Holmes struck a match and held it to the bowl of his pipe, his actions deliberate and measured. "You underestimate your contribution to our partnership, Watson. You provide not merely assistance, but perspective. You see what I, in my singular focus, might miss. You understand people in ways that I do not."

"You flatter me, Holmes."

"I do not flatter. I observe and deduce." Holmes drew deeply on his pipe, the smoke curling upward in the still air. "But I also understand the pull of one's original calling. Medicine was your first love, was it not? Before the Army, before Afghanistan, before you ever heard the name Sherlock Holmes."

Holmes stood and walked to the window, gazing out at the gaslit street below. "You have always been driven by a desire to help others. In our cases, you help by supporting me, by chronicling our adventures, by providing the human element that makes our work meaningful. But I understand your need to return to more direct healing, for the satisfaction of placing your hands on a patient and making them well."

"You understand perfectly," Watson said, relief flooding through him. "I worried that you might think me ungrateful or—"

"Ungrateful?" Holmes turned from the window, his expression almost shocked. "Watson, you have given me years of your life, your friendship, your unwavering loyalty. You have stood by me through cases that brought danger to your very doorstep. You have chronicled our adventures with skill and dedication, making them accessible to the public in ways my own reports never could. If anyone has cause for gratitude, it is I."

Holmes returned to his chair, leaning forward with an intensity Watson had rarely seen directed at him. "But more than that, you have given me something I had not realized I needed until it was gone— companionship. Not mere assistance, but true friendship. Before you came to Baker Street, I was... well, I was rather like a calculating machine, efficient but cold. You brought warmth to this place, Watson. You brought life."

Watson felt his eyes growing damp and cleared his throat roughly. "Holmes, I—"

"No, let me finish. You brought life, and laughter, and the occasional bout of exasperation that kept me grounded. You challenged my methods when they grew too callous, and you provided the emotional understanding that solved cases mere logic could not touch. You have been far more than a assistant or chronicler. You have been the finest friend a man could ask for."

The silence that followed was not uncomfortable, but full of the weight of years shared, dangers faced together, and the deep understanding that comes only from true friendship.

"So," Holmes said finally, "when do you begin with Dr. Pemberton's practice?"

Watson started. "You mean... you approve?"

"Approve? My dear Watson, I could no more disapprove of your return to medicine than I could disapprove of a bird taking flight. It is your nature, your calling. To deny it would be to deny who you are." Holmes smiled, and Watson was surprised to see genuine warmth in his expression. "Besides, a medical practice is hardly the other side of the world. And I cannot imagine that your patients would object to their doctor occasionally consulting on a case of particular interest."

"You mean... you would still want me to help with cases?"

"Want? Watson, I would be lost without you. But I would no longer ask you to choose between medicine and our work. Perhaps we can find a way to honor both callings."

Watson leaned back in his chair, feeling as though a great weight had been lifted from his shoulders. "Holmes, I cannot tell you how much this means to me."

"Then don't try. Simply return to being the doctor you were meant to be, and when the game is afoot, know that there will always be a place for you at my side."

An Offer from Collier's

May 5, 1902

Arthur Conan Doyle found himself pacing the terrace of Undershaw with the restless energy that always accompanied momentous business decisions. In his hand, he held a cablegram from New York that had arrived that morning, bearing an offer so extraordinary that it threatened to upend every arrangement he and James Watson had carefully established for their literary collaboration.

The cablegram, signed by Norman Hapgood of Collier's Weekly, was characteristically American in its directness:

PREPARED OFFER UNPRECEDENTED TERMS THIRTEEN HOLMES STORIES. FIRST PUBLICATION RIGHTS AMERICA ESSENTIAL. SUGGEST MEETING LONDON EARLIEST CONVENIENCE. OPPORTUNITY CANNOT AWAIT. - HAPGOOD

Arthur paused in his pacing to reread the message for the dozenth time, his mind working through implications that grew more complex with each consideration. Collier's Weekly was prepared to pay nearly three times what The Strand Magazine offered for Holmes stories, but their terms required first publication in America—a dramatic departure from the arrangement that had made The Strand the exclusive home of Sherlock Holmes in the English-speaking world.

The sound of carriage wheels on the gravel drive announced Watson's arrival for their scheduled meeting, and Arthur felt both relief and apprehension at the prospect of discussing this development with his collaborator. The American offer represented unprecedented financial opportunity, but it also challenged the loyalties and professional relationships that had sustained their partnership for nearly two decades.

Watson emerged from the carriage with the measured stride Arthur had learned to associate with his friend's most thoughtful moods. At fifty-one, Watson carried himself with the quiet confidence that their recent successes had restored, though Arthur detected immediately the careful attention that suggested awareness of significant business pending.

"Arthur," Watson called out as he approached the terrace, "your message mentioned urgent developments requiring immediate consultation. I confess myself curious about what could demand such pressing attention."

Arthur handed his friend the cablegram without preamble, watching Watson's expression carefully as he read through Hapgood's proposition. The silence that followed suggested Watson was working through the same complex calculations that had occupied Arthur's thoughts since the message arrived.

"Good Lord," Watson said finally, looking up with obvious amazement. "Arthur, these figures... they're extraordinary. Nearly three times our current arrangements with The Strand."

"Indeed. Hapgood's offer represents more income from thirteen stories than we've earned from our entire previous collaboration." Arthur's voice carried a mixture of excitement and concern. "But James, the terms require first publication in America, ahead of The Strand. That would represent a fundamental change in our publishing arrangements."

Watson moved to the terrace railing, looking out at the Surrey countryside while contemplating the implications of such a shift. "How long has Collier's been interested in obtaining Holmes stories?"

"This is their first direct approach, though I've heard rumors of American interest for months." Arthur joined Watson at the railing, his expression growing more serious. "The success of 'The Empty House' last October exceeded every projection. Hapgood apparently believes American readers are prepared to support Holmes stories on an unprecedented scale."

Watson nodded thoughtfully. "The resurrection story did generate remarkable response, both here and in America. But Arthur, what does Herbert Greenhough Smith say about this development? Surely The Strand has some claim to continued priority?"

Arthur's expression grew more troubled. "That's precisely the dilemma, James. The Strand has been our partner for over a decade, providing consistent support even during the years when Holmes was supposedly dead. But their current terms... well, they simply cannot compete with what Hapgood is offering."

"And Greenhough Smith's reaction to the American interest?"

"He's requested a meeting for tomorrow, though I suspect he already knows he cannot match Collier's financial offer." Arthur turned to face Watson directly. "James, this decision will affect our entire future collaboration. The question is whether we pursue this opportunity despite our loyalty to The Strand."

Watson was quiet for several minutes, his medical training making him naturally systematic in considering complex decisions. When he finally spoke, his voice carried the careful precision Arthur had learned to respect.

"Arthur, what exactly does Hapgood require for first publication rights? Would The Strand be permitted to publish the stories at all?"

"Yes, but only after a delay—typically three to six months after American publication. The Strand would become secondary rather than primary." Arthur consulted his notes. "Hapgood wants to establish Collier's as the premier source for Holmes stories in the international market."

"And the practical arrangements for our collaboration? Would working with an American publication create additional complications?"

Arthur had clearly given this considerable thought. "Actually, the arrangements might prove simpler. Hapgood is prepared to accept our stories based on our established reputation, with minimal editorial interference. The Strand's review process, while generally supportive, does occasionally require revisions that delay publication."

Watson moved to the chairs Arthur had arranged on the terrace, settling into his customary seat with the deliberate manner of someone preparing for extended discussion. "Arthur, before we consider the practical aspects, I think we need to address the ethical implications. The Strand has supported our work consistently, even during the difficult years following Mary's death when my contributions were irregular at best."

"I share those concerns completely, James. Greenhough Smith has been more than fair in his dealings with us, and The Strand provided the platform that made Holmes's literary success possible." Arthur's voice carried genuine conflict. "But we must also consider our responsibilities to ourselves and to the continued quality of our work."

"How so?"

Arthur settled into his own chair, his expression growing more animated as he developed his argument. "James, the financial security that Hapgood's offer would provide could transform our entire approach to the collaboration. Rather than working under the constant pressure of monthly deadlines, we could select only the finest cases, develop them with unlimited care, and create stories that set new standards for detective fiction."

Watson felt the appeal of such creative freedom, recognizing how financial pressure had sometimes forced them to adapt cases that were merely adequate rather than exceptional. "The artistic benefits would certainly be substantial. But Arthur, wouldn't accepting the American offer damage our relationship with The Strand permanently?"

"Not necessarily. Greenhough Smith is a businessman as well as an editor. If we explain that Collier's terms make their offer impossible to refuse, while assuring The Strand of continued access to Holmes stories after appropriate delays..." Arthur paused, studying Watson's expression.

"I believe we could maintain that relationship while pursuing this extraordinary opportunity."

The afternoon progressed with detailed discussion of practical arrangements, financial projections, and creative possibilities. Hapgood's offer included not just unprecedented payment terms but also guaranteed publication schedules, international distribution rights, and promotional support that could expand Holmes's audience far beyond anything they had previously achieved.

"Arthur," Watson said as they paused for tea, "I'm beginning to see the broader implications of Hapgood's offer. This isn't simply about better financial terms—it's about establishing Holmes as a truly international literary phenomenon."

"Precisely my thinking, James. Collier's has distribution throughout America, Canada, and increasingly in other English-speaking territories. Publishing Holmes stories there first could introduce him to audiences that might never encounter The Strand." Arthur's enthusiasm was building as he outlined the possibilities. "We could be creating a global readership for authentic detective fiction."

Watson found himself responding to Arthur's vision despite his continued concerns about their obligations to The Strand. "The educational benefits you mention—Mycroft's point about public education in proper investigative methods—would certainly be amplified by wider distribution."

"Indeed. And James, there's another consideration that may interest you." Arthur consulted his correspondence files. "Hapgood has suggested that Collier's success with Holmes stories could lead to opportunities for other collaborative projects—perhaps articles on criminal investigation, or even book-length works on detective methodology."

Watson looked up with obvious interest. "You mean non-fiction works? Serious discussion of investigative techniques?"

"Exactly. Hapgood believes there's substantial American appetite for authentic information about crime-solving methods, presented by the same team that created the Holmes stories." Arthur's eyes gleamed with possibility. "Such work could serve the educational purposes Mycroft identified while establishing us as authorities on criminal investigation beyond the realm of fiction."

As the afternoon wore on, both men found themselves increasingly convinced that Hapgood's offer represented more than just financial opportunity—it was a chance to expand their influence and educational impact on an international scale. The practical arrangements were complex, but the potential benefits seemed to justify the risks involved.

"Arthur," Watson said as their discussion approached its conclusion, "I believe we should pursue this opportunity, provided we can negotiate arrangements that maintain our relationship with The Strand. The financial security alone would allow us to focus on quality rather than quantity."

Arthur felt a surge of relief at Watson's support. "I was hoping you would see the possibilities, James. But you're absolutely right about maintaining our relationship with The Strand. Whatever arrangements we make with Collier's must include provisions for continued publication in Britain."

"Then you'll meet with Hapgood when he arrives in London?"

"I will," agreed Arthur, "and I will keep you informed."

Dr. Watson's New Practice

June 29, 1902

The June morning had brought perfect weather to London, with clear skies and a gentle breeze that carried through the tall windows of what was now Dr. James Watson's fully established medical practice on Queen Anne Street. The brass nameplate beside the entrance—"James H. Watson, M.D., F.R.C.S."—gleamed in the morning sunlight, marking the official beginning of a professional chapter Watson had never expected to write again.

The transformation of Dr. Pemberton's former surgery had required three months of careful renovation, updating equipment while preserving the atmosphere of medical competence that had served the practice well for over twenty years. Watson stood in his consulting room, adjusting the position of his diploma on the freshly painted wall, marveling at how natural it felt to be surrounded once again by the instruments and arrangements of active medical practice.

The morning's first patients had been a deliberate selection—longtime clients of Dr. Pemberton who had agreed to serve as a gentle introduction to Watson's resumption of medical work. Mrs. Ashworth's chronic bronchitis, Mr. Thompson's gout, young Sarah Mitchell's seasonal allergies—familiar conditions that had allowed Watson to rediscover his diagnostic skills without the pressure of complex or critical cases.

But this afternoon would bring the formal celebration that marked not just the opening of a medical practice but Watson's return to the professional life he had abandoned in grief eight years earlier. The small reception planned for three o'clock would include colleagues from the local medical community, valued patients who had agreed to the transition from Dr. Pemberton, and—most significantly—the friends whose support had made this renewal possible.

Earlier in the day, Watson had received a telegram from Sherlock Holmes sending his regrets for not being able to attend today's grand opening. Although disappointed, Watson understood better than most about the occasionally urgency that Sherlock's cases often required. He would be missed, but at least he had heard from his friend.

Watson checked his pocket watch: half past two. Miss Ann Hunter's train from Birmingham had arrived in London that morning, arriving in time for the reception that would officially mark his return to medicine. The past eight months of regular correspondence had deepened their acquaintance into something approaching genuine intimacy, while her two subsequent visits to London had confirmed the compatibility they had discovered during that memorable evening at Simpson's.

The sound of carriage wheels on the gravel drive announced the arrival of the first guests, and Watson moved to the window to see Arthur and Louisa Doyle approaching with the warm smiles that had characterized their friendship through triumph and tragedy alike. Arthur had insisted on attending this celebration, declaring that Watson's return to medical practice deserved recognition from all who valued his friendship and professional abilities.

"James!" Arthur called out as Watson opened the door to greet them. "At last—Dr. Watson properly returned to his natural element. The surgery looks magnificent."

Louisa embraced Watson with genuine affection, her face showing the pleasure of someone witnessing a dear friend's recovery from prolonged difficulty. "James, you look absolutely radiant. There's something about you today—a vitality I haven't seen since before Mary's illness. This return to medicine has clearly been exactly what you needed."

Watson felt moved by their obvious joy in his achievement. "Thank you both for making the journey from Undershaw. Having you here today means more to me than I can adequately express."

Arthur studied the renovated surgery with obvious appreciation for the care Watson had invested in its preparation. "You've created something remarkable here, James. Modern equipment, excellent lighting, comfortable arrangements for patients—exactly what a quality medical practice should provide."

"Dr. Pemberton left me an excellent foundation," Watson replied, guiding them through the various rooms. "The challenge was updating equipment and procedures while maintaining the atmosphere of trust and competence his patients had come to expect."

As they completed their tour, additional guests began arriving—Dr. Morrison from the village practice, Dr. Stephens from Guildford who had agreed to provide consultation for complex cases, and several of Watson's new patients who had insisted on attending to show their support for their new physician.

"James," Arthur said quietly as they watched the small gathering develop, "how are you feeling about this transition? Eight years away from active practice—surely there must be some anxiety about resuming such responsibilities?"

Watson considered the question carefully, recognizing its importance for his own understanding of what he had undertaken. "Surprisingly little anxiety, actually. The skills proved to be more durable than I expected, and the satisfaction..." He paused, searching for adequate words. "Arthur, I had forgotten how meaningful it feels to use one's abilities in direct service to people's immediate needs."

"And the combination with our literary work? Are you finding the balance manageable?"

Watson smiled at his friend's practical concern. "More than manageable—complementary, actually. The regular intellectual stimulation of medical practice enhances rather than detracts from my ability to contribute to our Holmes collaboration."

Their conversation was interrupted by the arrival of another carriage, and Watson felt his pulse quicken as he recognized the elegant figure of Miss Ann Hunter alighting with the composed grace that had characterized all her movements since their reunion. She wore a dress of pale green silk that spoke of careful preparation for this significant occasion, and her face showed the warm anticipation of someone genuinely pleased to share in a friend's important moment.

"Miss Hunter," Watson called out, moving quickly to assist her from the carriage. "How wonderful that you could join us. The journey wasn't too taxing, I hope?"

"Not at all, Dr. Watson," she replied, accepting his offered hand with a smile that seemed to illuminate the entire afternoon. "I wouldn't have missed this celebration for anything. To see you properly returned to medical practice—it's exactly the sort of achievement that deserves recognition from one's friends."

Watson felt the familiar warmth that had characterized all his interactions with Miss Hunter since their correspondence began. "Miss Hunter, may I present Arthur and Louisa Doyle? Arthur, Touie—Miss Ann Hunter, Head Mistress of Queen Mary's Grammar School in Walsall."

Arthur stepped forward with obvious interest, having heard Watson speak of Miss Hunter with increasing frequency during their recent meetings. "Miss Hunter, what a pleasure to meet you at last. James has spoken of you with such admiration—your educational achievements, your remarkable correspondence, your understanding of our... collaborative work."

Miss Hunter accepted Arthur's greeting with the intelligent composure that Watson had come to appreciate so deeply. "Dr. Doyle, the pleasure is entirely mine. Your literary work has brought such joy to so many readers, and I'm particularly grateful for your assistance in facilitating my reunion with Dr. Watson."

Louisa moved forward with the warm smile that had made her immediately beloved by all who knew her. "Miss Hunter, James has told us how much your friendship has meant to him during this period of professional renewal. We're so delighted you could be here today."

As the reception continued, Watson found himself observing Miss Hunter's easy integration into the gathering with growing satisfaction. She engaged Dr. Morrison in thoughtful discussion about educational health programs, shared amusing anecdotes with Louisa about the challenges of managing large institutions, and demonstrated exactly the kind of intelligent social grace that made her such valued company.

"Dr. Watson," Dr. Stephens approached with obvious professional interest, "I've been reviewing the case files Dr. Pemberton provided, and I'm impressed by the thoroughness of your diagnostic approaches. Your medical training clearly emphasized systematic methodology."

Watson nodded, appreciating the recognition from a colleague whose opinion carried weight in the local medical community. "Military medical service requires precision under challenging circumstances. Those habits prove quite valuable in civilian practice as well."

"Indeed. And I understand you've maintained scholarly interests during your years away from active practice? Dr. Pemberton mentioned some involvement with medical literature?"

Watson felt a moment of careful consideration about how much to reveal regarding his true literary activities. "I've provided some consultation for writers attempting to portray medical and investigative procedures accurately. Ensuring scientific authenticity in popular literature seems worthwhile."

Dr. Stephens nodded approvingly. "Excellent approach. Too much popular fiction presents medicine and criminal investigation in ways that mislead the public about actual professional methods."

As the afternoon progressed, Watson found himself repeatedly drawn into conversation with Miss Hunter, their exchanges ranging from professional observations to personal reflections on the changes the past year had brought to both their lives.

"Dr. Watson," she said during a quiet moment when they had stepped onto the surgery's small terrace, "I hope you don't mind my saying that you seem transformed since we first met again last October. There's a vitality, a sense of purpose about you today that speaks of genuine contentment."

Watson felt moved by her perceptive observation. "Miss Hunter, you're quite right. The return to medical practice has provided exactly the kind of meaningful work I needed to feel complete again. But..." He paused, choosing his words carefully. "I believe the renewal has as much to do with the friendships that have developed this past year as with professional considerations."

Miss Hunter colored slightly at the implication, though her expression showed pleasure rather than discomfort at his words. "Dr. Watson, your friendship has been equally meaningful to me. Our correspondence, our meetings when I visit London, the way you've encouraged my own professional aspirations—all of it has enriched my life considerably."

Before Watson could respond to this observation, Arthur approached with obvious satisfaction at finding them in such animated conversation. "James, Miss Hunter—I hope you'll forgive the interruption, but I wanted to propose a toast before our gathering concludes."

Arthur gestured to the assembled guests, raising his glass of champagne with ceremonial purpose. "Ladies and gentlemen, we gather today to celebrate not just the opening of a medical practice, but the return of a valued colleague to the profession that has benefited so greatly from his skills and dedication."

The small group gathered closer, recognizing the significance of the moment Arthur was marking.

"Dr. James Watson brings to this practice not only exceptional medical training and years of diverse professional experience, but also the character and compassion that make healing possible," Arthur continued, his voice carrying genuine emotion. "Those of us privileged to call him friend have witnessed his courage under the most challenging circumstances, his loyalty to those he serves, and his unwavering commitment to using his abilities in service to others."

Arthur turned to face Watson directly. "James, your return to medicine represents more than professional renewal—it demonstrates that the finest qualities of human character can survive any trial and emerge stronger for having been tested. We celebrate not just Dr. Watson the physician, but James Watson the man whose friendship has enriched all our lives."

The assembled guests raised their glasses in enthusiastic agreement, and Watson felt overwhelmed by the warmth and support of people who had witnessed his journey from despair through recovery to this moment of genuine renewal.

"Thank you all," Watson replied, his voice thick with emotion. "Your presence here today, your support during the months of preparation, your confidence in my ability to resume the work I love—all of it means more to me than I can adequately express."

Watson paused, looking around the gathering that represented different aspects of his renewed life. "Eight years ago, I thought my useful professional life had ended. Today, surrounded by colleagues who inspire me and friends who sustain me, I understand that the most important chapters may still lie ahead."

As the reception concluded and guests prepared to depart, Watson found himself walking Miss Hunter to the carriage that would take her to the station for her return journey to Walsall.

"Miss Hunter," Watson said as they paused beside the carriage, "thank you for making such an effort to be here today. Having you present for this milestone meant more to me than you might realize."

Miss Hunter turned to face him directly, her expression serious despite the obvious pleasure the afternoon had brought her. "Dr. Watson, I hope you know that witnessing your return to medicine, seeing you surrounded by colleagues and friends who value your contributions—it's been one of the most meaningful afternoons of my recent years."

Watson felt himself drawn to speak more openly than their public setting might typically permit. "Miss Hunter, our friendship has become one of the most valued aspects of my life. Your understanding, your encouragement, your own example of professional dedication—all of it has contributed to whatever success I've achieved."

Miss Hunter's eyes held warmth that transcended mere friendship as she prepared to enter the carriage. "Dr. Watson, whatever the future holds, I hope you know that your friendship has given me a happiness I had thought might be beyond my reach."

As her carriage disappeared toward the station, Watson stood for a moment in the evening light, reflecting on a day that had exceeded every expectation. The medical practice was established, his professional renewal was complete, and the friendship with Miss Hunter had evolved into something that promised possibilities he had never dared contemplate.

Arthur and Louisa emerged from the surgery to find Watson still standing in contemplation, his face showing the complex satisfaction of someone who had successfully rebuilt a life he had thought permanently destroyed.

"James," Arthur said gently, "how are you feeling now that the celebration is concluded?"

Watson turned to his friends with a smile that reflected genuine contentment. "Grateful, Arthur. Profoundly grateful for the friends who made this day possible, for the opportunity to resume meaningful work, and for the reminder that life retains the capacity for renewal even after the greatest losses."

"And Miss Hunter?" Louisa asked with the gentle interest of someone who had observed their interaction throughout the afternoon. "She seems to have become quite an important part of your renewed happiness."

Watson felt himself coloring at Louisa's perceptive observation. "Miss Hunter has indeed become... very dear to me. Her friendship has contributed immeasurably to whatever contentment I've achieved."

Arthur clasped his friend's shoulder with obvious affection. "James, today has been a triumph in every respect. The practice, the colleagues, the patients, the friends—and perhaps most importantly, the evidence that you've successfully found your way back to a life worthy of your finest qualities."

As evening settled over London and the three friends prepared to conclude this memorable day, Watson felt the profound satisfaction that comes from having achieved something genuinely significant. The medical practice would provide the professional fulfillment he had missed, the Holmes collaboration would continue to serve their educational purposes, and perhaps most importantly, the friendship with Miss Hunter would continue to develop into whatever possibilities the future might hold.

The brass nameplate beside his door would greet tomorrow's patients with the promise of competent, compassionate medical care, while the letters from Birmingham would continue to bring the correspondence that had become such a valued part of his weekly routine.

Dr. James Watson had returned to medicine, but more than that, he had returned to life—complete with meaningful work, valued friendships, and the prospect of happiness that honored his past while embracing whatever future awaited.

A New Years Eve Proposal

December 31, 1902

The ballroom of the Langham Hotel had been transformed into a glittering celebration of the approaching New Year, with crystal chandeliers casting warm light over London's most distinguished gathering. Dr. James Watson stood near one of the tall windows overlooking Portland Place, his evening dress impeccable despite the nervous energy that had characterized his demeanor throughout the evening. At forty-eight, he had regained the confident bearing that had once marked his military service, though tonight a different kind of anticipation filled him with an excitement he hadn't felt since his youth.

Beside him, Miss Ann Hunter radiated the quiet elegance that had first captured his attention during their reunion one year earlier. Her gown of midnight blue silk, chosen specifically for this most significant of evenings, complemented perfectly the dignified beauty that had matured during her years of professional achievement. At thirty-nine, she had reached the height of her career as Head Mistress, but tonight her attention was focused entirely on the man whose friendship had transformed into something far deeper during their months of correspondence and carefully chaperoned meetings.

"Dr. Watson," she said softly, her gloved hand resting lightly on his arm, "you've seemed rather... preoccupied this evening. Are you quite well?"

Watson felt his pulse quicken at her gentle concern, the small leather box in his waistcoat pocket seeming to weigh more with each passing moment. "Perfectly well, my dear Miss Hunter. Simply... contemplating the significance of the evening. The end of one year, the beginning of another."

The past fourteen months had brought changes to both their lives that neither had dared anticipate during that first tentative reunion at the Criterion Bar. Watson's medical practice in Haslemere had flourished beyond his most optimistic projections, while his renewed collaboration with Arthur had produced a second successful series of Holmes adventures that had cemented the great detective's permanent return to literature. Most significantly, his friendship with Miss Hunter had evolved through weekly correspondence and monthly meetings into an affection that honored his past while promising a future he had thought forever beyond his reach.

"The year has brought remarkable changes," Miss Hunter agreed, her voice carrying the warmth that had made their correspondence such a treasured part of his weekly routine. "Your medical practice established so successfully, the Holmes stories achieving such acclaim, our own..." She paused, coloring slightly. "Our own friendship developing in ways I never dared hope possible."

Watson turned to study her profile in the ballroom's golden light, marveling once again at the intelligence and character that had first drawn him to her during that memorable dinner at Simpson's. The months of courtship—conducted with all the propriety their respective positions demanded—had revealed depths of compatibility that transcended their shared appreciation for meaningful work and mutual understanding of personal loss.

"Miss Hunter," Watson said, his voice taking on the careful tone that indicated matters of genuine importance, "there's something I've been wanting to discuss with you. Something rather... significant."

Before Miss Hunter could respond, the sound of applause drew their attention to the small stage where the hotel's orchestra had been providing musical accompaniment throughout the evening. The conductor, a distinguished gentleman with silver hair and an obvious flair for dramatic presentation, raised his baton to command the room's attention.

"Ladies and gentlemen," he announced in a voice that carried easily across the crowded ballroom, "as we approach the final moments of 1902, we invite you to join us in welcoming what promises to be a year of unprecedented possibility and achievement."

Watson felt his hands trembling slightly as he consulted his pocket watch: eleven fifty-five. The carefully planned moment was approaching, and despite months of preparation, he found himself overwhelmed by the magnitude of what he was about to undertake.

"Dr. Watson," Miss Hunter said gently, having noticed his obvious agitation, "whatever it is you wish to discuss, surely it can wait until we're in more private surroundings? You seem quite... anxious about something."

Watson took her hand in his, feeling the warmth of her touch through their evening gloves. "Miss Hunter, what I have to say can't wait. Indeed, I've chosen this moment quite deliberately."

The conductor's voice carried across the ballroom once more: "Ladies and gentlemen, as we prepare to bid farewell to 1902, let us take a moment to reflect on the friendships, the achievements, and the love that have made this year memorable."

Watson guided Miss Hunter to a slightly more secluded alcove near the window, where the sounds of celebration provided a backdrop without overwhelming their ability to speak privately. His heart was beating so rapidly he was certain she must hear it, but her expression showed only the gentle patience that had characterized all their most important conversations.

"Miss Hunter," Watson began, his voice steady despite the profound emotion that threatened to overwhelm him, "when we first met again after all those years, I was a man who had given up hope of ever finding happiness again. The loss of Mary and our child, the grief that had consumed so much of my life—I thought such darkness was my permanent condition."

Miss Hunter's eyes filled with understanding as she recognized the significance of what he was sharing. "Dr. Watson, you know how deeply I've come to value our friendship, how much your correspondence and your companionship have meant to me."

"But it's become more than friendship, hasn't it?" Watson continued, his gaze fixed intently on her face. "For me, certainly, and I hope... I dare to hope... for you as well."

The conductor's voice interrupted once more: "Sixty seconds until midnight, ladies and gentlemen! Sixty seconds until we welcome 1903!"

Watson felt the weight of the moment settling upon him with an intensity that rivaled any crisis he had faced during his years with Holmes. But this was a different kind of courage required—not the bravery needed to face physical danger, but the vulnerability necessary to offer one's heart completely to another person.

"Fifty-five seconds!"

Watson withdrew the small leather box from his waistcoat pocket, his hands steadier now that the decisive moment had arrived. "Miss Hunter, you have brought light back into my life when I thought it would remain forever dark. You have shown me that love can honor the past while embracing the future, that happiness can be found again even after the greatest losses."

Miss Hunter's eyes widened as she recognized the significance of the small box he held, her hand moving unconsciously to her throat in a gesture of surprise and growing wonder.

"Forty-five seconds!"

"Miss Ann Hunter," Watson said, his voice carrying all the conviction and affection that had been building for months, "you are the most remarkable woman I have ever known—intelligent, compassionate, brave, and beautiful in ways that transcend mere physical appearance. You have made me remember what it means to hope, to dream, to believe in possibilities I thought forever beyond my reach."

"Thirty seconds!"

Watson opened the small box to reveal a ring of elegant simplicity—a perfect sapphire surrounded by small diamonds, chosen specifically for its understated beauty and lasting quality. "Miss Hunter, would you do me the extraordinary honor of becoming my wife?"

The noise of the countdown seemed to fade into the background as Miss Hunter looked into Watson's eyes, seeing there the depth of feeling that had grown from friendship through affection into something that promised the kind of partnership both had thought might be beyond their reach.

"Twenty seconds!"

"Oh, Dr. Watson," Miss Hunter whispered, tears of joy glistening in her eyes, "yes! Yes, of course, yes! Nothing would make me happier than to spend my life as your wife."

"Ten seconds!"

Watson slipped the ring onto her finger with hands that trembled with excitement rather than nervousness, both of them oblivious now to the celebration surrounding them as they became absorbed in the profound significance of their mutual commitment.

"Five! Four! Three! Two! One!"

"Happy New Year!"

As the great clock struck midnight and the ballroom erupted in celebration around them, Watson drew Miss Hunter into his arms with the tender reverence appropriate to such a sacred moment. Their kiss was gentle but profound, carrying within it all the hope, affection, and promise that had brought them to this perfect beginning.

The sounds of celebration—champagne corks popping, horns blowing, voices raised in joyful song—provided a festive backdrop to their private moment of commitment. But for Watson and Miss Hunter, the noise seemed distant and unimportant compared to the quiet miracle of having found each other again after so many years, of having discovered that second chances at happiness were possible for those patient enough to wait and brave enough to believe.

As they finally separated from their kiss, Miss Hunter looked up into Watson's eyes with a smile that seemed to illuminate the entire evening. "Dr. Watson," she said softly, then paused, her expression growing more tender. "Actually, I believe that after such a moment—after accepting your proposal and sharing our first kiss as an engaged couple—perhaps it's time you called me Ann. And I should very much like to call you James."

Watson felt his heart soar at this gesture of intimacy, understanding that she was marking not just their engagement but their transition from formal courtship to genuine partnership. "Ann," he said, testing her name on his lips with obvious pleasure. "My dearest Ann. And yes, please—James. After all we've shared, all we've promised each other, such formality seems unnecessary."

"Happy New Year, my beloved James," Ann replied, her voice thick with emotion. "The first of what I hope will be many, many years together."

"Happy New Year, my dearest Ann," James murmured, raising her hand to admire the ring that now marked their engagement. "I can hardly believe our good fortune."

As they held each other in the alcove that had become their private sanctuary within the public celebration, both felt the profound satisfaction that comes from having made a decision that honored their past while embracing their future completely. The sapphire caught the ballroom's light as Ann raised her hand to admire the symbol of their commitment, and James felt his heart soar with a happiness he had thought lost forever.

"When shall we marry?" Ann asked, her practical nature asserting itself even in the midst of such overwhelming emotion.

James smiled at her characteristically thoughtful question. "As soon as propriety and your professional obligations permit. Though I confess, my darling, that I would marry you tomorrow if such haste wouldn't scandalize the educational authorities."

Ann laughed, the sound musical above the continued celebration around them. "James, you know I must complete the academic year before making such a significant change to my circumstances. But perhaps... a June wedding? June has always seemed the most hopeful of months."

"June 1903," James agreed, raising her hand to his lips to kiss the ring that now marked their engagement. "Ann, I can hardly believe our good fortune. To have found each other again, to have discovered such compatibility, to be offered this chance at happiness..."

"We've both learned that joy can follow sorrow, that life retains the capacity to surprise us with blessings we never dared hope for," Ann replied, her voice carrying the wisdom earned through her own trials and recovery. "James, I believe we're going to be extraordinarily happy together."

As the evening continued with dancing and champagne toasts to the New Year, James and Ann found themselves the center of congratulations from friends who had observed their growing attachment with approval and delight. Arthur and Louisa Doyle, who had traveled up from Surrey specifically for this celebration, embraced them both with tears of joy at news they had been hoping to hear for months.

"James, my dear fellow," Arthur said, clasping his friend's hand with obvious emotion, "I cannot tell you how delighted Touie and I are by this news. Ann, you are gaining one of the finest men I have ever known, while James is gaining a woman whose character and intelligence make her worthy of his deepest affection."

Louisa embraced Ann warmly, her face glowing with happiness for friends whose courtship she had watched develop with such careful discretion. "My dear Ann, I am so very happy for you both. You and

James have found in each other exactly what was needed—not just love, but true partnership."

As the celebration gradually wound down and guests began making their farewells, James and Ann found themselves once again in their quiet alcove, reluctant to end an evening that had transformed their friendship into an engagement and their hope into certainty.

"Ann," James said as they prepared to part for the evening—propriety demanding that she return to her hotel while he traveled back to his own lodgings, "I hope you know that this proposal represents not just my love for you, but my profound respect for everything you've achieved. I would never ask you to sacrifice your professional accomplishments for marriage."

Ann's eyes filled with gratitude at his understanding of what her career meant to her. "James, that's precisely why I know our marriage will be so successful. You understand that love enhances rather than diminishes our individual achievements. Together, we'll be stronger than either of us could be alone."

As they stood in the hotel's elegant lobby, preparing to part until they could meet again the following day, both felt the deep satisfaction that comes from having made a decision that promised to enrich every aspect of their lives. The New Year stretched ahead, full of possibilities neither had dared imagine when the evening began.

"Until tomorrow, my dearest Ann," James said, raising her hand once more to his lips.

"Until tomorrow, my beloved James," she replied, her smile radiant with the happiness that had transformed an evening of celebration into the beginning of their shared future.

As James's carriage carried him through the London streets toward his hotel, he reflected on the extraordinary turn his life had taken. Two years ago, he had been a broken man living in exile from everything that had once given his life meaning. Tonight, he was an engaged man with a thriving medical practice, a successful literary collaboration, and the promise of marriage to a woman whose love honored his past while embracing their mutual future.

The New Year had begun with the kind of blessing he had thought impossible—the chance to love again, to build a new life with someone who understood both his history and his hopes. As London settled into the quiet hours after midnight, Dr. James Watson carried with him the knowledge that 1903 would bring not just professional satisfaction but personal joy that had once seemed forever beyond his reach.

The sapphire on Ann's finger caught the lamplight as her own carriage carried her toward her hotel, and she touched it gently, marveling at how completely her life had changed in the space of a single evening. Tomorrow would bring the practical arrangements that an engagement required, but tonight had provided the emotional foundation upon which their marriage would be built—love, respect, understanding, and the shared recognition that they had found in each other exactly what was needed to make the future bright with promise.

As 1903 began its first quiet hours, two people who had separately overcome significant trials looked forward to a year that would unite their lives in marriage and their hearts in the kind of love that survives every test time might bring.

The Perfect Wedding

June 3, 1903

The bells of St. Bartholomew's Church in Haslemere rang out across the Surrey countryside with a joyful clarity that seemed to announce not merely the approaching noon hour, but the beginning of what promised to be the most significant day in Dr. James Watson's recent memory. The morning mist had lifted early, revealing a perfect June day with gentle sunshine streaming through the ancient stained glass windows of the Norman church, casting jeweled patterns of light across the stone floor where, in less than an hour, he would pledge his life to Ann Hunter.

Watson stood before the mirror in the church vestry, adjusting his morning coat with hands that trembled only slightly—a marked improvement from the previous evening, when nervous anticipation had made even the simplest tasks challenging. Arthur Conan Doyle, resplendent in his role as best man, watched with the amused tolerance of a man who had observed his friend's transformation from confirmed bachelor to eager bridegroom with something approaching wonder.

"James, you've straightened that same cravat at least six times," Arthur observed with gentle humor. "I believe it was perfectly acceptable after the second adjustment."

"Forgive me, Arthur," Watson replied, finally stepping away from the mirror with a self-conscious smile. "I find myself rather more nervous than I expected. It's been... well, fifteen years since I last stood at an altar as a bridegroom. The sensation is both familiar and entirely foreign."

Arthur moved to check his friend's appearance with the careful eye of a man who understood the significance of the moment. "You look absolutely splendid, James. More importantly, you look happy—genuinely, thoroughly happy in a way I haven't seen since those early days when you first began writing about Holmes."

The observation was more perceptive than Arthur might have realized. Watson had indeed rediscovered not merely contentment but active joy during his courtship with Ann, finding in her intelligent companionship and warm affection exactly the partnership he had thought lost forever after Mary's death. Their relationship had developed with the careful deliberation of two people who understood both the value and the fragility of love, built upon shared experiences, mutual respect, and the kind of deep friendship that promised to sustain them through whatever trials marriage might bring.

"It's remarkable, isn't it?" Watson mused, gazing out the vestry window toward the church garden where early guests were beginning to arrive. "One year ago, if someone had told me I would be standing here today, preparing to marry Ann Hunter, I would have considered them quite mad. And yet here we are, and I cannot imagine any other outcome feeling so completely right."

The guest list was deliberately intimate, reflecting both the couple's preference for simplicity and the practical considerations of Watson's medical practice. The professional obligations that had initially prompted their move to early June had been resolved satisfactorily, allowing Ann to complete her academic year at Queen Mary's Grammar School while still permitting a summer wedding that honored the traditional associations Watson had mentioned during their planning discussions.

The superstition about Wednesday weddings being "the best day of all" had appealed to both their practical natures and their shared appreciation for the wisdom embedded in folk traditions. "Monday for wealth, Tuesday for health, Wednesday the best day of all"—the old rhyme had decided the matter when they discovered that June 3rd fell on a Wednesday, providing what Ann had laughingly called "supernatural endorsement" of their chosen date.

Dr. Reverend Marcus Thornton, the Pastor of St. Bartholomew's, appeared in the vestry doorway with the serene expression of a man who had conducted hundreds of such ceremonies and had developed an intuitive sense for distinguishing between matches likely to prosper and those doomed to struggle. In Watson's case, his professional assessment was unambiguously positive.

"Dr. Watson, Arthur," Reverend Thornton said warmly. "Everything is prepared. The bride arrived ten minutes ago and is with Mrs. Doyle in the bride's room. I must say, I've rarely seen a couple who seem so perfectly suited to each other. Miss Hunter appears radiantly happy, and you, my dear fellow, look like a man who has discovered treasure he had given up hope of finding."

Watson felt his heart quicken at the news of Ann's arrival. They had agreed to follow the traditional prohibition against seeing each other on the morning of the wedding, but knowing she was so near, preparing for the same ceremony that would unite their lives permanently, filled him with an anticipation that was both thrilling and deeply moving.

"Thank you, Marcus," Watson replied, using the given name that reflected their friendship rather than merely their professional relationship. The Pastor had indeed become one of Watson's closest friends since his establishment of the medical practice in Haslemere, their mutual respect having developed through shared concerns for the welfare of the local community. "I confess I'm rather more nervous than I expected, but also more certain than I've ever been about any decision in my life."

Arthur checked his pocket watch with the precision of a man accustomed to managing important schedules. "James, it's eleven-fifty. Shall we take our positions? I believe your bride is ready to make her entrance, and frankly, keeping a woman of Miss Hunter's intelligence waiting seems inadvisable under any circumstances."

The three men moved toward the church proper, where the soft murmur of conversation indicated that the modest congregation had assembled. Watson was touched to see that despite the limited guest list, several of his most important patients had arrived to witness the ceremony, along with colleagues from his medical school days and neighbors from both Haslemere and Ann's former residence in Walsall.

Most significantly, he noted with deep gratitude, Dr. Stamford had made the journey from London—the same friend whose chance encounter outside the Criterion Bar had first led to his meeting with Sherlock Holmes all those years ago. The symmetry seemed appropriate; the man who had inadvertently introduced him to the greatest friendship of his youth was present to witness his entry into what promised to be the great love of his middle years.

As Watson took his position at the altar, Arthur beside him with the rings safely secured in his waistcoat pocket, he found himself reflecting on the extraordinary path that had led to this moment. The grief that had once seemed insurmountable, the years of exile from everything that had given his life meaning, the gradual rebuilding of purpose through medical practice and renewed literary collaboration—all of it had been preparation for this day, for this woman, for this chance to discover that life retained the capacity to surprise him with blessings he had never dared imagine.

The church organ began the opening notes of the processional, and Watson felt his breath catch as the congregation rose to their feet. In a moment, Ann would appear at the far end of the aisle, and the formal ceremony would begin that would transform their careful courtship into permanent union.

But first came Louisa Doyle, moving with the graceful dignity that had made her such a perfect choice as Maid of Honor. Her gown of soft lavender complemented perfectly the floral arrangements that decorated the ancient church, and her smile as she caught Watson's eye conveyed both her personal happiness for the couple and her confidence in the rightness of their decision.

Touie had been one of Ann's strongest supporters throughout their courtship, providing the kind of feminine perspective and practical advice that had helped navigate the occasionally complex etiquette of a relationship between two people of mature years and established professional reputations. Her presence as Maid of Honor represented not merely friendship but genuine approval from someone whose judgment both bride and groom valued enormously.

As Touie reached the altar and took her position, the organ swelled into the traditional bridal march, and every eye in the church turned toward the back of the nave. Watson felt his heart stop completely as Ann Hunter appeared in the doorway, transformed by the simple elegance of her wedding gown into a vision that exceeded even his most romantic imaginings.

Her dress was of ivory silk, cut in the fashionable Gibson Girl style that emphasized her natural grace while maintaining the dignified simplicity that characterized everything about her personal presentation. The modest train and delicate lace veil spoke of traditional values without sacrificing contemporary sophistication. But what took Watson's breath away was not the perfection of her attire but the radiant joy that illuminated her features as their eyes met across the length of the church.

Ann had chosen to walk unescorted down the aisle, a decision that reflected both her independent nature and the fact that, at thirty-nine, she was entering marriage as a fully autonomous woman rather than being "given away" by male relatives. The symbolism was not lost on either of them; their union represented the free choice of two equals who had found in each other exactly what was needed to make their individual lives complete.

As she moved toward him with the measured pace appropriate to such a sacred moment, Watson found himself marveling at the extraordinary turn his life had taken. Two years ago, he had been a broken man living in exile from everything that had once given his existence meaning. Today, he stood at the altar of a church where he was valued as both physician and friend, waiting to marry a woman whose love honored his past while promising a future bright with shared possibilities.

Ann reached the altar with the soft rustle of silk that seemed to Watson the most beautiful sound he had ever heard. As she took her place beside him, their eyes meeting with the profound understanding that had characterized their relationship from the beginning, he felt a peace and certainty that had been absent from his life for longer than he cared to remember.

Reverend Thornton's voice carried clearly through the ancient church as he began the familiar words that would transform their careful courtship into permanent union: "Dearly beloved, we are gathered together here in the sight of God, and in the face of this congregation, to join together this Man and this Woman in holy Matrimony..."

As the ceremony progressed through its traditional elements—the exchange of vows, the blessing of the rings, the pronouncement of their union—Watson found himself profoundly moved by the recognition that he was not merely reciting ancient formulas but making promises that carried the full weight of his mature understanding of love's responsibilities and rewards.

When Reverend Thornton finally pronounced them husband and wife, and invited him to kiss his bride, Watson took Ann's face gently in his hands with the tender reverence appropriate to such a sacred moment. Their kiss was soft but profound, carrying within it all the hope, affection, and promise that had brought them to this perfect beginning.

The church erupted in applause as the newly married couple turned to face their friends with expressions of joy that needed no interpretation. Arthur stepped forward to offer his congratulations, his own eyes moist with the emotion of having witnessed his dear friend's transformation from solitary widower to happy husband.

As they moved down the aisle together, Ann's hand resting lightly on Watson's arm, both felt the profound satisfaction that comes from having made a decision that honored their individual histories while embracing their shared future completely. The bells of St. Bartholomew's rang out once more as they emerged into the June sunshine, their clear notes carrying across the Surrey countryside like a declaration of joy that had been too long delayed but was now finally, perfectly realized.

It was as they paused on the church steps, accepting congratulations from the departing congregation, that Watson noticed a tall, lean figure standing somewhat apart from the crowd near the ancient lych gate. Even at a distance, the angular silhouette was unmistakable. Watson's breath caught in his throat as he recognized the familiar profile, the hawk-like nose, the penetrating eyes that seemed to take in everything with a single glance.

"Holmes," Watson whispered, almost to himself, but Ann heard him and followed his gaze.

"Is that...?" she began, understanding immediately from Watson's expression who the distant figure must be.

"Yes," Watson said, his voice thick with emotion. "It's Holmes."

Without conscious thought, Watson began walking toward the figure, Ann beside him, their steps quickening as they approached. The man who had once been the most important person in Watson's life stood motionless, his hands clasped behind his back, his expression unreadable as always.

"Holmes," Watson said again as they drew near, his voice carrying all the complicated emotions—grief, joy, uncertainty, and above all, a deep and abiding affection that no amount of time or distance could diminish.

Sherlock Holmes stepped forward with that familiar, economical grace that Watson remembered so well. His appearance was unchanged—still the same piercing gray eyes, still the same lean, aristocratic features, though perhaps there were a few more lines around the eyes, a touch more silver at the temples.

"Watson," Holmes said simply, and then, with a slight bow to Ann, "Mrs. Watson. I trust you will forgive the intrusion."

"Holmes, how did you—" Watson began, but Holmes raised a hand with the ghost of his old smile.

"My dear fellow, did you truly think I would miss such an occasion? I have been keeping a distant but watchful eye on your welfare since your... relocation to Surrey. Your happiness has been a matter of considerable importance to me."

Ann stepped forward with the grace that had first captivated Watson. "Mr. Holmes, I'm delighted to see you again."

Watson felt his heart swell with love for this remarkable woman who could extend such gracious hospitality to a man who had once freed her from a problem that she thought was insurmountable.

"Holmes," Watson said, his voice steady despite the emotion that threatened to overwhelm him, "I cannot express how much it means to me that you are here. That you came to witness this day."

"My dear Watson," Holmes replied, his voice carrying the warmth that had always been reserved for his closest friend, "there are very few things in this world that could have kept me away. Your happiness has always been of paramount importance to me, and I can see that you have found in Mrs. Watson exactly what you deserve—a partner worthy of your loyalty, your courage, and your generous heart."

He paused, then reached into his coat and withdrew a small, elegantly wrapped package. "A wedding gift," he said, offering it to Ann. "Something I believe you will both appreciate."

Ann accepted the gift with evident pleasure, unwrapping it to reveal a beautiful leather-bound volume. "The complete works of Winnie-the-Pooh," she read aloud, then looked up with a smile of genuine delight. "However did you know I was fond of children's literature?"

"Elementary," Holmes replied with the first genuine smile Watson had seen from him in years. "A woman who chooses to teach at Queen Mary's Grammar School, who has dedicated her life to the education of young minds, would naturally appreciate literature that speaks to the imagination and wonder of childhood. The inscription," he added, "is from both the author and myself."

Watson looked over Ann's shoulder to read the inscription: "To Dr. and Mrs. Watson, with warmest wishes for a marriage filled with adventure, laughter, and the kind of friendship that makes all things possible. A.A. Milne. P.S. From one who has observed the profound loyalty and devotion that true friendship can inspire. - S.H."

"Holmes," Watson said, his voice thick with emotion, "I don't know what to say."

"Say nothing, my dear fellow. Simply be happy. You have found in Mrs. Watson the partner you have always deserved, and I have the satisfaction of knowing that my dearest friend has discovered the contentment that has so long eluded him."

Holmes turned to Ann once more. "Mrs. Watson, I entrust to your care the finest man I have ever known. His loyalty is absolute, his courage unwavering, and his capacity for love deeper than perhaps even he realizes. You have chosen well, and more importantly, you have been chosen by a man whose friendship has been the greatest privilege of my life."

"Mr. Holmes," Ann replied, tears glistening in her eyes, "thank you for sharing him with me. I promise you that I will treasure the gift of his love and do everything in my power to ensure his happiness."

Holmes nodded, satisfied by what he had observed. "I have no doubt of that. And now," he said, stepping back, "I must take my leave. I have intruded quite enough upon your special day, and I believe you have a honeymoon to begin."

He tipped his hat to Ann, gave Watson a look that conveyed volumes, and then turned and walked away with that familiar, purposeful stride. Within moments, he had disappeared around the corner of the church, leaving Watson and Ann standing together in the dappled sunlight, still holding the precious gift he had given them.

"What an extraordinary man," Ann said softly, watching the place where Holmes had vanished. "I understand now why your friendship with him has meant so much to you."

Watson nodded, unable to speak for a moment. Finally, he said, "He came. After all these years, after everything that happened between us, he came to my wedding."

"Of course he did," Ann replied, taking his arm. "He loves you, James. Perhaps he cannot express it in conventional ways, but his presence here today speaks more eloquently than words ever could."

As they walked back toward the church where Arthur was waiting with the carriage, Watson felt a profound sense of completeness. The two most important chapters of his life—his friendship with Holmes and his love for Ann—had been blessed and united by this unexpected encounter. The future stretched before them, bright with promise and possibility.

The luncheon in the church fellowship hall proved to be exactly the intimate celebration both had envisioned—elegant without being ostentatious, joyful without being overwhelming. The menu featured local specialties that reflected the community where Watson had established his new life, while the decorations honored Ann's preference for natural beauty over artificial display.

Arthur's toast, delivered with the wit and warmth that had made him such a valued friend, captured perfectly the sentiment shared by everyone present: "To James and Ann Watson—may your marriage be blessed with all the happiness your individual characters deserve, and may you find in each other the kind of partnership that makes every challenge bearable and every joy complete."

As the afternoon progressed with conversation, laughter, and the gentle celebration appropriate to such a significant occasion, both James and Ann found themselves repeatedly catching each other's eyes across the room, sharing the kind of silent communication that promised well for their future understanding. The memory of Holmes's unexpected appearance and blessing added an extra dimension of joy to the day, a sense that all the important elements of their lives had been harmoniously united.

When the last guests had departed and they found themselves alone in the carriage that would take them to the railway station for their honeymoon journey to the Lake District, Ann reached for her husband's hand with the natural gesture of a woman who had found in marriage exactly what she had hoped it might provide.

"James," she said softly, using his given name with the pleasure that had never diminished since that magical moment of their engagement, "I believe we're going to be extraordinarily happy together."

"My dearest Ann," he replied, raising her hand to his lips to kiss the gold band that now marked their permanent union, "I have never been more certain of anything in my life. And having Holmes's blessing... it makes everything perfect."

As their carriage rolled through the Surrey countryside toward London and the beginning of their married life together, both carried with them the profound satisfaction that comes from having found, after patience and trial, exactly the person needed to make the future bright with promise. The wedding day that had begun with superstitious hopes for the best day of all had indeed provided the foundation for what both believed would prove to be the great blessing of their mature years— made all the more precious by the unexpected benediction of friendship renewed.

Behind them, the bells of St. Bartholomew's continued their joyful celebration, their clear notes carrying across the peaceful countryside like a blessing on the union of two people who had separately learned life's most difficult lessons and now looked forward to discovering together its most enduring rewards. And somewhere in the distance, a tall, lean figure walked the quiet country roads, carrying with him the satisfaction of having witnessed the happiness of the man who had been, and would always remain, his dearest friend.

Mrs. Hudson's Retirement

November 15, 1903

The autumn fog hung thick over Baker Street as Sherlock Holmes descended the familiar seventeen steps for what had become his morning routine of collecting the post. At forty-nine, he moved with the same economy of motion that had characterized his younger years, though recent months had brought a contemplative quality to his bearing that suggested a man beginning to take stock of his accumulated experiences.

The morning's correspondence proved unremarkable—a few inquiries from potential clients, several letters from editors requesting comments on recent criminal cases, and the usual collection of admirers' notes forwarded by Arthur Conan Doyle's publishers. Holmes sorted through these mechanically, his mind already turning toward the day's planned experiments in chemical analysis, when Mrs. Hudson's voice called softly from the ground floor.

"Mr. Holmes? Might I have a word when convenient?"

Something in her tone—a careful formality that differed from her usual comfortable directness—made Holmes pause on the landing. In the fifteen years since he had first taken lodgings at 111 Baker Street, Mrs. Hudson had become as integral to his daily existence as his violin or his beloved chemical apparatus. Her steady presence, her unflappable response to the constant stream of visitors, and her remarkable ability to maintain domestic order despite the chaos that inevitably surrounded his investigative work had made this modest Georgian townhouse feel unmistakably like home.

"Of course, Mrs. Hudson," Holmes replied, making his way to the sitting room where she stood waiting beside the morning fire, her weathered hands clasped before her with obvious nervousness. "Please, do sit down. You look as though you have something of significance to discuss."

Mrs. Hudson accepted his invitation gratefully, settling into the chair that Watson had occupied during his years of residence at Baker Street. The sight of her in that particular seat struck Holmes as somehow symbolic, though of what he could not immediately determine.

"Mr. Holmes," she began, her voice carrying the careful deliberation of someone who had rehearsed this conversation extensively, "I find myself in the position of needing to inform you of a decision that will, I fear, cause considerable disruption to your comfortable arrangements here."

Holmes set aside the morning post entirely, giving her his complete attention. "Mrs. Hudson, in all our years together, you have never been anything but direct with me. Please continue in that same spirit."

She took a deep breath before speaking, as though drawing courage from his encouragement. "My nephew Thomas in Cardiff has written to inform me that my sister-in-law Margaret has taken seriously ill. The doctors believe it may be consumption, and she requires constant care. Thomas has a young family of his own and cannot manage both his work and the nursing that Margaret needs."

Holmes nodded with immediate understanding. "And he has requested that you come to Wales to provide that care."

"Yes, sir. But it's more than just the immediate crisis." Mrs. Hudson's voice grew stronger as she continued. "Thomas has been after me for years to retire and come live with the family in Wales. He's done quite well for himself—he owns a small but prosperous ironworks—and he's built a comfortable house with rooms specifically intended for me. He says I've spent enough years caring for other people's homes and should let family take care of me for a change."

The implications of her words settled over Holmes with remarkable clarity. "And you find his proposal attractive."

"I do, Mr. Holmes. I'm sixty-three years old, and while my health remains good, I feel the weight of the years more each morning. The thought of spending my remaining time surrounded by family, helping to raise my grand-nieces and grand-nephews, appeals to me more than I can adequately express."

Holmes rose from his chair and moved to the window, looking down at the familiar bustle of Baker Street while processing this information. The prospect of losing Mrs. Hudson represented more than mere domestic inconvenience—it meant the end of an era, the dissolution of the household arrangements that had provided the foundation for his most productive years.

"When would this transition need to occur?" he asked, though he suspected he already knew the answer.

"Thomas hopes I can come before Christmas, sir. Margaret's condition is deteriorating, and they need assistance immediately. I would, of course, provide you with adequate notice to secure alternative arrangements."

Holmes turned back to face her, noting the mixture of excitement and regret in her expression. "Mrs. Hudson, in all our years together, you have shown me nothing but loyalty and consideration. I would never presume to stand in the way of your happiness or your family obligations."

Relief flooded her features. "Oh, Mr. Holmes, I was so worried about how to tell you. This house has been my life for so many years, and you and Dr. Watson have been like family to me."

"We have been extraordinarily fortunate to benefit from your care," Holmes replied with genuine warmth. "But tell me, what are your plans for the property? Will you be selling, or seeking new tenants?"

Mrs. Hudson's expression brightened considerably. "That's actually the encouraging part of this situation, sir. My nephew has offered to purchase the house as an investment property. He plans to renovate it completely and convert it into a modern boarding establishment for professional gentlemen. The sale would provide me with a comfortable income for my retirement."

Holmes absorbed this news with mixed emotions. The thought of 111 Baker Street transformed into something unrecognizable felt almost sacrilegious, yet he could hardly object to arrangements that would secure Mrs. Hudson's future comfort.

"I see. And when might this renovation begin?"

"Thomas would like to take possession by the first of the year, sir. The workmen would begin immediately after that, as he hopes to have the property ready for new tenants by Easter."

Holmes found himself moving restlessly about the sitting room, his mind automatically cataloguing the accumulated possessions of fifteen years— his books, his scientific instruments, his extensive files of criminal cases, the comfortable furniture that had witnessed countless conversations with Watson during their years of collaboration.

"Mrs. Hudson," he said finally, stopping before the fireplace where so many important decisions had been made, "I believe this may be an opportune moment for me to consider some significant changes as well."

She looked at him with surprise. "Changes, sir?"

"I have been thinking recently about the direction of my future work. The constant stream of clients, the irregular hours, the necessity of maintaining a London address for professional purposes—all of this has begun to feel less essential than it once did." Holmes paused, organizing his thoughts. "Dr. Watson has established his new household very successfully, Arthur continues to find ready publishers for our documented cases without requiring my direct involvement, and my reputation in criminal investigation has reached a point where it largely sustains itself."

Mrs. Hudson listened with the careful attention she had always given to his more significant pronouncements. "Are you saying you might consider retirement yourself, sir?"

"I am saying that your decision may provide the catalyst I have needed to pursue some long-deferred interests." Holmes moved to his desk and withdrew a letter that had arrived several weeks earlier. "I have recently received correspondence from a Sussex estate agent regarding a small property that has been offered to me under quite favorable terms."

He handed her the letter, watching as she read it with growing interest. The property in question was a modest farm in the South Downs, complete with a comfortable farmhouse, several outbuildings, and extensive grounds that offered both privacy and spectacular views of the countryside.

"It sounds lovely, Mr. Holmes, but what has sparked your interest in rural property?"

Holmes smiled with genuine enthusiasm—an expression that had become increasingly rare in recent years. "The previous owner was something of an expert in apiculture—the keeping of bees. He established several hives on the property and developed quite a reputation for the quality of his honey. The present owner is anxious to sell but would prefer that the buyer continue the beekeeping operation."

Mrs. Hudson's eyes widened with surprise. "Bees, Mr. Holmes?"

"Indeed. I have long been fascinated by the social organization of bee colonies—their methods of communication, their division of labor, their remarkable efficiency in food production. The study of their behavior offers the same intellectual challenges that have always attracted me to criminal investigation, but with the advantage of subjects who are entirely predictable once one understands their governing principles."

The idea had first occurred to Holmes months earlier during a particularly mundane case involving insurance fraud. As he sat in his client's garden, waiting for a suspect to appear, he had found himself observing a beehive with the same intensity he typically reserved for criminal behavior. The intricate social structure, the precise allocation of roles, the sophisticated communication systems—all of it had struck him as worthy of serious scientific study.

"And you believe you would be content with such a quiet life?" Mrs. Hudson asked, though her tone suggested she found the prospect rather appealing.

"I believe I would find it restorative," Holmes replied thoughtfully. "The constant mental stimulation of criminal cases has served its purpose, but I find myself increasingly drawn to pursuits that offer knowledge for its own sake rather than knowledge applied to human failings."

Mrs. Hudson returned the letter with obvious approval. "It sounds like exactly what you need, sir. And the timing could hardly be better."

Holmes nodded, feeling a sense of rightness about the decision that had been crystallizing in his mind throughout their conversation. "I shall write to the estate agent this afternoon and arrange to view the property next week. If it proves as suitable as the description suggests, I could be settled there well before Christmas."

"Oh, Mr. Holmes, I'm so pleased that my retirement won't leave you feeling displaced. I've been worrying about that for weeks."

"Mrs. Hudson, you have given me fifteen years of exemplary service, and now you have given me the impetus to pursue a new phase of my life that I might never have had the courage to attempt otherwise. I am, if anything, grateful for your decision."

They sat in comfortable silence for several minutes, both contemplating the magnitude of the changes ahead. The sitting room, which had witnessed so many significant conversations over the years, seemed to hold their shared memories in its familiar furnishings and well-worn comforts.

"There is one matter I should mention," Holmes said eventually. "Dr. Watson should be informed of these developments, though I suspect he will find them less surprising than we might expect."

Mrs. Hudson smiled knowingly. "Dr. Watson has always understood you better than you sometimes realize, sir. I believe he's been waiting for you to discover what would make you truly happy."

Holmes considered this observation with interest. Watson's recent marriage had demonstrated his friend's remarkable capacity for adaptation and growth, and perhaps it was time for Holmes to show similar courage in pursuing his own path toward contentment.

"I shall write to him this evening," Holmes decided. "And to Arthur as well. They both deserve to know that Sherlock Holmes is ready to embrace a rather different sort of adventure."

As Mrs. Hudson rose to return to her domestic duties, she paused at the door to look back at the sitting room that had been the center of her professional life for so many years.

"Mr. Holmes," she said softly, "I want you to know that caring for this household, watching you and Dr. Watson solve so many important cases, being part of something that mattered—it's been the greatest privilege of my life."

Holmes found himself unexpectedly moved by her words. "Mrs. Hudson, the privilege has been entirely ours. You have created a home here, not merely lodgings, and both Watson and I have benefited immeasurably from your care."

After she departed, Holmes remained in the sitting room, contemplating the remarkable turn his life was about to take. The prospect of leaving London, of abandoning the profession that had defined him for nearly two decades, should have felt like defeat or surrender. Instead, he found himself filled with anticipation for the challenges and discoveries that awaited him in Sussex.

The bees, he suspected, would prove far more fascinating than most people imagined. And perhaps, in studying their industrious society, he might discover something about the kind of life he wanted to build for himself in the years ahead.

The November afternoon was fading into evening as Holmes took up his pen to begin the letters that would announce the end of one chapter of his life and the beginning of another. Mrs. Hudson's retirement had indeed provided the perfect catalyst for his own transformation, and he found himself grateful for the courage she had shown in pursuing her own happiness.

Change, as it turned out, need not mean loss. Sometimes it simply meant the beginning of something better.

Arthur's New Literary Venture

January 20, 1904

Arthur settled into his study chair at Undershaw on a crisp January morning, the winter light streaming through the windows as he contemplated his correspondence with considerable satisfaction. The final proofs for the last of the Collier's stories had been reviewed and returned to New York the previous week, marking the completion of their most successful American publishing venture to date.

He withdrew his finest letterhead and began composing a letter to James, his pen moving steadily across the paper:

My dear James

I write with news that should interest you greatly. Our collaboration with Collier's has reached its intended conclusion, with all thirteen stories now completed and moving through their publication schedule in America. Hapgood's enthusiasm remains undiminished, and the financial arrangements have exceeded even our most optimistic projections.

But this letter concerns an entirely different matter—a new literary venture that, for the first time in many years, does not require the services of our consulting detective friend. I have begun work on a historical novel tentatively titled 'Sir Nigel,' set during the early campaigns of the Hundred Years' War, specifically during the reign of Edward III.

You may recall that some thirteen years ago I published 'The White Company,' a novel set during the later phase of the same conflict. 'Sir Nigel' is intended as a companion piece—indeed, a prequel—that will provide the background story for young Nigel Loring's early adventures before he joined the famous White Company of archers. The character proved popular enough that readers have long requested more of his story, and I find myself drawn back to that magnificent period of English military history.

The research has been extraordinarily engaging, James. The early fourteenth century offers such rich material—the development of English military tactics, the social transformation following the victories at Crécy and Poitiers, the emergence of the professional soldier class. Unlike our detective stories, which require careful attention to contemporary investigative methods, this project allows me to immerse myself completely in historical documentation and period detail.

I have already secured preliminary interest from two highly regarded publishers. Bernhard Tauchnitz in Leipzig, with whom I have maintained excellent relations since our German editions of the Holmes stories, has expressed enthusiasm for including 'Sir Nigel' in his Continental series. Similarly, Smith, Elder & Company here in London—my publishers for several previous historical works—have indicated strong interest in acquiring the British rights.

Both firms have suggested publication in 1905 or early 1906, with the possibility of initial serialization to build reader anticipation. The serial approach proved remarkably effective for 'The White Company,' and I believe it would serve this new work equally well. The advantage of working with established partners like Tauchnitz and Smith, Elder is their understanding of my working methods and their willingness to provide the time necessary for proper historical research.

James, I confess there is something liberating about returning to purely fictional narrative after our years of adapting actual criminal investigations. With 'Sir Nigel,' I am constrained only by historical accuracy rather than the need to protect privacy or disguise actual locations and individuals. The freedom to develop character and plot without such considerations has renewed my enthusiasm for historical fiction considerably.

The financial security provided by our Collier's arrangement has made this new project possible, allowing me to pursue historical fiction without immediate commercial pressure. I can take the time necessary to ensure that every detail of medieval warfare, social customs, and period atmosphere meets the highest standards of historical authenticity.

I hope you will find this departure from our detective collaboration understandable, if not entirely welcome. Holmes will undoubtedly return to our literary partnership eventually—his methods continue to evolve, and I suspect the American public's appetite for his investigations remains considerable. But for now, I am thoroughly engaged with the world of fourteenth-century England and the young knight whose adventures preceded his famous service with the White Company.

The contrast between documenting Holmes's scientific detection and crafting historical adventure has proven remarkably stimulating. Both require meticulous attention to detail, but of entirely different sorts. Where Holmes demands accuracy in investigative methodology, Sir Nigel requires authenticity in historical period and military practice.

I shall keep you informed of the novel's progress, and naturally I hope you will review the manuscript when completed. Your medical training provides valuable perspective on the realism of combat descriptions and period medical practices, both of which feature prominently in medieval military fiction.

With continued gratitude for our successful collaboration and anticipation of future projects together,

Arthur

P.S. I have been wondering whether Holmes might find the forensic challenges of medieval criminal investigation interesting subject matter for future consideration. The absence of modern scientific methods would require fascinating adaptations of his deductive techniques to period limitations.

Arthur sealed the letter carefully, reflecting on how dramatically his literary career had evolved since that first meeting with James in Southsea nearly two decades earlier. The success of their Holmes collaboration had provided both financial security and literary reputation sufficient to pursue the historical fiction that had always been his first love.

As he prepared the letter for afternoon post, Arthur felt genuine excitement about the creative possibilities ahead. 'Sir Nigel' represented not an abandonment of his detective partnership with James, but rather an expansion of his literary horizons made possible by that partnership's extraordinary success.

The historical novel would allow him to explore themes of honor, courage, and adventure in ways that detective fiction simply could not accommodate, while the research itself promised months of enjoyable immersion in one of England's most dramatic historical periods.

News of Touie's Passing

July 4, 1906

The morning of July 4th, 1906, dawned with the kind of brilliant sunshine that made even the modest Surrey town of Haslemere seem to sparkle with particular charm. Dr. James Watson sat in his consulting room, reviewing case notes from the previous day's patients while enjoying his second cup of tea and the relative quiet that preceded his morning appointments.

At fifty-four, James had settled into the comfortable rhythms of a well-established country medical practice. The partnership with Arthur Conan Doyle in documenting Holmes's investigations had provided both financial security and literary satisfaction, allowing him to maintain his medical work without the financial pressures that had once driven him to accept less desirable cases. His practice now consisted primarily of local families he had served for years, along with occasional patients from neighboring villages who sought his particular expertise in matters requiring both medical knowledge and discretion.

The telegram boy's sharp knock at the front door broke the morning's peaceful atmosphere with the particular urgency that always accompanied such visits. James heard Kathryn, his housekeeper, answer the door and exchange brief words with the messenger. Her footsteps approached his consulting room with a hesitation that immediately drew his attention.

"Dr. Watson," she said, appearing in the doorway with an expression of concern, "a wire has arrived from Surrey. The boy said it was marked urgent."

James accepted the yellow envelope with the mixture of curiosity and apprehension that telegrams inevitably generated. In an age when urgent news traveled by wire, such messages carried equal possibility of celebration or catastrophe. The sender's address—"Undershaw, Hindhead"—told him immediately that the message came from Arthur.

He opened the envelope carefully, unfolding the thin paper with its distinctive Western Union markings. The message, transmitted in the abbreviated style that telegraph costs demanded, struck him with the brutal efficiency of its brevity:

DEAREST FRIEND. TOUIE PASSED PEACEFULLY THIS MORNING AFTER LONG STRUGGLE. TUBERCULOSIS FINALLY CLAIMED HER DESPITE ALL EFFORTS. FUNERAL ARRANGEMENTS ST LUKES CHURCH GRAYSHOTT. YOUR PRESENCE WOULD MEAN EVERYTHING - ARTHUR

James read the message twice, the formal language of telegraphic communication somehow making the devastating news feel simultaneously immediate and distant. For a moment, he simply sat holding the thin paper, his mind struggling to process the loss of a woman who had become central to his understanding of friendship and courage.

Louisa Doyle—Touie to all who knew her well—had been battling tuberculosis for thirteen years. James recalled with painful clarity that first diagnosis in 1893, when the disease had seemed like a death sentence that might claim her within months. Instead, her quiet determination, Arthur's devoted care, and the beneficial climate of various health resorts had granted them more than a decade of additional life together.

During those years, James had watched Arthur make every possible sacrifice for his wife's health. The move to Switzerland, the construction of Undershaw specifically designed for her recovery, the careful attention to climate and medical care—all had been undertaken with the single purpose of extending and improving Touie's life. Her gradual improvement in the Surrey air had offered genuine hope that the disease might be held at bay indefinitely.

But tuberculosis, James knew from his medical training, was a patient enemy. It might retreat for years, allowing victims to believe they had conquered it, only to return with renewed virulence when resistance was low. The fact that Touie had survived thirteen years with the disease spoke to both her remarkable constitution and Arthur's unwavering devotion.

James rose from his desk and walked to the window, looking out at Haslemere's quiet High Street where ordinary village life continued despite the personal tragedy that had just entered his world. Just a few miles away at Undershaw, Arthur was dealing with arrangements for his wife's funeral while simultaneously grieving the loss of the woman who had been his constant companion for nearly twenty years.

The friendship between the Watson and Doyle households had deepened considerably during Touie's long illness. Ann had corresponded regularly with Louisa, sharing the particular understanding that existed between women who had learned to live with uncertainty about their husbands' demanding careers. James had provided medical consultation whenever Arthur needed professional advice about Touie's care, and both families had visited frequently during the periods when her health permitted social calls.

Beyond the personal affection James felt for Louisa, her death represented the end of an era in his relationship with Arthur. So much of their correspondence over the years had included Arthur's updates on Touie's condition, his careful attention to treatments and climate, his fierce determination to provide every possible comfort during her illness. Without that central concern, Arthur's life would necessarily take a dramatically different direction.

James returned to his desk and withdrew his finest writing paper. A telegram in response would be appropriate and expected, but the gravity of the situation demanded something more substantial. Arthur would need practical support for immediate arrangements, but he would also need the kind of thoughtful consolation that only a close friend could provide.

He began writing carefully:

My dearest Arthur,

Your telegram reached me this morning, and I confess that despite our knowledge of Touie's condition, the news has struck me with unexpected force. To lose someone who has fought with such grace and courage for so many years seems particularly cruel, even when we understand that her suffering has finally ended.

Ann and I will travel to Surrey immediately upon receiving details of the funeral arrangements. We wish to be present not only to pay our respects to Touie's memory, but to provide whatever support we can during these difficult days. Please do not hesitate to call upon us for any practical assistance you may require.

I have been thinking this morning of that first Christmas we spent at your home in Southsea, when Touie welcomed us with such warmth despite barely knowing us. Her kindness that day established the foundation for a friendship that has enriched our lives immeasurably. Over the years, we have watched her face her illness with a dignity that inspired everyone who knew her.

Arthur, your devotion to Touie throughout her long struggle has been exemplary. The care you provided, the sacrifices you made, the hope you maintained even during the darkest periods—all demonstrated the finest qualities of both physician and husband. That she survived thirteen years with tuberculosis, thirteen years that included so many periods of relative health and happiness, stands as testimony to your unwavering commitment to her well-being.

Please give our love to Mary Louise and Kingsley. This loss will be particularly difficult for them, having grown up with constant awareness of their mother's fragile health. They will need your strength in the days ahead, just as you will need the support of friends who recognize the magnitude of your loss.

We shall depart for Surrey as soon as we receive word of the specific arrangements. Until then, please know that our thoughts and prayers are with you.

With deepest sympathy and continued friendship,

James

James sealed the letter carefully and rang for Kathryn to arrange immediate posting. As he waited for her response, he contemplated the broader implications of Touie's death for Arthur's life and work. The man had spent thirteen years organizing his career around his wife's health needs. Now, at forty-seven, he would need to reconstruct his daily existence around entirely different priorities.

The literary collaboration between them would undoubtedly continue, but James suspected that Arthur's approach to both writing and life might change significantly. The constant responsibility for Touie's care had provided structure and purpose beyond his literary success. Without that central organizing principle, Arthur might pursue the diverse intellectual interests—spiritualism, politics, social reform—that had always competed with his fiction writing for attention.

When Kathryn appeared to collect the letter, her expression showed the concern of someone who, despite having worked for him only several months, had quickly learned to read the significance of her employer's correspondence.

"Serious news from Surrey, Doctor?" she asked with the privileged directness of a longtime servant.

"Mrs. Arthur Doyle has passed away," James replied simply. "After a very long illness."

Kathryn's face immediately softened with genuine sympathy. "Oh, the poor dear woman. And Mr. Doyle—he was so devoted to her welfare."

"Indeed. We'll be attending the funeral and likely spending time with the family over the next few days. Please adjust my appointments accordingly and ensure that any urgent cases can be handled promptly."

As Kathryn departed to post the letter and adjust his schedule, James returned to his contemplation of the morning's tragic news. In the space of a few minutes, a telegram had marked the end of Louisa Doyle's long struggle with tuberculosis and the beginning of a new chapter in Arthur's life. The friendship that had sustained both families through thirteen years of uncertainty had now entered a period where different kinds of support would be required—support that James was uniquely positioned to provide, given their close proximity and long-standing relationship.

Outside his window, the July sunshine continued its gentle illumination of Haslemere's peaceful streets, while just a few miles away at Undershaw, Arthur Conan Doyle faced the first day of life without the woman whose courage and grace had inspired his devotion for nearly twenty years.

The Years Ahead

July 20, 1906

Arthur Conan Doyle sat at his writing desk, not with pen in hand as had been his custom for so many years, but simply gazing out at the Surrey countryside that Touie had loved so dearly. Four days had passed since her funeral, and the house seemed to echo with a peculiar emptiness that no amount of family presence could quite fill.

James Watson occupied the chair opposite the desk—Holmes's old chair, as they had come to think of it—his own grief evident in the careful way he moved and spoke. The two men had spent much of the morning attending to practical matters: correspondence with The Strand, arrangements for the remaining stories in their current series, the inevitable business that death leaves in its wake. Now, in the quiet of the afternoon, their conversation had turned to weightier matters.

Arthur sat in contemplative silence, his gaze fixed on the distant hills where Touie had so often walked during her better days. The weight of recent loss was evident in his posture, yet there was something else there too—a sense of a man beginning to look toward the future.

Watson leaned forward, his medical training evident in his assessment of his friend's constitution. "You're only forty-seven, Arthur. A strong man in his prime, with many productive years ahead. The question is what you wish to do with those years."

Arthur finally turned from the window, his expression thoughtful but no longer bearing the acute grief that had marked the past week. "I've been considering that very question. Our partnership has produced thirty-nine Holmes stories thus far—a respectable body of work by any measure. Yet I find myself wondering if the detective's career might continue considerably further than we originally envisioned."

"Further how?" Watson asked, though something in his tone suggested he already sensed the direction of Arthur's thoughts.

"More stories, certainly. How many, I cannot say." Arthur's voice took on the cadence of a man thinking aloud, working through possibilities that had been forming during the long nights since Touie's passing. "Not immediately, you understand. I need time to process this loss, to find my footing again. But eventually... Holmes has become something larger than either of us anticipated, hasn't he?"

Watson smiled for the first time since arriving at Undershaw. "Indeed he has. The letters from readers continue to arrive by the dozen. Children write asking for Holmes's autograph. Adults inquire about consulting him on real cases. We've created something that has taken on a life quite independent of its creators."

"Exactly." Arthur rose and moved to the bookshelf where the bound volumes of their published works stood in neat rows. "And I find myself thinking that perhaps this creative partnership—this strange collaboration between a physician who knew the real Holmes and a writer who could bring him to life—perhaps it needn't end with my current grief."

The two men sat in comfortable silence for several minutes, each lost in his own contemplation of the future. Through the open window came the sound of children playing in the garden—Mary and Kingsley, Arthur's son and daughter, their laughter a reminder that life continued its forward motion even in the face of loss.

"There's something else I must tell you, James," Arthur said eventually, his voice carrying a note of hesitation. "I don't expect you to understand, and I certainly don't expect you to approve, but I believe I shall marry again."

Watson's eyebrows rose slightly, but his expression remained carefully neutral. "Arthur, you need say nothing more than you're comfortable sharing. Your personal life is your own affair."

"No, I think I should explain, if only because our friendship has always been built on honesty." Arthur returned to his chair, his hands clasped before him. "There is a woman—Jean Leckie. I've known her for some time, and our... understanding has remained entirely proper throughout Touie's illness. But I believe, when sufficient time has passed and the proprieties have been observed, that she and I may find happiness together."

Watson nodded slowly. "A man in his prime, with many years ahead of him, should not be expected to live them in solitude. Touie would have wanted your happiness above all else."

"Jean is young—younger than I—and comes from a good family. If we do marry, I hope that we may be blessed with children to join Mary and Kingsley in creating a household full of life and laughter." Arthur's expression brightened as he spoke, the first sign of genuine optimism Watson had seen since his arrival. "The thought of young voices in this house again, of watching children grow and learn..."

"It would be a blessing indeed," Watson agreed warmly. "And it occurs to me that children might provide excellent inspiration for new types of stories. Adventures that capture a younger imagination, perhaps."

Arthur laughed—a sound that seemed to surprise them both with its naturalness. "Already thinking like a writer, James. Yes, I can see how family life might influence our work in unexpected ways."

The conversation was interrupted by Mrs. Leckie calling from the garden, summoning the children for tea. As their voices faded into the distance, Arthur and Watson found themselves contemplating the strange turns that life could take—how grief and hope could coexist, how endings invariably became beginnings in ways that no one could predict.

"The years ahead," Arthur repeated, his voice now carrying notes of anticipation rather than melancholy. "Time enough for a second marriage, for more children, for many additional Holmes stories. Time enough for new adventures in both literature and life."

Watson stood and moved to the window, watching the shadows lengthen across the familiar landscape. "You know, Arthur, when I first approached you with the idea of writing about Holmes, I never imagined we would still be discussing new stories more than twenty years later. The detective has proven remarkably... resilient."

"As have we all, it seems." Arthur joined his friend at the window. "The game, as Holmes would say, is far from over."

Outside, the Surrey countryside basked in the golden light of a summer evening, while inside Undershaw, two men who had shared the extraordinary experience of bringing Sherlock Holmes to life began to envision the years ahead—years that would bring new stories, new joys, and the continuation of a literary partnership that had already far exceeded their most optimistic expectations.

The future, stretching out before them like an unwritten page, held the promise of many more years of creativity, family, and the endless fascination of chronicling the adventures of the world's most famous consulting detective. It was, Arthur reflected, a prospect that filled him with something very much like happiness.

The End

About the Author

Thomas (Tom) Campbell resides in Wilmington, North Carolina with his dog Watson. Tom's professional background includes sales and marketing as a Account Executive - Industry Consultant with AT&T Information Systems, operating a computer repair shop, and managing a statewide legal software business. In his spare time, Tom enjoys attending Sherlock Holmes scion meetings, and teaching Sunday school.

Tom's Sherlockian Website:

www.SherlockHolmesSociety.com